The White Company

Book 3 in the Sir John Hawkwood Series

By

Griff Hosker

Contents

The White Company

SWORD
BOOKS

Published by Sword Books Ltd 2021

Copyright ©Griff Hosker First Edition

A CIP catalogue record for this title is available from the British Library. Cover by Design for Writers

Dedication

To my latest grandson, William, welcome to the family!

Real People Used in The Book

King Edward Plantagenet
Prince Edward of Wales and Duke of Cornwall- his son
Lionel of Antwerp, Duke of Clarence and Earl of Ulster, King Henry's third son
Lord Henry Plantagenet- Earl of Derby, Earl and Duke of Lancaster
Thomas Montague, the Earl of Salisbury
Thomas Beauchamp, the Earl of Warwick
Sir Robert Knolles- Mercenary Captain in the Loire
Arnaud de Cervole- Leader of the White Company
Margaret of Flanders- wife of the Duke of Burgundy and heir to the County of Flanders
Phillip de Rouvres- Duke of Burgundy
Jean de Grailly, the Captal de Buch, a Gascon lord
King Charles of Navarre
King John II of France
Crown Prince Charles, the Dauphin of France
Phillip the Bold, Duke of Burgundy
Queen Joan I- Queen of Naples, and Countess of Provence and Forcalquier
John II- Marquis of Montferrat
Amadeus-Count of Savoy
Bernabò Visconti -Duke of Milan
Galeazzo Visconti- Duke of Milan

Prologue

Bordeaux 1356

The Battle of Poitiers was a great victory and Prince Edward now had the King of France, King John as his prisoner but despite that, we were still heavily outnumbered and forced to retreat to the safety of Bordeaux. That did not sit well with many of the Gascons in the army but for me, newly knighted, Sir John Hawkwood and the men known as Hawkwood's men, it mattered not for we had been well paid and had suffered few losses. We reached Bordeaux in October and the first thing I did was to buy a manor on the outskirts of the city. I had learned the advantages of doing this when I had wintered at Hartburn during the Black Death. The city itself would be filled with the whole army. There would be fights and more chance of disease. I was the Captain of my company and I gave them a simple choice, follow me or find another commander to follow. All but four chose me and the four who left me did not take another leader but returned to England with their money. I now had a fortune and a manor with a hall we could defend was the best place to keep it. The manor was a large one for I anticipated hiring many more men. The owner had been a French sympathiser who had perished in the battle. He had chosen the wrong side and his family had fled fearing repercussions. It cost me two hundred florins but that was a bargain. The farmhouse was more of a hall than a rustic dwelling. I was no farmer but the peasants who remained in the manor seemed quite happy to continue to tend the vines, fields and animals. Robin, Roger, Michael and Dai would share the hall with me. We converted a large barn into a warrior hall.

Although we were one company, I had a group I kept close to me. They were the three whom I regarded as friends. Robin had been with me the longest and was the archer I might have been, had I not chosen the sword, Michael had been an English youth we rescued in Normandy and was the one I had trained as a man at arms. He now acted as my squire. The last was a youth, Dai. We had met him in the Welsh borders and he had begged to become part of our company. I had thought he would become an archer and, indeed, he had skills but he was also handy with a blade. I suppose he acted as a sort of page for me. The difference was that, unlike most pages, Dai could kill! He was ready to be a warrior in his own right. Roger of Norham was also a friend and a shield brother but he had been wounded and I was not sure what lay in his future.

My choice of home proved to be prescient for while the rest of the army, and indeed the Prince, caroused and tried to drink Bordeaux dry we husbanded our wealth and we trained for we were warriors and war was our work. Many men thought that the achievement of a knighthood was the summit of my ambitions. After all, I had started out working as a tailor's apprentice and then an archer. I had risen higher than any that I knew and yet I had plans for my future and I had many ideas. I had seen how a good leader could meld together archers and men at arms to make those two arms greater than they were individually. Whilst mounted men at arms could sweep an enemy from a field, mounted archers could be used to trap and capture the men who fled from the men at arms. Archers could be used to devastate dismounted men at arms whilst being protected by the pole weapons of men at arms. Poitiers was both the start of my life and the end of part of it. That battle saw me cease to be one who served the King of England and begin to serve Sir John Hawkwood, mercenary!

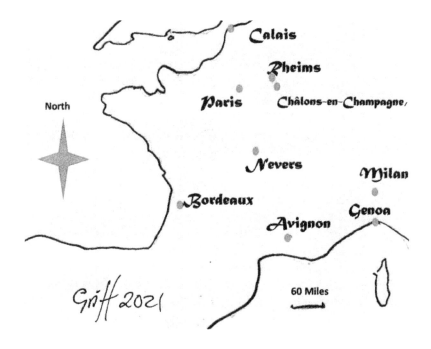

France 1356

Chapter 1

Bordeaux 1357

Peace, carousing all night and idleness did not sit well with me. I was a man of war and I confess that I enjoyed it. My men fell into two camps. There were those who felt as I did and then the others who, whilst they enjoyed fighting were more than happy to do nothing. That winter helped me to decide which warriors I wished to keep and which to let go. Prince Edward was still paying us and as ransoms were still forthcoming then our chests continued to fill with gold and silver. However, I could see that Prince Edward wished for some accolades from England and was desperate to take King John and his other captives back to London for a victory parade. I did not blame him. Weather and the wild winter seas dictated that he would not be able to leave in winter and when he concluded a truce in March, I knew he would be leaving soon. He did not depart as quickly as he would have wished as the Gascon lords were desperate to retain the King of France as their prisoner and a bargaining counter. Prince Edward gave them a hundred thousand crowns to silence them. The amount was a drop in the ocean for the ransom which had been set at two million ecus had been deemed too low by King John himself and was now three million ecus.

The decision did not please the majority of the English soldiers in Gascony. Henry Plantagenet had been forced back into Brittany and, to all intents and purposes, we were without an employer. The day after Prince Edward had also departed, in the middle of April, left me with a dilemma. I called together my company to address them.

"We are warriors for hire and our paymaster, the Prince, has returned to England. We are paid until Midsummer Day." I looked at the faces. To me it mattered not if they were archers or men at arms or a mixture of the two, like Dai, they were my men. I knew who I wanted to continue to follow me but I would force none. I was arrogant enough, in those days, to believe that men would wish to follow my banner and my new banner, which

I had paid a seamstress from the town to make up for me, now bore my coat of arms; the three scallop shells. My men all dressed, as I did, in white. Some other swords for hire had thought me foolish as it was hard to keep clean. They were wrong. We bleached it with urine, and we could always buy white cloth to replace any damaged material. If you tried to match a colour then it became a lottery.

Roger of Norham had been severely wounded in the battle. He was alive but I did not think he would wish to go to war again. When I asked them what they wished then it was he who was the first to speak, "Sir John, what do you have in mind? I was one of the first to follow you and, despite my injuries, I would follow you again."

"I intend to hire my sword out and those of the men who follow me to any who will pay us."

Eustace of Loughborough asked, "Even the French?"

I sighed, "If the French wish me to fight against Italians or Germans and can afford us then I would fight for them but if you are asking me would I fight English or Gascons then, Eustace, you do not know me!"

Eustace was punched playfully on the shoulder by those around him.

"I owe all of you pay and those who wish to leave me can have their horse and the pay which is due to them."

Roger asked, "And is there any likelihood of action soon?"

"I know not but we shall still train, and I will actively seek an employer."

By the time May arrived my company had been pared down. Robin, of course, remained as my captain of archers. More of my archers sought to remain and I had: Martin the Fletcher, Peter Longbow, Ned the Wanderer, Walter of Barnsley, Jack, Luke, and Joseph of Chester.

Fewer of my men at arms wished to stay and I could understand that. Some of them were good enough to make a living at the tourneys and jousts. Roger of Norham, Stephen and Henry the Luckless, joined Michael and the versatile Dai. We were sad to see the others go but it was necessary for a man with doubts was of no use in battle.

I spoke with Roger of Norham separately from the others. Apart from Robin, he had been with me longer than any but I knew I could not use him as I might wish. It was a pleasant early summer's evening and we went to the small stream which ran alongside the hall where we could talk privately.

"Roger, do you like it here?" I waved a hand around the land. There was a field of vines that were covered in grape blossom and there were beans growing in another field. It was a large manor and comfortable; I had bought it because all of us could be accommodated. There was also a huge stable as well as a paddock.

"Aye, Sir John, and after Norham, a veritable paradise!"

"You and I know that you can never be the warrior you once were."

His head hung and he nodded, "I knew when I said that I would stay that you might not be able to use me."

"I did not say that and I like it not when men put words in my mouth. I asked you if you liked it here for a reason. When I go to war, I need someone to look after this and, more importantly, to find new men to serve me. I need someone I trust and you are a shield brother. If I cannot trust you then all is lost. I will be leaving my treasure here and I know that you will keep it safe. Bordeaux is where all new English archers and swords for hire arrive. I would have you frequent the ships when they dock and find any that you think might be suitable. You can train them here. When others become unfit or unable to fight, they can join you." I lowered my voice. "I have chests of gold and I need them protected; you alone cannot do this and you need others to help you but you are one I can trust. What do you say?"

He smiled, "As much as I would like to go to war again, I know that you are right. My body now has weaknesses, and some poxy Frenchman might just best me. I should not like that. I will accept your kind and generous offer."

"Good and you shall be the paymaster too. I am a knight now and such things are beneath me."

I had already spoken of my decision with Robin and it was he suggested that Roger be the paymaster. With that in place, I rode with Dai into Bordeaux. The great lords of Gascony lived there, and they would be the first place I would seek work. Jean de

Grailly, the Captal de Buch was a man I not only trusted but respected. I also knew that he liked me and that was important. I had made enemies amongst other English and Gascon lords for I did not suffer fools gladly. Robin had often advised me to bite my tongue, but it was not in my nature to do so!

With the Prince so recently departed the Gascon lords could now be found at the palatial home of the Governor of Bordeaux. It was not that he had much power, but he had the finest home in the city. Thanks to my capture of the Oriflamme all knew me, and I was admitted immediately. I joined the other knights and lords who were there for a whole variety of reasons. Dai was learning how to move in such circles. He had enjoyed a rural upbringing and the Welsh borders had not prepared him for this. He had been with us long enough to have picked up some French and I had impressed upon him the need for him to listen more than he spoke. He played the part of a squire and until I needed one that would do but I knew that one day and soon, he would be a man at arms like Roger of Norham, but he would also be like me and be able to pull a longbow. As such he was invaluable.

Other lords, knowing that I was a favourite of Prince Edward sought my favour. I confess that I paid them little attention. If they needed my favour, then their company was not worth courting. As I say, in those days I was arrogant. Some say that I still am. I have, I believe never changed since the day I walked through the Chepe all those years ago to become an apprentice tailor. That was a lifetime ago.

A couple of Gascon lords emerged from what passed for a court. I smiled and nodded. One spoke to me, "Hawkwood, did you not return to England with the Prince?"

I shook my head, "No, my lord, I stay here plying my trade."

He laughed, "With the ransom you received you need not."

I shrugged, the man had no work for us, "I am a warrior. What else is there?"

When the Captal de Buch emerged, however, it was a different story. Even before I could think about approaching him half a dozen Gascon knights descended on him like seagulls on a crust of bread. I frowned but that frown turned to a smile as he flapped his arms to disperse them and made directly for me, "Sir John, just the man I seek!"

"Yes, my lord, how may I be of service?"

"I had thought you returned to England with the Prince, but I heard last night that you had stayed. That is fortuitous for I need your bows and your swords."

"Work?"

He nodded and, putting his arm around me said, "But not here. I wish a private conference with you away from prying eyes and ears." He saw Dai and cocked an eye.

"This is Dai, my squire. As with all my men, he is completely trustworthy, and you can speak freely before him."

"Good then let us retire to my hall."

His squire and page waited without and the five of us mounted our horses and rode to a large walled house by the river. "Dai, see to the horses and then occupy yourself." The look I gave him told him to find out all that he could about Jean de Grailly's plans.

The house, as I expected, was sumptuously furnished. I knew he had a wife but the two women who scurried upstairs as we arrived were patently not her! He waved me to a padded chair by the fire and snapped his fingers. A servant arrived with a jug of what I knew would be a fine wine. Since we had been in this part of France, I had learned to know the difference. I would still drink any wine, but it was good to know when I was being offered a good one. In this part of the world that showed you what your host thought of you, I always served the best wine I could afford. The fact that I had few visitors helped but by doing so I made certain that all my guests thought I respected them… whether I actually did or not.

I took a sip of the wine. It was, as I had foreseen, a good one.

"How many men do you have, Sir John?"

"Fewer than I did but I can still muster eight archers and four men at arms."

He frowned, "I had hoped for more but it is your archers I really need." I waited for him to continue. His eyes bored into me almost as though he was trying to read my thoughts. "I can trust you."

It was almost a question but not quite.

"My lord I have never yet let down any lord I served, and my men and I are closed-mouthed. So long as the work we do is not against the interests of King Edward and England then we are happy to do whatever we are asked."

He seemed relieved, "Good. You know that I captured James de Bourbon, Count of La Marche at the battle of Poitiers?" I nodded. "There were four others captured that day. I sold their ransom to Prince Edward for twenty-five thousand ecus and they are now in England with the Prince and King John." He smiled, "It seemed politic and suited the Count for this way he could enjoy the company and favour of his king whilst a captive. The Count has blood links to the royal line."

I emptied the goblet and he poured me another. "Forgive me, my lord, but I cannot see how this requires a sword!"

He sighed, "La Marche is historically part of Gascony. Now it is an island of France in the middle of Aquitaine. They will struggle to raise the ransom and the richest man in La Marche who was not captured is Gilbert de Bellac. His town is close to the River Vincou. There is no castle and I plan on making a chevauchée. There is no peace yet and we would not be attacking the land of a knight or lord taken at Poitiers." I said nothing but the knight felt he had to explain himself. "It is why I needed to be sure that I could rely upon you. I need men who can be quick and ruthless. You and your men have shown that. Your mounted archers are without peer and although you have few their effect far outweighs their number."

"I am quite happy for a chevauchée, my lord, and I have no qualms about raiding for you are quite right, there is no peace yet and as the Dauphin is still fighting in the north then there is no question of dishonour. I just need to know the pay."

He smiled, "I knew I could rely upon you. I will give you the choice, my lord, a single payment of a thousand crowns or a share of the profits."

A thousand crowns was a huge amount, but the profits could be far greater. I doubted that the French would expect an attack for the prince had returned to England. "We will take the profits, my lord. When do we leave?" We were still being paid by Prince Edward in any case.

"I would leave by the last day of May. I want to ensure that they have a full treasury at Bellac. I have a castle in Chalais. You and your men need to be there by the last Sunday in May."

I smiled, "Then we shall be there."

I did not tell my men our exact destination, just that we had work and not that long to ready ourselves. Martin the Fletcher organised the men to make arrows and Roger of Norham took on his new role with vigour. Since the battle, there had been a surplus of horses and they were cheap. He used, with my permission, some of my money to buy as many horses as he could. I found myself in much better humour than I had been just a month or so earlier. The reason was obvious, at least to me, I now had a purpose in my life. Robin and Michael, who were the closest to me, noticed it and commented upon it.

"Well, Sir John, you have a spring in your step once more, eh?"

I shook my head, "Robin, I have told you and Michael before that you need not bother with the title when we are alone!"

He smiled, "Before I called you Sir John, I called you Captain. I am comfortable with that and besides it is a bad habit to get into, using your Christian name for I might slip and use it in battle. Your company will grow once more. The losses from Poitiers and those who took their pay and returned to England will be replaced."

"You think so? I am not so sure."

Robin laughed, "The men who returned will tell all that they can of the money they made serving you. Most will waste it and they may even return for more but what I do know is that there will be archers and swordsmen who seek Sir John Hawkwood, the warrior who took the Oriflamme. When we return from this raid, no doubt richer, then men will begin to flock to your banner."

That was the day I began to plan for that eventuality. I needed order for my men. Robin was already my Captain of Archers and Roger my trainer of men but I needed a Captain of my men at arms. The choice was clear. Michael was young but so was Stephen. Henry the Luckless was a good warrior but he was no leader. The night before we left, I approached Michael, "Michael, I would have you as my Captain of Men at Arms."

He was so shocked that he took a step back, "My lord, have you taken leave of your senses? I am young and have much to learn!"

I nodded, "And in you, I see me when I was your age. The difference is that had I been offered what you have then I would have leapt at the opportunity." Smiling I said, "I believe, Michael, that you are a better man than I am, not a better warrior but a better man. That too helps for the men like you. Anyway, that is my decision. You will be paid double the pay of the others." I saw him start, "Robin enjoys the same privilege. Believe me, you will earn the extra pay. I will no longer have to worry myself about the preparations for war."

"I will do as you ask, my lord but what else is there to do?"

"Find ways for us to make money and profit from war. Do you remember when we rode with the Prince on the raid to Toulouse?" He nodded, "I saw then the potential for men such as we. The Prince is a good leader, but his mistakes cost us men. Those mistakes were made because while he was happy to raid, he had his eyes on a different outcome. He wished to bring the French to battle. My view is that we avoid battles if we can. We are hired swords who fight under my banner. I am happy to retreat before a superior force if we must. I intend to choose my battles and to fight as few of them as I can. In my world, Michael, we will all grow old and rich together."

The castle at Chalais was a strong one but it was not large and I knew that it was not the Captal's main home. It was just convenient for the raid. It was fortunate that we were not a large company of men. Jean de Grailly was taking with him some one hundred men. They were all mounted and all were men at arms. Now I saw why he needed me. He needed my mounted archers and, once more I put my thoughts to increasing the number I led.

His lieutenant was Roland de Limoges. I had never met him, but I knew that he had done well at Poitiers. Like many Gascons, he was impressed that I had been the one to capture the Oriflamme. Whilst the English contingent had just seen it as the capture of a banner, the Gascons knew the symbolism of the French battle standard. The three of us dined alone so that the Captal could give us his plan.

"Bellac has no castle but there is a bridge over the River Vincou. There is a hill that rises from the river and the Lord of Bellac has his manor close to the Église Notre Dame at the top of the slope. It should not be defended for they know not what we plan, and I would keep it that way. Sir John, I want you and your men to ensure that the bridge is cleared of our enemies. You will ride ahead of the main column and clear away any guards."

"Can the river be forded?"

The Captal looked at his lieutenant who shrugged and answered me, "I know the area but I have always used the bridge. I have never needed a ford and you should not need one either, Sir John. They have no defences on the bridge."

I smiled, "Good. Then all is well." I would find a ford. Crossing a bridge with armed men is always a risk for all it takes is a couple of guards with crossbows and I could lose a few archers. My archers all wore a metal coif, helmet and a padded tunic but riding across a narrow bridge meant that any bolt sent at them would penetrate. Archers hated crossbowmen but they recognised how deadly the missiles could be.

"Once you have secured the bridge then we will ride to take the hall, as quickly as we can. You and your men will support us and ensure that none leave the town with the ransom. Roland, you and your men will lead the assault on the hall. Our aim is to take the chests containing the gold. When we have that we will take all else that the town has. I believe that there are some rich merchants there and the town has managed to avoid war," he smiled, "until now."

I saw then that Jean de Grailly was weakening the area of La Marche so that he might be able to take it back. He planned on doing so not for personal gain but for Gascony. I could see that he was an honourable man who was forced to do something dishonourable for the sake of his land and his home. I would learn, as we rode north to Bellac and we spoke, that Jean de Grailly was single-minded. I think that was why we got on so well. I was as single-minded about my company.

We stayed at Saint Junien on the way north. I had my own plans for this was my company. "Sir Jean, my men and I will leave before dawn. If the bridge is defended, I want to clear it before the main column arrives."

He looked at me with surprise, "But if it is defended then will you not need the support of the rest of my men to help to clear it?"

I smiled, "You have given me my task, my lord. I will do as you ask but I will do it my way. All that you need to know is that the bridge will be in our hands by the time you arrive."

"Very well."

It was dark when we left and headed up the road. Had I been in command then I would have scouted out the bridge and the area well before I launched an attack. I intended to find a ford. Robin and I rode at the fore and when we came to the large wood just to the south-west of Le Vignaud, that was the hamlet which lay before us, we left the road. The Roman mile markers told us that we were just two miles from Bellac, and I intended to head upstream and either find a ford or to swim the river. We picked our way through the woods using hunter and game trails. When we emerged, we saw a few farms and tended fields. A line of dark green just a mile ahead showed the course of the river. Robin and I headed directly for it. I intended to rest, for it was coming close to noon, at the river. There the archers could string their bows and we could water our horses.

The river was completely covered by trees and we were hidden. I sent Dai upstream and Martin the Fletcher, downstream. The river was only twenty paces wide and we could swim it, but it made sense to seek a better crossing point. It was Martin who found the crossing. The river was just five paces wide and while faster-moving was the best place to cross. We could see, rising above the trees the tower of the Église Notre Dame. We were close to the town and therefore the bridge. Once ashore we dismounted and let the horses graze while we prepared for war. My men at arms had shields but they would hang from our cantles. My plan was to approach the bridge from the Bellac side. If there were no defenders or just a few then my men at arms would simply take the bridge. On the other hand, a defended bridge could be cleared by my archers.

Once we were ready, we walked our horses down the road. Unless we were very unlucky, we would not meet any soldiers but as we had weapons drawn and arrows ready to be nocked then I was confident that if we did then we would emerge triumphant. If the Lord of Bellac had been forewarned, then he would be expecting us over the bridge and not down this very small road. This time I let Robin lead with my archers. They had fast reactions. When Robin held up his hand and waved to the side then we took the trees which lined the road. We were so close to the river on one side and rising ground on the other that they had not bothered to cut down either the trees or the shrubs. I could hear the hum of noise from the town and so I signalled for my men to tie their horses. We had no one to guard them and that was something I would have to remedy. We did not need warriors to watch them but horses gave us an edge over most enemies and I wanted to keep that edge sharp!

Robin came to me, "The bridge is guarded, Sir John. It is just two hundred paces down the road. There is cover until a hundred and ten paces from the end of the bridge."

"How many men?"

"They are expecting us. There is a wagon drawn across the road and I counted more than twenty men. Numbers were hard to estimate because of the wagon and the parapet of the bridge."

"Then there is a traitor."

He nodded, "If there is then it is not one of ours."

I waved a hand as though to dispel the thought, "That is for a later time. You lead the archers, and we will follow. You will send five arrows each and then we will rush them. As soon as it is clear then I want you and the archers to mount your horses and ride around the town to stop any escaping with the ransom."

"Will you have enough men?"

"I will have enough!" I sounded more confident than I was as I had no idea how long it would take the Captal and his men to reach us.

Robin and my archers moved through the trees and I walked down the road with Michael, Dai, Stephen and Henry the Luckless. I had a sword in my right hand and a broad-bladed slashing dagger in my left. My men and I all wore the open-faced bascinet. There was a risk in wearing one but that was outweighed, in our opinion, by the vision it enabled. Every one of us, even Dai was protected by metal. In our cases, it was plate covered mail and in Dai's case, it was a cut down mail hauberk. Still, a youth, Dai had much growing to do.

I saw the men at the barricade. They had crossbowmen as well as men with spears, swords and axes. I recognised four men at arms amongst them but the rest were just warriors from the town. Without being told Robin and my archers would send their bodkins at the greatest threat: the crossbowmen and then the men at arms. Robin, as ever, judged it to perfection and the eight arrows struck all but two of the crossbowmen. The next eight remedied their earlier omission even as the two crossbowmen were turning their weapons around to face the new threat. We were able to keep moving down the road and the defenders saw their dual threat. Even as one of the men at arms was falling to the floor, dying, he shouted a command and I saw a swordsman run back to the town. He never made it as an arrow slammed into his back and from the fletch, I judged it to be Robin's.

"Charge!" It sounds ridiculous to shout charge when you lead just three men and a youth, but we had the desired effect and the defenders tried to flee. None made the safety of the town for Robin and his archers had easy targets.

"Robin, ride!"

"Aye, Sir John. Dai, collect our arrows eh? Come on my lucky lads, let us leave this to Sir John!"

"Henry, Michael, Stephen, shift this wagon. We shall use it as a fort if they are foolish enough to try to shift us. Dai, when you have collected the arrows, search the dead!"

We would be paid for this day's work but whatever we could take from the men who had been defending the bridge would augment it. The men at arms had mail and some plate as well as good swords. We would even take the crossbows. We would not use them, but they could be sold. It was all profit.

"Michael, take charge."

They had moved the wagon and I heard him say, "Henry, fetch our horses. Stephen, take the spears and pikes. Put them in the wagon."

I walked over the humped bridge and looked back to the town. We had been seen and I knew that they would be preparing either to flee or to defend themselves. The town needed a wall around it for the river, as we had demonstrated, was not an obstacle. There were many places we could have forded it and even men on foot could have waded across. The river only stopped wagons! I reached the far end and satisfied myself that there were neither defences nor men there. That there were not, showed me that Gilbert of Bellac was not a warrior to be feared.

He had made the most elemental of mistakes and assumed that his men at the bridge would eliminate our threat. He had no backup plan. In the distance, I could hear hooves and I took off my helmet and coif while I waited. It was too hot to wear it when I did not need to. My mind was always working, and I wondered how many other places there were in France which had such poor defences. It came to me that my company could continue to serve the English Crown and make war on France, but we could do it as freebooters and mercenaries. We would not have to answer to any higher authority, but we would need numbers. At the moment I had too few men.

Jean de Grailly reined in and I said simply, "They were warned, my lord, and had a barricade and almost thirty men waiting for us." He frowned. "We lost none and I have sent my archers to close the back door!"

"Thank you, Sir John. You have earned your pay this day. Let us ride!"

I stood to the side as the column of men at arms galloped past me. This was the easiest day's pay I had ever earned. I had drawn my sword, but it would not need sharpening. By the time I reached my men and the wagon, I heard the shouts and screams as the Gascons poured into the town. Their swords would not remain unsullied!

Chapter 2

The wagon was almost full, and our horses were tied there. "Dai, stay here with your horse and the wagon. The rest of you mount. There is treasure to be taken. We will use the wagon as our base. Whatever you find fetch it back here. A pair of draught horses would be useful."

Dai was disappointed but he obeyed his orders. Every one of my men knew that none questioned my orders. We rode up the winding road into the town. I saw that some men had been foolish enough to defend their homes against the Gascons. They had paid for their error with their lives. Unarmed townsfolk stood little chance of defeating mailed and plated men at arms. Instead of riding up to the church and the hall, I waved my men to the right shortly before the square. I guessed that there would be houses here that were owned by rich merchants. There were no bodies in the road and so I led my men down it. One house was set back from the others and looked large and imposing enough to promise riches. I saw that it had a high wall and large double doors which were big enough to accommodate a wagon.

The doors were closed. We dismounted and after trying them to see if they yielded, I said, "Henry, take your axe and break them down. The rest of you be ready to rush any who try to defend them!"

I drew my sword. I left my coif hanging down and my helmet on my cantle.

Henry struck the middle of the doors where they joined, and his accuracy meant that within a short time he had broken through the bar. Stephen and Michael put their shoulders to it, and we burst into their courtyard. There were eight men waiting for us. Four were warriors and the rest were servants with weapons.

"If you fight us then you will die. Put down your weapons!"

The older man who looked to be overweight and was, probably, the owner spat out, "You Gascon dogs killed my son at Poitiers. Try to take me who fought you at Crécy!"

His men, inspired by his words, rushed us. I whipped my broad-bladed dagger out and while blocking the spear thrust with my sword gutted the warrior with my dagger. I stepped into the gap left by his body and turned sideways so that the next spear slid along my breastplate. I hacked across the neck of the spearman. I saw, from the corner of my eye, the overweight owner as Michael slew him. As three others lay dead the rest quickly threw down their weapons and abased themselves before us.

I was taking no chances, "Stephen, bind them so that they can do no harm nor flee."

"Yes, Sir John."

The three of us entered the house. The door was wide open. Inside it was opulently decorated. The merchant, for he had never been a warrior despite his boast of having fought at Crécy, was rich. I entered the large hall to my left and saw the women of the house with half a dozen house servants before them. Some of the men held cleavers and knives. I shook my head, "Throw them to the ground or you will suffer the same fate as your master!" The family all screamed and ran from the hall. The servants quickly did as commanded. Sheathing my sword I pointed to the one who looked to be the oldest. "You, what is your name?"

"Henri."

"Good. Now that you have come to your senses, answer me some questions and then you can leave." He nodded. "Are there any more servants or family members in the house?"

He had a furtive look on his face as he answered, "There are no servants or family left in the house."

In two strides I was next to him and had my dagger at his throat, "Do not play games nor lie to me."

A woman, portly enough to be the cook stepped before him and said, "Leave my husband alone! He is not lying to you but there are two others in the house. They are not family and they are not servants."

I sheathed my dagger, "Then what are they?"

The man said, "Prisoners, my lord. The man is an Englishman who tried to defraud our master and the woman is his sister. They are held in the cellar."

I nodded, "Then take me to them. Michael, you and Henry search the rooms upstairs. Henri, lead on and remember that any more attempts to deceive me will result in pain for you."

"Yes, my lord."

He took me through the kitchen and down to a large cellar. There were doors leading off and I guessed that one had to be the wine cellar. The man took a key from a hook and opened the cell door. The smell which hit me told me that they had not emptied the night soil for some time. It was pitch black and I saw nothing. I spoke in English, "Whoever is in there come out. I am Sir John Hawkwood and I promise that you will be safe."

I heard movement and then a man, he looked withered but I guessed that was just his ill-treatment and a woman who, had she been clean would have been stunning came forward. Both of them had matted hair and skin covered with sores. The man dropped to his knees, "My lord, our prayers have been answered. I beg you to give us sanctuary."

I nodded, "Of course. We have no time for your story now, but I will hear it later." I turned to Henri. "Where does your master keep his gold?"

Henri shook his head, "I do not know."

The woman leapt up and tried to rake his eyes with her broken nails, "You lie! You know exactly where it is kept!" She had drawn blood and I waited for a few moments before I pulled her from him.

I grabbed the man by the throat, "I warned you of the consequences of lying to me and now I see that a fellow countryman and an English lady have been abused. Would you like to die now or wait until your wife can see your death?"

He dropped to his knees, "My lord, I beg you, spare my life and I will show you where the master hid his gold. I did nothing to these two!"

"But you knew of it and this lady's reaction told me that you did nothing. Lead on. Are you two able to walk? If not, I will have my men carry you."

"We can walk." The man's voice displayed his weakness and I wondered what had been his crime that he had been punished in this way.

Henri did not lead us far. We went into the next cellar, which, once again, required a key. It was as I had thought, a wine cellar. I said nothing but I noticed the woman and her brother were not surprised. I saw that the corked jugs of wine were stacked on every wall but one. There the shelves were empty. Henri went to the shelves and pulled at them, I saw that they swung and there had been a facade on the back which had deceived me. Now that it was moved, I saw a door. Once more it required a key and when it was opened, I saw chests inside. We had our gold. Even if the ransom had been collected and there was an empty treasury, we would be paid. I took the keys from the man and knelt to open one of the five chests. It was filled with coins. Most were silver but there was gold.

"My lord!"

I turned as the woman shouted and saw that Henri had run. I smiled as I stood, "He cannot get far, now come, I will need my men to carry this treasure." As we headed up the stairs, I allowed them to go first, I asked, "What was the merchant's business?"

"He dealt in cloths and spices from the east."

"Then it is no wonder that he is so rich." I wondered, however, why he had based himself so far from the sea. I would have expected him to be close to a port on the southern coast of France.

I met Stephen and Michael in the hall. There lay the body of Henri. Stephen said, "He tried to escape and as you were not with him, we feared he had done you harm."

I gave him a thin smile, "You think I could not handle an old man? I am disappointed in your opinion of me. Never mind. We need the wagon and my archers. We have found coins and there must be fine cloth and spices somewhere. We will stay here. You can let the people go but do not let them re-enter."

Stephen nodded and Michael looked at the couple, "Are these the prisoners?"

"They are Michael. Find them some food and drink while I seek the Captal." I turned to the man, "I do not know your name."

"I am William Thornton, my lord, and I am in your debt. This is my younger sister, Elizabeth."

"Then, William, you and your sister can be my guests in Bordeaux until you decide what you plan to do."

I did not give him the chance to answer me then for I turned on my heels. Henry was helping Stephen lead two draught horses from the stables when I emerged.

"Henry, when Stephen goes to fetch the wagon then close the gates. You and Michael will be in charge until I return. Dispose of the bodies. The river seems best but do as you wish with them. I go to seek the Captal."

I rode my horse up to the hall. There were more bodies the closer I got to it but fewer than I had expected. I dismounted at the hall and tied Roman to the wagon which was being loaded. I nodded to the men at arms who were loading it, "Have you seen the Captal?"

"He is inside, my lord. He is not a happy man."

I wondered what could have annoyed him for I had seen no Gascon dead. Men were busy carrying chests, swords and goods from the hall. It was being emptied of all that was valuable. I saw Gilbert de Bellac. He had a bloody coxcomb and was curled into a ball. Jean de Grailly was scanning documents when I entered, "Where have you been, Hawkwood?"

I heard the anger in his voice, and he had addressed me as Hawkwood rather than giving me my title. My answer was curter than I really intended, "Doing as you asked me to do, securing the bridge and searching the town. Why, what should I have been doing?"

The hall fell silent. He had not accorded me my title and I had not even used his name. If we were dismissed without pay it would not bother me for I had made more already than I had been offered in the first place.

He shook his head, "I am sorry, Sir John, I was a little short with you and you deserve more respect. We have been betrayed. They knew we were coming, and half of the ransom has been moved out already." He waved me closer, "It was Roland de Limoges. He and his men have fled. I have questioned the Lord of Bellac and he confirmed it. Now the traitor will be with his French masters. I have learned a lesson this day. That is why I intend to empty the town. I fear your share will not be as great as we might have anticipated."

"No matter for I lost no men. Did my archers secure the gate?"

"Aye, they did and managed to capture the wagon outside which had some of the ransom on board. They are good fellows. I sent them to find you."

"Then I will leave you and continue to search for treasure. When do we leave?" He cocked his head to one side. "If the traitor finds French allies then they may try to stop us on the way back. I would have my archers scout out the land."

"You think they might?"

"They obviously thought to delay us at the bridge and get the rest of the treasure away."

He lowered his voice, "Then we leave early tomorrow. If your archers could ensure that the road is clear, we will be in your debt."

"Of course."

As I mounted my horse to head back to my men, I decided that I would choose my paymasters even more carefully next time. Jean de Grailly was a good knight and leader, but his misjudgement might have ended disastrously for us.

When I reached the hall my archers were there as was the wagon which was being loaded. "You did well Robin, the Captal is pleased."

He grinned at the wagon, "I think you have done even better, my lord."

I nodded, "Take your archers and search the other houses which lie close by. I doubt that there will be much opposition. We will be sleeping here this night and then, on the morrow, you will be the scouts when we head back to Bordeaux. We were betrayed by Sir Roland."

He did not seem surprised, "I never trusted him, Sir John. His eyes were too close together!" he turned to his archers, "Right lads, leave your bows and horses here. We go to lift some purses!"

"Dai, go inside and tell the English brother and sister that they can take any clothes they want and clean themselves up. We will join them as soon as we can."

"Aye, Sir John."

With my men at arms and Dai, when he returned, we packed the wagon with all that we could find. It was getting on to late afternoon when we had finished. "Stephen and Henry, stay on guard at the gate until Robin and the archers have returned then secure it for the night. We will go and prepare food." It was the Gascons I feared taking our treasure rather than the French. I knew that most of the French would have fled with whatever they could carry as soon Jean de Grailly and his men began to clear the hall and the centre of the town of whatever they could find. Thanks to Sir Roland's treachery the raid had not been as successful as had been originally planned.

We entered a kitchen filled with the smells of food being cooked. William and Elizabeth, now cleaned up and in clothes which, no doubt, belonged to the former owners, were busily preparing food. William said, "We thought it the least we could do."

I sat on one of the benches which ran along the servant's dining table, "And that has saved us a job. Dai, wine! And now, William, I will be intrigued to hear your story."

He looked a little shamefaced, but he nodded and, taking a deep breath, began, "I am not a completely innocent man, my lord, but we did not deserve the punishment we received. We were treated like slaves!"

I drank some of the wine poured by Dai and said, "And I can see that you are no storyteller for you begin the story in the middle! Start at the beginning! How do an English brother and sister find themselves in Gascony?"

He nodded and seemed a little more relaxed as he began, "I am a clerk and bookkeeper by trade, and I worked in London for the Archbishop. I kept a record of his transactions and I was good at what I did. We are orphans and I was responsible for Elizabeth. She acted as a servant for the Archbishop. It was greed that brought us to this sorry state. Lord Guillaume and his son came to London with a view to selling spices directly to the Archbishop. He had a taste for such things. His son, Geoffrey, took a fancy to Elizabeth and…" he looked at his sister.

She turned from stirring the pot and said, "I was flattered for he was a young noble and did not know that he was such a venal man. He took away my maidenhood and treated me like a slave. His father employed my brother and..."

William continued, "I was flattered too for when he saw that I could both read and write as well as adding up columns of figures he offered me twice the amount I was being paid by the Archbishop. We leapt at the opportunity to have secure employment. This was two years before Poitiers, lord, and we did not know that war was coming. Almost as soon as we reached France and his home then Sir Geoffrey showed his true colours. Elizabeth was to be his concubine. I tried to stop his treatment of my sister, but I was beaten. I then devised a plan to escape. I knew that we needed money and I began to take small amounts from Lord Guillaume. It was easy, or so I thought, to hide the amounts from him. It all changed when his son went to war. We were happy for a while as Elizabeth was free from his paws but when he was killed then Lord Guillaume and his wife changed. They vented their fury at the loss of their son on us for we were English. We were thrown into the cellar where you found us and when they searched my room, they found the coins I had secreted beneath the floorboards. We were beaten even more. We are in this position because of my mistakes and I am grateful that you rescued us."

I nodded, "An interesting story and you are right, you did make mistakes." I thought back to my time as a tailor's apprentice and knew that I had made similar mistakes. "Tell me, William, why was this lord, who imports and exports, living here far from the sea?"

He lowered his voice, "He was a Cathar, or rather he and his family are from Cathar stock. They still have those beliefs. His grandfather fled here when Carcassonne fell in the crusade. That is the reason for the high walls and gates. The family kept to themselves. When Sir Geoffrey fought for King John it was because the Lord of Bellac was suspicious of this family which kept to themselves. Sir Geoffrey did not want to go to war but his father thought that with the overwhelming numbers his son would gain glory and not have to do much fighting."

I laughed, "Aye well, the battlefield is not the place for amateurs!" I appraised the young man. I saw that I could use the two of them. The girl had skills for the food smelled delicious and my home in Bordeaux could benefit but the young man seemed the answer to my prayers. I needed one who could read and regulate my finances. However, I needed to be able to trust him. I decided to proceed cautiously. "William, Elizabeth, I am touched by your tale. I have need of a bookkeeper and someone to be a housekeeper. I have a home in Bordeaux. What say you?"

William looked at his sister and said, "I would say yes, my lord, so long as my sister's virtue and honour would be safe."

I laughed, "You think I am another Sir Geoffrey?" I shook my head, "If I need a woman, William, I know where to find one to satisfy my needs. Elizabeth would be as safe in my home as in a nunnery." I did not add that the sores on her face and her still matted hair would have deterred me in any case.

That seemed to satisfy them, "Then we accept."

"Good, then when we have eaten, take any more clothes you need from this house and tomorrow, when we return to Bordeaux you two can ride in the wagon. William, find yourself a sword for until we reach Bordeaux we may have to fight!"

"I am no swordsman, lord, I am a man of letters."

I shook my head, "Do not believe that you cannot fight. If you had held a sword would Lord Guillaume have escaped injury? Had your sister held a weapon would Sir Geoffrey have violated her? No, William, keep a weapon close by you and if you are fated to die then you can hurt those who would hurt you."

When Robin and my archers returned with even more coins, we barred the gates and ate in the main hall. I left William and Elizabeth in the kitchen for I knew they would have much to speak about. They might even consider fleeing and making a new start. I would not blame them. I had made my offer which, unusually for me, was for the benefit of others. If they chose to spurn it then so be it. I put them from my mind.

Robin and the others were in high spirits, "We did not find as much treasure such as you took, my lord, but we managed to find little pieces here and there. We took clothes, weapons and goods as well as a few purses of coins. You were right. This area was where the high and mighty of Bellac lived. Most had fled, alerted no doubt by the news from Sir Roland but they could not carry all their riches."

Henry the Luckless said, "And will we do more of this, my lord, for it is easy money?"

I shook my head, "All turned out well but that was good fortune more than anything. Jean de Grailly made too many mistakes. We have enough money now to hire more men for our company." I saw them all look expectantly at me. "You should know that I plan on organizing a free company of warriors. We can do, if we have enough men, what the Captal de Buch planned. However, we need more men if we are to succeed where he failed. I will have papers drawn up so that each of you knows what he can expect from the riches we hope to reap. There will be rules and regulations for us to follow. Too many of our men left us and I need new men to follow me whom I can trust. When we return to Bordeaux, we will seek men who were left behind when the Prince returned to England. Roger of Norham is busy buying us horses. We now have gold and silver to pay for more. You men here are the ones I can trust. Each of you archers will be a vintenar and paid accordingly." I smiled, "I know now that seems a little pathetic for you command no one but that will change. Stephen and Henry, you will be my captains under the command of Michael. You will command the lances who join us. Henry, I think that we can now dispense with your unfortunate title eh?"

The men all banged the table with the goblets and cheered. Henry nodded and said, "Aye, lord. I should like that!"

Robin said, "And what do we call our company, lord? Hawkwood's men?"

I shook my head, "As I said I want rules writing for us. It is my company but I do not wish to be the head which every man seeks to take in battle. This is your company too, what do you think?"

I had taken them by surprise for they did not expect to be consulted. They were silent until Michael said, "With the exception of Dai we all have one thing in common, Sir John, we are English. Why not the English Company?"

I looked around and saw nods. Robin said, "We all wear Sir John's white, why not the White Company?"

I shook my head, "I like Michael's suggestion. Let us be the English Company!"

Chapter 3

My archers headed down the road an hour before the wagons were ready to leave the town and cross the bridge. Jean de Grailly had twenty men at arms with the wagons whilst the rest followed my archers. Dai drove the wagon and we four guarded it. The Captal had come to see me as we had prepared to cross the bridge. He nodded to the wagon. We had placed the furniture we had taken on the top. The chests of coins and spices were cleverly hidden at the bottom. "You have done well out of this. I fear that I have but a thousand ecus for you. You might have been better to take a fee."

I shrugged, "You were not to know that you could not trust your own man, my lord. We lost no one and we are content. The furniture will make our home a little more pleasant."

"Then you have no intentions of returning, like Prince Edward, to England?"

"No, lord, for we are warriors and there is no war in England!"

"Then I may have employment again for you."

I smiled, "The English Company is always open to offers!"

He smiled and joined his men at the head of the column. I did not like being separated from my archers and I did not like being at the back. Nor was I happy when the Captal and the majority of his men at arms allowed a gap of four hundred paces to develop between us and him. He was staying too close to Robin and my archers. The purpose of scouts was to range ahead. The men at arms had no need to be so close to their horses' tales and we could go no faster with heavily laden wagons. I knew that we had forty miles or so where there might be the danger of an ambush. After that French horsemen would be vulnerable to an attack from the Gascons whose castles lay along the border with La Marche. I rode next to the wagon so that I could speak with William and Elizabeth. My night of sleep had set my mind working. Once I got to know him and knew that I could trust William, and that would require a test, then he could find some way to make my coins grow. Certainly, the spices and silks we had brought from Bellac would make my company richer. In my head, there were two sorts of money: there was my money, money I had earned and there were the company's coins. I would not cheat my company as I realised how valuable they were to me. I had good men who would lead whoever came to serve with me and I wanted them to be as fair a man as I hoped I was.

"William, the spices and the silks we took from Bellac, where would be the best place to sell them?" This was William's first test.

He nodded and stared off into the distance. I wondered if he had heard me and then he said, "London. The Archbishop whom I served had a palate which yearned for the spices from the east and the prices would be higher there than even Bordeaux. The same for the silks. English ladies would happily spend their husband's money on such items."

I nodded. Henry Plantagenet had made almost as much in his chevauchée as Prince Edward. I knew because I had benefitted from it. Many other lords had gone home as rich men with fat purses for their wives and mistresses to spend.

I looked at William, "There is a but?"

He nodded, "There is the risk of the voyage. The seas can claim a ship easily and you would have lost all. And then you would need an agent to sell it for you. Is there such a man in England that you trust?"

"If I choose to hang on to my treasures for a while, what then?"

Elizabeth spoke, "The silks if they were kept safely in a cedarwood chest and regularly aired, would not suffer. The spices might last a year before they began to deteriorate. They are not yet ground and so they still have their power and pungency. Of course, as my brother will tell you, the English," she smiled, "the English lords and ladies will pay whatever they have to but if the spices are in the best of conditions then you can charge as much as a knight's ransom."

"How do you know this?"

"Before Poitiers, I helped my brother and I saw the amounts we received from the trade with England compared with the trade from France."

It was ironic that Guillaume's best market was the one which had taken his son!

Michael was behind the wagon with the other two and he was alert. It was as we ended the conversation that he shouted a warning, "Sir John, riders coming up behind and fast!"

I knew it was better to prepare for war and look foolish when it was just a messenger riding along the road. I chose caution, "Arm yourselves. William, Elizabeth, take cover in the wagon!"

I pulled up my coif and donned my helmet quickly and then whirled Roman. The rearguard knights were tardier. Their coifs still lay upon their shoulders and their helmets on their cantles. They looked at me as though I had gone mad as I raised my sword. I pointed it north for I had seen that it was not a messenger but a column of French men at arms, "The French!"

There was confusion. Jean de Grailly was at the fore and he had not put a lord in charge of the rearguard. They whirled and milled as they tried to do too many things at once. I saw that the French were led by the treacherous Sir Roland. That in itself caused confusion. Not all of the Gascons knew that he was a traitor and the first four knights who fell to French swords and spears, did not even defend themselves.

I shouted, "Form a line and defend yourselves!" Michael, Stephen, and Henry were next to me and our backs were protected by our wagon. Some of the French were busy fighting the carters and trying to capture the two wagons which were behind ours. I saw Sir Roland and a handful of knights carving their way towards my wagon. I saw their plan as clearly as the sun in the sky. They had allowed us to get some way down the road and now intended to recapture the treasure whilst our best men were at the front for we were still close enough to Bellac for them to return there. I pulled up my shield and raised my sword as the first lance came at me. The Frenchman punched with the lance and it barely cleared Roman's head. My horse was a good war horse, but the movement startled it and he snorted and raised his head, knocking the lance up. I accelerated the movement with my shield and as the knight closed with me brought my sword down diagonally to hit at his neck. The knight was well protected by plate and coif. There was little chance that I would break flesh but I had been an archer and the blow broke the bone at the knight's collar. His shield dropped and I stood in my stirrups to smash my sword down upon his helmet. The lance was useless in close combat and my blow hit without any defensive blow in reply. He fell from his horse.

Behind me, I heard horns as Jean de Grailly led his knights to come to our rescue. I was not reliant upon them but on Robin and my archers. When the bodkins slammed into three French knights, I knew that they had arrived. I saw Sir Roland attempting to lead away the rearmost wagon. His plan had failed but he could still hurt his former leader.

"Michael come with me. You two guard the wagon!"

I spurred Roman and used my sword to sweep the horses and men at arms from before me. Michael and I were helped by the arrival of the vanguard. Jean de Grailly would be angry with himself for his oversight. The French would not be treated well, and I saw men at arms, realising that their attack had failed, attempting to disengage. Sir Roland and four men at arms had succeeded in grabbing the traces of the last wagon and having turned it, were leading it back to Bellac. The problem was that two of the men at arms could not fight for they were pulling at the lead horses. Michael and I had just three men to fight and with help coming from behind us I was confident that we could recapture the wagon. In those days I had yet to lose and I was arrogant.

Wagons are slow to get moving and having had to turn this one we caught up with it just forty paces down the road. Sir Roland and one of the men at arms came for me as I neared the rear of the wagon. I had my shield up and neither of them did. I rode at Sir Roland and I planned on fighting him to my right. True knights, and by that I mean those trained as such from an early age, have rules about combat. I was not one of those. I had learned to fight the hard way and having blocked the blow from Sir Roland's sword I brought my sword down to hack deeply into the neck of his horse. As it tried to get away from the blow it smashed its head into the wagon and that accelerated its death. Sir Roland was thrown from his horse. The man at arms had managed to get a good hit on my shield and my arm was numb but I whipped Roman's head around so swiftly that the man was taken by surprise as he turned to get away from us. I smashed my sword across his back and gave him a second blow before he could react. I managed to sever one of the leather straps and the backplate shifted. He was becoming unbalanced and as he tried to control his horse and turn, I lunged with my sword for I saw a gap. The blade came away bloody and I turned again to see Sir Roland, on foot, coming for Roman with his sword held in two hands. Martin the Fletcher's arrow struck as true as any I had ever seen. It hit his nose and the bodkin came out of the back of his skull. He fell dead. Michael had easily taken the other man at arms and was racing after the wagon. When I joined the pursuit, and the horses of my archers thundered the two men at arms holding the wagon's horses let go and fled. We reined in next to the wagon and I turned to look at the scene of the ambush. It had failed and French men at arms were fleeing in all directions pursued by Jean de Grailly and his vengeful men.

Robin and my archers reined in. I nodded my thanks, "A fine hit, Martin the Fletcher. I did not know you could use a bow from the back of a horse."

He laughed, "Neither did I, Sir John. It was a lucky strike and had the range not been so close then I would have missed. I would not like to have to use the skill too often, but I feared you were going to lose your horse."

I nodded, "Sir Roland should have coins on him, and his sword and plate are well made. They are yours!"

He grinned, "You are generous my lord!"

I dismounted and went to the man at arms I had slain. He had a purse, which I took, but his plate was not worth taking. I lifted his sword. Dai could use it. "Robin, take the wagon back to the others." I smiled and winked, "Check to see that the French did not help themselves to any of the treasure."

"We will do so, my lord. Although it seems to me that the wagon is not as laden as it was. We shall see."

"Michael and I will return to our wagon. Catch us up when you can!" I hung the sword and its scabbard from my cantle. The dead of both sides lay around the wagons. By my estimate, the Captal had lost eight men at arms and the French just five. He would pursue the French survivors until he had exacted his revenge. I knew that he did not enjoy defeat. There were enough men left at the wagons for them to be safe. I said, "Tell the Captal that we will push on to Saint Junien and await him there."

The man at arms who had been in charge of the rearguard was still in a state of shock and just nodded.

I handed the sword to Dai, "Here, a little present from the French."

His eyes widened for it was a well-made sword, "Thank you, my lord."

William and his sister had come out of hiding and were staring at the bodies. He shook his head, "A dangerous world, Sir John!"

I nodded towards one of the dead Frenchmen, "If I were you, William, I should take that dead man's sword and then have Dai here or Michael teach you to use it." For a moment I thought he was going to refuse then he jumped down and, unfastening the baldric, took the weapon and climbed back aboard.

"Right, Dai, let us push on. We shall be in Saint Junien first and I intend to acquire the best accommodation."

My men at arms had already taken all that they wanted from the dead and, after putting the weapons, plate, mail, and helmets in the wagon, we began to move down the road before Robin and the others had fetched the recovered wagon. I threw my helmet into the wagon and dropped my coif. Elizabeth took the helmet to secure it, "Were you not worried when you were attacked, my lord?"

I shrugged, "Worry gets you nowhere, save, perhaps, to hasten your death. You just deal with the enemies before you and we were better than those they brought."

She nodded towards the helmet, "You do not think you will need it again?"

"Not today. Sir Roland gambled and lost. He did not count on my presence at the rear of the column. Had we not been there then he might well have succeeded and taken at least two of the wagons."

William then spent the next few miles questioning me about his job when we reached Bordeaux. The questions pleased me for they showed that he was diligent. They even helped me for the questions he asked made me think about the way I ran things. As we neared, in the late afternoon, Saint Junien I had come up with a better plan than when I had left for this raid. Thanks to Prince Edward we now had a secure Gascony. There might come a time when we might lose it but for the foreseeable future, it was ours. I would make the farm my base until I had enough men in the English Company to raid deeper into France. Until Gascony was actually threatened then I would use it to train men and to channel the goods we wished to sell back to England. William was right, that was where we could make the greatest profit, but I needed a captain I could trust and an agent in England. That meant I had to get to England. I would wait until autumn and then sail. It would give me the chance to hire archers and men at arms. I liked to plan and lay out a future. I knew that events could conspire to alter those plans but that did not worry me. I knew where I was heading and that my future and that of my company was in my own hands!

Jean de Grailly found us in the early evening. His bloody clothes told me what he had been doing. Rather than staying in the monastery we had used heading north, we had chosen an inn. We paid for our rooms and food with the coins we had taken from the dead Frenchmen. I had nothing against a monastery for they were safe places, but we now had a woman with us and monasteries sometimes frowned on such visitors amongst such a large number of men. I sent Dai for a jug of wine and waved the Gascon and his four men over to our table.

He sat and looked weary, "I am glad you ended the life of that snake. He cost me some good men." I said nothing for I knew the fault lay in the master. He had appointed Sir Roland just as he had paid for me. I had proved trustworthy while Sir Roland had not. "Tomorrow we will keep the wagons in the centre, and we will be closer together." I did not state the obvious that he and his men at arms had followed too closely to my fast-moving archers. "I have learned my lesson."

Dai poured him a goblet of wine which he drank almost in one. Was it to get rid of the bitter taste of his losses?

"And what are your plans, Sir John, when we reach Bordeaux?"

"Hire more men." I decided to speak plainly, "Had we employed more archers then we could have had some at the rear and your losses would not have been so grievous. We are men of war and I will seek employment. A sword that is idle in its scabbard becomes just a useless metal bar! It is the same with men."

"There are tourneys and jousts. Prince Edward is very fond of those."

"We do not play at war, we make war, my lord."

The journey was incident-free and when we reached Bordeaux, I was paid my share and we parted. Once we were back at my manor I sat down with William and Roger. I needed the two of them to know my mind. "I need a safe room building." I had been impressed by the hidden chamber in Bellac and sought something like it. I outlined what I required and left it to the two men to come up with a plan. "We also need accommodation for men as well as a separate room for you, William and your sister. I will leave the running of the house to her. She seems to know her mind. If, Roger, you have to use some of the cultivated fields for the new buildings then do so. I am no farmer and what we can take will give us a greater income than crops or grapes. Keep some vines for we can continue to make our own wine."

"And you, Sir John, what are your plans?"

"Tomorrow I will ride into Bordeaux to find men. I also need to ask about a ship. William, when I sail to London in the autumn, before the storms begin, then you will come with me."

"And my sister?"

"She is my housekeeper, and she shall keep house." I did not want to risk them running. I trusted them but only to a point. I did not want others to know about my coins and I did not yet know if they were loose-lipped!

As soon as we arrived in the commercial heart of the city, the port and the markets, I knew that I had chosen a good time to hire. With the Prince returned to England and Henry Plantagenet's adventure ended there were disillusioned soldiers attempting to return to England. I saw then the problem I would have in acquiring a ship for there were few to be had and the ones that there were already had cargoes of wine destined for England. The full purses of men at arms and archers who were trying to get back to England would soon be empty as the alehouses emptied them. I had Michael and Dai with me. Roger and William would both be busy for the foreseeable future. I had promised Elizabeth that I would buy those things she needed for the house. I would use the share of money paid to me by the Captal.

Archers were the most urgent requirement and I sought them first. They had all gathered close to the harbour at a tavern that was run by an old English soldier. Thanks to Poitiers and my time as an archer, I was well known. Many of the men I saw had been at Poitiers but had fought under different captains. The result was that I was given the respect which was not always accorded to men at arms. They knew that I could pull a bow as well as most of them. I was greeted with the knuckling of foreheads and oral greetings.

"I am here, archers, to hire as many archers as wish to join my company."

One archer, grey-haired and with knotted forearms asked, "Is there war, Sir John?"

I recognised him as Gerald of Tarporley, "No Gerald. I am not fighting for the Prince who is now in England. I am fighting for Sir John Hawkwood and his English Company!"

A Welsh voice piped up, "Then that rules me out!"

I laughed, "It is the name of the company and not the nationality. Any who join me will have a share of the profits and a vote on the leader."

I looked at Gerald who shook his head, "If the Prince needed me then I would fight for I am an Englishman, but I have a family I have not seen for three years and a full purse. I would spend time at home."

I handed him a silver coin, "Then have a drink for me when you reach home. I want only those men who have no ties. I know not where we fight but I know that there will be profits."

We found twelve archers who were happy to join me immediately and another ten who said they would need to think about it. I sent the twelve with Dai back to the farm. It was a better start than I had hoped. In truth, I suspected that I would find more when I went to England. I wanted the younger archers who might have missed out on Poitiers; young archers that I could mould.

Michael and I were on our way to buy the goods we needed for Elizabeth and were passing a quiet tavern just off the market when we heard the clash of steel. Our hands went to our weapons for we were soldiers. Suddenly a figure was thrown from a door and landed in the street on his back. As he stood, dagger in hand I saw that I knew him, it was Giovanni d'Azzo. Four men faced him and they had drawn swords.

I drew my sword, knowing that Michael would copy me and watch my back. Keeping my voice easy and calm I said, "Four swords to one does not seem like fair odds. What has this man done to deserve such treatment?"

My livery was well known in Bordeaux, even by those who had not fought at Poitiers and it arrested the movement of the swords towards my friend's head. "He tried to get out without payment, Sir John. He has little else on him so we thought to take the payment out of his Italian skin."

I took a silver coin from my purse and flipped it in the air. One of them caught it. "Does that pay the bill?"

"Half only!"

I flipped another, "Now that is done. Come with us." I saw Giovanni glare angrily at the men and I said, "Friend, either come with me now or I will leave you to your fate." He turned and looked at my face. I nodded, and he sheathed his sword and spat out some Italian. I guessed that it was a curse. We did not speak until we were in the square. "Michael, go and buy the goods we came for. I will speak with Giovanni."

"They robbed me!"

I smiled and shook my head, "The last time I saw you, you wore plate and mail. You had a good sword and now you wear worn buskins and have a dagger. The Giovanni d'Azzo I knew would not have been robbed by four such as we just left. What is your tale?"

He sighed, "A woman, what else? I earned a good living fighting against your Lord Henry and when I had made enough, I came south." He shrugged, "I like the wine. I met a beautiful woman with ebony hair and green eyes. She bewitched me, I swear that she did. She was a witch. I was infatuated with her and she spent all my money and left for England when Prince Edward departed. I found solace in the bottom of a jug and then when I had sold my weapons, mail, and plate I was forced to sweep floors. Those men took the last of my coins."

I raised an eyebrow, "How?"

"I gambled and I lost."

I shook my head, "I may regret this, but I have my own company now and I need men at arms. Time was I would have offered you a place but the man I see now who stinks of piss and vomit seems to be a shadow of that man."

He looked down at his clothes and nodded, "You are right, I am not the same man but inside I am still a good warrior. Give me the chance, for old times' sake."

"As I recall the last time we met I gave you your life back. How many times do I need to save you?"

"You are right but, my friend, perhaps this is fate. Give me a chance and if after a month you think me a hopeless case, then throw me back on the street. I can still fight!"

I laughed, "Aye, I saw that back there. A dagger against four swords does not seem like the act of a rational man. Come, let us find Michael!"

When we reached the farm Robin recognised the Italian. He shook his head, "Is this well done, Sir John? You saved him once and had the King discovered it then it would not have gone well for you."

"We will give him a chance and he is a good warrior. It will cost us a month of food and that is all. If after that time he has not shown himself worthy then we throw him out."

The next day Dai, Michael and I returned to speak with the other archers in Bordeaux while Robin assessed the new ones. Roger was charged with helping Giovanni to regain some of his skill. Six of the archers we had spoken to the previous day wished to join us and I kept them with us as we trawled the town for others. We found no more archers, but we did find two English spearmen who were down on their luck. Both had fought at Poitiers but their lord had been killed and they had stayed on in the hope of employment. Like Giovanni, they had sunk low enough to be night soil men and had no weapons, but I saw their potential. John of Stroud and James of Southampton were young enough to be malleable!

That night I spoke with Robin, Roger, and my men at arms. "The archers, Robin, what is their worth?"

He nodded, "All have talent. Two cannot ride but we can teach them. I am happy."

"Roger, Giovanni?"

"He too has potential. I can see that he has skills and a cunning mind, but we have a year of drinking and indolence to overcome."

I nodded, "The two I found today are just spearmen, but I thought to give them to Henry and Stephen. They need squires and when they are trained, then who knows, they may become men at arms."

We had our start and as the summer passed, we began to train as a company and to begin to look like soldiers.

I was happy and, perhaps, that affected me, perhaps even changed me. Elizabeth and William had both responded well to good food, the chance to wash and clean bedding. When Elizabeth's sores disappeared and with her hair brushed and combed, I saw that she was, indeed, a beauty and could understand why she had been treated as she had. I determined that I would treat her well and indeed I did, perhaps too well.

Chapter 4

It began with what I saw as harmless flirting. I would compliment her on her clothes; she had a fine wardrobe which we had fetched from Bellac. For her part, she would flutter her long lashes and give a coquettish smile when I did so. We laughed a lot when we were together, and I found myself looking forward to her bringing the food to the table. Robin noticed and counselled me, "Sir John, tell me it is none of my business, but you and Elizabeth seem to be heading down a path I do not think you wish to take."

I laughed it off, "She makes me smile, that is all." And, indeed, that was all that I thought it was.

It was the night of the storm which changed everything. August was hot and the storm clouds had been gathering for days. When the thunder and lightning began it was as though a battle was taking place above our heads. When the door was flung open, I grabbed my sword, but it was just Elizabeth who ran to me and threw herself into my arms, "My lord, I am afeard! Is the world ending?"

I laid the sword down and pulled her close. I swear that I just meant to comfort her. "Of course not, it is just a storm and like all such storms it will pass." I stroked her hair to calm her and as I did I smelled the rosemary she had used when washing it. Her arms came around my back and squeezed me. I just wore my night shift as did she and I could feel her firm breasts pressing into me. I swear I meant nothing, but my body seemed to have a mind of its own and I began to become aroused. A man can do nothing about such things. I was aware that neither of us had spoken. She looked up at me and stood on tiptoe. I kissed her and she kissed me back. Nature took over and we sank to the bed.

When I heard her breathing heavily, I knew she was asleep. Her head lay on my arm and I could not move. I was forced to stay there. This complicated matters and Robin had been right. I tried to think how I could have dealt with it in a better fashion and realised that I could not. Had I barred my door there might have been a chance. This was fate and I would have to deal with it. Even as I lay there, she turned her head and nestled into me. Her naked breast was next to my chest and I found myself becoming aroused again. I realised that it had been a long time since I had lain with a woman. I had lain with a woman by the Spanish border and she had borne me a child. I think that was the last time and was so long ago that I could barely remember the woman's name or her face.

In the morning I was spent. She woke and began nibbling my ear, "My lord, that was…"

I turned and raised myself on my elbow, "Elizabeth, I did not plan this."

She nodded, "I know but I have been yearning for this since I came to live here. Sir Geoffrey was a beast and an animal. I felt nauseated by his touch but you… you were different."

"This can lead to nothing, Elizabeth, you know that."

She smiled, "I know that, and you should know that I am happy to lie with you any time that you wish. Last night was something I would do again. Do not worry, my lord, I will not be a burden to you, but I am a woman who, until now, has only known the beast that was Sir Geoffrey. Last night you exorcised that ghost, and I am grateful to you."

I nodded. It was fate and so we began to lie with each other. It did not take long for the others to know what was going on but they said nothing. Robin gave me a reproachful shake of the head but that was all. In truth, I was happier than I had been in a long time. I enjoyed our time in bed together and it made me a better lord during the day for I was less prone to lose my temper. We still flirted but less often and she reserved her attention for the times we lay together.

We found four more archers and I was happy. I even found a captain I felt I could trust. It was William and Roger who found him. They had been to Bordeaux to buy cedarwood to make chests and metal to make weapons. While they had been at the port, they had met an Englishman. He was originally from Whitby and had gone to sea as a deck sailor. Now, Old Jack, as his crew named him, owned his own ship and travelled each month from London to Bordeaux. He was one of the few who sailed even in winter. It was our connection to Stockton and the time of the plague which forged the link. He had a sister who had lived in Hartburn and she had told him how we had saved the village when Stockton had suffered; he knew my name. Robin was convinced we could trust him and so we arranged to travel with him when next he was in port. He said that would be October.

We needed Elizabeth to advise us on the chests we would need and so she worked closely with us for the next weeks. It was when, one day, as we had finished lining a cedarwood chest that she asked if she could have a word. I wondered if she was going to ask for something from England.

"My lord, I am with child. Your child."

It was not the words I had expected but then as we had been together every night since the August storm it should have come as no surprise. "When is the babe due?"

"We lay together in August," she shrugged, "I would say, May or June."

I did not insult her by asking if she was sure it was mine, I just nodded, "I cannot wed you; you know that?"

"That is understood but you will raise the child will you not?"

"Of course!"

She beamed, "Then all is well!"

I wanted no bad feelings and so I called in her brother. He was remarkably stoical about the whole matter. "Sir John, you have given us a home and for that we are grateful. More, we now have work, and a man needs work. I would be lying if I said I would be happier if you wed my sister, but a man cannot have everything and when I was incarcerated, I learned what was important in life."

We sailed for England, Robin, Michael, Dai, William and I. We had chests of spices and silks as well as a chest of gold. I intended to visit Southampton and Balin the weaponsmith. I wanted a new suit of plate. Michael had now grown as much as he was likely to grow and he could have my other suit. I wanted one made of white metal to reflect my new livery. I had told my men that I might be away until the new year. We had chosen our time to travel well. Ships carrying spices and the like travelled during the summer months and then prices would be low. By travelling what was, in effect, the start of winter, meant that we could achieve the highest prices.

We reached London close to the end of October after a voyage which I would not relish taking a second time. The ship, *The Swan*, had been heeled over so much at one point that I swore the tips of the crosstrees touched the waves. We were lucky that our chests contained nothing that would be damaged by such violent moves whereas the captain's cargo of wine would not benefit from the buffeting it had received. Captain Jack kept a house in London, and it meant we could discover if he was in port quickly. We would travel back with him but that, very largely, depended upon concluding our business satisfactorily. As well as selling our goods we needed to hire more men and find where we could benefit from the hiring of our swords.

The voyage had taken it out of us and when we reached London, we found a tavern with rooms and stayed inside for a whole day. I did not relish the voyage back. The captain had no plans to sail for another fortnight and so we were able to leave our goods on board. When we had recovered from the voyage, I sent Robin and Michael to seek warriors. They would be found in the less salubrious parts of London but as Dai, William and I headed through the stinking streets of London I was not sure there were any pleasant places. I had lived close to the Chepe when I had been an apprentice which was a rough place. I had rarely ventured anywhere else in the capital of England. My assumption was that there had to be better places to live. As we headed towards the east side of the city to the warehouses and offices of the merchants we had been told were there, I kept my hand on my sword for I did not feel safe. It was no wonder that King Edward and his family chose Windsor as their London home!

William led us. I would have gone to the Chepe, but I bowed to his local knowledge. He had worked for the Archbishop and I trusted his judgement. We left the city by the Aldgate. I confess that I was enjoying stretching my legs on solid land. I had felt at sea for the first day ashore. We passed the Abbey of St Clare and headed down towards the river. The Tower stood like a white bastion ahead of us, but we turned before we reached it and after passing another monastery found the river with the wharves and the jetties. The warehouses all had guards upon them and that showed me that this was not a place a man could feel safe. William nodded, "The man I seek is a Jew."

I stopped, "But they were all expelled by King Edward at the end of the last century. It is illegal for them to live here! We cannot do business with one!"

He smiled, almost patronisingly and shook his head, "If you have money then your secret beliefs remain just that a secret. The French lord I served was a Cathar and none knew. John Braynford does not look like a Jew and he dresses like an Englishman. He married an English woman whom he met in Outremer. Her father was a knight and her mother was from the east. They returned to England and they have a daughter. To all those outside he is English."

"And how do you know he is not?"

"The Archbishop knew, and he kept the man's secret so that he could reap the reward of lower prices."

I was reassured. If the Archbishop used the merchant, then I should be able to.

The armed men on the door looked handy. They had short swords, but it was the cudgels that they held which told me of their skill. William handled the negotiations which had us admitted. He used my name to gain admittance. Once inside the darkened warehouse, we saw perhaps twelve people busily working. They were examining boxes and chests whilst others were taking goods out to the wagons. From the outside, the warehouse looked almost deserted. The guard who escorted us asked us to wait outside a large metal-studded door. We were not kept long.

John Braynford had grey, thinning hair but I saw that his eyes were as sharp and piercing as a good blade. I saw, too, that he had not gone to fat. He looked fit for a man who had to be in his forties. William was right, he looked nothing like a Jew and had I not been told then I would not have known.

"Harry, fetch chairs for our guests. Sir John, I am honoured."

The guard went outside. I had not seen chairs, but he returned with three of them held in his mighty paws.

"Would you care for refreshments? I have a fine wine from Lusitania which you might enjoy."

I shook my head, "It is a little early in the day and I would like to keep a clear head." He nodded and spread his arms intimating that I should speak. "Some goods have come into our possession which we would like to sell to you. There are spices and there are silks from the east." I leaned forward, "I confess that we are seeking a merchant who might purchase other such goods in the future."

He nodded, "Your timing is impeccable for I have need of such items. I had a supplier, but he has let me down. I expected a consignment some months ago." He shrugged, "Frenchmen, eh? And where are these goods?"

William said, "They are still on the ship we used to bring them here."

For the first time, the merchant's smile left his face and he frowned, "And how were they transported?"

"In cedarwood chests."

He beamed, "I can see that I am dealing with men of wisdom. Could I view the goods for I have clients who are keen to have them? When I have seen them, I can give you a price I am willing to pay."

"It is but a short walk…"

He shook his head, "I do not risk the streets of London. I have a wherry. It is safer to travel by water and my home is to the west of the city. It is safer there for my family."

I nodded, "But unless the price is right then there will be no sale."

He smiled, "Sir John, would I try to rob the hero of Poitiers? I am honoured that you sought me out. You will find me a fair and honest man. Merchants who are dishonest do not last long in this land. Besides, it is known that Prince Edward thinks highly of you. Indeed I heard that it was he who gave you your spurs."

"He did."

"Well then let us visit this ship of yours." As he left, he waved over a clerk, "Edgar, I shall be gone for the rest of the day. When I have visited with Sir John, I shall continue home."

"Very well master. I will see that all is locked up and our deliveries made."

I saw that two of his guards doubled as sailors. That made sense for working the agile little boat on the busy Thames would take strength and the two looked to have it in abundance. There was enough room for us as it looked to be a larger than normal wherry. We seated ourselves close to the mast and headed upstream. William pointed out the ship and the merchant nodded, "He is a good captain and I have dealt with him before. I am intrigued that you found him for he operates out of Bordeaux and yet you have eastern goods for sale."

I smiled, "I did not say that we had them from the east just that we had them."

"You are an intriguing man, Sir John." We had reached the quay and while one man tied us up the other lowered the sail. "Wait for me here. I will not be long."

He was quite agile for someone his age. The First Mate had been left aboard and warned that we might return. He led us to the hold. He held a glass-enclosed lantern and took us to the chests. Ours was the only cargo remaining aboard. The merchant insisted upon opening each one. He was not a fool. Satisfied he nodded, "I am content. Indeed this looks to be the very cargo I was expecting." He shrugged. "I will give you five hundred ecus for the cargo. That is my only offer."

I looked at William who nodded.

"Then we have a deal."

"Where are you staying?"

"The Lamb just off Leadenhall Street."

"I know it. I will bring the coins tomorrow; shall we say noon?" I nodded. "Until tomorrow."

He strode off. I turned to the First Mate, "Keep it guarded until we return."

The First Mate said, "You can trust him, Sir John. The captain has dealt with him before and he keeps his word."

We headed back to the inn. I would not spend money before we had it in our possession, but I planned on visiting the Chepe the next day before the merchant arrived to see the prices. I knew how to haggle. My time as an apprentice had served me well.

Robin and Michael arrived back in the late afternoon with little to show for their efforts. They had found neither archers nor men at arms, but they had heard of places where they gathered. They were not in the city for it was expensive to live there, as we were discovering. Robin had the most hopeful lead, "Rochester,

Sir John, has the archers of the Weald living close by and we were told that there are some who could be hired."

"Men at arms?"

Michael shook his head.

Dai said, "Sir John why search all the flowers for nectar? Your name is known. Why not spread the word that you are hiring. Then we could simply sit here and let them come to us?"

I looked at Robin who nodded, "A good idea, Dai! I will still go with Michael to Rochester but we will spread the word twixt there and here."

"Very well. The merchant is coming tomorrow at noon with the payment. We have done well."

"I will need to hire a couple of horses, my lord."

"And that is another reason that Dai's idea has merit. William, go to the innkeeper and negotiate a longer stay. Try to get a better price and let him know that we are seeking archers and men at arms so his profits should rise."

William gestured around at the empty inn, "The Prince has a tourney on the day after Christmas, St Stephen's Day, until then London will be empty. I will see what I can do."

For London, the food was not bad. I had eaten far worse but the price of everything was far higher than even a mile or two outside the city. William was persuasive and managed to extend our stay at a better rate. He even managed to hire two hackneys from the innkeeper so that Michael and Robin could make their journey as soon as it was dawn.

I went with Dai and William to the Chepe. We passed the tailors where I had served my apprenticeship. It was a young tailor who now ran it. We did not buy, as we viewed the items on display in the market, but we made a note of prices. I was not recognised as the tailor's apprentice, but my coat of arms was and some old soldiers who had been at the battles in France spoke to me. All had some wound or other. In the case of two archers I remembered they had lost their drawing fingers and in the case of a man at arms from Poitiers he had lost his left hand. I gave them coppers, but I could not offer employment!

John Braynford and four of his men arrived promptly at noon with a chest containing the coins. Dai took them to our rooms where I would secure them later. The merchant and I celebrated the deal with a flagon of wine. When the men returned, I sent William and Dai with them so that they could take them to the chests of spices and silks. When we were alone the merchant said, "Now that there are no ears to overhear, Sir John, I would speak in confidence to you."

"I have no secrets from my men."

He laughed, "I cannot believe that, but I will let it pass. I have asked others about you. You are more than a simple warrior. The spices you took and the silks were, I believe, taken in Bellac." He saw my face, "Do not deny it and I do not mind. I thought I recognised your man, but it was some years since I had seen him. Sir Geoffrey and his father were unpleasant men, and they were French. They were of no use to me. You on the other hand are."

I did not like the idea of being used and I stiffened.

The merchant held up his hand, "I am sorry. That was the wrong phrase. I meant we could be of use to each other. I need someone who can acquire for me goods in France which, shall we say, belong to others. They may not be spices or silks but they could be wines, fine furniture and the like. All I am saying is that if you come across such items then I will buy them from you. As you no doubt realise, prices are far higher here than you could be paid in either France or Italy. It would be mutually beneficial."

I nodded, "You know that if you tried to cheat me then you could expect violence and the men you hire to guard you would be no hindrance to me."

"I know your reputation and it would not be in my interests to cheat you for then my supply would dry up. Look, why not come to stay with me in my home for a few days. It is far more comfortable than here and we could speak more openly. I should like you to meet my family. What have you to lose?"

"I need to be here, certainly for a few days but I am intrigued. Let us say that I will come in a fortnight, the eleventh of November."

He beamed, "I will send one of my men here to take you to my wherry. Will you be bringing your men?"

"Perhaps. Is that a problem?"

"Of course not. My house is palatial!"

I did not tell the tale to Dai and William. I decided to wait until all my men were there. Robin and Michael did not arrive back until early evening. Their faces told me that they had enjoyed more success than on the previous day. I waited until they had eaten their food before I questioned them closely.

"As soon as we were in Kent, we found men who would be willing to follow you, my lord. We told all the ones who were interested that we would return to Rochester on the first of December. We would not hire until then." Michael looked a little worried, "Did we do wrong, my lord?"

I shook my head, "No, that was a good decision. It gives them time to decide if this is really what they wish and allows those who might have doubts to think it through here, rather than in France. I want committed men!"

"This will work out for the best," I told them of our trip in November. "It gives us two weeks to find any men who might seek us here and then we can return to Rochester. If we have enough, Robin, before December, then I propose to send them back to Bordeaux with you and William. Dai, Michael and I can go to Rochester and then sail when our business is concluded. There is nothing spoiling in Bordeaux."

Robin nodded and drank half of his ale, "Yew staves, lord and bodkins. We need those two items. You cannot get the right ones in France and I would have at least two spare bow staves for each man. Bowstrings we can get and Martin is able to fletch but yew bows will make all the difference."

"Then tomorrow you can get those while Michael and I ride to Southampton to see Balin of Bitterne." I had also decided to see Basil of Tarsus. He held money for me and I knew that it would have grown. I was unlikely to return very often to Southampton and I wanted to consolidate my treasure in one place, Bordeaux."

We saw Balin first and he was more than happy to make me a new suit of plate armour and mail. He still had my measurements. "And when it is made then I wish it sent to John Braynford in London. He is a merchant with a warehouse close to the river and to the east of the Tower. He will have it sent to me."

"Aye, lord." I paid him the coins and went to mount the hired horses, "It is a long ride back to London, my lord."

I shook my head, "I have business in Southampton with Basil of Tarsus."

He paled, "Did you leave money with him, my lord?"

I nodded, "He had some of my chests of gold which he invested for me."

"He is dead, lord and his house burned down. He and his men were attacked for being Jews."

My fortune was gone.

"When was this?"

"Even as the news of the Battle of Poitiers reached us so he was attacked."

"And who was responsible for this attack? Was it the king's men?"

"No, lord, a German. There were those who said he did it to steal the money that Basil of Tarsus had. Everyone knew he was a Jew, but he did good works for the people. I thought it was a shame."

"And the name of the German?"

"I am not sure, lord. I think he was a count, and he might have been called von Landau."

I gave an extra coin to Balin, "I will still visit Southampton and see who stole my money!"

Michael knew when to speak and when to stay silent. He was silent as we rode to Southampton. It was not that I disbelieved Balin, but I wanted to see for myself. He had not lied. The house was still a burned-out shell and the neighbours confirmed the story. None knew the name of the German except that he was a warrior.

The inn in which we stayed gave us more information. The German, it seemed, had landed with a number of other men about a month before the arson. I deduced that they were mercenaries and that made sense. If they heard that Basil of Tarsus kept money then it would have been an easy way to become rich quickly.

"Count Konrad Wirtinger von Landau, my lord. That was his name. They stayed a week after the fire and then vanished into thin air. Folks were not happy for Basil was well thought of, but you don't argue with twenty armed Germans."

It was clear to me that the story about Jewry had been concocted. I now had a name. There were German mercenaries, Giovanni had told me about them. He said they operated in Italy. I now had a name and when time allowed, I would have vengeance on this thief!

Chapter 5

By the time we reached London once more, I had cheered myself up. I had thought the money I had left with Basil was a fortune. When I invested it then it had been but now it was a drop in the ocean compared to all that I had taken since. However, it was my money, and I would extract it piece by piece from Count Konrad Wirtinger von Landau or his body if it was all spent.

My spirits were raised when we reached the inn, for Robin had hired three archers and asked for the two men at arms whom he had found to return the next day. I gave them my news and Robin suddenly leaned forward. "I have heard of a German Count. I believe he was von Landau."

"You have heard of a German Count? When?"

"Today. One of the men at arms who came seeking work said he had served in Italy with a man called Fra Moriale, a Frenchman, whom he liked but after he was executed in Rome a German took over the company and he did not like him. He left."

Fate sometimes works that way or perhaps it was that ours was a very small world. I had run into Giovanni d'Azzo on a number of occasions and met other warriors on the battlefield. Whatever the cause I now had a clue!

I barely slept that night so keen was I to meet and speak with this man at arms. Robin had asked him to return at noon. Even though we found another two archers and a man at arms in the morning I was still waiting for the man known as Robert Greengrass. It was the other who arrived first, Peter of Poole who was a seasoned warrior. He had been at Poitiers but the knight he had followed had been killed after the battle in a brawl at Southampton. He had a horse and a page, it was his son. He was the only one who had met that requirement. In a perfect world, all my men at arms would have been accompanied by a page and a squire. I had already decided on a compromise. Until they had a squire and a page they would have a pair of archers to act as a page and squire. As we had discovered on the road back from Bellac, it was a mixture of horsemen and archers that was important.

When Robert Greengrass arrived, I saw a type of soldier I had seen since the first battles in which I had fought. He was a real professional. While his plate armour was not the best I saw that everything about him showed him to be one who had learned, as I had learned, to be a soldier just by fighting. His sword was not richly decorated but I knew that it would be sharp enough to shave with and would be well balanced. The two daggers I could see were of different types, one was Italian and the other French and I did not doubt there were two others I could not see. The man had travelled.

"A curious name, Master Robert." He nodded, "I am guessing it is because there was always greener grass somewhere else?"

He grinned, "That is the size of it."

"You are hired for I like the way you bear yourself but I seek information too. My Captain of Archers tells me that you were in a company of mercenaries commanded by a German count."

His face turned sour at the thought of it. "Aye, my lord, Konrad von Landau and a more unpleasant man I have yet to meet." He shook his head, "I have nothing against Germans, the rest of the Great Company were either Italians or Germans and I got on with them, in the main. Fra Moriale was a rogue but he was an honourable rogue and it was his honour that had him captured. This Count left us for a while and when he returned, he had amassed a fortune. He began to take over the Company by hiring more Germans who were loyal to him."

I interrupted, "Was this around the time of the battle of Poitiers?" The news of the victory had resonated throughout every Christian land and was remembered.

He nodded, "Aye, lord, how did you know?"

"I know whence he gained the money."

"The man was ruthless, and he made it hard for men like me to stay. I came back to serve with the Prince, but he appears more interested in jousts than anything else."

"Thank you for your news. Where is the Great Company now?"

"When I left them, they were in Pisa and Florence. Those two city-states fight each other constantly and there is always coin to be made."

"Welcome to our company." I turned to William, "Make sure that all the men we hire have payment for signing on. Robin, find the sea captain. You will sail back to Bordeaux with the new men we have hired. It will be cheaper for us to keep them there. I will return to Bordeaux in January."

When I was alone with my inner circle Robin asked, "Why stay until January, Sir John? We will have the men we need by then. Elizabeth will be missing you and there is nothing else for you here."

"There is Prince Edward! He will be here for a tourney after Christmas and I hope to see him. I doubt that he will go to war this year but," I lowered my voice, "he may have plans for the next and if we can be in a position to be where he campaigns then we might find our first contract." I leaned back and smiled, "Besides, it will just be a month or so after you and as our ship is not large, we will all be more comfortable travelling in two parties.

By the time he had arranged the passage we had more men. We had four more men at arms and ten archers. The prospect of a winter in a warmer and less expensive clime appealed to many. As fate would have it, they left just days before my proposed visit to John Braynford. I gave William presents to take to his sister and I let Robin take the chest with the bulk of the coins which still remained. We had virtually filled the hold with all that we had purchased. The staves and arrowheads were guarded as closely as the chest of gold for they were our livelihood.

We paid the innkeeper when we left. I could see that he was sorry to see us go. His inn had been full most nights with our men and I had spent well. "If you return, my lord, then I will ensure that you have the best of rooms and the most reasonable of prices."

"Good. I know not where my business will take me, but I will consider your offer." Our trip down the river would only last a couple of days but I had plans on travelling to Rochester. From what Robin had said that appeared to be the best place to find the sort of men we needed. We had only managed to hire forty men and I needed more.

We were fetched from the inn by the merchant's men. They carried our bags. The day was a typical November one, it was blustery and flurries of sleet flecked rain spattered us as we headed to the wherry. There was an awning close to the mast and we took shelter there. As we passed down the river, we saw the city from a different perspective. The river was a safer mode of travel than the roads and every house and monastery had a jetty where they could board boats such as ours. The blustery wind helped us down the river and the tide was on the turn but, even so, it still took time. When we saw the house on the river it looked like the home of a mighty lord. It was not a castle, but it looked like a place that could be defended easily. I saw that there was a moat that fed from the river and that there were two towers above the gatehouse. Slits in the walls told me that both bows and crossbows could be used to defend the merchant's home. We approached from the river, of course, and I saw that on that side there was glass in the wind holes. They would afford a fine view over the river. I later learned that the ones facing the land, the ones which were seen from the road had no glass. That was the side of the house where the servants lived. The wherry pulled into a wooden jetty. I saw, closer to the house, a boathouse and there was a second wherry within.

John Braynford strode down to meet us. I saw that he wore a fine fur about his shoulders. The functional and nondescript clothes he had worn in London were now replaced by expensive boots, hose and all the trappings of a lord. On his fingers he wore rings and there was a golden chain around his neck.

"Sir John, thank you for coming."

"This is Michael, one of my men at arms and Dai, a sometime squire."

"Gentlemen, you are all welcome. Come let us go inside for this is not a day to stand and admire the river."

As we headed towards his hall, I was intrigued. This merchant had it all, money and security. Why did he need me? Unlike the other Jew I had known, Basil of Tarsus, John Braynford did not live in a crowded street where he could be attacked. It would take an army to assault this hall and the wherries meant that he had the means to flee. He did not need me for my men so why was he being so effusively generous?

The entrance had been cunningly crafted so that it could not be breached by a ram and yet did not appear to be a defensive structure. The door was opened by a man with tanned skin. He was not native to these lands. "Antoninus, have our guests' bags taken to their rooms."

"Yes, sir."

There was a finely carved staircase that led to an upper storey and we walked on a floor made of wood. When he opened the door to his hall, I saw that it was a room where twenty people could dine. Sitting by the fire were two women. The older of the two was patently the merchant's wife and she was stunningly beautiful. With jet black hair, almond eyes and skin which displayed the eastern origins of her own mother she took a man's breath away. The other woman was, obviously, their daughter, and had I seen her alone would have thought her a pretty young thing but next to her mother she paled into the background.

"Sir John Hawkwood, this is my wife, Katherine and my daughter, Antiochia. My love, this is Sir John Hawkwood and his men, Michael and Dai."

I took the proffered hand and kissed it, "My lady, your beauty warms a man on this cold day."

Katherine laughed, "A smooth-tongued gentleman! He is a cut above the men you normally bring here, my love."

I took Antiochia's hand and kissed that also, "And I can see that you have inherited your mother's looks."

The young woman flushed and then beamed, "I have looked forward to this visit since my father first mentioned it. I eagerly anticipate hearing about the great battles in which you have fought."

Before I could say anything Antoninus returned and said, "Gentlemen, if you would follow me then I will take you to your rooms."

"Do not be tardy, Sir John, we wish to make the most of every moment that you are with us." Katherine's perfectly enunciated voice was as mesmerizing as her looks. As I ascended the stairs I could understand, even more clearly, why this merchant kept his family so safe. His wife was as precious as the gold he had accrued!

We had been given two rooms and three beds. A door led from the larger room, mine, to the one with the two smaller beds. Like the rest of the furnishings in the house, there was quality everywhere. There were three bowls with scented water and drying cloths for us to use. Our clothes had already been hung.

Antoninus said, "There is a bell, lord, pray to ring it for anything you require. The garderobe is on the north wall." With that, he left us.

Dai looked around and said, "It is like a palace."

I nodded, "Aye, but until we discover this merchant's motives keep your ears open and say as little as possible." I did not need to warn them about drinking too much.

As we entered a hall with a heaving table already laden with food our host took my elbow and said, "Tomorrow will be the time for our business. For tonight my family, starved of good company, would hear your tales of life serving Prince Edward and our king."

"Of course."

The regaling of bleached and sanitized tales was no hardship although I could not yet see how we would benefit. The food was the finest I had enjoyed and laden with spices. The wine was superb although I drank sparingly, and my tale flowed like the river outside. The ladies were attentive and when I told the tale of Michael and he added his part, tears sprang to the eyes of Antiochia. Even Dai, who was mesmerized by it all was asked for his story. By the time we came to the sweet treats at the end of the meal I was satiated and felt I needed a rest. I turned the tables on our host.

"And you sir, what is your tale for this house, your family, your table have all the hallmarks of a noble and yet you have no title?"

For the first time, our host and hostess lost their smiles. John looked at his wife who nodded. "We come from what was once called Outremer. Now it is ruled by Muslims but we both come from families which lived there since before the last crusade."

Katherine said, "My father was a lord with lands close to Antioch. He came to an arrangement with the Muslims and we lived in peace for a while. It did not last. Had not John here, come to our aid we might have not only lost our home and our lands, but we might also have lost our lives. I owe everything to this man."

He nodded as his wife touched his hand, "It was nothing. I had already decided that my business could not continue for the new lords of the land were imposing taxes on all those, not of their faith. I managed to sell up in secret and I hired men, warriors like yourself, Sir John, to escort us to the coast where we took ship to Cyprus. There I was able to continue my business and I married Katherine. We lived in some style and I continued to prosper. The Empire ruled kindly for some years but the German governor who came, a couple of years after Antiochia was born, made life difficult for us and when my wife's parents died it seemed the moment to leave and we headed as far away from Cyprus as we could get. Once again I hired men to help us and we reached England not long after your great victory at Crécy." He smiled, "You can see why we needed to know about that battle for our fortunes changed in that year. We were kept safe here from the great pestilence and were able to profit when it left us."

"And yet you are still not a lord."

He looked me in the eyes, "I can never be a lord, I know that but I have enough influential friends who will keep me safe. It was Henry Plantagenet, to whom I have been of some small service, who spoke highly of you. When you arrived at my place of work it was as though God had sent you."

He had skirted around his religion whilst explaining to me the real reason I was here. He needed me for some sword work. I did not mind for it was work and I knew it would be well-paid work. That night as I lay in a very comfortable bed I found my thoughts drifting to Katherine. She was a little older than I was, but she was an incredibly attractive woman. Perhaps Elizabeth had made me realise that I was still a man and getting no younger!

The breakfast was huge and it was just the men who ate, "Tomorrow, Sir John, I would take you and your men hunting. I pay Sir Ralph, the local landowner for the privilege of hunting in his woods. He is well paid, and I never abuse it. Today I thought we would walk by the river. I own all of the lands to the east and west of my home and I have something I would show you."

We dressed for the weather. The rain and sleet had ceased but the wind was still scything along the black waters of the Thames.

It was one thing soldiers knew how to do and if nothing else my men and I were protected from the cold and the rain. The merchant pointed out features as we headed down the pebbled path that had been laid along the river. It was wide enough for a wagon and I saw not only the ruts but the piles of horse dung we occasionally found. He flicked them into the grass and undergrowth. I noticed that his men were not with us and I guessed his land was protected by piquets at the periphery of his grounds.

We had gone half a mile when I heard hammering and the sound of men working. As the path passed beneath some willows, shaped by the wagons which had passed along the track, I saw that half a dozen men were labouring on a house. It looked to be almost as substantial as the merchant's own. The men stopped work when we approached and he waved at them, "Continue, I pray. We come to see the progress is all." We stood while he pointed out the features of the house. "This will be for Antiochia when she marries. I have seen enough villainy in the world to keep my daughter safe. I would see her as a lady." I turned to look at him and he smiled, "There are many nobles who have lost fortunes either through the pestilence, ransom or bad investments. So long as they have a title and Antiochia wishes to marry them then I will be content. Money is not a problem. Were I to live a dozen lifetimes I could not spend all that I have accrued." He pointed to the stone chimney which was being built. "That will be the heart of the house. Even now, having lived in England these many years, I still find it so cold that I barely bear it in winter. There will be four bedrooms as well as a fine kitchen, hall and outbuildings. Whoever marries my daughter will do well for himself."

We wandered around the workings and I found it interesting. One day I would build a home but first I had to find a place where I could live. My home in Bordeaux was temporary, we all knew that, and England was no good if I was to be a hired sword. Speaking with John and Katherine I had realised the potential of fighting closer to the Empire. If a man led a good-sized company then it would be equal to most city-state armies.

We headed back towards the main house and I said, "I still cannot see why you wish to court my favour, for that is what you are doing. I cannot believe that you give this level of attention to all those with whom you do business."

He nodded, "And you are right. I do not need your sword. I do like you, Sir John, and did so from before I even met you. It made me interested in you. The stories you told last night were stirring ones but they do not tell the whole story. I know of your raid into Scotland and I know about your early days as an archer."

I whipped my head around, "How?"

"The men who serve me are all warriors. It was not hard to find someone who served with you in Captain Philip's company, and another knew of you at Carlisle. When you began to serve the King and Sir Walter Manny then your trail was even clearer." I must have started but he shook his head, "I think better of you for some of the things you have done. I know that others might frown on your actions, but I think that a man must look out for himself first or he cannot then look out for others. I think you are a man who gets things done. I can help you. I am not sure if you need money now but if you do then I can provide it for a share of the profits. If you do not need it then when you are earning your trade in…" he waved an arm, "wherever it is then I will do as I told you before, I will pay for all that you find. I will tell you where you may send the goods you take for I have sea captains all over the east coast of France and Flanders." We had reached the moat and the river. Dai and Michael had walked a discreet distance behind and I am not sure they had heard anything. The merchant lowered his voice, "And in return, there may be occasions when I use your swords and your bows to my own ends."

I could not see a problem with that for I doubted that it would be in England and if it was abroad then, as far as I knew, I had no friends there. "On those terms, John Braynford, I am your man, and my company are your men."

"Excellent. The walk has given me an appetite!"

The food that night was excellent and the conversation both easier and engaging for Michael and Dai now spoke more. They got on well with Antiochia who was just a little younger than Michael and I found talking to Katherine easy. John just watched us all and I could see that he was happy!

The hunt went well. Despite the fact that Dai and I were only using borrowed hunting bows and not our war bows our skill was such that we slew four deer with just four arrows. The merchant's men who were with us were hard men to impress but the looks they gave us showed that we had done what few others had done.

We left to travel upriver just three days later. Antiochia was sad to see us leave and wept but I genuinely believe that both the merchant and his wife would also be saddened by our departure. He agreed to send my plate armour to me and gladly offered his wherry to take us to Rochester. Meeting the Jew had proved to be one of the most fortuitous events in my life.

Chapter 6

We now had to go back to work. Once we had visited Rochester then we would be able to sail home to Bordeaux. Rochester inn in which we stayed, The Three Lions, was far cheaper than The Lamb and the food better. It was winter and the pilgrims heading to Canterbury were far fewer. There were, however, many men who sought an employer. When King Edward had failed in his foray in the north of France and Flanders then the men who had been released had gravitated from Dover, further west. Some had managed to make it further than Rochester, but a large number had spent the money they had and been forced to stay. Some were patently unsuitable. They had spent all their money on ale and women. Whilst in itself that was not a bad thing a real warrior always kept enough money so that he was not forced to beg. The beggars I ignored. The ones I looked for were the ones who had retained their weapons. Robin's visit meant that there were archers and men at arms who courted my favour. I sent Dai around the town to tell all those interested where I was to be found.

It was the third day of my recruiting that I met Albert Sterz. We had found six archers but no men at arms and, as there was no one waiting in the square, Michael and I went for a walk around the other inns. It was as we walked, I asked him about Antiochia, "You and she seemed to get on, Michael."

He laughed, "My lord she only had eyes for you!"

"She is a child!"

"She is the same age as Elizabeth!"

"Even so! The two of you were chattering like magpies."

"As was Dai and it was all about you. I think she sees you as a great knight and hero."

"But I am not!"

Michael, despite his age, was wise and he was very observant. He shrugged, "The girl never leaves the house and just hears the tales her father brings home. She sews and she reads. The books are romantic stories about knights and dragons. What else should she think, my lord?"

I knew the books of which Michael spoke. They were not stories as such but pieces of parchment written by clerks who wished to earn a little money. William had told me about them for he had done some of the copying. That explained much. I had never read one but I knew they were not written by warriors. They were written, originally, by priests who were making them into tales of good and evil where the dragon represented the Devil. There were a number of such conversations about the crusades and great deeds performed by Christian knights. I would have to remedy the situation if I had the chance to speak with her again.

We saw the German warrior trying to persuade some men at arms to join him. We were standing in the shadows for it was late afternoon and the brands had not yet been lit. I had seen him before on the chevauchée led by Prince Edward. I knew he fought for England, but he spoke with an accent. He was older than I was and by his weapons and his mail was successful. Like me, he had two companions. One was a swordsman and the other looked to be his squire.

Two of the men at arms he was speaking with turned and one said, "I am sorry, Lord Albert, but I would rather serve an Englishman. I hear Sir John Hawkwood seeks soldiers. I will find him."

The German said, dismissively, "Hawkwood? I hear he has a handful of archers and some old men at arms commanded by a stripling of a boy! What can you hope to gain from service with one such as he?"

I was angry, not for myself, but for Michael who had been insulted. I stepped from the shadows, "Repeat that, German, and you and I will trade blows."

The two men at arms turned and the one who had refused Lord Albert's offer said, "You are Sir John Hawkwood?"

I pointed to the chevron and scallop shells on my surcoat and said, "Aye. If you wish to serve me then head to the Three Lions. I gave one a silver coin. Ask for Dai and he will take your details."

The other man at arms had disappeared, sensing trouble. I did not think that there would be.

The German gave me a silky smile, "I am sorry Sir John, had I known you were here…"

"Then you would have put on a false face and lied to me. This is better for I now know your opinion." Michael's hand was on his sword and I shook my head.

"We have got off on the wrong foot, my friend. Let us have a drink for we both served Prince Edward. I am Albert Sterz and I too have my own company."

As much as I wanted to walk away, I knew that this man might have information that was useful to me. I nodded, "One drink!"

We entered the inn. A small crowd had gathered in anticipation of violence and I sensed the disappointment as they dispersed. We went inside the inn, The Hops, and he led us to a table. The room was filled with warriors, perhaps eleven of them and I saw some who had come to me, but I had dismissed. Albert Sterz did not have quality. I had the measure of the man.

We sat and Michael and I remained steadfastly silent. Sterz had asked for the drink and it was incumbent upon him to begin. "Let me start again. I am gathering a company of men. I have more than two hundred." I pointedly looked around. He shook his head and smiled. "Most are across the Channel, in Calais. When I have enough, I have a plan. You should join me?"

I laughed, "You mean '*a handful of archers and some old men at arms commanded by a stripling of a boy*'? Why should you need us?"

"I was trying to persuade them to join me. All is fair, is it not, Sir John?" I said nothing. He leaned forward, "The peasants in France are unhappy with their nobles. They say that they abandoned their King. King John is highly thought of." I nodded. "I propose to go to the heart of France, close to Paris and take advantage of the situation."

I was intrigued, "How?"

"You fought at Poitiers. Did you see any French noble who made you fear for your life?" I shook my head. "When the peasants rise, because they are fed up with working for nothing repairing the French nobles' castles, then they will not just stop with the nobles. They will take what they can. I propose to take my men and offer protection to towns."

"French nobles?"

He shook his head, "There will have to be some bloodletting but that will just encourage the ones who are not nobles but have money to pay us to protect their property. It may well be that the mere presence of my men might be enough."

"And you need me because?"

"Because I have men at arms aplenty, but you know archers. I saw you on the Great Raid. You and your mounted archers were a force to be reckoned with. Added to which you are the knight who captured the Oriflamme. That would give you standing amongst all the French for it was a heroic deed." He drank some of his wine, "I would give you an equal share in the profits."

I saw two of the men sat with us start and scowl at that.

It was an intriguing prospect, and I could see that it might work. We would not be fighting English men or Gascons and we would be increasing the chance of Prince Edward finally conquering France. We might even be seen as heroes. I finished the wine. The wine brought me to my senses. Such an action would never be seen as heroic. I stood, "I will give your words the study they deserve. I will be returning to Bordeaux soon. Send me a message if you leave Calais. I assume that you would not be beginning this commission until spring?"

"The peasants will be quiet until then. Even the nobles do not ask them to work on their castles in the winter."

"Then you will have my answer by Easter." He nodded, "But do not slander me or my men again!" I glared at the two who had scowled, "We have short tempers and well-honed swords!"

Albert Sterz was a pragmatic man and he smiled, "I would not choose to cross swords with you when we could share in riches beyond our wildest dreams."

Back at the inn, Michael shook his head, "I do not like the man. Why should we join with him?"

"Because, Michael, he has more men than we do and I cannot see this visit yielding the sorts of numbers we need. Besides, we learned much. We know France and if there is unrest then we are already in a better position to exploit it than he is. Let us put it from our minds. We give this area another three days and then head back to London and take a ship to France."

When we returned to the inn, the two men at arms were there already and they happily joined us. They knew the German and said that he was a good leader but as both men had been at Poitiers and were English, they wished to follow my banner. We had been right to name the company the English company. In all we found twelve men to follow us back to France. It would have been too expensive and impractical to hire horses for all of us and so I sent Dai to book horses for the three of us so that we could ride directly to London Bridge and I found a wherryman who agreed to ferry the men the next day back to London. It cost less than the hire of the three horses!

The weather when we left was atrocious. A wintery storm swept in from the east and brought flecks of snow as well as sleet and rain. Its only saving grace was that as we were heading west the wet came behind us and we were able to raise the cowls on our cloaks and wrap them tightly around us. It meant that the main road to London, the one built by the Romans, Watling Street, was largely deserted. That suited us as it meant we did not have to constantly navigate around carts, wagons and knots of people using it.

The attack, when it came, was close to Cobham, which lay to the south of us. The woods there were thick, and the ambush came from the side. Dai was hit in the leg by an arrow sent from our right, the ground to the north of the road but, being a game youth he held on to his reins and gritted his teeth. The other arrows sent at us missed and that told me two things, these were not good archers and they had not known that we were warriors.

Drawing my sword I shouted, "At them!" Michael drew his sword and we both wheeled our horses to the right. These were not warhorses nor even palfreys, but they obeyed us. My sudden charge must have panicked the men who sought to attack us for the arrows which flew at us missed. It was not by much, but it was enough. I aimed my horse in the direction of a beech tree from which I had seen an arrow sent. I held my hand with my sword behind me and when the face and chest emerged to send another arrow my sword swept up, hacking through his arm and into his jaw. I heard a voice cry, "Run!"

I knew that it could have been a trick to make us stop and so I wheeled the reluctant hackney to the right and as the man who was trying to flee looked up, he saw his death as my sword sliced down to split his skull. The noise and the movement disappearing in the distance told me that the ambush was over and the handful of men who had sought to take an easy purse were leaving.

I pushed back the cowl of my cloak and turned. Michael was wiping his sword and even Dai had killed an ambusher. I sheathed my sword and rode to Dai. "Come let us get you attended to." I pointed south. "There is a hall at Cobham. I believe it is just a mile or so south of the road. Michael, watch our backs."

We knew better than to try to remove the arrow. There appeared to be little blood coming from the wound and that meant no artery had been cut. The arrow had been stopped by the girth on the hired horse and it had sealed the wound. I found the signposted road which led to the hall and we headed down it. Michael nudged his horse next to mine. "I think there were ten of them, Sir John. We killed five and I think that other travellers will be safer now."

"Aye, but Dai has paid the price. How is the leg, Dai?" I could see that he was pale and in pain.

He shook his head, "I think the arrowhead hit the bone, lord. That is where I feel the pain, in the bone!"

The sound of our hooves on the cobbled yard outside the hall drew men from inside. They had weapons. "I am Sir John Hawkwood and we have been attacked by bandits on the London road. One of my men is hurt."

The grey-haired man sheathed his sword, "I am Edgar, lord, the steward. Sir Richard is away but my wife has skills, and she will tend to your man. Hob, take the horses to the stables, Peter, fetch wine and a poker. Alice!"

Michael and I dismounted and lifted Dai from the saddle. It was not quick for the arrow was stuck in the leather. Dai was lucky, had it been a better arrow strike then it might have pricked his horse and he would have been thrown. Such injuries were, generally, worse than wounds. As we carried him inside, I saw that the missile was a poorly made hunting arrow.

"Fetch him to the kitchen, my lord, it is warm there and I have all that I will need,"

We laid him on a table normally used for chopping meat. It seemed appropriate. Alice went to fetch her vinegar, honey, and bandages. I had been an archer and knew about such wounds. I took my dagger and sliced away the breeks and then down the two sides of his buskins. I slid the boot off as gently as I could, but I knew that it hurt him. "I will break off the head and then when this lady, Alice, is ready I will pull the shaft out. Michael."

Michael knew what to do and he took Dai's knife out and put the wooden handle in Dai's mouth.

"Ready, my lord."

Holding the head and the shaft of the arrow where it emerged from his leg, I snapped it off. I tried to be gentle, but I felt him wince. Holding my left hand tightly against the wound I grasped the fletched end of the arrow, "Now!"

I pulled the arrow out in one swift movement and Dai's back arched. Alice was ready with a vinegar infused cloth and she rammed it against the wound. "There is a brave boy!" Her maternal voice made Dai smile. She turned to me, "Thank you, my lord. My husband has some ale for you. I can see to this now." She shook her head, "Bandits! Hang them all I say!"

The steward nodded to me and we followed him to the hall. The ale was welcoming. "We did not fare badly, Edgar, but lesser folk might have died. The nest of bandits needs rooting out."

He nodded, "Sir Richard scours the forests every year or so but …Men need employment, lord!"

"Aye and before the pestilence there might have been an excuse but now there are jobs for those who are willing to work. Your wife is right, Edgar. Now is not the time for sympathy but a strong arm."

When the ale was gone, we returned to the kitchen. "I have stemmed the bleeding, lord, but the bone is broken. I have fashioned a splint, but he needs a healer."

"Is there a house of healing close by?"

She shook her head, "The nearest one is at the south end of London Bridge, my lord, St Mary Overey's Priory. They are good people."

I took a coin from my purse, "Here Mistress Alice."

She shook her head, "No, lord, it was my Christian duty."

"You showed the youth kindness and it helped. Take it for I am in your debt. Come, Michael. We will be a human chair for our friend. Dai, the next miles will be hard. Endure it."

"Aye, lord."

I felt every bump on the road as we headed down the ancient highway to London. The ends of the broken bone must have constantly jarred but Dai made no sound. He was white as a sheet and I feared that he would faint. Michael tried to help by chattering away. It was dark when we reached the priory and we had to ring the bell to gain access.

"Yes, my lord?"

"We were attacked in the forests by Cobham and my squire was struck by an arrow. The arrow was removed and splinted but the leg is broken."

"Fetch him within. Walter, a light!"

There was what I would have called a guardhouse had it been a castle and a table. The priest cleared the table and we sat Dai upon it. The priest nodded, "She has done a good job, my lord, but the ride has aggravated the injury. Do you want your man healed or would you have him walk in the future?"

"Why the latter, of course."

"Then he will need to be here a month so that we may set the leg. He will not be able to move it for four weeks at least."

"Just wrap a bandage around it, lord. I will be fine!"

Shaking my head I said, "I would have him whole again." The priest held out his hand. I knew there would be a charge. I held a gold ecu in my hand. He nodded. "I will be staying at the Lamb. I will call again tomorrow."

"No, my lord, come back in a week. We have many patients at this time of year, and we cannot be bothered by constant visits." He added by way of explanation, "The old and the poor are malnourished and succumb to the coughing sickness. The boy will be well treated. Next week."

I was defeated, "Take care, Dai."

He forced a thin smile, "I will be fine, and I have my purse. You and Michael return to Bordeaux."

I laughed, "You are of the English Company, Dai, and we do not abandon wounded warriors. I will stay."

The innkeeper was pleased to see us as the inn was almost deserted. He even promised to have the horses returned to Rochester for us. As we ate before a most welcoming fire, Michael and I discussed our plans. "When the men arrive, you shall take the ship home. I will stay here until Dai is healed." I shook my head, "We make plans and then..."

Michael tried to persuade us to switch roles, but I was adamant. Dai and Michael were like sons to me. I could have done nothing about the ambush, but I felt guilty.

The next day we went to the captain and discovered that he was due to make his last voyage of the year in two days' time. We had no choice. The men and one of us would have to return. When the men arrived on the wherry the next day, we took them aboard the ship and Michael joined them. He was my captain, and he would take charge.

"Are you sure that you will be alright here alone, Sir John? You need a servant!"

I laughed, "Michael, I thank you, but I will be fine. I intend to visit with John Braynford at his offices and when Dai is healed, we might ask if we can stay with him until the ship is ready for its next voyage. I just feel bad about missing Christmas with Elizabeth, but this cannot be helped."

I wrote a letter to Elizabeth and gave Michael presents to give to her. I made my instructions clear and went with them to the ship. I watched *The Swan*, slip down the grey Thames and headed back to the city. When they left, I suddenly felt lonely. This was the first time I had really been alone since I had been a tailor's apprentice! I decided that I would visit with John. It was for the company more than anything else. I did not head for the Aldgate as I was not riding. The walk would do me good. The skies were clear, and the air was crisp. I thought it might rouse me from my melancholy. It meant I used the postern gate which was close to the Tower of London. I would be heading along the north side of the Tower and pass the Abbey of the Cistercians. This was the main road into London from the east and a crossroads for the road to Essex.

I was lost in my thoughts when I heard hooves behind me. I was afoot and so I moved across the ditch to allow them to pass. As I looked up, to my surprise, I spied Prince Edward. It was only when I turned that he recognised me for my cloak hid my surcoat but as soon as he saw me, he reined in and arrested the progress of the knights behind him, "Sir John Hawkwood! This is well met, my lord!"

I bowed, "Indeed it is!"

"And what brings you to London at this time of year? I would have thought that Gascony was a more clement clime."

I nodded, "It is but my men and I were attacked in the woods near Cobham and my squire was injured. The healers say he cannot be moved for a month. I was just taking a stroll."

He dismounted and handed his reins to his squire, "Then this is truly well met. I have a tourney planned for St Stephen's Day. I will be leading men who followed me at Poitiers. Sadly, many of them will be in Gascony. We will be jousting with my brother's men from Ireland. He is returned to England to see our father. I would deem it an honour if you would join my company."

I spread my arms, "Prince Edward, these are the only weapons and mail I brought, and I have no horse."

He laughed, "I have a new suit of black armour. You may wear my old one." Grinning he said, "It may cause confusion eh? In addition, I have many war horses. We can find one to suit you. Come, sir, I will not take no for an answer!"

I nodded, "It would be an honour, my lord."

"Good, I return to London on the Eve of Christmas to prepare. Have you rooms in London?" The Prince never had to worry about accommodation. When he progressed around the country, he expected to be given the best of rooms.

"I am staying in The Lamb, my lord."

"Then come to the Tower on the twenty-third. I will leave word to have a chamber prepared for you. The horse and the mail will be there for you! This is a most happy meeting! My brother, the giant, will not be expecting the knight who took the Oriflamme! Farewell!"

He mounted and galloped off. My plans would now have to change. His brother, the Duke of Clarence was reputed to be the tallest Englishman for he was almost seven feet tall. I doubted that for I had met archers who were that size, but it was true that on a battlefield, mounted on a horse he was hard to miss! As I walked, I realised it changed what I would say to John Braynford.

I was admitted directly for the two guards had hunted with me, "This is a surprise, Sir John, the master will be pleased you have come. Your visit to his home is oft the subject of conversation."

"I am pleased that he is here."

"Aye, you are lucky, Sir John, for in winter he works three days and has four days at home."

The merchant was busy with a clerk and poring over parchments when I entered. He did not look up but growled, "Whatever it is I am too busy!"

I said, quietly, "Then I should go?"

He looked up and put down his quill. The joy on his face was clear, "Forgive me, Sir John, I was not expecting you!" He glared at the guard who had brought me, "I should have been warned!"

The guard was not put out and shrugged, "We thought, master, that you would be pleased to see him!"

"And I am, Peter, go. I will send for you when I am free, sit, Sir John, sit!" I did as he asked, "Katherine and Antiochia will be delighted that you are still in London. Where are your men?"

I spread my hands, "Therein lies a tale!"

I told him all up to and including the meeting with the Prince. It seemed to please him. "But Dai will recover? My wife and daughter thought him a charming and polite boy. They were both taken with his manners."

"The healers say so, but movement might undo their work. I have some more days before I can see him. Perhaps then I will have a better idea."

He nodded, "I know the prior at St Mary's. He has a fondness for figs and French cheese. If you would be agreeable and if he believes it will help, we could take Dai to my home. So long as it is not medical help that is needed and just attention then I can guarantee that my hall can supply all that he needs, and you could stay too. I had heard of this tourney and if you are involved then I know that my family would wish to attend."

"I do not like to impose!"

He laughed, "And you do not for you are a friend of the Prince and people like me need friends in such places. I will be honest with you, Sir John, your coming is like the opening of a door I thought was closed."

I nodded for I now saw that his friendship was not purely altruistic. He wanted something from our friendship, and I preferred that. "Then I am happy for you to speak to the Prior."

"You are still at The Lamb?"

"I am."

"Then I will send word to you." He rubbed his hands. "There will be a great celebration in my home this night!"

Chapter 7

Ralph, one of John's men came for me the next day with another man I did not know. "Master has arranged all, my lord. We are to take you to the wherry and thence to the Priory. Garth and Edward are there already. We have a litter, and the wherry has a harness to make the journey upriver smooth."

"The Prior was happy?"

He grinned, "Oh, aye, my lord. The cheese and the figs which the master gave him were very persuasive."

The priest who had greeted us when we had brought Dai was there with the Prior. The priest did not look happy and he wagged a finger at me, "I will not be responsible for the injury if you take him away! I said a week and it has been just days!"

I held up my hand, "Then we will not take him! I only agreed to this on the condition that he would not be endangered by it."

The Prior snapped, "Brother Bartholomew, these four men have made a litter and, as you can see, the harness on the wherry means he will not be jolted." He shook his head, "When he empties his bowels, we have to move him and these four look far stronger than the two who tend to him." He turned to me, "So long as the leg is not moved and remains supported then all will be well. He is young and bones should begin to knit well after four weeks, however, I would not advise his walking on it for at least two months." He flashed a look at Bartholomew who gave a reluctant nod. He handed me a flask.

"This will help him to sleep but only one swallow and then just before he sleeps!"

"Of course, and I thank you."

The litter was well made, and I wondered at the ingenuity of John and his men. Each one of the four took one of the handles and lifted it together. They had practised. The frame above Dai supported his leg. They walked to the wherry and gently, as one would with a babe, laid it in the centre where space had been cleared. I sat next to Dai.

They pushed us off and with a reefed sail we headed upstream. Ralph said, "The voyage will take us longer as speed is not important but being smooth is."

I had plenty of time to tell Dai all that had happened since I had deposited him at the Priory. "It is a shame, my lord, that I will not be able to attend the tourney." His voice told me that he hoped I would say that he could attend.

Shaking my head I said, "Your leg is more important. I do not wish to jeopardise your chances of becoming a man at arms someday. We have all invested much time in you, Dai, and we have high hopes for you."

"I have never been to a tourney, what happens?"

"It is a fight between two teams. It has rules which means that men should not be seriously hurt nor killed but if men are fighting on horses then there is a possibility of that outcome. The aim is to unhorse an opponent or make him yield. The last team standing wins."

Dai looked confused, "So men could be hurt or even killed?" I nodded. "I do not see the point."

"It is all about honour and prestige. Neither the Prince nor the Duke will be injured. As for the rest?" I shrugged.

"And why do you participate, my lord?"

"Who knows when I may need the patronage of the Prince. I do not burn bridges, but I will build them."

It was dark by the time that Dai was securely in his new chamber which was on the ground floor of the Great Hall. He was tired but he had suffered not a twinge of pain. When he arrived Katherine and Antiochia made a great fuss of him so much so that I saw none of them until the food was served. It gave my host the opportunity to speak with me.

"I have secured our place at the tourney, Sir John, and my daughter, especially, is excited for she has never seen one before." I nodded. "Dai will receive the best of treatment. Antoninus is something of a healer himself. Your squire will be well looked after while he is under my roof."

And so my life settled into a comfortable routine where I ate well and enjoyed good company. It soon became clear that Dai was healing when, a week after we had arrived, he complained of his leg itching! Antoninus assured us that was a good sign. I went riding with my host and we hunted once. Every day I practised with his guards. It suited us all for they were strong men and whilst they lacked sword skills they were far fitter and more cunning than any noble I might meet. For their part, I think it made them feel better about themselves as they were training with a real knight.

We were all sad when I prepared to take the wherry back to the Tower. I would not be enjoying the Christmas celebrations with the family. Katherine and Antiochia, not to mention the servants were all Christians and the day was an important one. I took my farewells and saw tears from both ladies this time. I sat in the wherry and we sailed down the Thames. I had enjoyed my time at John's home but now I would have to learn to put on a face and I knew that I would not be able to relax until I returned from the Tower.

Ralph steered us to the grand entrance close to the centre of the castle. St Thomas' Tower and gate meant the least number of barriers to enter the castle. He winked at me as we approached, "Stand up, if you please, Sir John, let them see your surcoat. I know these guards. They drink close to the Master's offices and they are full of themselves."

I did as I was asked, and the two huge water gates were pulled open and we entered a basin where I was able to step ashore away from any prying eyes on the south bank. One of a trio of equerries wearing the Prince's livery, inclined his head slightly, "Prince Edward told us to expect you, my lord. If you will follow me."

He turned to go, and I said, "And my bags?"

The man frowned but I made no attempt to pick them up. I saw Ralph grinning. He was enjoying their discomfort. Normally I would have carried them myself but Ralph's words had told me much about the men who would think themselves superior because of their position. Eventually, he nodded to the other two who, reluctantly, picked them up.

I waved at Ralph, "I will send a message when I need to be taken back upriver."

"Do not worry, Sir John, we will be ready!"

We passed through the gate into the bailey and I saw horses being exercised on the grass. We did not have far to go and I was led to a wooden building close to the wall. "This used to be the warrior hall, Sir John. King Edward plans on knocking it down and rebuilding it in stone." We entered and I saw that it was a large room which had been partitioned. I saw the suit of armour the Prince had promised, and I guessed which was my bed.

The equerry was telling me that it was for low-status guests. If he thought I would be intimidated or angry then he was wrong. I had just been staying in a palace so anything less than the Prince's own accommodation would have been a comedown. I nodded, "And do we eat in here?"

"No, my lord, you will dine in the Great Hall. You are one of the first to arrive and so tonight there will be few guests."

"When does the Prince arrive?"

I could see that he did not like the questions and was keen to leave but I towered over all three of them and in the confines of the hall I intimidated them. "Later this afternoon, my lord."

"Then I shall see him when I dine? Good. One last question and then you can scurry back to your watery nest." I saw them bridle at the implied insult. "The Prince promised me a horse."

"Master Gilbert is the Horse Master. He is exercising them on the green."

"Thank you, you have been most helpful." If he was offended by my tone he wisely said nothing.

I headed directly for the green. Gilbert, in contrast to the three popinjays, was a down to earth man and I took to him immediately. Even before I had reached him, he had waved a groom over with a fine chestnut courser. "Sir John, you come for your horse I believe?" I nodded. He took the reins and said, "Matthew, fetch a simple saddle for Sir John so that he can get used to Ajax." He smiled, "Prince Edward warned me of your arrival and your surcoat is a distinctive one."

I stroked the horse's muzzle. He was at least fourteen hands and one of the largest horses on the green.

Gilbert nodded approvingly at my stroking and said, "He is one of the bigger horses. Prince Edward said you are a big man." He smiled, "I fear the armour will be a tight fit, my lord."

I said, "It is not as if I have to wear it all day and in battle. I can bear the discomfort for an hour or so."

"He is a good horse. Prince Edward took him to Gascony but did not ride him."

Matthew fetched the saddle and after I had ensured that it was fitted firmly, I mounted. I knew that in a tourney, which would be held in a confined space, I would not need to gallop the animal, but I would need to twist and turn. That was what I practised for an hour and I was delighted with the horse. He was responsive and nimble which were two qualities I needed. More, he seemed to be quickly attuned to the slightest of movements. I was pleased. I saw that Gilbert was too.

"You can ride, Sir John, and do not mistreat your mount. Some of those who are given royal horses to ride seem intent on merely showing them that they are a master and the animals come back with scars down their flanks. Spurs are there to encourage and not to injure!. You will do well."

"Where is the tourney to be held?"

He pointed to the west, "About a mile or so from the city wall and south-west of Clerkenwell is a flat meadow just north of Watling Street. There are workmen there now building. The French King, John, as well as King Edward, are to attend and must be protected from the elements. The great and the good will have to pay for the privilege of shelter!" He laughed, "Why they have a tourney in December is beyond me, my lord. The ground will be hard and the falls, painful. If you add either snow or rain, then I think it might be a dismal day!"

"Perhaps Prince Edward hopes to brighten the day with our mêlée."

He shrugged, suggesting that he didn't think so, "Will you be riding on the morrow, my lord?"

"Aye, but early. I would give him plenty of rest."

"Very wise, my lord."

There were just thirty of us who dined that evening. I was relegated to a lowly table for there were two kings as well as Prince Edward and his brother. I did not mind. I never went in for such functions. Prince Edward had seen me, and I had done as he asked. He nodded to me. I had an ally in a high place and that was all I needed. I knew that my company might well stray across the line between lawful and illegal. Whilst this would not be on English soil if I had the backing of a member of the English royal family then it could not hurt. I left the hall as soon as I could and went directly to my bed. After the one in John's house, it seemed a pauper's cot!

The next day I rose early and exercised Ajax before going for food. Then I donned my armour for the first time. I had to use the last holes on the leather straps. There were servants sent by Prince Edward to help us to dress. The one who helped me was strong otherwise the plate would not have fitted. I knew that if I wore it to war then I would not be able to do so for more than a couple of hours. When I began to sweat and my body swelled, then my breathing would be affected. The helmet was, however, a good fit. It had a visor but was well made and I could see clearly. By early afternoon I had made all my preparations and walked the walls of the castle. It was the largest castle I had seen outside of Windsor and the White Tower, rising high above the river, seemed to make it even larger. I spoke to the sentries for that was my way and asked them where I might find men at arms who sought work. They gave me another couple of places we had not discovered. I was grateful. There was a prize of money for the winning team and I had decided that we would be on the winning team!

The equerry came for me as I descended the walls. I was escorted to a chamber above the river gate. It was Prince Edward's quarters. Thomas Montague, the Earl of Salisbury, was there as well as Thomas Beauchamp, the Earl of Warwick. Both were young knights. Indeed Sir Thomas had been knighted in the same ceremony as I had at Poitiers. The difference was that I was sixteen years his senior.

The door closed and the wine poured, Prince Edward began, "You three are the key to our victory tomorrow. That my brother's men will come for me is clear and you two," he smiled, "my Thomases will be my bodyguards. You, Sir John, will be my secret weapon. The knights we face were not at Poitiers. They are all from Ulster and Ireland. Duke Lionel was also absent from the battle and they will not know you. They may have heard of your name but the fact that you are not of noble blood and began life as an archer will mean that they could well underestimate you. They will see you as a late replacement. I want you to unhorse my brother!"

My face hid the fear I felt. All my good work might be undone. If I failed to unhorse him then Prince Edward might lose but if in unhorsing him, I caused a wound then I would become an outcast. I nodded, "That is my only role?"

Prince Edward laughed, "You say that as though it was easy!"

"No, my lord, but if they do not know me then I can play the coward and back off. I can attack the Duke of Clarence when he least expects it."

"You are a true tactician, Sir John. Yes, of course, that is your only task. That and ensuring that you do not injure him!"

I forced a weak smile, "A tall order, Prince Edward!"

"But you are the man for it and know this, the victory purse will be shared by the victors of my team. I will not need my share."

Thomas Montague laughed, "With millions of ecus coming for King John then that is no surprise."

Prince Edward said, "Sadly for both the King and for me, that is unlikely to happen in the near future." He lowered his voice, "I have heard that parts of France are on the edge of rebellion and while they want their beloved king returned, they are unwilling to shoulder their burden of raising the money."

So, Sterz had been right.

The feast that night was a good one. There was a great deal of wagering from the knights on both sides. I remained silent and kept my coins in my purse. Thankfully, I was allowed to retire early. I was the oldest knight who would participate in the tourney and I needed my sleep. Consequently, I was one of the first awake and that allowed me to breakfast well, dress and be at the stables before anyone else. I did not mount Ajax but walked him around. Prince Edward looked magnificent in his new black armour. He stood out because the rest had shining plate and we all looked the same. When his brother emerged we mounted. I saw the disappointed look on the face of the Duke of Clarence. Already Prince Edward had an advantage. This was a battle between young cockerels and better plumage always helped! By the time all were ready, the bailey was festooned with standards and banners. My rather plain white surcoat looked out of place. I was also one of only two who did not have a squire with a banner. The other was an Irish knight on the Duke's team, Sir Eoin. He looked young and hungry and I wondered if he was the Irish surprise.

It was like a parade as we moved through the city. Two kings and the elder nobles like de Vere and the Earl of Suffolk preceded us and with helmets on our cantles we were cheered and applauded on a day which, mercifully, whilst cold was not threatening rain. It was perfect weather for me. I would not sweat, and the ground would be firm enough to allow Ajax to jink around the other horses. I had seen the Ulster knights looking at my mount and the large knight who rode him. They would think us ponderous and heavy. I did nothing to disillusion them and I mounted slowly and kept a tight rein on Ajax to confirm their opinion. Many hundreds had gathered to watch. Those like John and his family had paid for the privilege of a seat but the greater numbers stood around the wooden hurdles which surrounded the circle where the fight would take place. The kings and the nobles rode in first and were acclaimed before taking their seats. The teams rode in together, in two columns. I was at the rear next to the young Irishman. It showed our status. The cheers were probably reserved for Prince Edward and his brother, but I did not mind. I needed no notoriety.

After we had paraded around the ring we lined up before the kings and bowed our heads. Prince Edward had taught his horse a trick and it also bowed. The acclamation and noise almost deafened me. It was like the sound of battle already. I scanned the seats for a sight of John and his family, but it was a sea of furs and cloaks! We then parted and rode to each end of the circle. Lances and spare weapons awaited us. There were no horses. If we fell or our mount was hurt then we were out. I dismounted and tightened my girths. That done I went to choose a lance. There was a great deal of choice and I chose the shortest one. It would be easier to control and as lances would only last for the first pass I counted on a wild charge by the Irishmen and that they would have little control over their lances. There were twelve men on each side. I think there was some religious significance to the number but all that mattered to me was which one would I unhorse first. I handed my chosen lance to a groom and then mounted. The rest of our company each had a squire or a page. I donned my helmet but left the visor open and the groom handed me my lance. I pulled my shield up. All the shields had the livery of the prince upon them.

When we were all ready, we faced the prince. He said, "Today we fight to entertain two kings and the people of London. More importantly, we fight for those we left at Poitiers. We represent the fallen!"

It was the right thing to say and I stored it for it stirred me and I was a cynic. There might be some battle, in the future, when such a battle cry might redeem a lost cause!

We wheeled our horses and the herald who waited in the middle shouted, "Any knight who deliberately harms a horse will be disqualified. Lances face lances. Hand weapons face hand weapons. Any deviation will result in disqualification. A knight who does not heed a cry of 'I yield' will be disqualified!" He looked at both sets of knights and we nodded to show we accepted the rules. Lances would only be used in the first pass and my choice appeared to be vindicated. We prepared to charge as the herald moved away. I was going to go for the Duke of Clarence but not in the first charge. He, like Prince Edward, was protected by a bevvy of knights. I placed myself anonymously on the left. I saw that the knight who faced me was already eager for the fight. He was roaring a challenge at our line and his horse was a wild one. It was frothing already.

I did not know the knight next to whom I was riding but I kept well to his left, allowing a gap between us. The rest all bunched up together making an arrowhead with the two earls at the fore. There was no command to charge but the Ulstermen just launched their horses at the two earls who led our team. The Irishman charging towards me must have thought, for I was slightly behind the rest of our men and travelling slowly, that I was nervous. He came straight at me. I heard the crash and crack as lances splintered when the two lines met and I watched the wavering lance as it neared me. His horse was travelling faster than mine was and normally the impetus given by such speed and a good strike would result in victory. I pulled my shorter lance back and brought my shield over to cover my chest. We were lance to lance and his shield was still on his left. In his excitement, he had either forgotten or not bothered to bring it around. I saw that the head of his weapon might hit my helmet and so as I lunged at his middle with my lance I flicked up the shield to deflect his lance. Not only was my strike a perfect one but his horse chose that moment to veer away from Ajax's rump. He tumbled from his horse and I heard a cheer from Prince Edward's supporters. One of the opposition was down.

I began to loop around and saw a knight who still had his lance. The ones who had cracked and crashed together all had broken lances. I rode at the knight from the side. He was blissfully unaware of my approach and his shield was on the other side of him. The Duke of Clarence's supporters all shouted a warning which he must have heard at the last moment when it was too late for he turned, with his lance to try to face me. My lance caught him square on and he tumbled from his saddle. The knight next to him still had his lance and he turned to ride at me. With a longer lance, he must have felt confident but perhaps the knight I had felled had been a friend of his for he spurred his horse at me and flamboyantly made the animal rear. It brought a roar of approval from the crowd, but it was a mistake as he was unsighted, albeit briefly and I jinked Ajax to my right so that when his horse landed, I was on the opposite side to the one he expected. As he had reared his horse he had, effectively, stopped and when I rammed my lance at his shield I reined in Ajax. My blow, delivered by an arm which had been trained at the butts, rocked him and before he could recover, I smacked him hard again but this time under the helmet and he, too, tumbled from his horse. There were more cheers and, as I threw away the lance which although still intact was the only one left on the field, I saw that there were now less than half of the men left on the field.

I was now behind the Irishmen and, once more, the Duke's supporters all shouted a warning. Drawing my sword I rode at them and saw that while the two earls protecting Prince Edward had fallen, the Duke of Clarence still had a knight before him. I rode obliquely from behind the Duke. Had this been war I would have said nothing, but this was a game, of sorts, and so I shouted, "Duke, defend yourself!"

I had a voice for war. When I shouted on the battlefield then my men heard me and so did the Duke. He wheeled his horse around to see who it was, but I was already bringing my sword down. The Duke was an accomplished knight, and he was young. He continued his wheel so that he could bring his shield around. He was a giant but that also brought problems for his arms were longer and his shield had more body to cover. My sword hit his shield so hard that some of the paint cracked and fell from it. Worse, from his point of view, was the fact that a crack appeared in the wood. I had quick hands and I raised the sword to hit a second blow before he could bring his sword over. His long arms were now a hindrance. The crack worsened and he wheeled his horse around to face me sword to sword. Ajax was a dancer, and his nimble hooves matched the huge horse of the Duke. I struck as we both danced around and hit his shield again. I saw metal through the crack. One more blow would see it break and the Duke recognised that. He stood in his saddle to use his great height and his unused sword to threaten a blow to my head. I was aware, even though I was not looking, that the tourney was almost over. I saw riderless horses and others led by fallen knights. The shouts of the crowd negated one another, and I could not tell if the cries warning of an attack were for me or another. This was like a battle and if I was in a battle then I would concentrate on the one before me. I stood and raised my shield. It had taken not a single blow and I gambled that even the giant before me could not break it with one blow. As I braced myself, I swung my sword horizontally. His sword strike was so hard that I was forced back into my saddle however mine not only shattered his shield but, as he was standing and unbalanced, knocked him from his horse.

The cheers roared around me and I wheeled to face whichever knight was left to come at me. As I turned, I saw the black knight with the raised visor. It was Prince Edward and he had sheathed his sword and held out a hand. I sheathed my sword and raised my visor.

"Sir John, you did exactly what you said you would. We are the only men left standing! The prize is all yours. Come let us go and receive the well-earned praise of two kings."

I took off my helmet and turned Ajax, "Well done, Ajax, you are as fine a horse as I have ever ridden."

The Duke of Clarence had risen and taken off his helmet. The young Duke walked towards us and I saw that he was smiling but his left arm hung at his side, "Brother, you chose your knights wisely. Sir John, that was a masterly display. I had been trained by the best tournament knights but you… if you chose you could earn a fortune."

I shook my head, "Duke, this is my first tourney. I am afraid I was taught on the battlefields of France, Scotland and Wales."

He nodded, "Just so. Go, brother and take the acclaim which is due to you!"

As we headed to the stand and the two kings who were waiting for us, I spied John and his family. They were not drawing attention to themselves, but their smiles seemed to glint in the winter sun.

"My son, you and your men fought well. King John here recognised your knight." He shook his head, "He bet me that Sir John would be standing at the end. I lost."

King John was smiling broadly, "I remembered you from Poitiers, Sir John, and you were terrifying. I have now had some recompense little though it is, for that defeat."

Prince Edward took the purse and handed it to me, "And tonight we feast and celebrate this day, St Stephen's Day, as friends!"

We dismounted and he went off to speak to his brother. The crowds were dispersing for many would be at the feast that night and needed to change into better clothes. I saw John making his way through them to the edge of the stand. "Sir John, it was a privilege to see you fight this day. I can see how you have been so successful. I will send Ralph to pick you up on the morrow."

"I will be ready!"

I walked Ajax to follow the other knights. I saw Sir Eoin who was trudging behind the other Irishmen. His head hung disconsolately down. I hurried to catch him, "Why so downcast, Sir Eoin? It was a good fight and neither knight nor horse was hurt."

He turned and gave me a weak smile, "Sir John, you now have the purse I hoped to have. I am a landless knight and I sought to make a living at tournaments. There are too few to earn a living. My horses and squires eat into the little money I have. If there was a war, then I might hire out my sword but as it is…"

I smiled and lowered my voice, "I have a company in Bordeaux. I need men at arms. Come to Gascony and join my company. I will be leaving in January on *The Swan*, from

London. If you wish to sail with me then be there. The captain is Captain Jack, and he lives by the Billingsgate."

We had reached the edge of the field and we mounted. It gave him, I think, thinking time. As we reached the city wall and people began to cheer again he leaned over to me, "I am tempted by your offer and if I can manage to live until January then I will join you."

I reached over to take his hand and, in doing so slipped him a gold piece, "Take this as a loan until you have earned enough. If you stay at The Lamb, in London, and mention my name I will know where to contact you and the innkeeper will not rob you."

"How can I thank you?"

"By being a loyal member of the English Company!"

I was pleased for I now had a second knight in my company, and I had found a way to recruit. There would be other knights who followed the tourney. I offered more opportunities for reward! I enjoyed the feast but not the attention. I sat with Sir Eoin but the other knights, especially the two earls, constantly came to speak to me. The earls knew what I had planned, and they were impressed that I had carried it out to the letter. For my part, I wished to be away from London and with my friends. That night, as I pulled my blanket over me I reflected that I had changed. I no longer sought the company of the high and the mighty. Friends, my company and Elizabeth were more important to me.

Chapter 8

The next day I was at the water gate as soon as the sun had risen. The gatekeepers looked at me in surprise. My name was now known and the disdain I had endured when I had arrived was now replaced by fawning attention. I smiled but I was not duped! It was a relief to step onto the wherry and sail, on a crisp December morning, up the river to the merchant's palace. By my reckoning, Dai should be almost healed and soon I could return to Bordeaux. My personal purse was now full and I could use it, if I had to, to subsidise the company. When I had spoken with the other knights, I had become even more aware of the potential for hired swords in both France and the Empire. The defeat of the French at Poitiers and the capture of their king had led to a breakdown in law and order. My company could exploit that and still be serving England.

My welcome astounded me. It was as though I was St George returned from the slaying of the dragon! It was as I entered the hall that I saw, for the first time, the love in Antiochia's eyes. I had not believed Michael but now I saw it for the truth and suddenly all became clear. I tried to remain aloof and distant, speaking more to her parents and Dai than to her but as the day became afternoon and then evening, when we dined, it was clear that she was infatuated with me and I had to put a stop to it.

After the meal, the merchant asked me to join him in his solar. I was happy to be freed from the attentions of the young woman. I had taken her for a girl but now I saw that she was indeed a woman. In the solar, John poured us some brandy. It was an expensive commodity, even in France where they made it. He drank it and then smiled at me, "Sir John, you, Michael and Dai are like the sons I never had. I know not why God made it so that I only had one child but he did. Perhaps he made me rich instead. I would choose sons over riches any day."

"I am to be a father in a few months."

He looked at me and nodded, "I know, Dai told us. We have learned much from your squire. He is an honest youth without a trace of dissembling. I know that you and your men have made the boy into the man and I approve."

I could not see where this conversation was going.

He poured us both another drink, "I also know, from Dai, that you know of my faith. It is not exactly a secret and it has caused problems. Antiochia has led a lonely life and, it seems to her mother and me that it will continue to be so for we wish a husband for her and a family."

"There must be young men who are suitable for she is attractive."

"They are not knights. I need a lord so that my daughter will be a lady."

I drank more of the brandy, "Then I see your problem, my friend. That is not easy."

He nodded and smiled, "And that is why I would have you marry her, Sir John!"

I almost choked on my brandy. "That is impossible! I live in France and if I were to marry any then it would be Elizabeth. This cannot be. I am flattered but no!" He could not make me do his bidding, and I determined to leave the next day whether Dai was fit or not and return to London.

"Hear me out, Sir John. I am a merchant and I know how to negotiate. My daughter knows that you will never live here, but we all know that you have seed within you and that if you married her then she would have a child and even if you were not here then she would not be alone. As Lady Hawkwood she would have prestige. The ladies who shun her now for they think she is the daughter of a foreign merchant would be persuaded to enjoy her company. The hall I am building for her would be yours and as she is my only heir then when I die you would be richer than you could possibly imagine."

I felt myself weakening, "But I leave for Bordeaux with Captain Jack and that is in three weeks!"

"And I can arrange for the banns to be read tomorrow. Captain Jack is a friend, and he will delay his voyage by one day for I will commission him to fetch me a cargo."

I had abandoned one woman and a second was relegated to the position of mistress or, at best a concubine. I did not feel like a gentleman. Of course, I had not been brought up by a father who showed me how to be and the men alongside whom I had fought were hardly father figures. Perhaps it was no surprise that

I had grown into someone so despicable. I understood Antiochia and her parents. When I married, I wished to marry an important family, perhaps with a title. Was I any different?

The merchant said, "Sir John, I am a practical man, and I can see that you are not convinced. I also know, from Dai and from hints that you have given that you see your future to the east of here. It is not unheard of for a man to have two wives."

I stared at him, "But Antiochia would never agree to such an arrangement."

He laughed, but it was a sardonic laugh, without any humour, "Then you do not know the lonely life she has led. A child, perhaps two, would give her a family, would they not? After Katherine and I have passed on she might find herself another man. As Lady Hawkwood she would be in a better position, would she not?"

"I know not."

"I tell you what, let us go to meet with Katherine and Antiochia, you can ask them yourselves and you can explain that which they both know already that this would be a marriage of convenience."

"And a hasty one at that!"

"Really? That someone would wish to marry the man who won the tourney for Prince Edward. If you went to half a dozen great houses, then you would find ladies who would be desperate to marry you. Single-handed you disposed of a third of the knights you fought! Those around us at the tourney had never heard the like! The haste will not seem overly unseemly but let us go and speak with them."

I was dreading this. I could face any number of armed enemies who were trying to kill me, but this was even more daunting than that! I could tell from their faces that they knew why we had returned. John was a man who knew how to get things done and this was well thought out. He had anticipated all my arguments and countered them.

Antiochia looked especially hopeful and I decided to be blunt and give her the truth immediately to avoid unnecessary suffering and hope. "Antiochia, your father has told me that you wish to wed me and that I have his approval for such an alliance. I am flattered and, indeed, honoured, but you must know that I do not love you. I suppose that in the fullness of time I might learn to love you, but I am a soldier, and my wars lie beyond these shores. If we were to wed, then I would leave almost straightaway to sail to some foreign land. At best I would find another war to fight and at worst I would die and leave you a widow. I think it is for the best if I simply leave."

I waited for the floods of tears but, instead, there was a beaming smile, "Then you might consider wedding me? Sir John, even one night with you would make me fulfilled. I knew I loved you the moment I saw you but having seen your courage and skill at the tourney I know what a great warrior you are. I understand why you need to go to war for if you did not then you would be unfaithful to yourself. I know that I may only have days with you and that I might never see you again but, with God's help, I will have something to remind me of you, long into the future."

I was dumbfounded, "But what if the banns cannot be read?"

She came over and dropped to her knees. She held my hands in hers and said, "I would lie with you tonight. I would not miss one moment of the time twixt now and when you leave."

"But I have not agreed!"

The merchant gave me a stare which, I guessed was the one he used when making a hard bargain, "Sir John, I need a grandchild. My wife and I are agreed that you and Antiochia should lie together until you leave here. I can see in your face that you do not understand the reasons for this but you are not yet a parent and a doting parent will do aught for their child."

I was defeated and knew it. I could not in all conscience deny the young woman what she wished. That I did not understand it was neither here nor there. She took my hand and, with her mother and father behind, went to her chamber. That they had anticipated my agreement was disturbing. The room was decked out with flowers. I knew not whence the merchant had acquired them, but he had. The door closed and we were alone.

I rose while she was still sleeping and went downstairs. John was already up even though it was not yet dawn. He smiled at me, "I have much to do! There is a priest to see and although we have few real friends they will be invited. I must also send a message to Captain Jack."

"I could still leave before the wedding."

I thought it might make him angry, but he merely nodded, "Of course you could but I do not think you will. If you did then I would tell the world that you had wed my daughter in any case. She would have the title I need and, I hope, a babe in her womb. If you do go through with this then apart from the legal record which we need, none outside of the priest and the few guests will know that you have married. You could tell others, but you need not do so. All else would still stand. You would have a property and be a part heir to my fortune."

"You are a clever man, John, and have thought all of this out well!"

"I almost lost all in the east and in Cyprus. I determined that when I came here, I would not lose again. You are my insurance against failure, Sir John!"

The days passed quickly for each night saw Antiochia fall even further in love with me and she seemed to need my company as a man needs air and food. After the first morning when I rose without disturbing her, she woke each time I stirred. I had, of course, to tell Dai and he did not seem surprised. "Sir John, in my village it was common practice for a man to take a woman and then leave. He sometimes only went as far as the next village but often they would take to the road. The woman would find a good man. You are famous. Antiochia can easily find another husband but there is only one Sir John Hawkwood."

The guests at the wedding were just a lawyer from London and his guards and servants. The merchant really meant what he said about small numbers. The lawyer was there so that I could witness the amended will although, as it turned out, he was John's only friend and, indeed, had suggested this course of action when the merchant said that he sought a husband for his daughter.

We left two days before the end of January. When I stepped aboard the wherry there were neither tears nor words of recrimination. There was just joy on their three faces. I wondered if I would change when I became a father.

Dai had recovered although he needed a stick and he sat whenever possible, but he was keen to get back to Bordeaux and his comrades. I had sent a message to Sir Eoin to say that I would be delayed, and Ralph skippered the wherry. I think that in an ideal world I would have stayed there, and we would have had a normal marriage but that would not have worked out. We sailed from London on the evening tide. I rarely returned to England and I never saw Antiochia again but all three were in my heart. I had never seen a more loving nor determined family and it made me think about my future!

Chapter 9

Bordeaux 1358

I did not tell all my men of my marriage, but I told my captains and, hardest of all I told William and his sister Elizabeth. What surprised me was that none seemed at all put out or upset by my actions. I was the one who thought I had acted badly. Neither my wife, her family nor those in Bordeaux seemed in the least bit concerned. The result was that I threw myself into the preparations for war to rid myself of the self-loathing and self-recrimination I felt. War had come to France but not from the normal source: the French peasantry had risen. Admittedly not everywhere but Paris and the major cities were all held for ransom by the people who were called the Jacquerie. The word just meant Frenchman although there were leaders such as Etienne Marcel in Paris and the enigmatic Guillaume Kale both of whom took advantage of the French peasants' desire to have more freedom. The question remained, where was the best place for us to go? It was Albert Sterz who helped us with that decision. He came in secret in the middle of March with just a handful of men. However, he also came with another warrior, a knight. I was introduced to him as Arnaud de Cervole. I did not like him not least because he was French. I also soon learned that he was Albert's superior!

Albert smiled and said, "Well, Sir John, have you decided to join our enterprise or has the success in the tourney turned your head?"

That he had heard about my victory was not a surprise. I would not underestimate the man. "The tourney was merely a diversion. And who is this?"

"I am Arnaud de Cervole and Albert was a little less than truthful when he said he commanded the company. He was in England recruiting warriors. It is I who command. All else he said was true and we would like you and your men to join our enterprise. I have done this before. Will you join us?"

"I would with certain conditions."

"Make all the conditions you like but understand that I lead." He looked at me, "I bring the majority of men and if I call a vote then I will win. It is as simple as that."

I stared at him and nodded, "Agreed, for you will bring more men but you will consult with me."

I saw some of his men frown at that but he shrugged and nodded, "Agreed."

"And the three of us have an equal share in the profits from our enterprise. The men all have their own share, but we will be equals."

"I would agree but that seems complicated."

"I can simplify it with my last condition. William Thornton becomes the bookkeeper for the company, and he is responsible for the accounts."

Albert nodded, "I have heard of this man and know that he is honest... now."

Arnaud said, "Then I am content and as for our name, we are called The White Company?"

I laughed and waved a hand at my surcoat, "It is my colour, so I am happy."

"Our men have white surcoats too. I care not what others think. You and I know the truth that while I consult with you, Arnaud de Cervole is the leader of the White Company."

"Agreed and where do we raid?"

"Champagne. The country is rich and close enough to Paris for us to frighten the French. We will meet at Arcis-sur-Arbe on the 1st of May."

"Why then?"

"Everyone will be busy in their fields and tending their vines. We will all need to travel as discreetly as possible. You should have no problem whilst you are in Gascony. The Duke of Burgundy is a youth and Burgundy will be an easy route for you to take. I will lead my men through the Duke's lands in the north, Flanders and Brabant."

"It is agreed then."

"It is agreed."

My men liked neither Albert Sterz nor Arnaud de Cervole. To be truthful neither did I and I saw conflict somewhere down the road, but it was a start. As a marriage, it was one of convenience!

I learned from some of the locals in Bordeaux when we went to pick up arrowheads that we had ordered from England, that Arnaud was a French noble and was known as the Archpriest for he had been ordained. That he had been defrocked was immaterial.

I was unhappy that my child would be born while I was away, but my men had been idle enough and we had suffered bruises and cuts from stupid rows. Roger of Norham was more than happy with Giovanni's improvement and the rest of the new men had proved to be good choices. All were delighted to have a second knight and so we left Bordeaux on the 18th of April. We had hired some locals to be spearmen. I left four with Roger to guard my home, but we departed with just under one hundred men. Thus far they had been a drain on my finances, but I hoped that would change soon. My marriage meant I had access to the merchant's funds, but my pride prevented me from thinking of that as a first resort. It would be the last one. Elizabeth wept when I left but that could have been her pregnancy. She was large with child. I had used some of the tourney money to hire women to help her and I knew she was in good hands.

Dai was now fully recovered and carried my banner. My new armour had not arrived when we left and so I continued to wear Prince Edward's which he had kindly given to me after the tourney. We kitted William out with a mail hauberk and helmet. He would not be fighting but it paid to have him protected. With our spare horses and the wagon containing the spare weapons, it was hard to hide us and so I did not try. In Gascony we told any we met that we were heading for Brittany. When we crossed the Loire, we told people we met that we were heading for the wars in Flanders and the Empire. As we did not steal and behaved well, we were believed and we reached the small town three days before the appointed time. I found a farmer who was happy to allow us to use his land, for a small fee. I obliged him knowing that once we began to raid, we could easily take back the payment we had made! The other reason we were welcomed in the towns we passed whilst heading north was that the presence of so many armed men made the peasants less belligerent. Every lord whose land we passed through was nervous as reports came from the north of lords and their families being burned alive in their homes. Law had broken down in France and we were about to take advantage!

When Albert Sterz and Arnaud arrived, they brought over a thousand men. Man for man mine had more quality for I had archers and plated men at arms. Arnaud had but one hundred men at arms and archers. His twenty crossbowmen were useful, but it was my archers who would determine our success or failure. My men were also better disciplined. It was the cause of our first major argument. There would be many more. There had been a woman abused. My men had behaved impeccably and the locals had warmed to us. This would set us back.

"Most of your men are a rabble!"

The man who had been accused was one of the brigands brought by Arnaud de Cervole and the Frenchman shrugged, "They will fight and that is all that matters."

"No, it is not! If we are seen as nothing better than brigands, then we will be treated in that way. We need rules and be seen to be an efficient fighting force. It will win us battles without having to fight them." I gave him some simple rules and he agreed. He was the leader, but I had the power. The man was dismissed without pay. I thought that would have an immediate effect, but it did not. We had to hang one of his men who knifed another in a stupid brawl. As the man died, I insisted upon hanging and we lost two men. The effect, however, was dramatic and we had no further instances of such behaviour. Had we hanged the man who had abused the woman then we might have had two men left alive to fight for us.

We chose as our first target Plancy-l'Abbaye. It was not a large town, in fact, it was little more than a village, but it only had a manor house for defence and, more importantly, lay along an extensive wood which stretched for miles in an east-west direction. It was defensible and we just needed somewhere we could defend which, in turn, was able to feed us. The Jacquerie were not in evidence and so we galloped in early one morning. I say we but the English Company, my men, were sent to guard the road from the north while the rest of the company did the riding. It allowed my men and me to operate as a single company. Our task was simple; to stop any from entering the village and only allowing out the women and the children. That was, once again, my suggestion. I knew that it would make us seem less evil and would spread the word about what we did. Our plan was to hold as large an area as possible to ransom and, eventually, cut the road from Paris to Orleans.

We took the village in less than an hour. The treasure was miniscule and was hardly worth the effort but there was plenty of food and later that night, in the house of the lord who had been killed by Albert in single combat, we planned the next stage of the strategy. I deferred to Arnaud as he had done this before, albeit on a much smaller scale. We would keep half of the men in the village, making the manor house defensible and then the rest would ride in columns of one hundred like the spokes on a wheel and tell every village within thirty miles that they were under our protection. We would tell them that the protection would come at a price. We kept the money, effectively a ransom, at a sustainable amount. Each day we would ride further afield until we had a large enough area under our command.

Arnaud, for all that I disliked him, was a realist, "Someone will come to rid the land of us. There will be some French lord, probably with lands close to Paris who will take exception to our presence. He will bring an army not least for they will fear that the Burgundians will take advantage of the situation and try to take the land for themselves." He looked at me, "That is when your archers and men at arms will earn their coin."

"So far, Arnaud, I have not seen anyone earn coin. Albert here is the only one with blood on his blade!"

I knew that Albert worried that the two of us, Arnaud and myself would clash for I never backed down whereas he did. For two weeks we had no problems and every town and village quickly agreed to our terms. The lords and the merchants did so because they feared the Jacquerie who had already taken over Paris.

It was the Dauphin, Charles, who tried to end our rule and we heard that he had raised an army from the northwest of Paris and was heading down to meet us. We had mounted men riding every day. They served two purposes: they would give warning of any danger and they would show the villages we controlled that we were vigilant. As my men were all mounted it was a duty we did every day. I already had plans to ask for better pay for those who were mounted. In fact, I had a new structure in mind but that would have to wait until we had defeated whoever was coming towards us. Our time in the village had helped to make it easily defended but our rides had shown us a better place to meet an enemy army. Sézanne lay just fourteen miles north and the road from Paris and the north had to pass through a large forest. We were about to leave for the town when a rider came from our farm in Bordeaux. It was one of the new men and I knew that it was important for Roger would not have risked losing a man for trivia. The letter told me that I now had a son, John and that he and Elizabeth were doing well. Robin, Michael and those closest to me knew how much a son meant to me. There would be another Hawkwood. He was not legitimate but that was unimportant. King William had been a bastard and had conquered England!

Leaving Arnaud with one hundred men in the village we took the other thousand to the road through which the Dauphin and his army would have to pass. Robin commanded not only my archers but also the crossbowmen. He was not happy about using them but with so few archers he had no choice. We arrayed ourselves between the trees of the forests. We occupied a frontage of just four hundred paces. Robin had his men spread out on either side. He took command of the crossbows and left Martin the Fletcher to command the archers. They hid in the woods and we all dismounted. William and the lightly armed men guarded our horses. I had offered William the chance to stay in the village, but he disliked Arnaud every bit as much as I did.

I had sent two of my men to ride up the road and ascertain the numbers and while we waited Albert and I organised our men. "Albert, put my men at arms in the centre. We will be a rock. If you put yourself and your best men on the right and have someone you can trust on the left we can put the weaker ones between us in two groups." I had not fought alongside any others thus far, in fact, we had not done much fighting at all but I recognised that the French rabble of Arnaud needed stiffening. As Robin said this was the easiest money any of us had earned.

"Karl von Württemberg is my knight, and he is anxious to prove himself. He can command my men on the left."

I nodded and set Michael to organising our men. He and Sir Eoin got on well and the knight did not appear to take umbrage at being ordered around by someone younger than he. Michael had an easy manner with him.

Albert and I stood apart, "Is this what you envisaged, Sir John?"

"You mean fighting real warriors and not terrifying peasants? Aye."

"It is easy money!"

"Albert, our men are in the prime of their lives. You and I have, between us, the finest mercenary force in France. We can take on anybody and yet Arnaud seems content to be a bandit king!"

Albert's silence told me he agreed with me.

"Let us get this battle out of the way and then you and I, Albert, can plan to take on more challenging and richer targets. Did I not hear that he was known as a castle taker?"

Albert nodded, "Aye, he was renowned as a knight for his skill in scaling walls."

"Yet we have avoided all castles no matter how mean."

Michael returned, "We are all in place, my lord, and Walter approaches. The French are close!" We knew that they had camped just five miles from the village. I suppose we could have raided them but I did not know the quality, yet, of the other warriors, German, Hungarian, and French, who made up our company.

I clasped Albert's arm, "We will speak further after this."

When Walter reined in, he said, "There are two thousand men coming down the road. The Dauphin himself leads them. They have sixty men at arms, mainly knights in the van and there are forty crossbows but in the main, they are just pressed men, the levy!"

"Good, tie your horses with the others and then rejoin Captain Martin and the rest of the archers."

I cupped my hands to shout to the others, "There are sixty men at arms. We break them and we win!"

No matter what the men had voted, the leader of this company was me! The cheers of the men told me that if I forced another election, I would have a better chance of winning. I would bide my time. It would not do any harm to impress the rest of the company with the prowess of the English Company. I turned to Dai who stood with my standard, "We will need every warrior we can this day, Dai, plant the standard in the soft earth and use a long spear. Watch my back!"

His grin told me that he was eager and he was as big as any of Arnaud's men but a much better warrior. He walked to the side of the road and rammed the standard into the earth. Michael and Sir Eoin flanked me then Harry and Stephen flanked them. Giovanni had shown himself to be a good leader and he was with the rest of my men at arms. We all bore polearms and wore our shields around our backs. We did not fear the missiles of the French for the archers and crossbowmen in the woods would hit those first. The lack of light horsemen meant that the only way for the French to dislodge our men from the woods would be to send in the levy. I prayed that they would for it would be the quickest way for us to win the day!

The French appeared and stopped three hundred paces from us. The Dauphin had learned his lesson at Poitiers. He would not make a reckless charge on horses, especially on such a narrow frontage. His men at arms and squires dismounted. I saw then that he planned on using men at arms backed by squires as his front line. With shields before them, they formed a line, sixty men wide. I watched with interest as a knight, not the Dauphin, organised the others on the flanks. He chose the ones with the better helmets, shields and weapons so that there was a line of two hundred men ready to advance. The crossbowmen nervously arranged themselves in the fore. The rest formed up behind. I marked the knight who had five golden stars on a red background as his livery. When he placed himself in the centre, while the Dauphin, his bishops and his priests stayed with the horses, I knew that he intended to come for me. I would have it no other way. I left my visor up. It afforded better vision and could be closed in an instant. Had their crossbows been a threat then I might have lowered it.

The French were too far away to make out words but when the knight who led them shouted an order and they cheered then I knew that they were on their way. I placed the butt of my poleaxe next to my foot. It was less of a strain on my arms and it allowed me to view their progress. Martin and Robin knew their business. The French crossbows would stop two hundred paces from us. If they were feeling braver, they might come closer to guarantee to hit us, but they would fear our archers and assume they were behind us. We had fought that way before. It was at two hundred paces when they stopped and knelt. The arrows and the bolts which hit them from the side scythed through them. The ones at the sides fell first and barely a dozen French bolts came towards us. Hastily released none of my men was hit although I heard a cry from my left. One of the Germans there had been struck. The knight who led shouted an order and men from the rear detached themselves to race to the woods. It allowed the crossbows, led by Captain Robin, to send another flight, this time into the lines of Frenchmen and for Captain Martin to send three flights of arrows. Coming from the sides the French shields were of little use. Only their armoured men at arms were unscathed. They reformed their lines and advanced, this time at a faster pace. They intended to hit us at the charge. With neither ditch nor stakes before us, they hoped their weight of numbers would drive us backwards and win the day for them.

"Brace and hold them!" I glanced left and right and saw that my English Company looked eager and that filled me with pride. This would be our first real test and would tell me much about their character.

The French knight had made a mistake. His knights still wore spurs and running in spurs is never easy. The ones who ran in the centre, on the road, had the easier journey and they were ahead of those who struggled on the flanks, crossing the scrubby shrub, and weed-infested ground. My men spanned the road so that we would bear the attack first. I saw that the French knight had his visor down and I risked leaving mine up. That he would come for me was clear. He held, in his hands, not a pole weapon but a long two-handed sword such as King John had borne at Poitiers. If he thought to hack through the shaft of my poleaxe, then he was in for a shock. I had asked my weaponsmith to encase the shaft in metal. The only wood he could strike was protected by my metal-backed gauntlets. I did not lift the weapon but supported it with my two hands. Still braced by my foot I was presenting an easy target for his sword. Dai's long spear was also braced against his foot and protruded between me and Sir Eoin. The French knight had two weapons to watch for and with a visor down he was at risk of not seeing one.

It is hard to stand and await a blow, but I had to trust that my poleaxe was longer than his sword. He began his swing when he was four paces from me and it told me that he had not practised the strike before. The edge of his sword was still a foot or so from my head when he ran first into the spike on the end of my poleaxe and then, more crucially, into the long spearhead of Dai's spear. His breastplate was a good one, but the poleaxe struck slightly below and to the right of his middle. Not a mortal blow it would hurt. Dai's spear, held at an upward angle found the space under the knight's arm, he did not wear a besagew. The spearhead must have found a tendon for the sword dropped from the knight's hands. I lifted the poleaxe and smashed the hammer head into the side of his helmet. His squire screamed and stepping over the knight's body tried to cleave my head in twain. I blocked the blow with my poleaxe as Dai rammed his spear into the screaming mouth of the squire.

That was the point when all order broke down, amongst the French at least. Sir Eoin and Michael had slain their opponents which meant their best three warriors were dead and we now faced squires or, at best, warriors who had weapons and mail but were not trained as well as we. The poleaxe is a mighty weapon with a spike, axe head and hammer. A sweep, if it connects, will cause a deadly wound. If it does not connect it means that the target has ducked and therefore cannot see. The first man I slew ducked and I reversed the poleaxe to bring the axe side down to smash into his back. I am strong and I think the blow broke his spine.

It was when my archers, having defeated the men sent to pursue them, began to rain arrows on the rear of the French mob that they broke. Fewer than half of the men at arms survived. I raised my sword, "After them! There are horses to be had!" I shouted in English. I had decided that the Germans would adapt to my language rather than the other way around. I planted my poleaxe in the ground and drew my sword. As I ran so the others followed me. I was surrounded by my men and I felt as safe as a babe in his mother's arms! We caught up with the wounded. If they asked for mercy, we took their weapons, otherwise, they died. More surrendered than died. I saw that the Dauphin, his bodyguards, and his priests had all fled before the first of the survivors reached the horses. My archers were there already, and their arrows plucked those who had mounted from their saddles. The wiser French warriors took to the trees to avoid pursuit. Martin and my archers had secured not only the horses but also the wagons containing food, wine, clothes, tents, camp chairs and the like. We claimed it.

When the dead had been stripped of all that was of value, we burned their bodies and those of our dead. The English Company had lost not a man and only two had slight wounds. The Germans and French, in contrast, had lost eighty men either killed or so badly wounded as to no longer be useful as warriors.

We left as soon as we could. Our wounded shared the wagons with the treasure and I rode at the van with my men. Captain Robin rode next to me, "Sir John, it is archers we need. The crossbows were useful, but they were so slow and could not send a bolt to soar and fall. The men were slower to run."

I smiled, "I knew you would not enjoy leading them but I thank you for doing as you did. You are right but we cannot get them here. We have to hope that the messages we left in London and Rochester, not to mention Southampton will reach the ears of archers who wish to follow my banner. I plan on returning to Bordeaux soon, to see my son and to see if my plate has arrived. I also need to send a shipment of the goods we have taken to John. I will ask Roger then if we have more archers. It may well be that I have to send someone to England, but I am loath to do so for I need every one of you!"

When we reached our camp Arnaud was waiting. On the ride back I had decided what I would say to him. I had spoken to Albert when we had burned the bodies and I knew that I had his support. The treasure we had taken was secured first. That would be divided up as per the rules we had agreed. The weapons, horses, mail, and the like went to those who stripped the bodies. The English Company had done well and when Arnaud saw the booty collected by both the German and the English Company his face darkened. That evening the three of us ate together in the hall we used. We ate well for the Dauphin had brought fine food and wine to celebrate his victory.

We chatted amiably about the food and when the women we paid had cleared the table we turned to more serious matters. Arnaud could not wait to vent his feelings upon us, "I guarded our stronghold and I was not rewarded. I want a share of all that you two took!"

I smiled, "The next time then, I shall stay here with the English Company and you can lead, Arnaud." I turned to Albert, "Who won the day today?"

He had his mouth full and he nodded to me and then swallowed, "Sir John's archers and his men at arms. We still might have won but our losses would have been higher."

"We are one company and we should all share."

"And we do but if a warrior kills another then what is on the dead belongs to the warrior."

"What of the horses?"

"The men who took the horses were the ones who had the most courage and raced to get to them. I took no horse."

Albert had remained silent. He had a horse for I had given him one. I had decided to court his favour. I wanted to control the company.

Arnaud was angry but he had no argument to counter ours. I took the bull by the horns, "While we are clearing the air, Arnaud, I think we have set our sights too low. Here are small villages. The money we take equates to the tax they would have paid their king. If we went further north, closer to Paris, we might be welcomed more and have more treasure."

He shook his head, "I am against that. You are right that there would be more treasure but there would be more risk and we have lost men this day. I will not sanction it."

I nodded and leaned back, "Then you would leave me no choice but to call an election and put it to the vote. If the men do not back me then I shall take my men and return to Bordeaux."

That upset both men but for a different reason. Albert knew that our success lay in my archers and Arnaud was no longer certain that he would win. Even worse if he did win then we would leave. He had no choice at all. I could tell that I had won when he put on a false smile and wheedled, "Sir John, you have no need to call an election but if we leave this area then we lose this income with no guarantee that there will be more forthcoming."

I nodded, "Then leave twenty or so of your men, the ones with horses. Have them ride the patrols that we do. The people will still enjoy our protection. Spread the word that the army we defeated was to come and make them pay taxes again!" We had deliberately set the rate for our protection at the old tax rate. The Dauphin had raised taxes to pay for his father's ransom!

I had given Arnaud a way to keep face and he nodded, "That is a good idea and where would we raid?"

I had spoken to Albert about this and I had a bold suggestion, "Châlons-sur-Marne."

Arnaud almost choked on his wine, "You might as well say Rheims! It has a wall!"

I nodded, "I did not say that Châlons-sur-Marne was our final destination, just the next."

"You are mad! It cannot be done!"

"And I thought you were the one who scorned walls! Besides, I did not say that we would assault the town. I am not a fool. There are other ways to take it through deception and deceit. If I can take it then more men will flock to our banner. There are many churches there and they will pay well to avoid us stripping them of their treasures and if the Dauphin is foolish enough to try to take it from us then we defend the walls."

I knew that Albert was already convinced, and Arnaud could not challenge me. Of course, I would have to sleep with a knife beneath my pillow for I had made an enemy. He would wait until I had taken the town. If I did not, then I would be dead in any case.

He shrugged, "As you will be the one getting inside then be my guest. You will take the risks."

I smiled, "And think on this, both of you, I have thought to have William draw up articles for payments. I believe we should pay, as they do in England, Brittany and France, for lances. A man at arms, squire, page and five archers make up a lance. How the lances are organised is up to the men but it means we have a better organisation. When horses are captured in the future then the lance will decide how they are apportioned. This way we will reward success and those who squat behind walls and allow others to do their fighting will be the ones who benefit the least. Of course, we will put this to the men." I looked Arnaud in the eye, "It is not a threat to your leadership and if the men disagree with the system then so be it, but I believe it will help us to recruit better men and make them more loyal. As I say, I have yet to speak to William but by the time we are ready to attack Rheims then the documents should be ready!"

While Albert smiled when he nodded, I saw blades in the eyes of Arnaud.

Chapter 10

An attack on Châlons-sur-Marne was not something to be considered lightly and I had to scout it out first. I took with me Dai and Giovanni. We all went in disguise. The knight I had slain at the battle of Sézanne wore a red surcoat and it was as far away from white as it was possible to get. There was no livery upon it. We had his shield too and Dai painted over the golden stars. Giovanni wore the squire's surcoat which was also red. We left at the start of July. I intended to keep as close to the truth as I could. If we were questioned, I would say that we were on our way to Italy to join the Great Company and had chosen a route through Châlons-sur-Marne to avoid Paris. It was why I had chosen Giovanni rather than Michael or Sir Eoin. His Italian looks, accent and language would make my journey more plausible. The town was known for its churches and so we would use that, making it almost a pilgrimage. St Étienne was revered in the town and one of the oldest churches was dedicated to him. As the town had been the scene of a battle against Attila the Hun then a visit to a church dedicated to a Christian martyr would seem appropriate. We planned on a single night's stay. We left our hall before dark and rode hard so that we reached the River Marne by the fifth hour of the day. There was a lot of traffic on the road for the crossing at Châlons-sur-Marne was the best way to cross the huge Marne. I had feared that the bridge over the river would be more heavily guarded, but it was not. The two men on the west bank just controlled the flow of people passing over the bridge. As I wore spurs I was allowed over ahead of the laden wagon which was stopped and searched.

On the far side, there were no guards until we reached the town wall. When we reached the gate, I saw that all were being questioned closely, especially those with weapons. It became clear why when we neared it. They were looking for Jacquerie. It was the poorer people who were searched. We were given a cursory inspection. My spurs marked me as a knight and as such unlikely to foster rebellion. I did not even have to tell my story while the farmer with the short sword had his wagon examined. It was a telling moment.

We found an inn close to the church. It was popular with pilgrims, but the recent unrest had meant that the inn had not been as full as normal and we were welcomed. The innkeeper told us when I had bought a large pichet of wine, that a close watch was made on all who entered the town. "The merchants and those with money are fearful that what happened in Paris will be repeated here."

"Does the lord who rules here not keep good order?"

"He is held in London with Good King John. Until he is ransomed then it is his wife who rules. She has a family." He shook his head, "She is in a difficult position. She cannot afford the ransom herself and she dare not raise the taxes for fear of angering the Jacquerie. As it is you will be paying a tax for the merchants and Lady Isabeau have put a tithe on all food, drink and accommodation."

"Does that not make you angry too?"

He shrugged, "I am not happy, but I know the Jacquerie would not make me any richer. If anything I would be worse off. It is like a plague of flies in summer. It will pass. Better times will come. No matter what we think we are better off with a royal family than the Jacquerie who seem to think that all men are equal. It is not true, my lord, I work hard as do my wife and my children. Many of these Jacquerie seem to think that it should be our right to share the riches of the rich. That is not the way it works."

As we walked around the town, after first visiting the church as pilgrims would, we could sense the tension. It hung in the air in the narrow streets. The town walls were manned a little more heavily than one might have expected, especially around the gates and much of the attention was within rather than without. Satisfied that we knew their defences we sought a second inn. I had my plan, and it entailed a return and a further night of stay. We could not stay in the same inn for it would arouse suspicion. We found a second one on the opposite side of the town. We did not enter, merely identified its position. We then found every gate, there were four of them. Satisfied we returned to the inn. Our next reconnaissance would be at night. That would be a trickier exercise as we would not be able to look as closely at the walls and the manning of them as we would wish.

We retired to our room to wash and to speak. "You have a plan, Sir John?"

I nodded, "Aye, Giovanni. Dai put your head around the door and see if any are close by." He did so and then closed it. "Anyone?" He shook his head. "We use twenty men at arms. It will have to be a mixture of English, French and Germans. Five enter at each gate. You, Giovanni, will lead three of my English men at arms and the other Italian speaking man at arms who joined us. If you speak then the sentries, if they are curious, might assume you are all Italian. You could always teach them a few words of Italian. Once inside some take rooms while others just stable their horses. None of us will be sleeping at night in any case. The next part depends upon what we find tonight. However, I am assuming that there will be fewer sentries than during the day. We need to coordinate opening the gates at the same time to allow in the rest of our men. Once we have our men in the town then it should be easy. We outnumber the armed men by at least eight to one and from the looks of the ones we have seen whilst they might be able to deal with a Jacquerie, one of our company would be a different matter."

The Italian nodded, "A bold plan but it might well work. Of course, Sir John, you realise that Arnaud will not be one of those who will enter. Nor will he be one of the first into the town. He is cunning and should not be trusted."

I laughed, "And I do not. This suits me, Giovanni. If he hides at the rear and does not draw a sword then when the time is right, and I demand another election the men will be more likely to vote for me. Would you vote for a leader who takes no risks and more of the treasure than you?" He shook his head. "I will bide my time. Albert is another matter. His Germans would vote for him. We need more English in this company. I hope that when we take this town it draws others here."

We left our weapons in our room and after we had eaten and when dusk had descended, we wrapped cloaks about our shoulders and took to the streets to wander, as others did. What we did not do was to stop and talk for we saw a patrol of the night watch, seven of them and whenever there was a gathering of townsfolk, even just one or two they were moved on. We did not loiter and, whenever possible, it was Giovanni who spoke. I wanted to learn Italian in any case and, I know not why, when he spoke Italian the guards appeared to relax as though he was not a threat. I saw that there were two men at ground level on every gate. Above them, on the town wall were another pair. It looked to me as though there were two men allocated to the walls between each of the gates. It was a heavier presence than there might have been but for the unrest. We headed back to the room and I was satisfied that the twenty men I used to enter the town would be able to take two gates, one at the bridge end of the town. It did not matter that there would be two more gates we did not take. The main ones were the northeast one and the bridge gate. The men who entered the town would need to be able to overcome the guards silently and, in a perfect world, none of the watch would be hurt. I did not want the populace roused against us because we had killed a father or a brother. I would have to choose the eighteen other men very carefully.

The next day we left by the northeast gate. I had told the innkeeper that we were heading that way and while I doubted that he would have us followed it suited me, for this way I could scout out the ground to the north. We swept around the town in a long circle using the roads which crisscrossed the fertile land. There were vineyards all around and there looked to be neither castles nor fortified manors. Châlons-sur-Marne was the citadel they would all use and if we held it then we could control a far larger area than we had at present. I had asked, in the inn, about bridges across the Marne and discovered that the nearest bridge to the north was four miles away close to Recy. When we reached it, I saw that there was no house closer than the village, a mile away. The bridge was not well made but looking at the river it was narrow enough for men on horses to be able to swim it if the bridge was guarded. I was satisfied that my plan could work.

It was dark when we passed through our sentries to the manor. Giovanni and Dai saw to the horses while I went to speak with Albert and Arnaud. Dai and Giovanni would tell my captains what we had discovered. Arnaud was grinning, "So, Englishman, have you now come to your senses and realised the futility of trying to scale the walls of Châlons-sur-Marne?"

I smiled and took the wine Albert proffered, "I am sorry, Arnaud, when did I say that we would scale the walls? You are quite right it would cost us men. That we would take the walls is immaterial. My aim is to lose as few men as possible for we have well-trained men, and they are as valuable to me as the gold that we take. If my plan succeeds, then we take the town without losing a man!"

"Pah! That cannot be done! This is not England, this is France and here men guard their walls well!"

I turned to look at Albert, "We need eighteen men at arms. My plan is to enter the town on the last day of July. We will enter at different gates and each group will have a different story. Some will say they are heading to Italy to join the Great Company. Others will say they are riding to Aragon and Castile to fight there or to Germany. The guards at the gates do not fear men at arms but peasants. Meanwhile, by using side roads you two will make your way to the land close to the northeast and the bridge gate. We will take the bridge gate and the northeast gate and hold them. We will give a signal and the two groups will enter and take the town."

Albert smiled but Arnaud said, "As simple as that?"

"And why does it need to be harder? There is not a garrison in the town and no lord. He is in England being held for ransom. The merchants all fear the peasants rising as they have done in Paris. We can do this but if you, Arnaud, wish to stay here again, then fine. I will have Sir Eoin and Michael lead."

"I did not say that. We will do as you suggest but I fear that we will just lose twenty men!"

"And as I will be one of them then that just removes a thorn from your side and might induce a smile, eh?" He had no answer to that but I saw him as he tried to work out if I had an ulterior motive.

It would take time to organise the attack. The first thing Albert and I did was to choose the men. I picked four English men and Sir Eoin. Michael would be responsible for the rest of my men at arms as well as a sizeable portion of the rest of the company. Robin would be with him and he would command all the archers. There were two other Italians in the company. They came from the land to the east of Nissa, but they could aid Giovanni in his deception. The other two were English men at arms. Albert chose the last two groups for me and they were from his personal entourage. They had been with him for many years and he trusted them. He and Arnaud would command the largest group, the one which would have to take the bridge gate. As they would have a shorter journey, they had the men who fought on foot whilst Michael and Robin's men were all mounted.

I explained to those who would enter the town exactly how we would do it. Half of them I was confident about for Giovanni had been with me. We used a wax tablet to explain to the Germans what was required. I intended to leave William in Plancy-l'Abbaye. He was still working on the new agreement which I would present to the men after we had taken the town. Even Arnaud was impressed with his work. William was honest and he now blossomed with the freedom I gave him. He had learned much working in Bellac and now he was able to use his clever mind to our advantage.

I knew from our time in Châlons-sur-Marne that they rang a bell on the hour. We would make our attacks at midnight. It was the signals which were the crucial part of the raid. The gatehouses all had lanterns hung from them. I devised a simple signal. When we had them, we would cover them with our cloaks, count to ten and remove them. We would do this three times. Only two men from each group would be needed for that task. I would lead my Englishmen and Karl von Württemberg's group would be with me and we would take the northeast gate. Giovanni would have his men and the other German group. We only needed one gate to be taken for even the small portion of our army, mine, would still outnumber the garrison. I was confident even if Arnaud was not. The night before we left, I had planned on leaving before dawn, I met with Albert, Robin, and Michael.

"I will not be with you but the journey twixt here and Châlons-sur-Marne is the most dangerous you will have to pass. When we were in the town, we were aware that they knew of our presence here, further south, but as we had not made any moves to extend our territory then they were unconcerned. So long as the men move in smaller groups then all will be well." I looked at Albert, "I have leaders amongst my men, archers like Captain

Martin and I know that they can lead smaller groups of men. Yours and Arnaud's are more of a mystery to me."

"I know and it concerns me. Arnaud's men are more like bandits but, thankfully, they are mainly afoot. I plan on having Arnaud lead them. That way if they all stay together then they will be at the rear. I doubt that they will be close to the town until well after dark. My fear is that some of them take off to raid isolated farms and hamlets. They are ill-disciplined."

"Then, if they do, we try and then hang them. Let us weed out the tares!"

We took a sumpter for I needed to be able to use my white surcoat once we had entered the town. The red one taken from the dead Frenchman had worked. The others also wore surcoats taken from the dead rather than our white ones. I knew that I had an advantage over the others for we would be leaving first, having the longer journey, and I knew the road. The Germans and I shared the road until we came to the Marne and while I crossed the bridge, they found somewhere to ford it. The longer journey meant we reached the gates in the late afternoon. We approached it down the Rheims road. I knew that it was twenty odd miles and that we could have done it, easily, in a day. As we approached the gate I said, "Study the gate when we pass through. Tonight we need to take it!"

"Aye, Sir John."

This time we were questioned at the gate for I was recognised. "My lord, I see you have returned to us quickly. Lady Isabeau has asked us to question all who frequent our town." There was suspicion in his voice.

I smiled, "I am passing through but, in these perilous times your caution is understandable. I went to Flanders to seek work but there appears to be peace there and so we will travel south to Italy. There is always work there for hired swords."

"Where will you be staying?"

I shrugged, "So long as there is a bed for us and a stable for our horses, then I care not. Where would you recommend?"

That seemed to satisfy him, "The Grapes is a fine inn. It is not cheap, but you and your companions look like you could afford it."

I now had the measure of the men. We would be rooked, and the sentry would share the profits. "Then that is where we shall be should anyone wish to speak with us."

My men had remained silent whilst I had been talking. Most could understand French but while I had a passable accent they did not. I said nothing to them, and they kept impassive faces. When we reached the inn it was as empty as the other had been, but the prices were twice what we had paid there. I paid knowing that I would be staying here for free once we took the town. I did not wish to risk walking the streets for a large number of armed men might be noticed. The fact that we had entered at four different gates would hide the numbers. Instead, we sat at a table and I ordered some food and a pichet of wine. Once more, it was overpriced and the food was not particularly good.

It was not long before the gates were closed for the night when a liveried servant came to speak to me. He must have been told what I wore for he ignored the others and spoke directly to me. "Lady Isabeau and the Council of Châlons-sur-Marne wish to speak with you, Sir Knight."

I saw through the open doorway that there were six armed men outside. "Am I in trouble?"

He smiled, "No, my lord."

I rose and said, slowly, "I will not be long. Finish off the wine and order more." Sir Eoin gave me a questioning look, but I gave a subtle shake of my head. Whatever trouble I was in I would handle it. When we were outside, I looked at the armed men and said, "I thought you said I was not in trouble? Why the armed guard?"

He smiled. This was a silky servant, "There are some troublemakers in the town, my lord, and it is after dark when the rats come from their holes. It is for your safety."

I patted my sword, "If anyone tried to do me harm it is they who would suffer!"

The Hotel de Ville was next to the manor house. There were six armed guards outside each building, and they were scrutinising all who approached them. One was obviously the Captain. He was a well-muscled man with a long scar running down his cheek. He wore plate and carried a long sword.

"I will take him to her ladyship." He turned to me, "Your sword."

I stared back at him, "Why, I was told I was not in trouble?"

"All visitors to her ladyship must hand over their weapons first."

"In that case, I decline to enter."

"What?"

"I was invited to meet her ladyship and the Council. Are you now telling me that I am brought here against my will?"

The Captain looked at the servant who had brought me. The servant shrugged. The Captain said, "Hand over your sword, now!"

I shook my head, "You have cleverly separated me from my men but as you have brought me here under false pretences then should you try to take it then I would draw it and believe me, I guarantee, Captain that you would die." I looked at the other sentries who were all looking nervously at me. None of them had plate and all carried spears, "And these men would soon follow. Now, do I return to the inn or shall you accompany me to her ladyship?" My hand rested lightly on my sword.

The Captain might be well-muscled and have a long sword but his eyes told me that he was unused to having his authority questioned and his confidence was no longer there.

"If it helps," I spoke to the servant who was now trying to edge nervously away from any swordplay which might ensue, "I will give my word that the Council and her ladyship will be safe and I will harm none of them!" I then looked at the Captain and smiled. He knew what I meant.

"Very well," he snapped. "Follow me!"

When we reached what must have been the place the Council discussed civic matters, I heard raised voices from within. I could only make out a little of what was being said but it sounded like there was a real danger of the populace rising. That explained the interrogation when we had arrived. We had been isolated in the inn and had not seen the streets. Was this a case of bad timing? Should we have come sooner? It was too late now to change our plans. The doors opened and the Captain led me in. I realised that thus far none had asked me my name.

"The man you wanted, Your Ladyship."

The woman was an imposing character. She sat in the centre of the table and had the stern look of one who brooks no dissension. "Captain Lafarge, you may leave us. Wait without." As he turned and passed, he glared at me. I smiled.

I did not give them a chance to begin to question me. As soon as the double doors closed I asked, "Why have I been summoned here? Your Captain Lafarge treated me as a criminal and yet I am just a sword for hire passing through your town."

Lady Isabeau frowned, "You are English!"

I nodded, "Sir John of… Bordeaux."

"You fought at Poitiers?"

I could have denied it, but something made me tell the truth, "I did."

"My husband was taken when the Dauphin treacherously fled the field!" I said nothing. She looked down the line, "Sir John, you have heard of the Jacquerie?" I nodded. "We thought we were immune from them but they are in Rheims and we believe that they are here. My Council and I are keen to keep the streets under our control. Sadly, we have too few soldiers to do the job. We would hire you and your men to help Captain Lafarge and his men."

"Five men?" I shook my head, "I confess that we would be better than anything I have seen thus far but five of us and the men you have would not be enough. However, I may know of others who might aid us, but it would take some days to organise. Is the threat imminent?"

One of the Council spoke, "We have days rather than weeks, Sir John. One of the Council had cause to speak to some of his workers and when he remonstrated with them, they attacked and killed him."

"Then arrest them!"

"Captain Lafarge tried but there were too many of them. He dispersed them." The man was all bluster!

"And that was the worst thing he could have done, my lady, better to have lost some of his men and caused the killers pain than this. The dog has bitten and should be punished. I can return in two days with some men who might be able to help you."

The relief on their faces made me feel guilty. Then I realised that our taking over the town would actually solve their problem.

Lady Isabeau would not be happy as the money she was raising for a ransom would now line our purses.

The man who had spoken said, "We would be most grateful, Sir John."

"Then the next time I speak with you we should have a solution to your problem."

That the Captain was less than happy about the situation was clear. For my part, I was delighted with the result. I now saw the opposition and it was not a threat. I felt confident that not only could we take the town but also that there was a good chance that we might be welcomed, by the Council and merchants at least. I knew that we could keep law and order.

Once we were outside the Captain said, "You had better watch yourself out there, Sir John, in here I can keep you safe but out there…" He leered.

I smiled, "I should find yourself another line of work, Captain! I cannot see Lady Isabeau keeping you on and if I cannot defend myself from peasants then I had no right to call myself a knight!"

I headed across the square. The streets had emptied and that was ominous for when I had been brought to the building there had been knots of two or three men here and there. I loosened my sword in its scabbard and took out my long dagger which I held close to my right leg. Once I left the square then I was plunged into darkness. There were inns and taverns but not down the road which led to The Grapes. There were other businesses nearby. The three men who stepped from the shadows were workers and they had been drinking; I could smell it on their breath and their clothes.

One growled, "Another rich stranger with a purse too large for one man! Hand over your purse so that we may feed our families and we shall let you live. Resist and you will be like the merchant we slew."

They were confident but it was a confidence that came from the dark and the drink. Both were an illusion. They stood in a half-circle blocking my passage. One held a wooden mallet while a second had a cudgel. The last, the leader who had spoken to me had a short sword. Even in the dark, I could see that it was pitted with rust and slightly bent.

"I will give you one chance and I pray that you take it. Turn away and vanish before my eyes. If you are still here when I have finished this sentence, then there will be blood and it will not be mine." I did not shout but the threat in my voice made the one with the mallet look worriedly at the leader. The leader, however, and the other laughed. As I was speaking I drew my weapons and I lunged at the man holding the cudgel. My dagger went through his arm and I twisted as I withdrew it. He screamed and it sounded like a vixen protecting her young. Even as the leader tried to gut me, my sword swept up and knocked the sword from his hand. I punched him hard in the face with the crosspiece of my sword and, with blood pouring from a broken nose and an eye hanging from its socket, he fell to his knees. I looked at the last man, the one with the mallet, "Drop it!" He did so. "Now take your friends to a doctor and then leave Châlons-sur-Marne. If I see you in the morning, then the three of you will be dead men."

The one with the gashed hand just fled and the mallet man helped the leader to his feet, and they hurried off. I heard the moans until they had turned the corner. No one had come from the houses to see what had happened and that, alone, told me that the law had broken down in Châlons-sur-Marne. Picking up the mallet and the cudgel I hurried to the inn.

When I reached the inn, I found my companions waiting for me. Sir Eoin said, "We were worried." He saw blood on my cloak and his eyes widened.

"It is not mine, now let us retire indoors. We have much to do and I have a great deal to tell you."

Chapter 11

It did not take long to tell them all, from the encounter with the Captain to the meeting with the Council and then to the attack by the Jacquerie. "It is clear to me that we are needed here. Of course, they will not like paying protection to us and Lady Isabeau will be angry that she was deceived but I am now convinced that our plan will succeed." Just then we heard the six o'clock bell. "And I will retire, just for an hour or so. I suggest that you four do the same."

I fell asleep almost immediately. My bladder woke me, and I saw that the others were still asleep. After I had made water, I took out my whetstone and sharpened both my sword and dagger. The cudgel and the mallet lay on the chair in the corner. I picked them up. The cudgel was better balanced and easier to use. Thanks to the attack I had a weapon and would not need the leather bags filled with river sand we had brought to use. While the others slept, I changed out of my red surcoat and put on my white one. I slipped my coif over my head and let it hang about my shoulders. I would not need my helmet.

Sir Eoin woke and seeing me dressed leapt to his feet, "You should not have let me sleep!"

I smiled, "You have not overslept. It is still early. We have plenty of time. I just wished to prepare." He nodded and went to make water in the pot. "Do you regret following me from England?"

"It is not the work I thought we would be doing, but the battle at Sézanne was more to my liking and I can see how things will improve, but I do not like our leader."

"Neither do I but it serves my purpose. This way it is Arnaud who is seen to be the one demanding the protection money. We still need more men and until we get them then we cannot be a force to match the Great Company. Sézanne showed me that archers are the weapon we need in greater numbers. The foot soldiers of de Cervole are just knight fodder and are little better than brigands. It is another reason that I wished to come here. We are closer to Paris and we will attract more attention. When others hear of our success then they can join us. This town is somewhere we can winter and who knows what the next year will bring."

The others woke when we spoke, and I waited for the eleven o'clock bell before we descended to an empty inn. We were the only ones in the inn and the owner and his family were asleep. I knew that we were in the part of the inn furthest from his rooms. He did not wish to be disturbed. We made our way to the front door and lifted the bar. Sir Eoin slipped out into the night and hurriedly returned. He made the sign for danger and we leaned against the door. It was the night watch and there were ten of them. Bearing in mind my conversation with Lady Isabeau and the Council I was not surprised, and it pleased me for the increased night watch meant fewer men on the walls. When the sound of their boots on the cobbles receded, we opened the door and slipped out. We hurried to the northeast gate and waited for the Germans to join us. We did not have long to wait and it was while we were waiting that I checked that the numbers at the gate were the same. I saw from the glow of the two burning brands that there were two men on the fighting platform. The other two were obligingly seated next to a brazier and they were drinking. They faced the street which might cause a problem.

When von Württemberg and his men joined us, I mimed for four of them to make their way further down the wall to the steps which led to the fighting platform. They nodded and disappeared. I did not think that we would need to use the cudgel I had brought. We moved into position unseen by the two men whose eyes were rendered night blind by the fire. As I heard the bell in the hall toll, I stepped out of the darkness with a drawn sword. The others followed me, and I had my sword pricked into one man's chest before they even knew. I hissed my words at him, "Friend, you do not wish to die, do you?" They shook their heads. "Bind them!"

From above me, I heard a double thud as the two guards there fell. We had briefed the men well. While the gate was unbarred, there were two bars, I signalled for two men to watch the street we had taken. I knew that two of the Germans would be hurrying down the fighting platform to eliminate the other guards. As the gates were pulled open, I nodded to Karl who said something in German. We peered into the darkness and then I saw a movement. It was Michael and Robin. They were leading our men. This part of the plan had succeeded. We now had a good chance of pulling off the rest of it. The sound of the hooves on the cobbles would alert those who lived close to the gate and Karl and I hurried, with the handful of men who remained to us, to frighten the burghers back into their homes. Only one man opened his door and seeing Kurt with a drawn sword, slammed it shut. From the other side of the town, I heard shouts. Albert and Arnaud had not been as quiet as we had been. We had planned this part of the raid before we had left, and Joseph and Luke would stay by the gate with those who were not of the English Company and the horses. Even though I was confident we would succeed I had planned on an escape should we need it, and our horses were our way out. With a drawn sword, I ran down the street. I knew exactly where to go: the hotel de Ville and Lady Isabeau's hall. Dai and Michael quickly caught up with me and it was reassuring to have the two of them by my side once more. The armed patrol we had seen must have heard the noise from the bridge gate and raced to the square for as we emerged, I saw Captain Lafarge on the crenulated roof of Lady Isabeau's hall shouting out orders. They were defending the centre. It was futile and would aid us as the men on the walls could be quickly overcome and we could establish control quickly.

I waved Captain Robin to my side, "Fetch our archers! Michael, I want a wall of shields before us."

I was without a shield and it seemed prudent, bearing in mind that the men we faced might have crossbows, to be prepared.

"Sir Eoin, Sir Karl, take your men and secure the Hotel de Ville."

As the men we had led followed the two knights I saw a couple of bolts fly towards them. That they not only missed but missed by a large margin told me that the men who used them were not very good. We advanced towards the hall. It felt strange not to be at the fore. I was behind Michael and Harry who held their shields just below their chins. A half dozen bolts were loosed but only one hit a shield and Robert Greengrass laughed, "If that is the best they can do, Sir John, we do not even need these shields.

When we were just a hundred paces from the closed and, no doubt, barred door, I said, "Stop." Our tramping boots had echoed across the square and when they stopped the silence around us was deafening. I could hear in the distance the muffled noises made by Arnaud and Albert and their men. I frowned for it showed they were not as disciplined as we were. I had advised them what were our priorities and they had ignored them.

I shouted, "Captain Lafarge, I am Sir John Hawkwood of the White Company. We have taken charge of your town. You no longer need to pay taxes to the Dauphin, and we will protect you from the Jacquerie. Lay down your arms, open the doors and admit us. I promise that none will be harmed."

He laughed, "You think me a fool! We will stay within these walls. Help will come and sweep your handful of men from our streets and deposit your corpses where they belong, in the gutter."

I realised then that he could only see the hundred or so men I had with me, "Captain Lafarge, fetch her ladyship."

I was greeted by silence and Sir Eoin said, "He has left the walls."

A few moments later Giovanni appeared behind us, "Sir John, we have secured the gates and the town is ours, but Arnaud has no control over some of his men."

"Michael, Giovanni, take twenty men and find the wrongdoers. Arrest them."

Michael turned, "What if Arnaud causes trouble?"

Just then a bolt flew from the walls and it hit the backplate on Michael's armour. I heard the thrum of an arrow and the crossbowman tumbled from the walls.

"Let me worry about that. You just stop the troublemakers."

We readjusted our line as the men chosen by Michael departed. I saw a female figure and Captain Lafarge appear on the battlements of the fortified hall. "Lady Isabeau, my men have taken your town. We hold your gates and the bridge. There are a thousand of us and resistance is futile. Thus far only a handful have perished, and it is my intention that no more die. We will protect you from the Jacquerie and you will not have to pay taxes to the Dauphin. Have your men lay down their arms and open the gates."

"Treacherous mercenary!" There was venom in her voice.

"Lady Isabeau, I can help you to raise the ransom for your husband." The idea just popped into my head but having met the lady I knew that she had steel in her. The single weakness I had seen was her love for her husband.

"You would do that?"

"Before my men and those within your hall I so swear."

"You all heard his words!" She pointed at me. "Lay down your arms and open the gates."

Robin asked as we headed to the door which was pulled open to admit us, "Why, Sir John?"

I shrugged, "It seemed a small price to pay and we can take it from those who come to retake their town. She is a strong-willed lady and with her on our side, the town will be easier to manage."

The servants who opened the door for us quickly disappeared. Robin shouted, "You six go and make sure that they take nothing!" Six of his archers disappeared.

"Dai, light the brands in the sconces, I want no treachery from any within."

Lady Isabeau, with her ladies around her and a fur about her shoulders, swept down the stairs. She paused halfway down, and I could not resist a smile. She was using the stairs so that she could look down on me, "You are the leader of this mercenary army?"

I shook my head, "I lead the English Company, my lady, and the promise I made was my own. Arnaud de Cervole is the leader."

"Then it is he to whom I must speak even though the Archpriest is a bandit. At least he is French!" she turned, "Come, ladies, let us dress appropriately." She turned and headed up the stairs.

I suddenly realised that I had not seen any of the soldiers, including Lafarge, descend. There had to be another staircase. "Karl, guard the door with some of your men. Robin, fetch the rest!" This was one building I had not scouted out, for obvious reasons, it was too well guarded. There had to be a stable. I ran with a sword in my hand. Dai's lights marked the way. We hurtled through the servant's quarters where Robin's archers had secured the servants who had fled and then we burst out of the hall into a darkened and cobbled courtyard. I heard and smelled the stables, and we ran towards them.

"Robin, cover the gate. You men at arms, come with me."

As we reached the gate it burst open and two riders tried to run us down. I just reacted and swung my sword. It bit into the side of the leading warrior and then he and his companion were plucked from their saddles by arrows. I ran inside and saw Captain Lafarge and another four of his men trying to saddle uncooperative horses. As I ran in he turned and drew his two-handed sword. He was going to fight, and I relished it. The stable was not the place for a two-handed sword, and it showed his lack of real skill. He tried to swing his sword overhand and it hacked into a beam. I had no such problem as I swung horizontally and hacked into his side below the breast and backplate. His mail slowed down the blade, but I still ripped through his gambeson and into his flesh. He pulled his sword free and tried a diagonal swing, but his wound made the blow weaker and I met it with my sword. They rang together and sparks flew. I was a fighter, and I had no compunction about punching with my crosspiece. He was not expecting the blow and I caught his cheek, laying it open to the bone. I could see, in his eyes, that he now regretted his decision to fight. Had he asked for mercy I might have considered it, but he did not and as he reeled, I hooked my right leg behind his left and he tumbled to the ground. I turned my hands and put all my weight behind the thrust which went through his nose and skull. His body shivered and then lay still.

The others had either surrendered or been slain. "Secure the stable and let us return to the square."

By the time the sun rose the town had been secured. In all twenty-three guards had died. A half dozen of our men had been wounded but Michael had arrested twenty men, all of them Arnaud's who had been caught pillaging and attempting to rape women and girls. He brought them to me after I had discovered that Arnaud and Albert had entered the hall to speak with Lady Isabeau. It was a deliberate insult to me. I would not give the Frenchman the pleasure of watching me run in and demand to be a party to the talks. I had said all I needed to say. Instead, I turned to the bound men, "My Captain has arrested you all for crimes against the innocent of Châlons-sur-Marne."

One large loudmouth whom I knew was a close friend of Arnaud's shouted, "We are not your men, Englishman, and the Archpriest approves of what we do!"

I stepped close to him, "There you are wrong for we are all one company now and there are rules. You are no longer a brigand. Hang them all!"

Robin had my men at arms and archers ready for he knew my mind. There were trees lining the square, they afforded shade in the summer. Ropes were thrown over the lower limbs and the men were hauled, their arms bound behind them, kicking and screaming. Their necks were not broken, they were, effectively strangled. When their kicking stopped, I said, "Leave their bodies there until dark so that all may see the punishment for breaking our rules."

The Jacquerie as well as those members of our company who had less than honourable intentions would now understand that I meant to have law. "Peter of Poole, take four men and ride back to William. Fetch him and our treasure. For the rest, we will use The Grapes and The Lamb as our homes. Take our horses there and inform the landlords of my decision. Tell the landlord of The Lamb that we will pay for our rooms." I signalled for Michael, Giovanni, and Dai to join me. "We will walk the walls. Arnaud and Albert can discuss the terms, but we will make sure that we can defend the town. They let us keep Plancy-l'Abbaye, but this is an important town and controls a major crossing of the Marne."

As we walked, I talked to Michael about my plans. "I will return to Bordeaux at the end of September. If there is an attempt to retake this town it will be by then. I need more English archers and men at arms. I hope that there will be men in Gascony who tire of inaction and seek the rewards which we have and will increase."

Dai asked, "We do not just hold Châlons-sur-Marne?"

"No Dai, this is a rich country, and we will offer our protection to the manors which lie around here. The Jacquerie may wish to extend their control and Paris is not far away. It is why I selected this as the place we would take. We use the threat of rebellion to our advantage, but we must be seen to be law-abiding."

"We take money for protection and we are law-abiding, lord?"

"Yes, Michael. Lady Isabeau offered to pay me to protect her town when she first met me." I laughed, "Of course that was before she knew my real intentions but those with money and power do not wish to give it to the peasantry. They want law and order, and we can give it to them." We had reached the bridge gate. I pointed to the far end of the bridge. "I need that fortified. Giovanni, take ten archers and ten of my men at arms. I want a barrier here. Move stones from the town if you like. I want to be able to defend the bridge from any who try to take it from us."

Michael pointed north, "The river is easy to ford."

"I know but the great lords who will come to test us do not like to get their feet wet. They will try the bridge first for it is what they know. We will destroy the bridge to the north and make the Marne our moat!"

By the time we had returned to the square Arnaud and Albert were still within and I wondered what was being said. Robin and Sir Eoin had organised patrols so that my orders would be obeyed. The hangings had served their purpose. The two of them strolled over to us and Robin asked, "We have the town, Sir John, how long do you think before we have to defend it?"

"I am not sure that any escaped to spread the word, but we know that this is the main road and eventually someone will come and wonder why there are men guarding the bridge. I would say a week and that gives us enough time to organise the defences and to ride to the manors close by."

Before either of them could answer the doors of the hall opened and a beaming Arnaud and Albert came out. They saw me first and Albert said, as he neared me, "You were right my friend, this is more lucrative than…"

It was then that first he and then Arnaud saw the bodies. Most were Arnaud's men but two of them were Albert's. "What is this?"

"Arnaud, these men were found abusing women. I tried and hanged them."

"They are my men!"

"And we agreed that we would not behave like bandits. This way the townsfolk know that they can be safe in their own town. The Jacquerie will also behave."

"I command here!"

"Do you, Arnaud? Would you like to make a contest of it?" I stared at him, almost willing him to draw his weapon. "Do not anger me, either of you! You chose to negotiate with Lady Isabeau even though it was my plan. You have the majority of the men but whose are the better? Would you like me to take my men back to Bordeaux? It would be the work of a moment to take the coins from the town and ride away. How long would you last when real soldiers came? Come, tell me, do you want our agreement to end?"

Albert shook his head, "I do not and, if you think about it Arnaud, neither do you."

He was defeated but I heard the anger in his voice, "Next time, ask me!"

"If there is a next time I will act as I did today. You either have rules and laws or you have chaos!"

He turned and went back into the hall. We had solved nothing and there would be more conflict in the future. This was not the mercenary company I had envisaged. It was a start and nothing more. Albert came with me as we set the sentries and ensured that all on the walls and the gates knew what they had to do. As we walked I cleared the air between us. We were united and Arnaud had begun to be isolated.

It was a risk but, the next day, I led my English Company, Hawkwood's men, to ride around the neighbouring manors to the east of the Marne, to tell them of the new arrangement. Crops were being harvested and in the three days we rode, not one farmer or lord offered us any opposition. They were unhappy about the situation, but my men were well armed and with the threat of archers too then no one refused to pay for their protection. After three days I deemed that we had enough farms for my men to protect. Albert had been doing the same on the south side of the town. That Arnaud did nothing was no surprise.

William had arrived on the same day that I had ridden forth. Although I had seen him each night, I had been too tired to discuss company matters. On the fourth day, I let Sir Eoin lead the twenty men who would patrol the manors I was protecting. Michael, Robin, and I sat with William and went through the new financial arrangement. It seemed fair to me but I knew that we would have others to convince. The most important part was that the lance would be led by one person. In the case of everyone not in the English Company that would be a man at arms. There were fewer men at arms and they were the ones who would bear the brunt of any fighting. The exceptions were the archers. William had recognised the fact and Robin, Martin, Ned, and my other archer captains would all lead a lance. In fact, William told me that he had used the model I had created of captains. No matter what the other two said the English Company would use William's suggestion.

It was two days later that I managed to get Albert and Arnaud alone. I went with William and he had the written agreements with him. Both of the others could read but we discussed the points one by one. Surprisingly neither man disagreed. Since the hanging, more than forty of Arnaud's men had deserted. They had stolen from the churches before they went and that had caused some ill-feeling. Arnaud had been forced to ride after them. He had hanged three of his own men. He now saw the need for a structure of leaders which we could use. It was Albert who made a suggestion I had not thought of, but which was a good one.

"The leader of each lance should be a knight." For once Arnaud and I were in agreement in that neither of us understood Albert.

"In my company, Albert, I only have two knights, myself and Sir Eoin."

He had smiled, "You miss my point, Sir John, we make them knights. It is we who give them their spurs."

"Can we do that?"

"Who is to stop us? Here we operate outside the rule of kings and dukes. Do we seek the approval of the King of France who is, in any case, a prisoner of King Edward? Think about this. I know how I felt when I was knighted and they will feel the same. It will be a way to encourage others to aspire to be the leaders of a lance. We all hope to recruit more men." He turned to William,

"Bookkeeper, you have been here some days, how sits our finances?"

"In one week we have taken more than in the month or more we were at Plancy-l'Abbaye."

Even Arnaud was impressed and Albert continued, "There you have it. Sir John, you were right to come here and you are right to reorganise the way we operate. My idea means that we will have fewer desertions and each new knight has more reason to hold on to his own men."

We did not disagree, and that meeting began a period of peace amongst our triumvirate. We even recruited from the town. There were orphans and abandoned children. They lived an almost feral existence and when Ned found some stealing, he did not beat them, as would have happened had others discovered the theft, he brought them to me. I saw the potential. Their ages went from those who were barely five summers old to older youths who were almost men. They were dirty and they were ragged but I saw what we could do with them. There were eighteen which was a good number for I led fifteen lances. I addressed them.

"You are thieves and there are punishments for theft. You could lose a finger for each offence." I saw the older ones looking for a way to run and escape. "Do not think to run for my men will stop you. I offer you an alternative. Instead of living in dark holes and stealing, I invite you to join the English Company. Each one of you would join one of my lances. You would be washed and dressed so that you look like Christians once more. You would become a page who served the lance but, in return, be taught to use weapons so that, in the fullness of time, you might become a squire and then... who knows?"

I had learned from Albert. A title such as a page cost nothing and yet, even as I said it, I saw hope appear in the eyes of the older boys. All agreed for they had nothing to lose and much to gain. Dai took charge of them and after speaking with them allocated them to the lances. The three youngest he kept, and he trained those very young ones himself. They served us and William. It was a good arrangement and once begun we continued to use it in the future.

It was Giovanni who, a few days after Dai began his training of the boys, found the Jacquerie. He returned early from his patrol and threw himself from his horse, "There is a column of Jacquerie heading from Rheims, Sir John. They are afoot but there are many hundreds of them."

"You think they are heading here?"

"They are this side of the Marne and unless they seek to take the manors which pay us it seems the only reasonable explanation."

Ned and Joseph were close by, "You two stay here. I will take all the rest of my men. William, inform Albert and Arnaud of the danger. We should prepare for a fight."

I had not ridden forth since the first week after we had taken the town and I relished the opportunity to ride out. I had expected some sort of attack, but I had assumed it would be lords and knights. We found the rest of the patrol ten miles from our walls. The mob, for that was what it was, of Frenchmen was a mixture of peasants, artisans, and old soldiers. They were the ones disillusioned with the Dauphin and having seen what had been done in Paris sought to shake off the shackles of a weakened aristocracy. The ripples from Poitiers were still in evidence. Giovanni's men had stayed out of sight. We had patrolled enough to know the roads well, however, as I led more than a hundred men, we were seen. The mob halted and I was able to view the leaders. They had helmets and mail. None were plated. Their lack of training and organisation was clear to be seen for they bunched together. We were at the top of a rise. The fields to the left and right were made up of vines and, as such were relatively open. Bunches of ripening fruits hung from them.

Turning to Robin I said, "Have the archers dismount. I will go to speak to them. I hope I can persuade them to return whence they came but if I fail then let us see if your arrows can do the job."

He nodded, "Archers, dismount."

The advantage of our lances was that we had horse holders and there was no need to issue an order. Each lance organised itself.

"Michael, come with me."

I had not taken my banner, but we all wore white and I no longer had to disguise my identity. In fact, using my name was a weapon. The English knight who had taken the Oriflamme was well known. Our helmets hung from our cantles and I slipped my coif over my shoulders. We reined in forty paces from their leaders. I had seen neither bows nor crossbows and I took the danger of a missile as an acceptable risk.

"I am Sir John Hawkwood of the White Company and both the land and the road upon which you march are under my protection. None use it without our permission. I ask you to disperse and return whence you came."

The one who spoke was the better-armed of them and I thought he might have been a former man at arms, "You are English, and this is France! I will give you a chance, take your brigands and leave Châlons-sur-Marne and you can live. We will liberate the town from the rule of despots and leeches." He spread a hand and raised his voice so that the others could hear, "I see less than a hundred men before us. We will sweep you away as though you were annoying rodents!"

I shook my head, "My friend, I can see that you have military training. Do not cause the people you lead to die because of your arrogance."

In answer, he raised his sword and shouted, "Kill them!"

Michael and I wheeled our horses and spurred them before the mob had taken a step. Stones rattled on our plate but, thankfully, none hit our heads. Our mounts were struck but that just encouraged them to run. I saw that Robin had the archers in a line and that there was a gap for us to pass through and join the mounted men at arms behind. The Frenchman was right, we did look like too tiny a number to withstand an attack by the mob but they had a slope with which to contend and were all bunched in the middle. Had they enjoyed any kind of leadership then they would have used their numbers to outflank us.

Robin waited until we had passed through before closing the gap and then ordering his archers to draw. There were forty archers which does not sound like a large number but it would be enough. As the forty arrows were released another forty were nocked and released. In the time it took for the mob to cover a hundred and twenty paces over two hundred arrows had been released. It was as though the front of the mob had been struck by a giant's scythe. All their leaders, including the former man at arms, were hit. The bodies were an obstacle and the mob slowed and almost stopped one hundred paces from us.

"One more flight and then we will charge them."

As the last forty arrows were loosed the archers stepped back and I led the men at arms through them. As soon as we were clear I shouted, "Charge!" There were just twenty-five of us but we were spread out and the steel of the Jacquerie lay dead and dying. The would-be rebels turned and fled. "Hold the line!" I used the flat of my sword to smack into the backs of the heads of the men I caught. I did not need butchery. I just wanted their spirits breaking. I stopped a mile from the skirmish. We had won.

The archers and the rest of my men had stripped the dead and made a pyre. We did not want to encourage vermin. As we headed back to Châlons-sur-Marne and the sun began to set, the column of smoke rose high in the sky. The first attempt to relieve the town had failed.

Chapter 12

Two days later a delegation of merchants and farmers crossed the bridge over the Marne. These lived outside our protection area. They came to Lady Isabeau's hall to speak to the three of us. Their leader spoke for them, "We would ask this company to protect us from brigands, bandits and the Jacquerie. We have been let down by the nobility and we cannot harvest our crops and fields as well as fighting them. We would pay you to do so for us!"

The look on Arnaud's face was a mixture of admiration for me as I had said that by being a force for law and order we would encourage cooperation, and hatred for I had been proved right again. With William, we agreed a fee and Albert took it upon himself to keep their lands safe. When they had gone Lady Isabeau came to see me.

"Sir John, you have kept all the promises you made to me save one. Where is the ransom for my husband?"

It was not a great sum and I could have paid it with my own money but as soon as William arrived, and I explained the problem he had solved it. By taking a miniscule amount from here and there as well as the pay he allocated to the men I had hanged, he had secured the money.

I smiled at Lady Isabeau, "I have the ransom, my lady, and as soon as we have the autumnal equinox I shall ride to Bordeaux and send it to England for you."

She nodded and smiled a thin smile, "Forgive me, Sir John, if I doubt you but I would have two of my people take it. Raymond and Guillaume are old family retainers."

"That is fine, but the ransom still leaves when I do. Not that I do not trust your men, my lady, but it is a long way twixt here and Bordeaux." I was determined that she would not dictate terms to me.

"That is satisfactory."

It was an honourable draw!

I told the other two and, for different reasons, I suspect, both were happy. For Albert, it gave him the opportunity to win over more men to his side for the moment when he called an election.

Albert had told the men at arms that the decision to knight them was his and I had not argued. For Arnaud, it was just that he did not like me and if I was away then he would be happy. My men did not wish me to go but I knew that with Robin and Michael in command my interests would be protected. The men gave me lists of what we would need to bring back from Bordeaux. All had agreed that I could stay until the New Year and that pleased me. I would like to spend time in the nearest thing I had to a home. I would take Dai and William with me. Dai had grown over the summer and while it would be some years before he achieved his final size, he was not far short already. The two men Lady Isabeau sent were old soldiers and when I met them, I was impressed with their attitude. I let them take charge of the ransom as it was one less thing for me to worry about.

We left the day after the equinox and stayed overnight at Plancy-l'Abbaye. It was a peaceful place now and the men who protected it were almost part of the land. The manor we had taken over was ours by right. The owner was dead, and the locals looked to the men there as their new landlords. Albert had chosen his men well. Of course, if a force came to try to take it there were not enough to withstand it but it was a start. We had a wagon for there were goods I had taken to send to John in England. I had promised I would keep my side of the bargain and it would be profit for me. It took sixteen days for us to do the journey. Without the two older warriors we would have made better time, but I did not mind. It was October when we deposited them in the port. I had them sign a letter saying that we had done our part and delivered them to a ship. If anything untoward happened now I wanted no blame attached to us. We then headed for my farm. I would finally see my son John and, I confess that I had been celibate in Châlons-sur-Marne. There had been women I could have taken but Antiochia and Elizabeth were enough women for me!

We were in good humour as we rode through the gate into the courtyard. I heard the sound of metal on metal and that told me that we had new men and that they were practising. That could wait. William pointed out the features which had been added since I had left. I nodded my approval. Dai said that he would take our horses to the stable and so William and I hurried inside.

Roger must have been with the men who were practising for it was Elizabeth and a chubby, pink-faced bundle who greeted me.

"Here, my lord is your son! He is a healthy babe and has a good appetite." She lifted him so that I could see him, and he screwed his face up as he stared at me.

"I am your father, son, and when you are a man you shall be as I am, a warrior!"

Elizabeth frowned briefly and then hid it. I knew that women did not approve of my way of life, but I enjoyed it and it was natural that I would try to ensure that my son followed in my footsteps. "He has just fed so if you wish to hold him…"

I shook my head, "I am dirty from the road and, I confess, I fear that I might break him!"

She laughed, "No, my lord, he is robust enough but you are right, I can smell horses on the two of you." She seemed to see her brother, "And it is good to see you, William."

"And you, sister. Motherhood suits you!"

"Then we shall bathe and change."

We waited until Dai had finished with the horses before we went to the room we used for bathing. The water was not hot, but it did not matter. The large tubs of water were big enough to accommodate a large man and it was good to be rid of the stink of horses and sweat. We dried ourselves and dressed. By the time we had done so it was dark, and Roger had finished for the day. He, too, looked content and he gave me his report as we enjoyed a jug of wine made on the estate. "We have recruited well. Your visit to England was productive. We have eighteen archers, all good men. Ten are from Cheshire! Not only did I manage to recruit ten men at arms but also squires for them."

"And horses?"

"And horses." He shifted uncomfortably, "Funds are running low here, my lord. The farm is profitable but buying horses and feeding almost forty extra mouths is difficult."

I waved at William, "William has brought money with him. We will be staying for a little while. I smiled at Elizabeth, "We shall be here for Christmas!"

She beamed, "Then I am content!"

I turned to Roger, "Did my plate come from England?"

He nodded, "I think that was what it was. It came a week since in a large chest. I had it placed in the armoury."

"Was there no letter with it?"

Roger suddenly looked embarrassed, "Lord, I forgot to look. There may have been, but we had new men whom I had brought from the port and I just thought to…"

I smiled, "It is no matter. I am here now. Come, Dai, while we wait for the food, we will open the chest."

The armoury, as we called it, was a room that had been used by the previous owner to store wine and was just off the kitchen. It had a door which could be locked although we kept it open. The Jewish merchant had sent the plate securely and the chest in which it resided was well made. Secured with ropes it looked to have made the voyage without any damage. We untied the rope and opened it. On top of the plate, which was wrapped in hessian sacks, was a piece of parchment and I recognised the seal of John Braynford. He had written it himself for I knew his hand. I picked it up and told Dai to unpack the plate so that I could inspect it the next day. I took the unopened letter to my hall. Elizabeth had just put John down to sleep in the cot she kept in the hall. She put her finger to her lips and went to the kitchen. I sat by the fire where I could watch my son and read the letter. Roger topped up my goblet and then headed to the kitchen. I smiled at my sleeping son. I was a father and I would be a better one than my own father had been. Taking my dagger I cut the wax seal and unfolded the parchment. I was not ready to read what lay within.

September 9th

My son,
Sir John,
I know not how to break this terrible news to you. This is news which a man should hear face to face and not separated by mountainous seas. You have a daughter, Antiochia, who was born three days since. She is hale and healthy but your wife, my daughter, Antiochia, died giving birth. It seems that the only son I shall now have is the one given to me by marriage. We can see now that Antiochia was too frail to be a mother. The pregnancy was a difficult one but she loved her unborn babe as much as she loved you. We had no time after the baby

was born for farewells, God took her mercifully quickly. It was as though the two lives were exchanged in that single instant of birth and death. Even though we had no time for goodbyes, her illness had meant that the three of us were all closer and she told us that the time since you had come into her life was the happiest and she regretted nothing. She had hoped that she would be able to lavish the love she wished to give to you on the child and I swear that my wife and I will ensure that your child, my granddaughter, has all that Antiochia would have wished for her.

You were not here when we named her, and I hope that you will forgive us for naming her after our daughter. I think I know your mind, Sir John, and that you would not wish to raise the child yourself. Our talks told me that you are a man of war and that is as it should be. The home we built for Antiochia is yours and none shall live in it but you. Should you return to England then it will be your home. Until she is of a legal age then you will be my sole heir. After that time then Antiochia will inherit all but your hall. I hope this meets with your approval.

Your wife, my daughter, Lady Antiochia Hawkwood, will be housed beneath a marble stone in the church. There will be space, should you choose, for you next to her. My wife and I will be buried close by. Should you ever need anything then I pray that you write to me. I am a rich man but what are riches without children? You are my son and I pray that God keeps you well.

Your friend,

John Braynford

    I read the letter twice for I could not believe it. I could not argue with any of the merchant's decisions. Indeed, I had no right to do so. I wondered, briefly, about taking a ship to England to see the babe but I dismissed it. I had a son. I looked over to John and standing over him, took his tiny fingers in mine. He was soft and smelled, well, like a baby.

    "My son, I swear that I will be a better father to you than I will be to your sister. I have learned the value of fatherhood and of love." I looked up and saw Elizabeth and Roger standing at the door. I handed her the letter. There was a chapel in the hall and I said, "I must go to the chapel, I need to speak with God!"

Roger put his arm around Elizabeth as she read. I went to the chapel and took out my sword. Holding it like a cross I prayed. "Lord, I beg that Antiochia is accorded a place in heaven for she was a good woman. I did not deserve her for her love was unbounded and given without any reservations. I will not be there for my daughter, but I beg you not to punish the child any further. She has lost her mother and deserves all the love that she can get. I promise to be a better man from now on and I will raise my son, John, to be a true gentleman and knight!"

Elizabeth said nothing when I entered the room but she ran to me and threw her arms around me. William and Dai approached from the outside and both were laughing. When they saw us embracing, they stopped and looked at the baby.

Roger said, "Sir John has had bad news from England. Any celebrations which we might have had we will have to defer."

I disengaged myself and shook my head, "No, we will celebrate the two births for Antiochia would have wished us to."

Dai's eyes welled up and I suddenly remembered that he and my wife had been very close, "Is she...?"

I nodded and took him in my arms, "She is with God now, but she left me a daughter. Let us celebrate that."

That evening was a celebration albeit a subdued one. I wondered how Dai would make it through the meal for I saw him suddenly force back the tears as he remembered something else about the lady. What surprised me was Elizabeth. She seemed to be genuinely upset that my wife had died yet Antiochia had been, as far as she was aware, a rival. She could not know that she was not. That evening as we lay together for the first time in many months emotion won over and, thankfully, John slept on through the night and we did not disturb him. It was as though it was a release for both of us. When I was able to, I wrote a long letter to John. I owed it to him. I told him that I would appreciate it if he brought up Antiochia. I said that when time allowed, I would return to England, but I knew that the astute merchant would see through that. My home would be wherever there was war. I gave it to Captain Jack and asked him to deliver it along with the goods I had brought to Bordeaux. I saw the captain each time he was in port for he not only brought those who wished to follow me but also the goods we ordered from England.

For the next few weeks, the death of my wife hung like a spectre over the house. I forced myself into work to dispel it. For a short time, I would be a landowner and a father. I threw myself into both roles. I did not, however, forget completely that I was a captain and I got to know the new men as best I could. William and I explained to them the new financial arrangements and the way we worked. My share of the profits thus far enabled me to have surcoats and jupons made for them all. It was an investment. William, however, worked out a way for me to equip my men but at their expense. He knew how to manipulate accounts and I was pleased that he did not appear to wish to rob me. It would have been very easy.

I spent some time each week in Bordeaux for I needed to know the mood both of Gascony and England. The port was a good place to do so. It was there in late November that I met a kindred spirit. I had served in the same army as Robert Knolles, but I had just been a man at arms. Now that I had been elevated, we could speak easier. He had been serving with the King of Navarre and the king's brother Philip. Robert actually sought me out. I had visited the city often and found an inn which I quite liked. It was run by a former archer who kept me a good table and gave me only the finest of food and drink. I had just begun to eat when Robert came in. He was excitable and exuberant, that was his way.

"Sir John! I heard you came here when you were in town! Do you mind if I sit here with you for I wish to learn from you?"

"Of course. Jack, another plate and a goblet of wine."

We spoke first of the raids we had both been on and he told me that he had been in Paris with the King of Navarre who was trying to establish some sort of order there. After we had eaten and he had emptied one goblet of wine he said, "I have been commissioned to raise a company of Gascons and Englishmen to raid the Loire." I nodded, in as neutral a manner as I could adopt. "I would like you and your men to join me."

"You wish me to lead men in a raid along the Loire?"

He looked embarrassed, "I would lead, and your men would be part of my Great Company. I have funds to raise two thousand men."

"Then that is a great company, but I fear I am committed. I am here raising men myself."

He gave a wry smile, "And that is obvious to me for I cannot hire Englishmen for love nor money. Gascons I have but I would like archers and most of the ones who come here seek you."

I was flattered but we had worked at this. Our winter in London had been to encourage archers and men at arms to seek us.

"Will Prince Edward be raiding?"

He was an honest man and when he shook his head, I saw no deception. "He still enjoys tournaments in England, but I have heard that he and his father are negotiating with their prisoner King John. Next year may see some movement."

"And that is when you will be raiding?"

He smiled, "It might encourage the French to negotiate. The Jacquerie mobs have got them worried. The French need a lasting peace so that they can regain control of their great towns."

I did not like the idea of following another. I knew that it was merely a matter of time before I was able to take control of the White Company.

Robert saw my hesitation and added, "You would be serving Prince Edward once more."

"He will be raiding the Loire? I thought his father had his eyes upon the French Crown."

He shook his head, "Prince Edward and his father will be coming to the north. With Calais in our hands, he has the opportunity to be close to France when the call comes to seize the crown. We weaken the French's resolve in the Loire. Come, Sir John, you are an Englishman of great repute and your presence would draw many men to the banner."

Thinking back I suppose that had Prince Edward been the one to ask me then I might have agreed for I felt I owed him something but the young man before me was different. It was at that moment that I decided that the three major battles I had fought for King Edward were enough. He was going to be landing at the town I had helped to take and where I had lost friends.

I shook my head, "I have a new son and I will spend time with him. When the spring comes, I will decide then but I wish you luck with your task."

I could lie with my face but not with my eyes. Robert knew that when the spring came, I would not be joining him. He smiled and nodded, "Congratulations on your son. We will be at the Loire by April should you decide to serve your Prince once more."

It was a barb, but I did not react to it. I had served England and more and I did not need to explain myself to him.

Elizabeth had a fine Christmas present for me. As we ate in our hall and I enjoyed another English Christmas, the second in two years, she told me that she was with child. "You know so soon!"

She smiled and said, "I knew the moment you lay with me. Your seed, husband, is strong."

Roger of Norham, Dai and William looked as delighted as I was, and the news made the Christmas merrier than any I could remember. The one with John and his family might have been a grander affair but I knew which one I preferred.

By the time February came the men arriving from England had long dried up for most were already signing up to follow Robert or they were joining Prince Edward who was in Kent. Since I had met him, I had managed to recruit another ten archers and five men at arms. My hall could not accommodate many more. Where I did find gold was in the poorer quarters around the inns at the quayside. Many English and Gascon soldiers had, over the years, taken local women and fathered children. Too often the children had been abandoned by fathers who went to fight in other wars and women who had to earn a living in the inns and taverns. Their lives were often short. The children lived as best they could. The prettier girls would, eventually, serve the customers of the inns while the boys who survived would become labourers or sailors. I had seen in Châlons-sur-Marne the opportunities they represented, and I recruited twenty of them. Fifteen were boys but I managed to save five girls. It was an act that pleased Elizabeth. She took them under her wing and trained them to be her servants. I left the younger boys with Roger of Norham so that he could train them but the ten elder ones would come back with the men at arms and archers I had recruited. We had a wagon and I hired two old ex-soldiers to drive it. Robin would need the arrowheads ordered from England and I had bolts of white cloth to further fit out my men.

Had this been England then we would not have dreamed of setting out in January but here, while the weather could be wet and unpleasant it was more benign and clement. We left in the middle of January. We were a large well-armed column and were safe from any predators along the roads. Of course, the journey was expensive, and William deducted the expenses from the accounts. This would cost the White Company but not Sir John Hawkwood.

The three of us rode at the fore when we travelled, I did not bother with scouts, and we spoke of hopes and dreams. The thought of a new child excited me, and it had set off thoughts and plans in the others. William opened up first, "I think I will take a woman, Sir John. I look at Roger and think I do not wish to be alone when I am his age."

Dai nodded, "Yet your sister and he are great friends. They laugh and they are company for each other."

William shook his head, "Dai, a man needs to do more than laugh."

"And you, Dai, what are your hopes?"

"I would be a man at arms. When the new men arrived in the hall, I saw that I am nearly as big as some of them. When I lived in Wales I was small but the good food and exercise have made me grow rapidly over the past months. All that I lack is the skills and they are coming. With the new boys you took on, I need to be a page no longer. You need a squire, and I would be that squire. I have carried the standard for you but…"

I realised that I had almost forgotten Dai, "And I will remedy that now, Dai. You shall be my squire and I do not think it will be long before you lead your own lance."

When we stayed in the inns, taverns and monasteries along the road the three of us would eat together. I made a point of speaking to all the men whilst on the road but the meals were times for friends and that was what William and Dai were. I knew, know, that men think me cold and uncaring. I am not but I confess that I have the ability to make hard decisions and to be ruthless. I believed I had a handful of friends, these two, Robin and Michael were the only others who were close to me. When I spoke with William and Dai I knew that I could speak in confidence and they would listen to my plans and offer suggestions.

William knew of the offer made to me by Robert, "If Prince Edward and his father come to France, Sir John, we may find ourselves in a difficult position. Suppose he is offered the French crown? The land we hold would be his. Would we fight Englishmen?"

"No, William, I may not serve Prince Edward, but I will not fight my countrymen. Giovanni has urged me to go to Italy and with the men I have now recruited then that is a possibility. His coming may, in the short term, aid us. We shall see."

By the time we reached Châlons-sur-Marne, I had got to know my new men well and I was happy that they would fit in well with my other men. On the road, we had explained to them our system so that they arrived better informed than any other recruits. The land around Châlons-sur-Marne was peaceful and I was relieved. Lady Isabeau's husband had arrived home before Christmas and even before I had time to speak to any of my men I was sent for. She thanked me and I saw that she had changed her mind about me. When I had come to her and made my offer, she had thought it preposterous and that I was little more than a bandit. Now she saw me as a man of my word. She gave me a necklace for Elizabeth, "Your men tell me that you have a son. This is for your wife. I know how much I missed my husband. She must miss you."

I did not tell her that I was not married, I just nodded.

When I finally got to speak with Robin and Michael my good feelings left me. "Sir John, Arnaud has been speaking with Margaret of Flanders, the wife of the Duke of Burgundy. He is taking the company to Nevers to fight against an English company which is heading there from the Loire."

When I had been on the road we had heard of this column. It was Robert Knolles and his men. Would we have to fight against

Englishmen? I just nodded and said, "You two come with me. We go to speak to our leader!"

Chapter 13

Champagne 1359

Arnaud and Albert still lived in the Hotel de Ville and even as I arrived, I saw a great deal of action and movement. Albert smiled when he saw me, but Arnaud just scowled. The Frenchman said, "You have finally returned and just in time. I have taken a commission to fight in Burgundy for Countess Margaret. I have asked Jean de Senonches to maintain our interest here. We leave in a week for there is a band of mercenaries heading for Nevers!"

"I am not leaving, and neither are my men."

"I am the leader and I say we are leaving."

"You are a leader in name only and you know it."

"I command the largest number of men and you will do as I say."

I laughed. Looking back it was the wrong thing to do but I found the situation ridiculous. His men were a rabble. "And how will you force us to join you? Will you fight? If you do then firstly you will lose and secondly, it will destroy the company!"

His knuckles were white as he gripped the edge of the table and his voice was cold. "Then the Company is dissolved, and Albert and I will take our men south to Nevers! That will leave you a handful of men to defend the town. You will lose for the French are already flexing their muscles. It is rumoured that there is to be a peace with England when King John is returned to the throne!"

In one way he was right. Even with the boys and the new men, I had less than two hundred men but mine were well trained. I turned to Albert, "You know you will be fighting an English company? They will have longbows."

I saw that it came as news to Albert. He had thought it was a band such as the one Arnaud had led before he met us, "How do you know?"

I held Arnaud's gaze, "I was invited to join but I chose The White Company and those I thought were my friends."

Arnaud laughed, "We were never and could never be friends, Englishman. Leave us now so that we may speak."

I nodded, "Before you leave you will leave my men's share of the money." I saw his mouth open, "And if you do not it will be a bloodbath!"

He said nothing but I saw that he would have to go along with it. As we left, I said to Robin and Martin, "Replace the men on the bridge and the bridge gate with our men. If he is going to Nevers, then he has to cross the bridge and we will examine every wagon which leaves. I will see William and have him work out what is due to us."

Michael asked, "Will we have enough to hold this town?"

I lowered my voice as we hurried back to The Grapes, "Prince Edward and his father are in London negotiating with the French King. Our hold on Châlons-sur-Marne may be tenuous at best. If the King is offered the French Crown, then he will not wish this town to be held against him. We may have to move."

Robin asked, "Where to?"

I smiled, "I have no idea, but we now have a core of men who will make the English Company the finest in this land. We will cross that bridge when we have to." I did not actually know where we would go but I was the leader and leaders led!

I spoke to William who gave me a smile, "The profits we made are stored safely, my lord. I do not doubt that Arnaud and Albert will have been attempting to steal us blind but unless they have sharper minds then I think we will end up the richer."

I was glad that William was on our side.

The situation in the city was a difficult one. My men held the two main gates and there was bad blood between the English Company and the Frenchmen led by Arnaud. There were fights but, fortunately, none led to a death.

The night before they were due to leave a messenger arrived. He was from the Dauphin and his words were for the Council. The envoy tried to sneak through a minor gate but we were watchful. We were watching out for treachery from Arnaud, but we were rewarded by the news. It reported that the King of France had signed the Treaty of London. King Edward was given the lands which had formerly belonged to King Henry II and he would not hold them in fief to the French crown. In addition, the ransom for King John was raised to four million ecus. The message informed the town that the Dauphin repudiated the terms of the treaty and there was war! I now saw the significance of Arnaud leaving for the south. The Dauphin might try to take Châlons-sur-Marne. Rheims had already been secured for the crown. It was my time for diplomacy. I hurried to Albert's quarters. We had been in the town long enough to know the ways around it and I entered without Arnaud's men seeing me. They were too busy packing booty to take to Nevers.

"Albert, there will be war with England."

"I know and we now have the chance to win."

"You know I will not fight the English."

"Of course and that means that you are doomed to lose."

"Do you think that Arnaud is the man to fight an English led army?" I saw the doubt on his face. "He will lose and if you are with him then you will lose also. You both know that and that is why you wish me to be with you. My longbows give you a chance."

"Then join us."

"No, but I have a proposition for you. Keep your Germans here and we will be as we were before Arnaud came. Between us, we have almost a thousand men and that is more than enough to maintain control over the town."

I saw his eyes widen and then he smiled, "I do not like Arnaud and, like you, I know that his men are unreliable. I will agree on the condition that I become the sole leader of the Company."

"There will need to be an election."

"And if you do not stand then I will be elected."

It was a bitter pill to swallow but the medicine had to be taken and I nodded. "Will you tell Arnaud?"

He smiled, "No, he will discover that he is alone when he has crossed the bridge and we are behind the river." He shrugged, "If I tell him then there will be bloodshed, for he is an unpredictable man and unnecessary deaths would benefit no one, save the French."

And so Albert Sterz became Captain of the White Company. When I told my captains none were happy, but they accepted the inevitability of it.

My men were on duty well before dawn. Arnaud de Cervole surrounded himself with his best men and headed across the square to the bridge gate. I waited there with my men. Half of my archers guarded the northeast gate. When he reached the gate the Frenchman said, "Where is Albert? What have you done with him?"

I was on my horse and I leaned down and said, "I have done nothing with him, but I do not think he wishes to ride alongside you."

The words had a dual meaning and Arnaud took the wrong one and thought I meant that Albert would follow, "The next time we meet, Englishman, it will be on the field of battle. First, I will deal with these raiders on the Loire and then I will return to deal with you. Tell Albert that I have left."

He and his horsemen headed out of the town first. I had archers close to the bridge in case he tried treachery, but he did not. Arnaud had more than fifteen hundred men for many Frenchman had joined over the winter. The food of Châlons-sur-Marne was an incentive. The last of the men had crossed the bridge and were hurrying the wagons on when Arnaud and his bodyguard galloped back.

He reined in as Robin and his archers each nocked an arrow. I had followed the last of his men to the bridgehead and I waited for him to speak. I did not need to draw my sword. If he made a move then there were twenty arrows that would empty the saddles of the Frenchman and his bodyguards, "Where is Albert?"

I did not turn for I wished to see his face, but I gestured behind me with my thumb. I knew that Albert was on the fighting platform. He pointed an accusing finger at me, "You are a treacherous dog!"

"From you, that is a compliment. The bridge is now barred to the, what is it you call yourselves, '*The Great Company*'? You know how good my bowmen are. Your men return at their own risk!" He wheeled his horse angrily and I waited until the column had disappeared from sight before returning to the town.

The next three weeks were peaceful. Albert was confirmed as the captain and we spoke with the Council. William reduced the tax the townsfolk paid to us as a result of half of our men leaving and they were happy as that was less tax than they would pay the Dauphin. I knew, for we had allowed them to leave the town, that messengers had ridden to the Dauphin to complain about the protection they paid us. When the Dauphin established control again, they could plead coercion. It was June when the rider came from Henry, Duke of Lancaster. It was one of Prince Edward's closest friends, Sir John Chandos. He rode in with half a dozen men at arms. Albert was put out when the English knight chose to ignore him and speak with me, alone.

"Sir John, I am come from Henry Duke of Lancaster but also with the permission of Prince Edward." I nodded. "You know that the French have refused to accept the terms of the treaty their king signed."

"I heard."

"Prince Edward and his father are raising an army to come and take what is his by right and under God. Before then Duke Henry is gathering all the companies of mercenaries to ravage and weaken this land. You followed the Duke before and both he and his cousin, Prince Edward, beg you to place your men under his banner."

I sighed, "I do not lead the White Company. That is Albert Sterz."

Sir John smiled, "All of this is known but you command the English Company, and your two hundred men would be the equal of any other knights and men at arms not to mention archers."

"How long do I have to decide?"

"We are weary, having ridden from Calais. We will leave to return to the Duke at first light. You have until then, my friend. We would like to fight alongside you again for you know this land well and Duke Henry remembered you from his Great Raid."

"I will give it due consideration you can be assured of that."

As I headed to speak with William and my captains, I reflected that I had a dilemma. If we abandoned Châlons-sur-Marne we would be losing our income. On the other hand, we had the prospect of not only plunder but also battle and that was badly needed to hone us into a sharpened weapon. Not surprisingly perhaps all were keen to fight alongside Duke Henry. Even those who had not fought with him before knew of his reputation and the incredible fortune he had amassed.

William pointed out the obvious, "Albert will not wish to fight against the French."

"I know but that does not concern me. I am happy to fight against the French if that is the wish of the English Company but it may mean the end of our hopes for the White Company."

Michael shrugged, "A setback that is all. Thus far we have been lucky and not lost a man, all of us are well off and we have hopes that we can be rich soon. Sir John, speak with Albert and tell him we intend to leave."

William nodded, "I will need to know as soon as possible." He said no more but I knew that he meant he would have to secure our savings.

Albert had taken over the Hotel de Ville. He got on well with the Council and had even gone into business with a couple of the more enterprising merchants. He helped them to move goods around, escorted by his men. He thought I did not know that he was making a profit from it. I did not mind. William was my secret weapon. He and his lieutenants were drinking, and they beamed when I entered. "Is this not more pleasant without de Cervole, Sir John?"

"It is. Could I have a word?"

He was a very clever man and was naturally astute. He knew something was amiss and he waved his men away so that we were alone.

"Is this about the leadership?"

I shook my head, "I made an agreement with you and I will stand by it. I, that is to say, we, have been invited to join a chevauchée with Duke Henry of Lancaster. I know you have fought with the English before, but I know not how you feel about abandoning Châlons-sur-Marne."

He smiled, "I am relieved, I thought it was something more serious. Why would we have to abandon this golden egg?"

"It will mean fighting the French and the town is French."

"We have fought them before, and we will do so again. However, I see what you mean." He stroked his beard and then smiled, "I have a compromise. I shall stay and guard the town with five hundred of my men, the ones who have no horses. You lead the others with yours."

He was a clever man. I nodded, "If you do not mind me leading, and perhaps losing your men then it is a solution. Who would lead your contingent?"

"Karl von Württemberg. He likes you and you have worked with him before."

I stood and clasped his arm, "Then we are agreed."

He smiled his usual silky smile, "We are agreed." He was clever and many men might think I was being used. He would not have to fight and the Dauphin could not take back the town while the English raided. I did not mind for it meant I had more of Albert's men to lead and there would be profit. When it was right to wrest control from him I would have secured more support.

I went directly to Karl and told him what had been decided. I know that it should have been Albert who spoke to him, but I wanted to know for certain before I gave my answer to Sir John Chandos. Karl was delighted. "I will choose the men. Unlike the English Company, the German one has some within its ranks whom I would not choose to have behind me. There are not many, but I will choose those who have the best horses and are good warriors. It will mean leaving behind more men than Albert promised you."

"We need well-mounted men. It is the right decision!"

Sir John was delighted with the news. "I will tell the Duke and he will be pleased."

"Where do we assemble?"

He smiled, "My lord. If you head towards Calais from here then we shall meet. This is a raid to hurt the French and make them regret their decision. Attack everything which lies between us. I believe that Duke Henry will attack Artois first but that is many miles from here and it would seem a shame if the English Company did not make a profit before ever it reached our main army."

Sir John had learned from Prince Edward. Our raid towards Toulouse had not only brought us great riches but forced the French to battle. When King Edward and his son arrived in Calais the French would be clamouring for their Dauphin to fight the English.

Sir John left before dawn and our preparations began. We could not simply pack our horses and ride. We had squires and pages now. There were horses as well as ponies to be prepared and arrows to be gathered. We were lucky to have the boys from Bordeaux we had adopted. Ponies were relatively cheap to acquire and meant that the older boys were more than capable of leading a packed sumpter loaded with arrows, but the boys all needed practice. The result was that it was not until July when we left and, before we did, I had news that my wife had given birth to Thomas, our second son. She had named him without reference to me, but William told me that Thomas had been their grandfather and had doted on Elizabeth. I did not mind. Roger's letter told me that she was well as was the bairn and both were well looked after. The two men who had brought the letter were three archers he had hired. William arranged for a messenger to take my reply. I would be too busy for the next months. William would be staying in the town. Albert had come to rely on him, and the men enjoyed the fact that they were paid regularly and on time.

I planned on skirting Rheims. The Dauphin had ruthlessly rid himself of the peasantry problem and installed a garrison. I would not choose to waste men on it. Soissons, on the other hand, was just fifty miles from us and was a rich and ancient town. It had a wall around it but as it was July, I planned on tricking the soldiery from the city into attacking us. I gathered my captains the day before we left. I gave them all clear instructions. It was not just my plan. Robin and Michael had helped me to create it.

When we left the city, I was surprised that Lady Isabeau came to wave us off. Her husband was still unwell, and it was she who was the public face of Châlons-sur-Marne. She said nothing but her smile told me that the investment of some coins for her husband's ransom had been well worth it. We crossed the bridge and headed for Monthelon. It was eighteen miles away and we had extracted no protection from it. As such it was fair game. There was a hall there and the lord kept ten retainers but there was no castle and no fortified hall. We simply galloped into the square and, obligingly, the lord, his men and his family abandoned their manor and fled north-west. To the great surprise of the villagers, we did not behave badly towards them. To be fair they had little but the hall was a rich one and we slaughtered the animals we found there. The lord had enjoyed a good cellar which we emptied, and he had raced out so quickly that he had left his mail, plate, weapons, and, best of all, his chests of treasure. I would send it back under armed guards the next day for William to keep safe. We also found spare horses.

It was Robin who suggested that we might use archers to range ahead of the main column and capture the next lords. Ransom was useful. I thought it a good idea and he sent two large groups of archers before dawn to scout out the river at the small town of Dormans which was our next target. There was a castle, but we had decided that if it was too strong to take without heavy loss we would just take what we could from the surrounding area.

Our archers used the woods which lay to the south of the small town to surround the men who were on guard at the road. The lord of Monthelon had alerted the men of Dormans. We reached the edge of the woods as Ned and his men were disposing of the bodies. I saw the castle which dominated the small town although it was not a large one. Martin and Joseph's archers were not to be seen but I knew that they would have forded the river and if any tried to cross the bridge then they would be stopped. Robin dismounted all the archers, and we left the mounts with the pages. I led the men at arms down the road toward the castle. We were seen from the tower and the fighting platform. They were waiting for us but eight men who might have been in the garrison had already been killed. The people of the town had not yet been admitted to the castle and when they ran to the gates, they were refused entry. From a sally port, I saw a man lead a horse, mount it and race towards the bridge. The villagers, when they saw us approach, followed him. There was a collective wail when the rider reached the middle of the bridge for he was knocked from his horse by two arrows. The villagers stood at the bridge end and milled around not knowing what to do. There were men on the walls of the castle and I saw sunlight shining from metal. There were crossbows too, but I could not see them.

Stopping a hundred and twenty paces from the small gatehouse, I lifted the visor on my helmet. I had not needed to keep it covering my face, but I knew that a dramatic gesture like that had an effect. "I am Sir John Hawkwood of the White Company and I urge the lord of Dormans to surrender his castle and town. If you resist, then it will go badly for you!"

In answer, I saw a figure rise and rest his crossbow on the crenulations. My shield was hanging from my cantle but even as the man released the bolt four arrows came from behind me and one hit the crossbowman throwing him backwards. The bolt arched in the air as he fell backwards and landed a few paces from my horse's hooves.

I laughed, "Do you really wish me to ask my archers to rain death upon your walls?" I turned and said, "Captain Robin…"

I got no further for a voice shouted, "No! No! We surrender!" He had little choice for the villagers, having seen what my archers could do were wailing and moaning. The lord of this manor could not know that we would not harm them. The gates creaked open and I rode in, flanked by Michael and Karl. As I dismounted, I said, "Sir Eoin, tell the villagers to leave but not across the bridge. Do not let them take animals."

"Aye, Sir John. You do take chances, my lord."

"I trust my archers. Time was I could have hit that crossbowman. I know the skill they all have."

We had a rich haul from the French lords. The one who had fled Monthelon had brought his jewels and best horses. They were now ours. The lord of Dormans, Geoffrey de Dormans was also a rich man, and we emptied his treasury as well as his larder and wine cellar. I sent him and his family from the castle after I had disarmed them all and took their surcoats from them. The bridge was barred, and they had to follow the villagers to Rheims. The town would soon have more mouths to feed. It was little enough but it might make it easier for Prince Edward and his father to reduce it when they came.

I sent more men back with the treasure and I dined with my captains in the Great Hall. "Tomorrow will be a more difficult day but our plan is a good one. There are no bridges twixt here and Soissons but the roads leading to it must be cut." We had taken a risk with the planning for it required taking the first two places without loss but now that we had I was sure that God smiled on our venture. I sent two groups of archers to cut off the main road north. With such a large town there were enough gates for some messengers to get through, but we would stop most. It had worked so far and I saw no reason to change our strategy. We had taken thirty surcoats from the French and that was more than we had expected. The two lords we had sent forth had been most unhappy that they had to change into other clothes while we took their liveried garments. We rested well that night and I left Michael in charge of the Company. I had Karl, Giovanni, Sir Eoin and twenty-six of my best men at arms dressed not only in French surcoats but also riding French horses and carrying French banners. With two large groups of archers ahead of us as a screen, we hurried towards the town. It was built on the south side of the Aisne River. We halted in the woods a mile away from Soissons. Our archer scouts meant we had arrived unobserved.

I nodded to Robin and then said, "We ride as though we are lily-livered Frenchmen fleeing English archers and men at arms!" My men laughed, "Michael, make sure there is a gap between you and the archers. I do not want the gates slamming in my face."

"Aye, lord."

"Ride as though the devil himself was biting at your heels!"

Sir Eoin laughed as he shouted, "No, Sir John, he is at Nevers!"

Our archers could easily have caught us, but Robin and the others kept the gap at a healthy four hundred paces. We were seen half a mile from the walls of the town, and I heard the bells tolling the alarm. Sunlight glinted off the helmets of the men running to the fighting platform, but the gates remained open. We were armed men and they thought we were French. They would not spurn our help and it would look as though they could close the gates before the archers reached them. All of us rode with our swords hidden at our side. We had a great responsibility. If we failed, then I would be captured, and all our good work thus far was undone. I was willing to take that risk. I had great confidence in myself and the men I led. Men see what they want to see and the sentries on the walls saw countrymen being chased by the hated English archers. The gates remained open. Our visored helmets hid our faces, and we were dressed as Frenchmen.

"Hurry! We need to close the gates!" The Sergeant at Arms holding the pike stood just outside the gates urging us in. He stood on our left and did not see the swords hanging from our right hands.

I did not risk speaking but merely urged my horse in. This was not a castle but a walled town and there was no gatehouse. There was an open area just inside, presumably to allow wagons to pass each other. There were eight men ready with the bar and two stood at the gate. I wheeled my horse around in the open area and when Sir Eoin, the last man in our column, had passed the Sergeant at Arms I brought my sword down on the shoulder of one of those holding the bar. Karl and Henry struck another two and when Giovanni and Stephen slew the two men at the gates then the rest of the men holding the bar dropped it to draw weapons. The danger was the sergeant for he had a pike and that was a deadly weapon against a horseman. Sir Eoin brought his sword backhanded to hit the back of the Frenchman's helmet and shoulders. He pitched forward.

From the fighting platform, I heard shouts as my archers neared. They knew nothing of what we were doing for their attention was fixed not only on the archers but the column, led by Michael which was now in sight and clearly gaining. As the last of the gate defenders were eliminated, I wheeled my horse to face the town. I shouted, "Giovanni, take four men and clear the top of the gate. Sir Eoin, take ten men and secure the gates."

I looked for danger ahead but there were no armed men racing to reinforce the gates. I glanced over my shoulder at the walls and saw that they had a man every ten paces or so. Soissons had a good view of the road and the people must have had a good system in play. The men on the walls would only have eyes for my men. They would assume we were friends.

As soon as I heard the men selected by my two knights I said, "The rest of you, follow me!"

I led them through the streets, which were wide enough to take a wagon and he hurried towards the centre. What I did not want was the town hall and square fortifying. If they did so we might still win but we would bleed men taking it. As we burst into the open square, I saw that we had been right to do so. A mailed and plated man was ordering wagons to be hauled into position where the roads entered the square. There looked to be ten or so of the garrison and the rest were shopkeepers and artisans from the town. They were taking no chances. Faces glanced up as we galloped in, but the surcoats were familiar to them and they resumed their work. I rode at the plated warrior who, by his spurs, was clearly a knight. I had learned to take out leaders first and then victory came much easier. He had his visor up and I saw him stare towards us as we showed no signs of slowing.

"To arms! They are enemies!" He lowered his visor and picked up his two-handed sword.

I rode at him. The horse I rode had been taken from the French castle at Dormans and was not one I was familiar with. I could not risk trying to use either his agility or his power for I did not know him well enough. I rode to the knight's left for that gave him two choices for his swing. Either a vertical one to slice down on me or a long sweep that might take my leg. His sword was a longer one and I would have to use skills learned over the last years to defeat him.

My men had spread out and gone for the warriors. The townsfolk had weapons, but they were no heroes and the men stood close to the wagons they had been pulling. I concentrated on the knight. He was looking for an attempt by me to move either left or right. He did not know I would do neither. He raised his sword over his head, and I held mine to the right. This was all about timing. So far, I had not used my spurs and I waited until I was a horse length from him before I dug the spurs in and started to lean out. Although he leapt forward, as I had hoped, the sudden shifting of my weight unbalanced him, and I felt him begin to fall. I had survived all these years because I could think on my feet, or in this case on a falling horse. I slipped my feet from the stirrups as the knight, committed to the blow, brought down his sword. It did not strike me but the unfortunate animal's head. The blade bit in and stuck in the neck. I could feel that I was falling and so I dropped my sword and held my hands out as I headed towards the cobbles of the square.

The animal was dying, and the knight and his sword were trapped as I hit the ground hard. I heard the crash as the horse fell on the knight. The air was knocked from me but I managed to roll away from the flailing hooves of the horse.

I had no sword, but I had my long dagger and as I rose I saw two of the artisans, seeing me apparently unarmed, run at me with their own swords. I drew my dagger and moved back towards the horse, dying knight and my sword. My men were busily trying to secure the square and I was on my own. The two men, masons by their aprons, were not fools and they approached me from two directions. Balin's plate had been a wise investment. The straps had held, and the fall did not appear to have damaged the plate, but I needed good vision and with my mailed left hand I raised my visor. The masons would be strong, but their weakness would be their lack of agility and their reactions. They held their swords in two hands and approached me steadily. Now that I had my breathing under control, I took charge, and I ran at the one to my left. He started to swing and, even as his companion ran to attack my rear, I raised my hand to arrest the sword with my mailed left hand whilst ramming my long dagger up under his ribs. The man was strong, but I caught the sword at the start of its swing and not the end. There was not as much power in it. The blow from the other, to my back, could have hurt me had it been better aimed but he hit the backplate and, as his friend slipped to the ground and began to bleed out, I pirouetted and swung my dagger horizontally. It was a blindly struck blow and perhaps a little lucky, but it tore across his throat and I saw his eyes widen as he realised that he was a dead man.

I did not wish to be struck by a lucky blow and I ran to recover my sword and transferred my dagger to my left. I saw that more townsfolk had entered the square and that they saw how perilously few of us there were. My men had all dismounted and our borrowed horses were milling around. I saw the Hotel de Ville and the Cathedral. They were just forty paces from me. "English Company, to me!" I ran towards the two buildings which would afford us some protection until Michael and my men arrived. There were men in my way, but I now had my sword. The raised visor helped me to see the dangers. The men did not stand before me in a line but, obligingly, came at me piecemeal. The first was a carpenter who came at me with an adze and a hammer. The hammer was the more dangerous weapon and I blocked it with my sword before ripping open his throat. His adze scratched ineffectually down my breastplate. The man behind was sprayed by the dying carpenter's blood and when he hesitated, I punched him hard in the mouth with the hilt of my sword. He fell to the ground with a broken nose and he was unconscious before he reached the ground.

The rest fled before me and I reached the Hotel de Ville and turned at the entrance. My men joined me. "Henry, go inside and make sure it is empty. Stephen, go with him and make sure no one is trying to take our treasure."

They raced off and the handful of men who were left stood shoulder to shoulder with me. We all wore plate and were well-armed. We had managed to slay all the warriors, or, at least, eliminate them as a threat. The square was filled with armed men but the bodies which littered the square were a warning to them. I heard hooves as Michael and the rest of my men galloped in. Seeing them the townsfolk turned and ran. They had lost and my gamble had paid off.

Chapter 14

Michael raised his sword and led my men to follow the fleeing townsfolk. The archers would be clearing the walls. It would be a slow process as they would have to work their way around them. Each gate would have a small tower which would delay their progress. I left two men to guard the entrance and sent four more into the Cathedral. Up to this point we had, largely, left churches alone but I knew that Soissons had a richly decorated Cathedral. We would become robbers of churches and all the richer for it.

I hurried into the Hotel de Ville. I passed four bodies which marked the progress of Henry and Stephen. I heard cries from ahead and when I entered the large chamber, I saw that there were four men holding swords and facing my two knights. With the men I had brought, we outnumbered them.

"Put your swords down or you will die!" They hesitated. "I have enough blood on my hands and wearing armour means that you cannot hurt us. You will die and for what? Money? Swords down!" The steel in my command made them obey. "Good, now show my men where the town's treasure is held."

They obeyed and I risked taking off my helmet. I sent the rest of my men to search the building and I sheathed my sword. I spied a jug of wine and a goblet. I poured myself a drink and sat on the chair. I was still there when Robin and Michael entered.

Robin laughed, "Now you look like a Captain, Sir John!"

Michael nodded, "The town is ours. Some escaped through the smaller ratholes but the archers at the north western gate caught the rich merchants trying to flee."

"Losses?"

"Walter of Lincoln died, lord, and four archers wounded. Nothing serious."

Michael added, "Cuts and bruises mainly. We were armoured. The plan worked."

"Good, then secure the gates and set a watch. I want three shifts. Michael, find Dai and have him and an archer ride to Duke Henry and tell him we hold Soissons."

He hesitated, "You do not wish to move on?"

"Not yet. If the Duke is too far away, we risk being cut off and if he is close we have a barrier to prevent him from being attacked. We no longer have to follow orders. I command this company and not Prince Edward nor the Duke of Lancaster. This town is rich, and we will have a great profit from it."

In all, we spent a week in the town and that was long enough to haul all the treasures taken from the town and the cathedral back to William and Albert. We did not have to win over the populace, in fact, Duke Henry would wish us to arouse them so that when Prince Edward arrived in the autumn he could do as he had at Poitiers and force the French to battle. Dai brought back the news that we were to join him in the assault on Compiègne, the next most important town to Soissons. Amiens and Arras had been raided and robbed. Artois was, effectively, under English control and still, the French did nothing. That was how I knew that Compiègne would be harder to take. The town was surrounded by bands of Englishmen who roamed at will. The gates would be barred, and the walls manned. There was a castle, and the Duke had a bridge over the Oise to negotiate. We had the easier task in that there was no obstacle to us, and our mission was a relatively simple one. We had to bar the road to and from Compiègne. As Soissons was just twenty-one miles away we had the luxury of being able to keep a third of our men in Soissons. We had taken many horses which meant we could let our warhorses graze and rest while we used the captured ones to patrol the land.

We did not dig a defensive ditch but we did hew down saplings to make stakes and our side of the town was ringed with them. We did not need a double row for with Soissons in our hands we were protected from the rear. Albert's Germans had proved to be good men and I enjoyed leading them. Karl was a good leader and it ensured that our camp and town were both well protected.

While we waited for the Duke to arrive a third of our men raided and hunted. The forests teemed with game and we ate wild boar and deer. I do not think I had ever eaten as well whilst on campaign. The hunting and the raiding not only brought us food and treasure it also stopped the men from being bored. I rotated the men so that each one only spent a day besieging, raiding, or resting. It kept them fresh and meant that we had no desertions. That had not been the case when Arnaud was in command. Even more importantly, the Germans seemed to embrace the idea and camaraderie of The White Company. Hitherto it had seemed as though the name was merely a convention but now there was an esprit de corps amongst them all. No longer did Germans and Englishmen squabble and fight over minor disagreements and there was harmony. I was not sure it would be the same when we returned to Châlons-sur-Marne.

It was the middle of August before Duke Henry arrived. This time it was the Earl of Warwick who forded the river to view our position. "Good to see you, Sir John. I see you have this side of the town under your control and you look to be well fed but I am concerned; is this the total sum of the men under your command?"

"No, my lord, it is one third." I did not elucidate for there was no need. I did not serve the earl and the duke. I was here as the leader of my own free company. I did not have to obey orders or even take advice. I was no fool and I would not ruffle the feathers of the men I might need in the future.

He seemed satisfied, "Good. In three night's time, when we have ravaged the land on the other side of the Oise, the Duke intends an assault. We will build rafts to cross the river, but we need a diversion from you."

"What time will you be attacking?"

"Does it matter? It will be the night!"

I shook my head. The Earl of Warwick was a good man but he was young, "My lord, if we are to create a diversion then we must do so before you attack. If the Duke chooses midnight then, after dusk, we can begin to create the diversion he needs and attract the attention of the defenders. If it is dawn then we would attack at midnight. We have been here for some time and I believe that hunger will be an increasing ally. Hunger and lack of sleep can make good men weaker and less vigilant. I shall use those to my advantage."

He nodded, "As ever, Sir John, you know your business." He hesitated, "You could join the Prince you know. He values not only your skills but your mind. There you would be a knight held in high regard."

I smiled, "And I am touched but I like being the captain of a free company. This suits me."

When he had left us and after we had eaten, I convened a council of war. My captains knew that they could make suggestions, but the basic idea would be mine. "I propose that the next two nights after this we make a show, just after dusk, of preparing to attack. Robin, we have plenty of arrows?"

"Aye, Sir John."

"Then for the next two nights, we shower the walls for an hour with arrows. The aim is to thin out their sentries. I want the archers to choose their targets. On the third night, the night of the Duke's attack, we do the same but use fire arrows and our men at arms will take kindling and place it by the gate. We fire the gate."

Michael nodded, "They will think that this is the real attack and that we have been softening them up."

"And a burning gate prevents them from fleeing. Any fires we start will need men to douse the flames and they cannot defend the walls." I pointed a finger at them as I swept a circle with my hand, "I want not a man to be lost. I will lead the fire starters on the gate. Is that clear? The profits from this will be much smaller than we are used to. Duke Henry is a good leader, but he always takes the lion's share. When this is done, we will head back to Châlons-sur-Marne. The Prince is coming in the autumn and we may be needed again. We have done well thus far, and I would not risk weakening our company."

To add further confusion each evening I had most of the men at arms mount their horses and ride to just beyond arrow range. It drew men to the walls and my archers, who had been hidden behind our horses, raced forward to loose flights of arrows before they could react. It yielded casualties. Crossbows were used against us but as darkness fell it was the arrows of my archers which struck flesh. One archer was hit in the leg by a bolt. It was the only casualty, but it was one too many. The next day I had pavise placed, during the day, where the archers would stand. That night they raised their pavise and we had no casualties.

On the day of the actual assault, I had the boys make up bundles of kindling. For the first time, I would be using them in war, and they were excited. I chose the oldest and made sure that they knew they had to stand behind the men at arms who would protect them with shields. Robin and his archers had spent all day manufacturing fire arrows. Men at arms would carry lighted braziers for them to ignite their missiles. The French were expecting the attack for we had come for the previous two nights. As the sun slowly set the walls were manned. Our smoking and glowing braziers were a warning of what we intended. As darkness fell Robin gave the command and the darkening sky was illuminated with more than a hundred fire arrows. As soon as they launched their second flight, I raised my sword and the twenty men and ten boys I led moved towards the gate. We were cloaked and would appear as shadows. Dai carried the lighted brand, but he would not join us until we reached the gate. The lighted brand would tell the French what we intended. The archers behind us were raining their arrows not on the fighting platform for the embrasures there afforded some protection, but on the rooves of the houses behind. Those on the fighting platform would either be sending bolts at my archers or watching the fall of arrows. Even so, there were some vigilant Frenchman and I heard, when I was twenty paces from the wall, the shout of alarm and a heartbeat later two bolts slammed into my shield. It was too late for we were at the walls and my men at arms and I raised our shields above the boys. Reaching the gate they packed the kindling as rocks were dropped onto helmets and shields. It sounded like a hailstorm. I whistled and Dai ran. He jinked and twisted as bolts were sent at the blackened shadowy figure. He handed it to me.

I shouted, "Now, Robin!" He had allocated twenty archers to the actual gate and they now switched to war arrows and sent them at the gate as I said, "Run!"

Dai remained with me and I let him ignite the oiled kindling. It caught and I raised the shield above our heads. We ran back together. The fire caused such consternation that not a single bolt was sent in our direction. We reached our lines and I saw that none had been hurt. We had done what we were asked. Robin and his archers kept up their arrows all night, but it was sporadic. As the fires were doused, new ones were started. We realised that the Duke had begun his attack when men were taken from our wall. I ordered Robin to save his arrows and we watched until dawn.

Michael and Karl came to see me as the first hint of sun appeared in the east. "Sir John, Karl and I think that we could force the gate." I raised a questioning eyebrow. "They have not completely doused it and it is glowing. There are fewer men on the wall to defend and we have found a tree that was uprooted. We have a ram."

"We do not need to. Our job was to cause a diversion."

Karl nodded, "But when the Duke breaches the walls his men will have the first choice of any treasure and loot."

"Very well but take volunteers."

Michael laughed, "Then that will be all of us."

"Dai as well?"

"He found the tree!"

I sighed, "Then I will come too and if I come then I lead!"

"You do not have to, my lord."

"Just as Robin feels responsibility for you so do I for Dai. I will lead."

I went to don my helmet while Michael organised the men at arms who would carry the tree. I waved over Robin, "We are going to break down the door. Cover us when we do so."

"It should be safe enough, Sir John, the fire has broken their spirits." We could see the smoke rising from our side of the town wall. Fire arrows do not always work but Robin and Martin the Fletcher had ensured that ours did. "Try to be careful, Sir John. You have a daughter and two sons now."

I smiled, "Two daughters and two sons but who is counting? I do not think I am done yet."

Robin laughed, "God alone knows how many I have sired." He hurried off to organise his men and I slipped first my coif over my head and then donned my helmet. I left the visor up. There would be neither arrows nor bolts coming in my direction.

"Ready, Sir John."

I hefted my shield and drew my sword. I saw Dai standing at the back of the tree. Eight of our biggest men at arms held ropes wrapped around it. On either side were more men at arms with shields held aloft. Michael led one side and Karl the other. Sir Eoin was behind Michael and Giovanni behind Karl. We had evolved a natural order and that meant we had a greater chance of success. I joined Dai behind the tree. Michael began to bang his shield with his dagger's pommel to help them to march together.

When he was satisfied, he said, "March!"

There is an art to using a ram and while we had not had to use the skill very often, we had practised. Our time in Châlons-sur-Marne had not been wasted. He began to increase the pace and we went from a walk to a sort of jog and then when we were just twenty paces from the still smouldering gate we ran. A few stones were thrown but the thrum of bows and the cries as men were hit soon slowed down the rocks. When we hit the gate it simply crumbled. We might have done it without a tree! The men with the ram kept running and their protectors used their swords to slay any who came close.

"Drop!"

The men dropped the tree where it would not be in our way and then we simply burst upon the defenders. Karl shouted, "Germans, with me!" A dozen men at arms ran with him to climb the steps and clear the gatehouse.

I raised my sword, "English Company, on me." All our men at arms were now inside the walls for the ones not using the ram had been waiting with Robin. Robin and the archers would follow and then Albert's spearmen would be the last through the gates. Even the boys would follow. They were trained to protect us with the slings whilst looking for booty and treasure we might have missed. The smoke from the fires, which, in some cases, were now burning out of control made it a confusing scene into which we ran. We all wore white and until we heard an English voice then anyone with a sword was a potential enemy. We had done what we had been asked and so when we came to the first house which had more than one floor, I held up my hand to stop my men. I signalled for four to go through the open courtyard to the stables and the kitchen and I led the rest through the main door. There were people in the house I could hear their movements and there was also noise coming from the kitchen. I waved Giovanni and Sir Eoin towards the kitchen and I led Michael, Dai, Stephen, and Henry up the stairs.

The man who emerged from the room at the top of the stairs had his arms laden with a large chest. He was rushing and it was simplicity itself to stick out a leg so that he tumbled, dropping the chest as he did so.

"Francois! Be careful of our treasures!" The unfortunate Francois lay unconscious halfway down the stairs. We followed the sound of the voice and entered a sumptuous bedroom. A man, a woman I took to be his wife, and a servant were busily packing another chest.

Smiling I said, "We can save you the bother of packing!"

His hand and that of his servant went to their swords, "Do you really wish to cross swords with five men at arms? Drop your weapons. Take your lives and be grateful." The man began to open his mouth and I said, mildly, "And any insults will be rewarded with a blade too. Your wife is lovely, she is a treasure I give to you!"

His wife gave me the sign of the evil eye and said, "Animal!"

I bowed and stood aside so that they could flee. "Dai, make certain that they leave empty handed!"

"Aye, Sir John!"

When they had gone, we saw some of the finest clothes and furs I had ever seen. I marked a dress for Elizabeth as well as a fur. There were other items I would send to John the merchant. The dazed Francois had the treasure in the chest but within the room were objects which were as valuable as gold. There was an ivory embossed chest as well as an intricately carved spice box. Not as big as the one we had found in Bellac, it was still worth a small fortune. "Collect all you can and secure it. We will stay here tonight. I expect he will have a fine larder. I will take Dai and find the Duke."

I saw that Francois had recovered and fled. Dai stood guard over the treasure. I grabbed one handle, "Let us take it downstairs where it can be guarded."

Peter of Poole and his son carried a small chest of coins into the large hall, "Buried beneath the kitchen floor."

I nodded, "This is a much larger one. Collect the treasure in here and put a guard on the door. This is the White Company treasure!"

"Aye, Sir John."

"I will seek the Duke. If you see any of our men, this is our bed for the night. Have Robert Greengrass take some men and search the houses on either side. They may not be as grand but anything we can take will be useful. Fetch the boys and their horses from outside. Let us use the stables and the courtyards of these houses. We can feed them oats!"

As soon as we stepped outside it was like trying to wade through a tidal race for people and soldiers were running in every direction. I spied Captain Ned and waved him over. He was a broad-shouldered archer, and he ploughed his way through the citizens of the town who were trying to escape. "Ned, the house I just left is ours and I want the two adjacent ones securing. I will seek the Duke."

As the two of us pushed our way towards the town square I reflected that if the taking of this town did not induce the French to fight then nothing would! The Duke was in his element. We had done this before in Aquitaine and he put behind him his failure in Brittany. He had done that which had been asked of him and there were now large swathes of France under English control. When the prince came, if he could draw them to the battlefield then by Christmas his father could be crowned King of France and he would control an empire even bigger than that of the second King Henry! He was in a good mood.

"Hawkwood, it is good to see you. You have become powerful since last I saw you."

"And I owe much to you and Prince Edward."

He nodded, "You did more than I asked of you and I am pleased."

"And now, my lord?"

"Why we empty this town and head back to the coast." He leaned into me, "The men have full purses and will wish to spend their coin. I have done that which was asked of me. You will return with us?"

Shaking my head I said, "We have a place in Champagne. Will the Prince need us?"

"He will but you say your company is in Champagne?"

"Aye, Duke Henry."

"And that is close to Burgundy is it not?" I nodded. "Then you may be useful to the prince. If his progress to Paris is as swift as I believe it will be then the only opposition will be in the east. We have seen nothing thus far to impede his progress and we have taken all from the land. There is not an animal to be eaten between here and Calais. I will send Sir John Chandos to you if you are needed."

And the brief campaign was over. It was the easiest one I had been on and not only had it brought us great wealth and prestige, but we had also lost but one man, Walter of Lincoln. Albert's men who had been sent with me would be richer and if I chose to challenge him would vote for me. That time was not yet nigh, but I was moving my chess pieces into position for the day when it would.

Chapter 15

We stayed for two days taking everything that there was to take. Even the boys had purses so full that they struggled to carry them. I had gained allies too for the spearmen of Albert who had ridden with us now had better arms and armour and I knew that they would vote for me. We headed first to Soissons and when we had taken all from there and the farms we had missed the first time, we rode back to Châlons-sur-Marne. We reached it by the first week of September. I do not know if Albert thought I might fail in my raid but when he greeted me it was not with as much joy as should have been merited by the wagon loads of goods we brought in. I had sent the spices and choicest goods to Calais where they would be carried to my father in law. He had left me the names of captains who frequented all the English ports in France. Ned and Luke escorted the wagons with their archers. Although they travelled with the Duke of Lancaster, my men were vigilant. We still had many other wagons full of food and goods which would not have benefitted from a sea voyage. True, the clothes and furniture we had brought were not the Company's nor were the gold and weapons, but the many wagons of food were. We had so much that the town could be fed over the winter. The point about food was that it was perishable, and we could afford to be generous and share it with the citizens. Perhaps it was the cheers from the men I had borrowed from him which made it look as though he had just sucked a lemon. When he forced a smile and said, "Well done." I saw it for the lie it was.

I told him that it was likely that Prince Edward would come with his father to fetch the French to battle. "And then, John, what then? Will we have to relinquish this honey pot?"

I shrugged, "Probably but there are others. What about Italy?"

He nodded, "Our old friend Arnaud is not enjoying himself in Nevers. Twenty of his men returned last week asking to be part of the company again. William swore them in for a second time and made them make a mark on a piece of parchment. Your English friend Knolles is winning!"

"We could always return to Bordeaux to winter there and see what jewels there are to be plucked come spring."

"Bordeaux is your home, not mine. I thought somewhere warmer and less English. If we are to winter, then I thought closer to the Mediterranean. It would fit in with your plan to go to Italy."

It was a good suggestion, and I could call at my home to see Elizabeth and my sons. I had planned on spending the winter there in any case but the plans of Prince Edward had wrecked them. I dared not, at the moment, upset the man who might be King of France one day. We had also to assimilate the new men who chose not to follow Duke Henry back to Calais but, in small groups, came to ask if they could join the White Company. Our time in the recently captured town meant our archers and men at arms met with those from other companies. When they learned of the rights of the members of our company and the way that they were paid, thirty archers, each with a horse and ten men at arms, asked to join us. After they were questioned all were sworn in and the men at arms given one of the spare boys we had. Compiègne and Soissons had yielded more orphans who were happy to be clothed and fed by us despite the fact that we were English. Their own people, it seemed, had either shunned or ignored them. The French towns' losses were our gain. Accommodation was now a problem and had we not brought so much food with us then there might have been issues with the locals. As it was, we had enough coin to pay for rooms. Of course, we recouped that from the taxes we charged.

The land around us was also peaceful and the autumn harvest a good one for the farmers had been able to work unmolested. They saw that the protection had worked.

Sir John Chandos arrived in the middle of November. To be honest, I had assumed that the expedition had been postponed and I had planned on returning to Bordeaux. The weather was typically autumnal, and rains had begun. It would not be easy for the King and his son, Prince Edward, to move his huge army around France.

Sir John's words showed that I was wrong, "The King has arrived and is progressing through the lands we subdued in August. He plans on taking Rheims and being crowned there in the cathedral. The pretender, Dauphin Charles is within its walls."

I poured some wine for the knight, "Sir John, I would not advise a siege, not at this time of year in any case. The Jacquerie may still hold Paris but all the nobles and warriors who had been there are now ensconced in Rheims. The men who fled Soissons and Compiègne not to mention all the other places raided by our men also fled there. They have a huge army."

Sir John gave me a patronising smile, "Sir John, this will force the French to fight us on the field and our archers will win the day once more."

It was when he said those words that I realised that my opinion mattered not because I was not a true noble. I was a sword for hire. Prince Edward and his cronies did not think I was worthy to make suggestions.

"Prince Edward wishes you to bring your men to Rheims by the end of November. Your task is to cut the road from the south. You are well placed to do so as you hold this town." I tried to persuade him that it was the wrong time of year and the weather would be against us. It was after the harvest and the granaries would be full. He would not listen, however. He was a good man but he was under the sway of the man people were now calling, The Black Prince. The magic of his two battles seemed to make many think that he could do no wrong. I had been at both of his great battles and knew that he won because of French mistakes, which were greater than the ones he had made and because of his archers who had won both battles for him. Archers cannot win sieges. He left and I knew we would have to spend months in a boggy camp haemorrhaging warriors.

That was the moment that I decided to sever my relations with Prince Edward and the English army as soon as I could. Albert was right, our future lay further south. Provence was ruled now by Naples and was close to the warring states of Milan, Pisa, Florence, and the like. I knew that there was scope for men like us. Arnaud had once held the Pope, who lived in Avignon, as a hostage. It seemed a place ripe for plunder and, more importantly, a land that had nothing to counteract our archers. Our numbers were increasing and in the latest letter from Elizabeth, she had told me that Roger had found another fifteen for me! I would serve the prince and his father at Rheims, but it was mainly in the hope of recruiting more archers. That he was likely to fail did not make me happy, but he had chosen that path. I wrote back to tell them that I planned on being back by February. It meant a Christmas away and my youngest son would have grown without me seeing him!

I told Albert who, once again, chose the easier task of remaining in the town with a few men. A few men were all that we needed. I took the opportunity after Sir John had left us, of sending William with a heavy escort of men to take our latest treasure to Bordeaux. My captains and I kept our monies there. Roger would watch over them and he always had plenty of guards for he was recruiting constantly. I gambled that they would be back before the attack began but as Prince Edward had no idea of our true numbers it was immaterial.

The prince and his father were being clever. He had been forced to pay for many of his lords and archers to fight for him but most, like Robert Knolles, were not fighting for pay but booty. It was a cheap way to make war and another reason I chose to distance myself from England.

We knew Rheims as we had scouted it out many times. There was no real river to protect it, La Vesle was tiny, but the walls were well made and even as my archer scouts reported back, I realised that the ground was boggy and in the winter that meant pestilential. I decided to do as we had in August. I would allow one-third of my men to return to Châlons-sur-Marne so that they could have a roof and hot food every five days. Being organised in lances with my leaders already in place made it easy to organise. Robin, Michael, and I would lead a third each. We were not being paid and I did not see why we should have to suffer when we had a home twenty-five miles away.

The progress of the English army was not as quick as it should have been. It was another reason I did not wish to serve with them again. They were less efficient than we were. We were all mounted and moved quickly. King Edward's soldiers marched and rode quickly but it was the rest, the churchmen and the entertainers the King took with him who slowed them up. I remembered when we had sailed to fight the French all those years ago; minstrels and singers were present on the King's ship in large numbers!

We did not rush to Rheims and yet still made it before the appointed time. When we reached the Abbey we were seen from the walls of the city and the gates were closed. I had received no orders about the Abbey from Sir John, but I guessed that King Edward would not wish it violating and so I told the men to avoid it. We stopped just four hundred paces from the south gate and began to build our camp. There was a farmhouse nearby, but the farmer and his family had fled with their animals inside the walls of the great city. We had our base and while William, now returned from Bordeaux, and the boys made it somewhere we could use, I went with my captains to dig our ditches and embed stakes. Unlike the nobles with King Edward, my knights and the men at arms were quite happy to toil like labourers for our archers did not dig but stood ready to repel any attack. It proved judicious for as we began to hammer in the stakes men rushed forth from the gates to stop us. We were without mail and plate for we were working although our weapons were to hand. They were not men at arms who raced out but a mob of men with swords, spears, pitchforks, axes, and the like. There had to be more than a thousand of them.

Robin shouted, "Nock and draw!" The creak of a yew bow being drawn in such numbers was, to me, a reassuring sound. "Release!" More than a hundred and thirty arrows soared in the sky and even as they descended their brothers were following. It was as though the mob had been punched by a giant. We drew our swords and stood behind the archers in case they needed to pass through us. It never came to that for after seven hundred arrows had been sent and more than two hundred men lay dead or writhing in pain, the rest turned tail and fled. While Robin and the archers went to collect undamaged arrows and give those who were too badly wounded a warrior's death, we went back to work. We left a guard that night and the bodies lay where they had fallen.

The next morning, mounted on my palfrey Mary, I rode with my hands open and my coif hanging around my neck, Dai carried my banner. I stopped before the gates and said, "You have one hour to remove the bodies of the dead, unless, of course, you wish to surrender to me!"

Dai said, "Do you expect them to?"

"Of course not but it will annoy them."

No one answered and I waited patiently for it was a good opportunity to examine the defences. The walls were well made but not all the mortar was sound, and I saw places where, if we had to use a stone thrower, we could damage them. The gates too were old. As we had already discovered at Compiègne we could use fire to weaken them. Eventually, an equerry came to speak to me. He bore the livery of the Dauphin and that told me that he was within or that they wished me to think he was.

"We will collect the bodies but your suggestion that we surrender is laughable. You will rue the day you came to Rheims."

I nodded and turned my horse. He was right of course, and I rued coming here in any case. As I dismounted at the farmhouse, I resigned myself to a wet and unpleasant winter.

The royal leaders and the army arrived on St Andrew's Day, the thirtieth of November. Inevitably it was Sir John who came to view what we had done and to tell me who would be adjacent to us. He was in good humour, "We have a huge army, Sir John. It is many times larger than the one at Poitiers. When the French come to relieve it, we will match them with numbers and this time King Edward will take the crown."

I smiled, for that was expected but I did not think that we would succeed. As if to make the point it began to rain and did so for a week. That slowed the digging of ditches and preparations for an assault. I sent the first of my men back to Châlons-sur-Marne and I spent as much time indoors as I could. William was with me, having brought another five archers who had turned up. We discussed the finances and then I turned to family matters, "And how are your sister and my boys?"

There was the slightest of hesitation before he answered, "They are well. The boys are both in good health and have fine sets of lungs on them."

I said, "You hesitated. What is wrong with Elizabeth?"

"Nothing! Nothing! I know not why I hesitated. Perhaps she does miss you. You have spent a short time with her since she conceived your first son." He shrugged, "Some mothers find it hard, especially when they are alone."

I was relieved for what he said made sense. "If these rains continue then I could be home for Christmas. We have only been asked to make scaling ladders and not war machines. These walls will not fall to an escalade!"

"I know nothing about such matters, lord. It was good that you brought so much back from the Artois raid for had we not then we would be without funds! You are paying for a large number of men."

I nodded, "And with no sign of recompense either." We had raided the land to the north and east before King Edward had come. We had plenty of food, but we had taken few coins.

As Christmas drew closer the rains abated a little but were replaced by cold and by the wind. Nature, it seemed, was not on the side of the English. My men, who knew the country well, roamed every day to hunt and we ate better than most. The days off also meant that my men were in a better frame of mind. The result was that men deserted not from the siege but to us from other bands. These were not knights and so we hired them and while the numbers of others were decreased by desertions and deaths, ours were rising. Sir John had asked us to scout and so my hunters also kept an eye open for an army to relieve the siege. None was forthcoming and I could see no reason why they would. By Christmas, we had not made a single assault on the walls. Some desultory and inconclusive battles between archers and crossbowmen had not had an effect on the outcome.

I was back in Châlons-sur-Marne by St Stephen's Day. Michael and his men had enjoyed a Christmas Day. I did not mind for The Grapes was now familiar and almost homely. It was better than the overcrowded farmhouse. On my second day of leave, I spoke with Albert. He was not in a happy mood, "The men who are here are becoming bored, Sir John, and they are becoming fat and lazy. I would leave."

I think he was looking for an argument, but I said, "I am happy to go. Will you be joining Arnaud?"

"He failed to hold the town which fell to your fellow as did Auxerre. He has been given his spurs and is now Sir Robert Knolles. I know not where Arnaud has gone. He married well and perhaps he has given up fighting for a while. I planned on finding somewhere further south. Are you interested? You know that I still see you and your men as vital to the success of the White Company?"

I nodded, "Thank you. We may be interested. My numbers are almost the equal of yours."

He smiled, "Did William not tell you? The reason I know that Nevers fell was that four hundred of Arnaud's men came back to seek work. They were very grateful to me!"

"Tell me what you plan and I will see if this is to be the parting of the ways."

His confident look left him, and he pulled a map from the satchel he had brought with him. He unrolled it. I saw that it was of south eastern France, Savoy and Provence. He jabbed a finger at the River Rhone, "This place is called Pont-Saint-Esprit. It is the junction of important rivers and it is situated on the river Rhône and the Ardèche. The bridge, as you can imagine, controls the entry into and out of France. I propose to take the town as we did Châlons-sur-Marne and Soissons. We use your cunning. I have heard that Pope Innocent hires mercenaries and we would be close enough to Avignon to make ourselves available to him. Fighting for God is never a bad thing, my friend."

I nodded, "In principle, I like the idea, but I have said we will stay with the English army until the siege is resolved."

He laughed, "It will never fall. I have spoken to the men who returned on leave and none believe that there is any chance of success. In any case, the weather is against us, but I would leave in February in any case. You have until January, my friend."

An outbreak of dysentery and sleety snow meant that the siege was abandoned on the eleventh of January and King Edward dragged his weary, weakened army south to Burgundy. This time it was Prince Edward who came to speak to us although he brought Sir John with him. I cleared the main room in the farmhouse.

"Sir John, your men emerged from the siege with fewer losses and in better condition than most of the other companies. We would have you join us as we head south to Burgundy."

I shifted uncomfortably in my chair, "Prince Edward, we have no lands in England and my men and I earn our living by the sword. For two months we have had no income. There was no plunder and no treasure."

He frowned and then nodded, "I forget that, sometimes. I still see you as I see Sir John Chandos here, as an English knight." He smiled, "I will pay you. Each day that you are serving me, even if we do not fight shall see you and your men paid."

That suited me as it meant I did not have to give an immediate answer to Albert, and we had an income once more. "In that case, Prince Edward, we will stay with you until the conflict in Burgundy is over." I wondered if Sir Robert Knolles would be involved and also if the victory at Nevers had been a deciding factor. "We will make our own way south."

He did not seem put out. "With Nevers in Sir Robert's hands that seems a good place for us to meet. We will be there by February the fourteenth."

I was pleased for that gave me the opportunity to ride home and see my family while Michael and Robin saw to our departure from Châlons-sur-Marne. "We will be there."

My men were more than happy to leave Rheims and when I told them of the new contract were even happier. I saw Albert myself to tell him the news. His eyes lit up when I said that we were being paid. "Does Prince Edward know how many men you bring?"

"Roughly."

"Then we could take more of the White Company and they would be paid. I would lead the ones who remain and make a little more coin from Châlons-sur-Marne."

"I am happy to take them, my friend, but with the siege lifted then I can see that the Dauphin will wish to reclaim Châlons-sur-Marne."

He shrugged, "At which point we shall leave!"

And so we packed for the journey south. With an escort of ten men at arms and ten archers William, Dai and I took the wagons with the last of our treasure to Bordeaux and I said goodbye, for the last time, to Châlons-sur-Marne.

Chapter 16

Bordeaux 1360

It was a long, wet, and miserable journey we endured but when we neared my Bordeaux farm it was worth it. A storm had been blowing from the sea and was driving rain into our faces. Normally I would have stayed with my men and archers but as darkness fell and we were still more than a mile from the farm I left the wagons under the command of Dai and William and spurred my horse down the road. With my cloak flying behind me I soon reached the farm. The guard on the gate was new and I had to dismount to identify myself. I was cross but then realised that this was a good thing as it meant my family were safer.

"There will be a number of wagons coming down the road soon. When you hear them open the gates for we have had a long journey."

"Yes, Sir John."

I led my horse to the stable and found another new man, this time a stable boy. "Tend to my horse. Dry her and feed her oats. I have ridden her hard." I had not introduced myself, but my spurs told him I was a knight and even in the dark my surcoat told the world my identity. The wind was still howling and rattling when I hurried to the door. I opened it and slipped in through the kitchen. Silently I took off my cloak and hung it from the hooks behind the doors of the small entrance hall. There was a mat to wipe my boots and I scraped the mud from them. Opening the door to the kitchen I was hit by a wall of heat and noise. I had good, solid doors in my home. The cook and her helpers looked up in surprise and all curtsied. I waved a greeting and after saying, "William and Dai will be dining with us tonight. We will need more food preparing," I strode through the door which led to my hall. After closing it I listened for the sound of my children but there was silence. I frowned. Was something amiss? I remembered William had been a little vague when he had last reported to me. Was that because something had happened to the boys? I pulled open the door to the room we used during the day and as I did so I was greeted by the sight of

Roger embracing and kissing Elizabeth. Now I understood why William had been less than truthful. I slammed the door shut behind me and my hand went to my sword.

They parted and Elizabeth hid behind Roger who faced me. I saw the man alongside whom I had fought in many battles and I took my hand from the hilt of my sword. I was angry but this was not the anger of war. This was the anger of betrayal. This was the anger I had felt when my father and brother had conspired against me. The difference was that there was no mother now for comfort. I said nothing but I felt my hands curl into fists almost without my thinking at the memory of my childhood pain.

Roger spoke and his voice was filled with sadness. Behind me, I was aware of the door to the house opening, for there was a cold blast of air and I knew that William and Dai had arrived. "My lord, this was not planned. This just happened."

I was about to say 'my wife' and stopped myself just in time, "So Elizabeth just happened to fall into your arms so that you could…" I could not bring myself to say the words.

Just then the door behind me opened and I turned to see William and Dai. I jabbed an accusing finger at William, "You knew and said nothing!"

"My lord what could I say? You need to know that Elizabeth has been lonely while we have been away. Roger has been kind to her, and it was a natural and inevitable thing."

Dai said, "Sir John, they are happy."

"You too! God's Blood, am I the only one who did not know?" Dai hung his head.

"My lord, I would marry Elizabeth and she wishes to have me. I did not intend you to find out this way but perhaps it is for the best. I do not think you would marry her, would you?"

That was the moment when my anger evaporated. For his words cut like a sword and he was right. I would never have married Elizabeth. This was pride. This was the same pride that had made Prince Edward plough on with a siege he could not win. I looked at Elizabeth as she clung to Roger's arm. She deserved a husband, but Roger was right I would not marry her, yet she was the mother of my children. I would have no more sons by Elizabeth. The same mind which planned raids and attacks began to work quickly. Four faces stared at me. The boys needed their mother, that was clear. I looked at Roger. He had served me as long as any and I would trust him to guard my back in battle. He would see that my sons were brought up well.

I heard a mewling behind me and I turned to see John, now toddling, being led by the hand of one of the girls we had employed and another babe, swaddled in white held by another. They had been elsewhere. In a way that was a comfort, and I don't know why. In my distracted state of mind, it seemed to detach them from the betrayal.

"Sarah, give Thomas to me." Elizabeth became the mother once more and she stepped forward to take the babe who was still making the noises I assumed were for his mother's attention, "Sir John, this is your second son, Thomas." She smiled, "He is as healthy as his brother." She took him and baring a breast let the boy feed. She stood facing me and began to speak. She spoke calmly and every word that she said felt like a blow for each one was true, "John barely knows you. He knows my brother more than his own father. This house is a lonely place when you are not here and I am, after all, a woman. Had you asked me to marry you I would have but that would not have changed the loneliness; you would still be away more than you are here. With Roger, the boys have someone they can look up to. He will never be their father, that will always be you but until they are old enough to ride to war with you, and ride they will, then Roger can make them the men you wish them to be."

Every eye was on me and I did not like the attention. I nodded, "I need to change and to eat. We will speak of this later." I know that I appeared cold, especially to the two girls but a man cannot change his nature. Perhaps I am cold. I had lost a wife and barely mourned her. I had not gone to see my daughter. As I climbed the stairs, I wondered what kind of man I was. It was as I took off the spurs that I realised; I was a man of war. That was where I felt most comfortable. I was not like some men who abhorred women, I liked women, but my trade was war and God had made me good at it. Perhaps I was like my father. I had thought him a poor father and I had wished to be a better one. I saw that Elizabeth was right, Roger would bring them up better than I for he would be with them constantly. He was a good man and would make sure that they did not take advantage of their mother. By the time I had changed and washed my face and hands it was as though I had cleansed myself of doubts. I now knew what I would say after we had dined.

When I entered the hall the rest were seated. My place at the head of the table, opposite Elizabeth, was empty. Roger was seated close to Elizabeth as was William. Dai was close to where I would sit. John was seated between Dai and William on the lap of his nurse, Maud, and Thomas was in his crib. There was silence. I saw the servants I had seen in the kitchen waiting to serve the food, but every eye was on me. I smiled, "Thank you for waiting. Let not the food go cold. Serve it and let us eat for the weather outside makes this the warmest and most comforting of places." I sat.

Dai poured me some wine and said, quietly, "Is all well, Sir John?"

I smiled at him, "It will be Dai, but it will take time to wash the taste of betrayal from my mouth."

I felt guilty when Dai recoiled as though he had been slapped. It was not his fault. William should have been the one to tell me, but William would not be riding to war with me. Dai would and I had to feel that I could trust implicitly all those alongside whom I fought. A thought struck me, "Michael and Robin, they knew?" There was hesitation and I added, "No more lies and deceptions, Dai, the truth."

He nodded, "We knew not how to tell you, Sir John, and once we delayed then it became impossible to find the right words and the right time."

I actually understood what he meant but it was a sad moment. I had brothers in arms but I was their leader and none could really be my friend. The only one who could really be my friend as an equal was Albert and I did not like him. I downed the wine in one. I was doomed to a lonely life. I had men who would fight alongside me but there would be no one in whom I could confide. John Braynford was the only man I could truly call a friend and he was in England.

The atmosphere around the table was, to say the least, subdued. That was my fault for I was silent. I think the others thought that it was anger but it was not. It was reflection, as I did what I did best, I came up with a strategy that would suit everyone and one where I would be a winner.

When the food was finished and the table cleared, I took John from his nurse and sat him on my knee. His clothes were covered in discarded food. Alone out of the whole table he had laughed and giggled as he had played with his food. The lamb bone he had gnawed, Elizabeth had said he was cutting teeth and it would help, had been wielded like a poleaxe and that had made the whole table smile.

I smiled at him as I spoke for I had noticed that when someone smiled at him, he smiled back. He did so now. "John, you are a bonny bairn and I wish you to know that I dearly love you and your brother. I may not be here as often as I would wish but Roger of Norham will ensure that you are brought up well so that when you are of an age and can join me, I will be proud of my son." Out of the corner of my eye, I saw Elizabeth grab Roger's hand. She knew what I meant. "You may not understand these words, but I hope," I stared at his nurse, "that Maud will repeat them when you are old enough to understand them."

She nodded, "Of course, Sir John."

I kissed him on the forehead, "And now, Maud, take him to his bed. Dai, you may leave us too."

He looked sad as he stood and nodded, "I am sorry, my lord, I was wrong, we were wrong, but the carrot is out of the ground and cannot be put back."

"You are right, but we can plant new ones and tomorrow we start again. The wax is smoothed clean." I saw the question in his eyes, "I swear that when I wake in the morning all will be put behind us. When I see the others this will be as it is the day after a battle. The dead will be buried, and we will get on with life."

I stood and went to sit by the fire, close to Thomas' crib. He was a healthy-looking baby and had not stirred since Elizabeth had fed him. He looked content and I stroked his head before sitting in my chair with my goblet in my hand. I did not look up but continued to watch my son as I spoke, "I understand why you have done this, but I am disappointed. I look back and I can see signs that this affection was there before Thomas was born. Roger, you should have spoken to me of your feelings." I sighed, "We have fought together too many times for me to be angry with you and, Elizabeth, I understand you but, as with Roger, I should have been told. Dai is right, that is in the past and we start again. William, if I can trust you, I would have you draw up papers. This farm is to be owned when they are of legal age by John and Thomas jointly. Roger and Elizabeth may live here so long as they live. I wish one-tenth of the money I earn put aside for the use of my children. The proceeds from the farm will be Roger's to use as he sees fit. When the boys are old enough, they can make those decisions."

Silence greeted my pronouncement. I had not taken my eyes off Thomas and I waited for their response. "This is your home, Sir John. This is where your sons live. Are you saying that you will not live here?"

I turned and looked at Elizabeth, "I came back, infrequently I grant you, but I came back to see you, Elizabeth, and my sons. I will now come back to see my sons, but war is my business, and I must go where wars are fought. I will visit but only when business so dictates. For a while, we will be relatively close by, in Burgundy, and later, at Avignon, and it may be that I can visit in the summer. Dai and I, along with the men I brought and any men you have for me, Roger, go to Nevers and fight for pay. William will remain here and organise somewhere for us to keep our money."

Roger came over to me, "I never meant for this to happen, Sir John."

"That I can believe but happen it did, and our world has now changed." I glanced at Elizabeth, "I assume you will share your bed this night with Roger." I stood, "That is good for I am tired."

She grabbed my hand and kissed it, "I am sorry, Sir John."

"You never promised to be faithful and I gave you no hope of a future with me but I just wish you had been honest."

As I closed the door, I heard tears.

I rose early and went to the kitchen to ask for food. The looks on the faces of those within told me that they feared me. My anger was in the past and I smiled, "We ride forth this day. A good breakfast for all!"

We did not leave until noon as we had ten new men and four boys to take with us. There were horses for the men but no ponies for the boys. I had to send William and Dai to procure them. I was not happy with Roger, "Is this what I can look forward to when you are married? You pick and choose what is important and what is not?"

He looked suitably contrite as he knew he had made a mistake, "Sorry, my lord."

I saw then that things could never be the same between us. I had said it was in the past and it was but times past I would have almost laughed it off. I hugged John and promised him a dagger when I returned and kissed Thomas who knew little about anything, it seemed to me. I turned my horse and left my farm.

Dai rode next to me and tried to make conversation. I forced myself to be as pleasant as I could be. All the time I was thinking how reasonable I had been. There were many men who might have drawn a sword and slain the two of them. I had not even raised my voice and the further along the road we were the more convinced I was that my behaviour had been exemplary. Five days later, as we neared Nevers, I had convinced myself that I had done nothing that was wrong. The road to Nevers was a long, cold and almost silent one.

My men were in the town already and had taken over some of the inns. Michael looked nervous while Robin just gave me his usual grin. "We have the best of the inns and the prices are reasonable but as the prince is paying it matters not. Messengers arrived to tell us that the main army will be here tomorrow, so your timing is perfect, my lord."

Albert would still be in the north. He would only leave when the French threatened. "Good!" I stared at the two of them, "You knew?"

Michael nodded and looked as though he simply wished to crawl away. Robin just said, reasonably, "Aye, but there seemed little point in upsetting you while you were on campaign. It would have done no good."

"What?" I was incredulous.

Robin's was the voice of reason as it always was, "It would have taken your mind off the siege and you could do little about it and besides, Sir John, you had no intention of marrying her did you?"

"That is not the point!"

He laughed, "Of course it is. If you had expressed an interest in her as a concubine even, then Roger would have kept his distance. She was the mother of your children and they need a father." I glared at him for he was speaking the truth and my righteous position was not as secure as it had been. "We are men of war. When you decide to settle down and be a husband and a father you will have to make a choice, war or the life of peace. Are you ready for that?"

"No!"

"Then I hope you left Roger on good terms. He is a shield brother, and you owe him that." My eyes could not disguise my guilt and Robin sighed, "Women come between brothers in arms, but the blame here lies with you, my lord, and not Roger."

"He took the mother of my children!"

"He gave her comfort. I am guessing that the first time he lay with Elizabeth was after you had left."

I knew, at that moment that he was right. I had been in the wrong and it did not sit well with me.

Chapter 17

When the army arrived I was glad, for it stopped the self-recrimination I put myself through. King Edward had returned to England and Prince Edward planned a short campaign. As such we had to be swift and ruthless. He divided us into columns. The White Company, under my command, was one. Sir John Chandos had another and Sir Robert Knolles a third while Prince Edward commanded a fourth. Our instructions were clear. Prince Edward wanted a chevauchée down the Saône towards the Rhône! Our four-pronged attack meant that even if the Burgundians brought a large army to fight us, four other bands would still devastate the valley and the band which was attacked would be mounted and so could escape. Any treasure we took would be ours to keep and with that incentive in mind my men and I headed for Beaune.

Arnaud had found the futility of trying to defend against Englishmen at arms and archers. For the people who lived between Nevers and Beaune, it was even worse for they had no wall to protect them. I had no intention of attempting to breach Beaune's walls which was the place we had been asked to reach. That would be a waste of men, but the vineyards and farms of the valley had enough to satisfy us. I took all my anger out on the farms and farmers we attacked. By the time we reached Sully all who could, were fleeing to Beaune, and the Duke of Burgundy had to accommodate many hundreds of refugees. The towns thought they were safe but, when my archers surrounded each town and village and my men at arms rode in, they realised that the defences of their towns were an illusion. We travelled so quickly that we took towns and villages before they had managed to dig up all their treasure. We took animals both to eat and to ride. By the seventh of March, we were at the outskirts of Beaune and we took over the tiny hamlet of Mersault, three miles from Beaune. The hamlet's inhabitants fled as we approached, and we had roofs! We threatened the city, but I did not build any siegeworks. There was a huge, wooded area less than half a mile to the west of us and we could use it to hunt and, if we were threatened, to take wood to make defences. I had no idea where the other columns were, but we and our animals were exhausted. In truth, we could ride little further, but it mattered not for we had done all that had been asked of us and done so in an incredibly short time. Burgundy had paid the price for my anger which, by the time we reached Mersault, was completely gone. For the loss of ten of Albert's men, we had made a fortune which dwarfed that taken in the north and I halted. I had no intention of besieging Beaune, but we pretended to, by riding to the walls and making the gestures which would suggest we intended to dig ditches. I sent riders to Prince Edward to tell him where we were and then we rested in the village which we began to fortify for defence.

The Burgundians sent a hastily gathered army to shift us from their town. My scouts brought me the news the day after the rider had hastened to Prince Edward. "Sir John, there are five thousand men heading from the south. There are at least eight hundred men at arms, all of them mounted."

I did not panic. Indeed I had time to think that we had moved far faster than the other columns. If the rest of the raiders had done as we had then this army would not be coming for us. Whence did they come?"

"We were close to Chalon-sur-Saône when we spied their tents. It looks like they were gathered there from further south."

It made sense now. They had heard of the chevauchée and the army was assembled to deal with it. Our success had drawn them to us. I nodded to Michael and Robin who were with me, "Then there could be more. Let us work on the assumption that they will be reinforced." My choice of the camp had proved to be a wise one. "Robin, have the archers cut down saplings to make stakes. If they come for us, then I want them forced to fight where I choose."

Michael said, "You think they may not?"

I shrugged, "If their intention is to rid the land of us then they will but they may think that numbers alone might drive us away. I want stakes from the wood to the hamlet. The main road lies a mile to the east of us and I will give them the chance to get to Beaune unopposed."

Michael asked, "Will that suit the prince?"

I nodded, "He is always happy for a battle. If they camp close to Beaune, then he can bring them to battle and garner the glory." I turned back to Robin, "I want the stakes thickest closer to the hamlet."

He smiled, "You will use the woods to hide archers."

He knew my mind well. "We will use our men at arms to draw them close and then archers can attack from the flanks and from behind us. Michael, we will put the horses in the woods. Half of our pages can watch them while the other half can use their slings from the eaves of the woods. If there is a fight, then this will be good practice for them."

While they set about obeying my orders, I summoned my other senior captains to give them their instructions. All thoughts of Elizabeth and Roger were banished to the far recesses of my mind for this was when I felt alive. I had a plan, but my mind was such that I would be able to modify it in an instant if I had to. My organisation of the English part of the White Company meant that I could give orders to one or two men and they would cascade them down through their lances. It was dark by the time we were finished, and the Burgundians had yet to arrive. I left just a handful of men on watch for I gambled that a rapidly assembled army would not risk a night attack.

Since speaking to Robin my relations with Dai had improved and it was as it always had been. I knew that I had bridges to mend with William but, as we sat in the farmhouse, it was good to laugh with Michael, Robin, and Dai and be as we once had been. My rapid ride and success had expunged the ill feelings I had harboured. That night I prayed to God to watch over my children. I knew that it was unlikely that I would ever see Antiochia, but I knew that her grandfather would see that she was brought up well. John and Thomas would join me when they were seven. It would break Elizabeth's heart, but I knew that by then she would have more children by Roger and that would be a good thing for all.

I rose early for I hoped the Burgundians would come. The raid thus far had not seen my blade bloodied overmuch and I knew that once I had fought then I would be as I had been before I had walked into my home. When I had made water, I wandered the lines to see the men on watch, and they said that all was quiet. I joked with them for I remembered what it was like to watch all night while others slept. By the time I reached the farmhouse again, I could smell the fire and food as it was cooked. We had slaughtered some pigs and it was the smell of meat sizzling in the pan that made me salivate. I did not think that we would see the Burgundians until noon. It was sixteen miles to Chalon-sur-Saône, and I did not think a hastily assembled army would be completely mounted. We had a whole morning to prepare while they would be tired from an early start and a march. We were not complacent and once we had eaten, I sent Martin and his mounted archers to watch the army as it approached. Their line of march would give us an indication of their intentions.

One of his men reached us in the middle of the morning. He grinned as he dismounted, "Captain Martin said that they will be here by noon."

"What makes you smile, Jack?"

"When they spied us, they sent a group of light horsemen to shift us. Captain Martin had half of us dismount and the twenty arrows we sent emptied some of their saddles. They turned tail. If that is the best that they can do, Sir John, then this will be an easy day!"

"There is never an easy day, Jack. When we fight, we do so as though we fight the finest warriors in Christendom." He nodded, contritely, "Their numbers?"

"As we expected. They are swollen by some of the men from Chalon-sur-Saône but the men at arms are roughly in the same number. They and about two hundred light horsemen are their only mounted men."

I waved him away and he headed back to the scouts.

The boys had brought the horses from the woods to graze on the grass and stubble before the stakes. It was not only to feed them but also to allow them to urinate and defecate on the ground. It would make it slightly wetter and slicker. I returned to the hall to don my mail and plate. A half dozen boys were in the farmhouse to help with the cooking and it was they who helped me prepare. They deemed it an honour and I wondered how many would grow to become men at arms. Robin had identified the ones he would train as archers. He was the best judge of

frame and attitude. The ones who had skills with a slingshot
were the ones he looked closely at. We allowed him to make his
choice before we started the practice with a sword for the others.
I was looking at them with a view to the future. Ten years from
now I would have men ready to hand rather than hiring ones I
did not know.

When Martin and his scouts rode in it was an hour before
noon. "They are behind us, Sir John, and they are coming here
rather than Beaune."

I knew that despite our precautions they had sent scouts to
discover where we were and that we were still a threat. I nodded
and waved to the trees. "Captain Robin will show you where to
place your men." He rode off and I cupped my hands to shout,
"To arms!"

Michael, Giovanni, Sir Eoin, Karl, and the other captains
knew my plans and their men hurried to their positions. We
would fight dismounted in three lines. The fourth line would be
archers who would loose over our heads. The thinner screen of
stakes between the woods and our right would invite an attempt
to outflank us and there the bulk of our archers would rain
arrows on their backs. The spearmen and those without plate
were in an oblique block on the right flank. Under the command
of one of Albert's Germans, Otto, they had long spears and
would be a barrier to hold them while Robin and his men thinned
their numbers.

I did not have my usual men at arms around me. I had spread
them out along my line to stiffen it. Dai held my banner and I
had some of the new men we had brought back from Bordeaux
with me. I had my poleaxe rammed into the soft earth and my
helmet hung from the spike. We had time. Looking down the
line I saw smiles and heard laughter. My men were not daunted
by the numbers which we saw approaching for we had yet to
taste defeat. There were many banners heading towards us and
that told each of us that we were facing knights. While that
might worry some warriors mine knew that it was a chance for
profit. Had we been part of an English army then the
Burgundians might have attempted negotiation, but they would
not negotiate with mercenaries. They formed up before us. I saw
that they had their knights and men at arms mounted and in a

block on their left flank, the one closest to the woods and furthest from the village which would be an obstacle to horses. They were walking into my trap. The largest element of their army, the dismounted men at arms and spearmen were in a massive block and it was they who would try to drive us back.

Half of our archers were behind us and were commanded by Martin the Fletcher. He did not need me to tell him when to loose his missiles. During the morning, my archers had measured the ranges and marked them with small cairns. The horsemen were not galloping towards us but heading to our right and I knew what they intended. They would allow their dismounted comrades to engage us and then try to charge our weaker flank. Much would depend upon the steel of Otto and his spearmen. I could count on Robin and the archers in the woods to choose their moment well and when they had loosed their arrows their swords were as deadly as any Burgundian's.

The Burgundians had yet to face mercenaries and it may have been that they thought their overwhelming numbers would make us take our booty and run. They certainly came on at us with steady confidence and seemed eager to close with us. I saw a great deal of metal in the front ranks of the men who advanced, and the level ground prevented me from seeing beyond their front ranks, but I could not see them having more than two or three ranks so well-armed. Martin's men would have bodkins ready for the first flight so that, descending from a height they would drive through helmets, mail and even plate. He waited until they were two hundred paces from us and the noise, as they were released, sounded like a flock of birds taking to the air. Our second flight was already in the air when, in the front rank, I had the luxury of watching their fall. They plunged down and I could see that the archers had concentrated their arrows on the centre of the line. A metal arrowhead striking a metal helmet makes a loud noise and as many men were hit it sounded like a busy weaponsmith's workshop. I saw men fall and then the second flight struck. This was not quite as effective as some arrows hit dead men. My archers' third flight was shifted slightly to hit the two sides of the men first ones had hit. The three flights brought the column to a halt and I heard orders shouted to belatedly bring shields up. In the time it took to do that Martin and his men had sent another two flights and there were men writhing on the ground who bore testament to the Burgundian's tardiness.

I saw that the horsemen had moved a little closer and that suggested they were nervous. Robin would judge when to loose his arrows. If the horsemen came close enough and were not moving quickly then they would be easier targets. Whoever led this army had made a grave error for they had not sent scouts into the woods. Their light horsemen hovered between the main column and the horsemen. Light horsemen could move very quickly and if they spied a weakness then they would take advantage! Once the shields were in place then Martin and his archers changed arrows and loosed into the mass of men following the shields. He had scouted out the enemy and knew better than any how they were armed and armoured. We saw the war arrows falling but not the effect. The Burgundians were now coming much more quickly to get close to us before the next arrows hit.

"Dai, plant the standard and be ready to defend my back."

"Aye, Sir John."

Dai was not yet ready to face plated men in the front rank, but he was quick and he could use his sword to great effect. His job would be to find the weakness in the armour of any who fought me whilst avoiding enemy blades. He would look for the places without plate where either his sword or bodkin dagger could find flesh!

Men were running now, and the slippery, dung soiled earth made some fall. Their falling caused others to move to the side or trip themselves and what should have been a straight and solid line of spears, axes, swords, and pole weapons was an irregular one. That and the stakes meant I could judge which man at arms would come to me. Using shields to protect them meant that the majority of those in the front rank were armed with either swords or axes. My poleaxe outranged them and as the man at arms with the yellow shield and red hawks twisted and turned through the stakes, I brought the poleaxe down to smash into his helmet and skull. All the men in our front rank had pole weapons and they knew how to use them. Martin and the archers were now sending their arrows at several targets. He still had some sending their arrows to strike blindly into the middle and the rear of the column but some were using a flat trajectory to send their arrows into the chest and faces of the men who made it through the stakes.

The men who had endured the arrow storm pushed hard and the line which made it to fight us was a more solid one. A spear was thrust at my head. The man who wielded it wore an old-fashioned mail hauberk and had an open sallet upon his head. I fenced away the spear with the spike on the end of the poleaxe and then swung the hammer head into the side of his helmet, punching hard. I saw the eyes roll into his skull as he fell, and I jabbed forward at the surprised Burgundian who was close behind him. The spike drove through his mail and into his chest. It was at that moment that I heard a horn and when the ground began to shake, I knew that the Burgundian horsemen had begun their charge. The horn seemed to encourage the men on foot who cheered and swarmed forward. The men in our second and third rank stepped closer to us. Dai remained behind my shoulder. The white standard drew the enemy like bees to nectar and both sides were packed closely together. Soon I would have to discard the poleaxe and draw my sword. Timing would be all. My poleaxe had metal protecting the wood for two-thirds of its length. That and my mailed gauntlets meant that I could use my weapon horizontally. As I blocked a spear and two swords a sword darted out from behind me and found the gap below the breastplate of the Burgundian. The man at arms had a surprised look as he realised he had been gutted. I swung the haft of the poleaxe to smack into the face of one man and then swung it the other way, driving the axe head into the face of another. Three men had sought to end my life, one was dead, a second so badly wounded that he might not last and the third one, who was stunned, was killed by one of my men at arms who stepped next to me. I drove the haft into the ground and drew my sword and dagger.

I heard, to my right, the screams and cries of both men and horses as Robin and Otto battled them. I had to trust my men and we would have to stem the flood of men trying to end the battle. We were aided by the fact that the men we fought were not real warriors. They still outnumbered us, but we knew how to use our weapons and even Dai was the equal of those who came. Some had shields but they made the mistake of just using them defensively. A good warrior used a shield for offence as well as defence. I raised my sword at the Burgundian who obliged by raising not only his shield to block the blow but his sword also. The dagger in my left hand drove under his armpit where there was little or no protection. Once I found flesh, I turned and twisted the blade before pulling it out. The man fell.

It was Martin who told me we were winning, "My lord, their horsemen flee!"

I shouted, "White Company! Forward!"

This was not a charge but my men, instead of standing to take the blows stepped forward when they had killed their enemy. We were all plated and well protected. As we pushed them back the Burgundians found themselves slipping on the blood-soaked ground and tripping over the bodies of the dead and dying. Skewering a prostrate man is easy and within a short time the Burgundians, now leaderless, fled! I halted the pursuit at the edge of the stakes. There was little point in trying to chase men who were discarding weapons as they raced to get away from us. The plate and purses we sought would be amongst those we had first killed. We had done all that I had hoped.

By the time it was dark the enemy had been stripped and their bodies piled on a pyre. We placed the fire so that the wind would take the smell of burning flesh across the fields to Beaune. Many of those who had fled, especially the horsemen, had fled there and the funeral fire would confirm that not only had we won but we had not been hurt. In all, we lost forty men and all of those were from the spearmen led by Otto. I gave the ones who lived the plate we had taken from the dead. We had also taken more than a hundred horses. Twenty knights had surrendered to Robin and his archers. I knew it galled them to have to do so but my men were killers and the Burgundians had discovered that to their cost. They would be ransomed.

The smell of burned flesh from the fire was still there in the morning but Joseph and his scouts found no enemy left alive within ten miles of us. They discovered the bodies of wounded men who had fled the battle but succumbed to their wounds. It had been a costly battle for the Duke of Burgundy.

Prince Edward led two of the columns of men to ride into our hamlet. It was three days after the battle although some of my men were so disparaging of the Burgundians that they just called it a fight! The prince first came to speak to us and to ask me for my account. He was delighted when I told him.

"And have you spoken to those in Beaune, Sir John?"

It was a test, and I knew it. Had I exceeded my authority? "Of course not, Prince Edward, I assumed that you would wish to do so."

He beamed, "I would have you and your standard-bearer come with me when I do so. It will do no harm to let them know that the man who destroyed their army is still close by."

We rode to the besieged town the next day. The prince wore his black armour and was accompanied by men wearing his livery. It was in direct contrast to Dai and me in our white jupons and with my white standard. It would draw attention to us and Prince Edward had planned it that way. We halted outside the gates and it was the Duke himself who spoke to us. I did not know he was within but then we had not kept a close watch on its walls. Once we had known the Burgundians were heading towards us, we had kept to the hamlet. I saw that the eyes of those with the Duke were not on Prince Edward but on me and there were hateful looks. I wondered how many fathers, brothers and sons had been killed by us.

The Duke said, "Prince Edward, you and your knights may come within Beaune's walls so that we may discuss terms to rid our land of you but that man, the mercenary, is not welcome!"

If they thought they had offended me they were wrong. The prince hid his smile as he said, "Sir John if you would return to the army, I would be much obliged."

"Whatever you wish, Prince Edward." I looked up at the walls and said, loudly, "If you need us then you know where we are!" It was a threat, and all knew it.

It was in the late afternoon when Prince Edward returned, and he was in high spirits. "They are paying us two hundred thousand gold pieces to leave! I am pleased I took you, Sir John, for it was a bargaining counter that swayed the Burgundians. They demanded that you leave their land. Forty thousand of the gold pieces are yours!"

He thought he was being generous, but I knew he was not. The other companies, who had done less, were being given an equal share and he was taking two. However, it was a good payment, and I would ensure that my men were well paid for their services. "Thank you, Prince Edward."

"And there may be more forthcoming when we head down the Loire."

I shook my head, "I fear, Prince Edward, that I will not be able to join you. I am expecting the rest of my company soon and we have plans."

The prince looked genuinely disappointed. He tried to persuade me but I would not move and, I think, his opinion of me changed. However, Rheims had been the moment when I had decided to sever the links with Prince Edward and it was only right that he knew sooner, rather than later. Over the next few days, while we waited for the gold, he tried all that he could to persuade me. It was only when Albert arrived with the last of our men, all one thousand of them, he finally gave up. Sir John Chandos appeared not only disappointed but offended that I chose the life of a mercenary rather than serving Prince Edward.

Once the gold arrived, I was given my share. Poor Albert was most unhappy for had he been with us then he would have had a share. Prince Edward and his knights left us with ill grace. I had plummeted in their estimation. The hero of Poitiers was now seen for what he really was, a sword for hire!

Southern France and Italy 1360

Chapter 18

Even though the Burgundians were desperate for us to leave we did not do so immediately. I sent Michael and twenty men to take my share of the gold and the coins we had earned back to Bordeaux. I needed William and any new men whom Roger had found. I also needed to send a letter to Roger and Elizabeth. Robin had been quite correct, and I owed them a letter and an apology… of sorts. After they had gone and having given them instructions where to meet us, we packed up and headed south. We had a long way to go to reach Provence and that was our target. We were shunned all the way down the valley for the word had spread of the mercenaries who had defeated their Duke. Gates were barred to us and so we took over hamlets along the way. We did not abuse the people but as our horses soiled their fields and we ate the wild animals in the woods close to their houses we let them know the reason. We had to eat, and the towns would not accommodate us!

We finally settled in the village of Jonquières in Provence. We were close to the home of Pope Innocent in Carpentras and that was deliberate. Arnaud de Cervole had ravaged Provence three years earlier and been bought off by the pope. The rulers of the county, Louis of Naples and his wife Joan did not get on and Queen Joan supported Pope Innocent. She lived to the east of Avignon at Forcalquier. We had the chance to do what we had done on the Marne and take advantage of an unstable dynasty.

The village welcomed us. In truth, they had little choice in the matter, but I had decided that we would need a base and we should be on friendly terms with some of the locals. It was while we were there and after William and Michael had returned that we heard of the disaster which befell the army of Prince Edward. He had left the army to return to England when, on a day known as Black Monday, the thirteenth of April, a hailstorm struck their camp killing over a thousand soldiers. It was the end of the push towards the Loire and effectively ended the war with France. The following May the treaty of Bretigny was signed. When we heard the news it vindicated our decision to leave Prince Edward's service. Who knows how many men we would have lost and for what purpose? William's arrival also brought news that was of great import.

"All the ransom which is being collected for King John is held in Pont-Saint-Esprit." He unrolled a map. "I had this made in Bordeaux. As you can see it is just twenty miles north of here. If you had travelled down the west bank of the river you would have seen it."

I remembered that Albert had mentioned the town, "And is there a castle?"

"No, but there is a wall around it." He smiled, "I believe, Sir John, that we could gain entry through a trick. Despite the fact that there is money there they do not appear to have a large garrison. Each month the money collected is gathered and taken by wagon to the north. All that we would have to do, once we have taken the town, is to squat there and wait for the money to arrive. We would not have far to travel, and I am sure that you could make the town more defensible."

I nodded, "Perhaps, and I like the idea. What do you think, Albert?"

Albert was still the official leader of the company, but I knew that when I asked for an election then I would win. That day was coming but I would pay lip service to him and appear to consult him.

"It is worth investigating and I had always planned on taking the town." He nodded to William, "I confess I did not know about the ransom and that makes it an even juicier target."

My mind had been working as soon as William fetched out the map. "We need to scout out the town as I did in Champagne. Albert, you, and the company can raid the area to the south of us and I will take a few men. We will say that we have been in the east fighting the Turks who are trying to take the Empire. We have spare jupons. We sew red crosses on them so that we appear to be Englishmen fighting for God. It should allow us to see how hard it would be to take the town."

All agreed that it was a good idea, and I chose my men, Dai, Michael, and Sir Eoin were obvious choices as was Robin. The other five were Englishmen who had served in the south and had tanned features. Three were archers and the other two were men at arms. We headed north the next day riding horses we had taken from the Burgundians. There were many knights who went to the east to fight against the Turks and our story was believable. Since Acre had finally fallen there were no more crusader states and the Turks had begun to eat into the Eastern Empire. I knew, from some soldiers who had joined us, that it was only a matter of time before Constantinople fell too and that was a terrifying thought. With more barbarians attacking Poland and Hungary men like my company would soon be in great demand.

The bridge over the river was guarded at both ends. The crosses we had sewn on our jupons meant that there were no weapons pointed at us. We had made sure that the red we had used for them was faded! We did, however, have to endure questions.

"When you were travelling from Italy, did you see any mercenaries?"

"Hand on heart I saw none but my men. We heard that there were some operating in Provence."

The sergeant at arms nodded, "That was what we heard. And how long will you be staying in our town for it is not a large one."

"A day or so." I patted my Burgundian horse, "We need to look after our mounts if we are to get back to England."

He laughed, "And we have heard that your Black Prince has been punished by God! More than a thousand of his men perished in a storm. Pass, friend, but do not expect a friendly welcome everywhere. We Frenchmen are still trying to raise the ransom so that our king may be returned to us. I let you pass because I know that if you fought in the east then you had nothing to do with his capture!"

We passed across the bridge. The examination at the other end was cursory. Had we tried to force it then it would have been a different story. We passed into the town and I saw that the walls had a good gatehouse and towers. An attack from the river side of the town was out of the question. We would lose too many men. After finding an inn with stables we split into five pairs. I took Dai. We had the whole afternoon to find out as much as we could about the town. I went with Dai to the west gate and I saw what the sergeant had meant. The town was very small. Its sole purpose seemed to be to guard the bridge. The other gate, which led north, was not as formidable as the bridge one and there was no ditch. While Dai pretended to take a stone from his boot, I looked at the walls which appeared low enough for a rider to climb. I decided that when we left, the next day, I would examine the western wall in more detail. We walked around the whole town in well under an hour. The church bell gave us the time. The inn had a tavern attached to it and we joined the others there to enjoy a jug of wine before we ate. We had to be circumspect with our conversation as I had no idea who did or did not speak English. What I had not seen was the place they were collecting the ransom.

Michael gave me the answer, "There is a fine church by the river, Saint Saturnin's. It is worth a look just do not let the guards there put you off."

I nodded and smiled, "I will do so when this jug is empty. I will light a candle to ask Saint Saturnin for his help on our journey." When the wine was finished, I stood, and Dai began to rise. "I shall do this alone." Prayers from a solitary visitor would seem less suspicious. I saw the spire of the church and headed through the narrow streets towards it. There were two guards on the main door but others were entering the church and I was allowed to pass. I saw no sign that gold was being gathered and I wondered if Michael had made a mistake. I knelt and went through the ritual of prayer. A priest stood in an alcove watching the half dozen worshippers in the dimly lit church. I went to the candles and dropped a coin in the box. The coin was suitably heavy enough to make the priest smile and I lit the candle, made the sign of the cross and left. The two guards outside seemed uninterested in any coming out. It was as I was heading up towards the centre of the town that I saw the two riders dismount. One held the reins of the other's mount and the second took a hessian sack that jingled to the side of the church. I used Dai's trick to lean my back against a wall so that I could see where he went. The crypt in this church had an outside entrance and that was where he descended. I saw a further guard sitting and eating there. Michael was right!

I headed back to the inn knowing that we had a chance. This would not be as easy as William made out but, to be fair, he was a bookkeeper and not a soldier. I arrived back just as Robin was ordering the food. My smile told them all that they needed to know. We could talk of inanities that night and I would give them my plan as we rode back.

We left not early, for that would have been suspicious, but with enough time for us to find a crossing of the Rhône River and get back to our new base. Once we left the town I stopped, ostensibly to tighten my girth. I saw that a tall rider could stand on his horse and reach the crenulations. What I did not know was how the guards were placed but as the small guard towers were just two hundred paces apart, I guessed that they would largely stay in the towers. I mounted and we headed north. I would risk two crossings of the Ardèche and the Rhône. The swim was not an easy one, but I knew we had riders who could manage it and that meant that I could get enough riders to the west of the town and that we could take the west wall. With the bulk of our army on the east bank, we would be able to cut off the town and with it the treasure. As we rode, bedraggled and wet back to Jonquières I explained my plan to my men. Four of them were as close to me as brothers and they were confident enough to modify my plan.

When we reached our new home more than half of the men were still raiding. That made me realise that we would not be able to use the whole company to attack the town. If retribution came our way, then we needed enough men to defend the first town we had taken. I would leave that to Albert. I would not need him for much longer. He did not arrive back for another day but already we had garnered much treasure. I had devised a plan which I hoped would be successful so that when we ate and drank together, I had a smooth and coherent outline to give to him.

I saw the smile of approval, "John, this is well thought out. If you can take this town then it will be like capturing a mint. We can almost produce our own coins."

I shrugged, "Perhaps, but eventually, they will stop sending the ransom and then they will seek to remove us from the town."

He laughed, "John, you have a mind like a steel trap. You will find a way to make money from this. Arnaud was a fool! You are the goose which lays the golden eggs."

That night as I lay in my bed, I knew that he was right but also, that I did not need him. Soon I would take the company and make it mine!

I chose the men carefully. I would need just five hundred of our best men. They were mainly English, but I liked Karl and knew him to be reliable. I took him to command the fifty Germans I had chosen. I had many archers with me for they would give us a distinct advantage. Albert had half of the men remaining to continue giving the appearance of raiding. One hundred would guard our new base and William would command them. The rest, all six hundred would wait out of sight and block the road to the river. We rode north and cut across country to reach the two rivers. We crossed in the late afternoon and the crossing was easier than I had expected. Perhaps the waters upriver had dropped a little. We dried off and waited for dark before we headed for the walls. While we rested, I went through the plan in great detail. I had men who could lead, and they were reliable. I had chosen every man I led, and I trusted them.

I took on the challenge of the gate. We walked our horses close to the walls. I had men at arms leading two horses and archers with arrows nocked. If they saw an inquisitive face peering over the wall, then they would loose. We walked one hundred and twenty paces from the walls knowing that we would be hard to see and then we turned and headed to the walls. We moved towards the gaps between the towers. I prayed for complacency from the sentries and we were rewarded. Dai led two horses and I prepared to stand on the back of Roman. I did not look for a white face in the night, that was Robin's task. Roman obligingly went next to the wall and I stood on his back. He was a well-trained horse, and he was as still as a rock. I stood on tiptoe and my fingers grabbed the crenulations. As I pulled, I put my feet into the mortared gaps between the stones and climbed. I was almost level with the top when I heard the arrow slam into the man who had peered over the wall to see what the noise was, and he fell to the street below. To me, it sounded like the crack of thunder but as I hauled myself over the wall there was no reaction. Once over I drew my sword and hurried towards the gate, I had to assume that I was the only one who had made it and that the whole success of the attack depended on me. I made the gatehouse tower, and I must have made some noise for it opened and the sentry who did so lived for a heartbeat before my sword ended his life. I hurried in and the second man who rose quickly just turned and saw death with a drawn sword. He made the mistake of attempting to draw his own sword as he opened his mouth to shout. The only sound was his body as he fell back into the wooden chair from which he had just risen.

I stepped as silently down the stairs as I could manage. I was glad that I had not worn my spurs for they would have rattled on the stone steps. I had seen, when we had passed through this gate, that the gates had two small open chambers, one on each side and, as I expected there was a sentry sitting there. He was asleep and I pricked him awake with my sword. I signed for him to remain silent.

Michael appeared behind me and I pointed to the other side of the gate. He nodded and left. I waited until he returned with the other gateman and I said, "Open the gate! Do so silently and you live. Make a noise and you die, and we shall open it ourselves."

They were not paid enough, I suspected, for heroics and they obeyed. The door creaked open and two more of my men at arms appeared from the upper wall. I stepped out into the dark and I waved my sword. I counted on the fact that my men would have taken the wall for the sound of the hooves, as my archers and horse holders rode towards the open gate, was louder than I would have liked. There were now fifteen of my men at arms gathered and I said, "Go to the other gate. Take it and hold it."

Sir Eoin and Giovanni led them. I waited until all my raiding party were inside the walls and then closed the gate. I left Robin in charge and I took just twenty men, a mixture of archers and men at arms. We headed to the church. The noise of my men had awakened people. Doors partially opened and faces appeared, but they ducked back inside as we hurried through the empty streets. The guards at the church, however, were awakened and they were ready. When I had scouted out the church, I had recognised them for what they were, men at arms. I saw two of them scurrying down the steps to the crypt and slamming shut the door. The crypt had a lock, but it was outside the door. I pulled open the door and stood to the side, but no blade emerged.

"Whoever is in there you are outnumbered. Surrender and you live."

"We took an oath to protect the gold intended for Good King John!"

"And you will die to keep that oath!"

A voice laughed, "And what would you know of oaths, mercenary! We may die but we will take some of you with us."

He was right. My men were good but there would be no light in the crypt. I had no intention of losing any of my men. "Harry, stay here with four men. Joseph, take another four and go into the church. See if there is another way in. I doubt that there will be."

He said, "What do you intend to do, Sir John?"

"Leave them within. They can do no harm and when they need to eat or drink, they will either have to come out or risk dying. There is no rush to this. I will be at the bridge gate. Keep me informed."

By the time I reached the bridge gate, it was in our hands. The men guarding the bridge were completely oblivious to the fact that they had lost the town. The dozen or so sentries we had taken were now bound and guarded. The townsfolk would awake and wonder if they had just dreamed badly.

"Dai, fetch me food and something to drink. I will watch from the gate." I took my coif from off my head. The air felt pleasantly cool. Michael was with me as were two other men at arms and Robin. I looked east to where I knew the sun would rise. Without turning I said, "The walls are guarded?"

"Yes, Sir John, and the Hotel de Ville is guarded. Do we have the treasure yet?"

"Not yet, Robin, there are some heroes within. We will starve them into submission. They are watched and guarded. They cannot do anything to hurt us."

Dai brought bread, ham, cheese, and wine for all of us and, as the sun rose, we finished off a pleasant breakfast. Albert and the rest of our men would appear soon for we had planned a dramatic entrance on the high ground above the river. As the sun rose there would be a long line of armed horsemen. It was probably unnecessary, but we planned to be here for some time and the effect would linger in men's memories. The story would spread, and we hoped that we would have an easier time holding on to this part of France. We were not demanding protection money, we were holding this rich corner to ransom. With our two strongholds just sixteen miles apart, it would take an army to shift us.

As the sun suddenly flared above the high ground I saw silhouetted there, Albert and our men. That they were seen from the bridge was clear for a bell sounded. It was obviously to alert the town end of the bridge and the town itself.

"Dai, it is time to raise our standard!"

"Aye, Sir John." He attached my standard to the flagpole and raised it. The faces from the bridge looked up and saw not the familiar visages of the rest of the garrison but the White Company and they would know that their town was lost.

I cupped my hands and shouted, "The town is taken. Leave your arms where they are and come back to the town. You will live. The walls are lined with English archers and you know what they can do."

The ten men who had been guarding the bridge opened their gates and walked disconsolately back to us. Albert led our horsemen and by the time the sun had risen in the sky the town and the bridge were ours. We disarmed the sentries, and they were sent on their way. They were useless mouths, and we did not need to feed them. We offered the same to any who would take it. Fifty or so people left. Most of them had family who lived to the north and west. Of course, word would then spread that the White Company had taken Pont-Saint-Esprit but that was inevitable anyway. Albert and I waited until late afternoon to return to the crypt. Joseph had not found another entrance to the crypt. He and the archers had taken everything of value from the church. I would even have back the coin I gave for the candle. The open door had been well guarded, and none had tried to come out.

Harry gave a shake of his head, "The coins within, my lord, will need cleaning. We heard them pissing earlier on."

I nodded, "When they come out, we will give them a bucket of water and they can clean it." I went to the door and shouted, "Are you ready to come out yet?"

"Cowards! Come in and fight us if you dare!"

"The town is ours and the rest of the warriors have left. You are the last. We have more than a thousand men. Throw your weapons out and then follow."

My words were greeted by silence. Then I heard murmuring. I had a sixth sense about such matters. It had helped me to survive as long as I had. "Have weapons ready." I had barely begun to draw my sword when the men burst from the crypt. They were going for a glorious death. In their haste, they had forgotten that the door was narrow, and they had to duck their heads as they came out. I saw the sword emerge first and, as I stepped back, I batted it up into the air. Harry swung his sword two handed and it hacked into the face of the first man. The second tripped over his body and I shouted, "Step back and surround them with steel."

The fallen man rose as his two companions emerged, blinking into the light. Albert used the flat of his sword to render the first man unconscious and I used my mailed glove to tear the sword from the hand of the second. The last man shook his head and dropped his sword. He nodded to the man whom Harry had slain, "Jean Francois said it was the only honourable thing to do!"

I put my arm around him, "My friend, you have done the right thing. How could any have faced these men? We are the White Company and even dukes and princes fear us."

We had the town, and we had the gold!

Chapter 19

We counted the coins and there were fewer than we had hoped. The French, it seemed, were finding it hard to raise the ransom for their king. The unrest in the towns was a clear sign that the people were reluctant to pay the ransom! The choice of town, however, was perfect. Even though there was no castle we controlled a vast area, and we were close enough to Provence to raid there as well as Burgundy. The Duke had paid off Prince Edward. If he wanted us to stop raiding, then he would have to pay. I suspect that we were not hurting the people too much, but we kept archers riding up to thirty miles from our twin bases to ensure that we were not surprised. Our organisation meant that we were more efficient than most armies of the time and certainly better paid.

Surprisingly, no one came for quite a while. In fact, we had more recruits before any attempt was made to shift us. The Treaty of Bretigny effectively ended all fighting in France and there were many Englishmen who still sought work. Our company was the one which had enjoyed success and so archers and men at arms made their way to Pont-Saint-Esprit to join the White Company. In all our numbers were swollen by one hundred and fifty archers and sixty men at arms. We housed them at Jonquières, and William organised them into lances. My original captains now commanded many men each and, as such, their pay increased. The summer passed and more recruits arrived. When I met with Albert and the captains, we worried that we might not be able to pay them unless we raided further.

Avignon was a tempting target. In late September William raised the subject, "The Pope is a rich man, and he has few guards. Have you not thought of raiding him?"

I had not. I had no objection to taking from the church for it was very rich and seemed to me to have come as far away from its original purpose, as preached by Jesus, as it was possible to get. "I do not object in principle but what are the dangers of doing so, Albert? Do we risk an alliance of Christian states?"

Albert laughed, "I do not think so. Even if they did, we are now strong enough to defeat them unless they came at us at the same time. The danger is to your soul."

Some of the young captains made the sign of the cross. Michael asked, "Why is that?"

"He could excommunicate you but as few of our men go to church in any case, I do not think that would worry any." He smiled, "I would say that it is something we could explore. If we leave the churches alone at first, we could levy a tax on pilgrims travelling through this land."

And so as summer turned to autumn, we looked to the papal lands for an income. We went in such numbers that there was no resistance for it would be seen as futile and our purses grew but, amongst my English contingent, there was also growing disquiet. Some of them, Michael and Dai included, thought that we had become little better than brigands and the days of the battle with the Burgundians seemed a lifetime ago.

"Sir John, is this to be our future? Are we to hold to ransom priests and the like?"

I nodded, "Until, Michael, we can find a paymaster who will pay us to fight his enemies then aye. I am resigned to this. We fought for Prince Edward and there is no pay there. This will not last long. Give it until the New Year and then see."

I was unhappy with the situation, but my reasons were different. I did not mind being paid without the prospect of fighting but soon I would have to make my move to become Captain of the White Company. I really needed some of Albert's Germans to vote for me. Despite the extra men who had joined us being largely English, Albert's men still outnumbered those who would vote for me. I had won some over, but I would only call an election when I knew that I would win. The pilgrims dried up. It was not only our presence but also the approach of winter. Whilst not as bad as further north it was still cooler and wetter than pilgrims liked.

I had no letters from Bordeaux except those forwarded on from England. My father-in-law kept me informed about my daughter and her progress. He also wrote to me about my investments and thanked me for the goods I had sent. We had sent more since coming to Provence. When I had married

Antiochia he had given me a dowry of five thousand florins. It had grown to be almost seven and he told me that if I wished more money to be invested then I should let him know. I would not, of course, send money without an escort. Had Michael and Dai expressed an interest in returning to England then I would have sent a chest with them. There might come a time when they would choose to return and then I would have my guards for my treasure. The last year had seen Dai grow into a man. We ate well and he exercised every day. We had a suit of armour we had taken when we fought the Burgundians and that fitted him well.

Our riders continued to press the papal lands even in winter and it paid off for in early February a papal column approached the town. There were just twenty men and the majority were priests. We allowed them in, and Albert and I spoke with them. I let Albert do most of the talking but he glanced at me frequently to ensure that I agreed. I was able to observe the men while I listened to the negotiations. There was a cardinal in charge of the talks, but I saw a hawk-faced priest who was studying Albert just as intently as I was studying them. He did not look like a priest to me and he had a lean and hungry look about him.

At first, the cardinal tried to persuade us to leave using God and the threat of excommunication. If the Pope could save money, then he would. I admired Albert for he knew how to negotiate and soon brought the talks around to the subject of money. We made a point of telling the priests that we had many more men now than when we had first arrived, and they would all need to be paid off or else they might stay. The cardinal increased the amount they offered. Albert then pointed out that the King of France's ransom could not be raised until we left and that we were comfortable in our winter quarters. The final inducement he used was the veiled threat of an attack on Avignon and the Pope's home to raise it still further. The figure which was agreed was a hundred thousand florins.

The cardinal was not happy that he had been forced to pay so much, "You will, of course, leave directly!"

Albert smiled, "Of course, just as soon as the gold is delivered here then you have my word that we will leave!"

"And leave completely! You will not move to anywhere within fifty miles of Avignon!"

"Of course, but that will take time, you do understand that."

He reluctantly agreed. We, of course, fed them and it was while we were eating that the hawk-faced priest approached me, "Sir John, is there a garderobe handily placed?" His English was good, and I doubted that he really needed such directions.

I was unsure of his title and so I elevated him, "If you would come with me, your grace, I will show you." I saw Albert give me a questioning look and I shrugged.

Once we had left the room and were out of earshot he said, "You are a clever man and knew that I wished to speak with you. I am not a churchman, as you no doubt deduced. I am a soldier. I was sent by the Pope in case you tried to hold us hostage."

"The Pope must have great confidence in your skills to enter a den of lions and expect to escape."

He smiled, "Like you, my friend, I am a sword for hire. The difference is that my position is one within the law and not without."

"And, I dare say, pays well."

"You have negotiated more money than I will expect in ten lifetimes, but I have enough and life is pleasant. I did not ask to speak with you just to share our experiences, I am here to offer you and your company a commission."

"Fight for the Pope?"

"No, for the Marquis of Montferrat." My face must have looked blankly at him. He smiled, "It is in Italy and a buffer between Savoy and Milan. It is famous for being in the centre of the nine holy hills. It is known for its fine wine and my cousin, John, is the Marquis. He wishes to hire your men."

"Can he afford them?"

"You do not know the area, I can see that. One of our ancestors led the Fourth Crusade and became King of Thessalonica. Sadly, the kingdom did not last but as with all crusaders King Boniface acquired a vast fortune. Montferrat may not have men, but the Marquis has money. You have heard of the Visconti family?"

"I have heard the name but that is all."

"There were three brothers but one died and now there are just two, Bernabò and Galeazzo. Bernabò rules in Milan itself and his brother in Pavia. Theirs is an uneasy rule for both want to be the sole ruler. Galeazzo has arranged for his son to marry the daughter of King John of France. Bernabò Visconti wishes to take over Montferrat for a whole myriad of reasons not least the treasury. Montferrat does not have a large army, but you have shown that you are capable of taking on Burgundy and France and defeating them. Amadeus of Savoy presses from one side and the Visconti from the other. What do you say? Is it a commission which you might relish?"

I nodded and then said, "Why speak to me and not to Albert?"

"You are the military leader, Sir John. I will leave one of my servants with you." He smiled, "Francisco is a soldier but, like the others I brought with me, is disguised as a churchman." Now I saw why so many had come with the Cardinal, they were warriors and we had let them in. I was being given my first lesson in Italian politics. "When you have discussed it with your co-leader then let me know. If you cannot then I will have to see if I can persuade the Great Company of Konrad von Landau to fight for Montferrat. They are good but not, I fear, as good as you. And now we must return else they will begin to wonder about two men being at the garderobe for so long."

The name of the man who had stolen from me made my blood run cold. Perhaps there was a chance that fate had given me a chance to have vengeance and retrieve my money.

The heads turned as we entered the room. The soldier was right. I never got to know his name. Francisco just called him Captain Giovanni and I often thought about him. He changed my life and our company. They left in the middle of the afternoon. Francisco seemed to disappear. Albert was both excited and concerned. He was delighted with the payment which, added to the money we had received from the Burgundians made the company even richer but worried for he did not know what I had said to the mysterious priest.

Before I addressed him, I said, "We need Giovanni d'Azzo for this, Albert." His face creased into a frown, and I smiled, "Trust me in this. All will become clear."

With our captains and Giovanni, we sat around the table and I asked Giovanni about the Visconti family. "Vipers!"

I smiled, "That would describe many leaders!"

He shook his head, "No, Sir John, the family crest is a viper swallowing a baby and it describes them completely. They intend to take over the whole of Northern Italy and then, I believe, the rest of the country. They are land-hungry."

"We have been offered a commission to fight for Montferrat against Milan and Savoy. What do you think?"

He drank some wine, "The land does not suit horsemen, Sir John. It is mountainous but our archers could easily control the passes. Bernabò Visconti is no general, but he is cunning." He nodded, "We could do it."

Albert said, "But how much would they pay? I have heard of a commission in Castile. There I know how much we will earn."

"We have until the florins arrive, but my vote is for Montferrat. We had always planned on heading to Italy and I believe that we can do well out of this."

"And if I overrule you?"

My thin smile was a warning to Albert, "Do you really wish me to call an election? I will do so happily, or I can take the English Company and William with me to Italy. As Giovanni has said the land will suit my archers. More are arriving each day, and this might be a good time to dissolve the White Company."

I saw Albert's knuckles, they were white as they gripped the goblet. "There is a compromise, John. We could send Otto with horsemen to Spain and you and I could lead the majority of our company to Montferrat and then if the Italian adventure does not pay as well, we can always go to Spain."

I had won and I decided to be magnanimous, "Then it is agreed, we go to Italy and fight for Montferrat. I will send my message."

I stood and Albert said, "Who with?"

"Did you not know? One of the priests did not leave. I do not doubt that he waits without." Albert must have known that the balance of power shifted at that moment. As soon as Otto led the Germans away, I would call an election. I would have the Company.

I sent William, Giovanni and three other Italians with Francisco. They would carry on to Casale Monferrato and negotiate a price for our work. In the two weeks it took for the

Pope to send the money he had promised, our numbers were swollen by another four archers and ten men at arms. The news of our success had spread. William and Giovanni returned just a day before the papal convoy. Even Albert was pleased with the result. We had a six-month commission, and we would be paid ten thousand florins. Savoy was the priority as its Count, Amadeus was already raiding Montferrat. We would also be able to raid the lands of Milan as well as Savoy and both Albert and I knew that our profits would be increased even further. We learned from Giovanni and Michael that the Visconti family had raided the lands around Asti and Alessandria and we thought to attack the enemy there.

Otto led five hundred Germans and French towards Spain. I was sorry to see Otto go for he was a doughty warrior, but I knew that I was one step closer to taking over the company. We were not escorted by papal soldiers but, as we headed slowly east, there were riders watching us to make certain that we did as we said. It was almost laughable for the nearest army which could hurt us was the French one and that was closer to Paris. We paid for food, grazing and accommodation on our journey. We were not robbed for who would rob the master thieves of the land? Once we hit Savoy, we changed our strategy. We no longer asked for food, we took it. Winter was not far behind us and Amadeus was not expecting us. The count did react, or at least some of his nobles did. We had just crossed one river and were preparing to ride to the next town, just two miles away. We were only sixty miles from Casale Monferrato and nearing the town of Saviliagno when our archer scouts rode in, "My lord, an army bars our path. They have raised the local levy and we counted four thousand men."

My scouts were observant, and I knew I would have answers to my questions which would help me formulate a plan. "Where exactly are they?"

"They are before the river. They have their men at arms and feditore in the centre guarding the bridge. The levy is to the side and they have archers and crossbowmen before them."

"They are not mounted?"

"No, my lord. They also have men on the town walls."

"Which is how far from the men who defend the river?"

"I would say three hundred paces."

"Then we can eliminate those as a threat. Joaquim, sound the horn for the captains to assemble." Michael and Robin rode with me, but the others were spread along the sprawling column. When they arrived, I gave them my assessment and my plan, "The men of Saviliagno await us. They bar our crossing and are prepared for a battle. I do not think that we can surprise them. Joseph, your company will guard the wagons. Robin, divide the archers into two. You will need the pages as horse holders. All the men at arms will be mounted and we need lances. As we do not have surprise on our side, we will use speed. Robin, you will take the archers ahead of my men at arms. Leave a gap of two hundred paces and then shower the enemy with arrows. We will attack on a two hundred pace frontage. Their best troops are in the middle guarding the bridge. We will hit them with our mailed horses."

I knew that there was a slight risk involved as we had not charged on horses very much before but I counted on the fact that they would not be expecting it. My captains merely nodded. The horses had just rested and drunk from the river. We put their mail shaffrons on and took our lances. The archers waited patiently for us. Timing would be all. When we were ready, I said, "Let us ride, Robin. Joseph, keep as close behind us as you can."

"Yes, Sir John."

Robin and the archers soon opened a slight gap. This was farm country and there were few trees. Perhaps that was one reason why the Savoyards had been so prepared. They had seen our movement as we crossed the open land. The fields having no hedges helped us, and I waved us into a one-hundred-man wide line. Michael rode on one side of me and Giovanni on the other. Dai rode behind me with my standard and next to him rode Joaquim who had a horn, but I did not think that we would be needing it. Sir Eoin and my other captains were spread out along the line. I heard the Savoyard horns and that told me that my archers had been seen and were spreading out. I realised as we neared the town that I had not asked about buildings and there were two small farms, each about a hundred paces from the Savoyards. They would be an obstacle, but my organisation meant that my captains would simply negotiate the houses and then reform their men. The thirty of us in the centre would not have that problem.

I saw the arrows of my archers begin to descend. The archers were spreading their missiles along the whole line but when we neared, they would concentrate those arrows on the flanks and leave the men in the centre to be dealt with by my men at arms. We would not have to waste valuable bodkins as the men on the flanks wore little mail. The feditores, the warrior class below man at arms, did wear mail and padded jackets and, aspiring to be men at arms and knights they would be hard to break. We were not yet galloping but I lowered my visor as the first arrows and bolts came our way. The mail hoods, shaffrons, on our horses afforded them protection and our shields deflected the missiles. The Savoyards were obligingly standing close together for mutual protection hoping that the barrier they presented would prevent horses from charging. Their closeness helped my archers for when we were still two hundred paces from the Savoyard line, plunging arrows hit men whose shields were facing our lances. The apparently solid line suddenly had holes appearing along its length and when one hundred paces from them we increased our speed the men replacing those in the front rank were also hit. Our archers ceased their arrow storm when we were fifty paces from the front ranks. I lowered my lance and, although I could not actually see, I knew that the other lances were being lowered.

This was a skill we had practised. Even when we held towns and raided, we found time, once a week, to practise charging with a lance. I rested my lance on my cantle and only pulled it back when we were forty paces from the enemy. Roman was now in his stride and the bolts which had struck his shaffron merely angered him. He would bite and kick when we struck. I chose the most dangerous man before me to strike. He held a long pike. My lance was longer. One advantage I had over almost every other man at arms was that I had been an archer and my right arm was very strong. My lance never wavered and when I punched, the spearhead went through the breastplate and into the chest of the pikeman. As he fell the end of the lance broke leaving me with a shortened lance but one which had not a single point but jagged shards. I saw men at the rear begin to run back across the bridge as the sound of our lances striking metal and men echoed against the town walls. I pulled back and punched the broken lance into the face of the feditore whose kettle helmet did not help him. Clutching his mashed face he fell backwards, and I used the broken lance again to strike the knight who swung his sword ineffectually at Roman's head. The knight had a full helmet, but the lance smashed into it and he tumbled to the ground. And then I was on the bridge. I galloped towards the gates which had opened to allow through some of those who had fled the battle already. I knew there were horses just behind me and that meant our men.

I heard a voice shouting to close the gates, but it was too late, for I hurled my shattered lance and hit the last man who was trying to get through the gates. He fell forward and his body blocked the closing gates. As they tried to pull his body away Roman crashed through them and I drew my sword. I made Roman rear and his flailing hooves smashed one skull and made the others fall back. As Michael, Dai, Karl, and Sir Eoin followed me in so the gatemen were either slain or surrendered. It had been a wild charge, but we now held the gate and the bridge. I raised my visor and I looked, from the gate to the battlefield. Those who could were hurling themselves into the river while the knights, nobles and men at arms threw down their arms to surrender. My men were not a rabble and their surrender was accepted. The feditore were the last to accept their defeat and less than an hour after we had begun our ride, we had taken the town and victory was ours.

Saviliagno was the largest town we had taken in Savoy and had they not defended it then we might have avoided it for the town walls would have cost us men to take. Thanks to their defence we had been forced to take it in a battle which I am sure they now regretted. We stayed for a week. That was partly to await the ransoms we had taken from some of their nobles but also because there was a huge amount of plunder. We left with even more wagons filled with all that we had taken and headed for the home of the Marquis of Montferrat.

Casale Monferrato was a good site to defend for it was on a river and, as we approached, I weighed up what would have to be done by the Savoyards if they were to take it. It was a formidable fortress. By the time Albert and I were riding through the gates I knew that the Count of Savoy, who was a young ruler, would also need to hire a mercenary army if he was to take it. The only other company which might be able to do so was the Great Company. It was then I realised how astute the young Marquis was; by hiring us he had forestalled an attempt by Amadeus to do so. The two leaders were similar in age but the Marquis of Montferrat knew how to win.

The marquis was a young ruler and he had powerful family connections. He was related to the Emperor of the East and had a claim to Mallorca. He was more than happy to accommodate my captains in the city, but we all knew there was not enough accommodation for our men. I sent Michael back to the company to begin erecting a camp. It would only be temporary for Albert and I did not intend to sit and wait for the Savoyards to attack.

He was beaming when he greeted us, "You have bloodied the Savoyards and taken one of their strongholds. Already you have done more than I hoped!"

"We were a little lucky, my lord. I suspect that Count Amadeus will be more cautious, and it will take more than luck to defeat him and make your land safe."

He nodded, "Well, gentlemen, do you have a strategy?"

Albert deferred to me, "We have, my lord. Chieri is a rich town. Whilst it has a wall, and it would be foolish to attack it, we could raid and ravage the land around it."

"That would provoke the Savoyards!"

"My lord it worked for Prince Edward of England. We will raid the lands around Chieri and Torino for they are less than ten miles apart. Our aim is to make Amadeus try to force us back here."

"You think you can beat him?"

"If we thought we would lose then we would come up with another strategy."

"Why do you need a battle?"

"Because your other enemies, the Visconti, are more of a threat. If we can defeat Savoy, then the Milanese will think twice about attacking."

We had devised this plan while heading east. Although most of it was mine the choice of Chieri had been Giovanni's. My men had stayed there on their way back from their meeting with the Marquis and Michael had agreed with the suggestion. Even in winter the land thereabouts was busy and looked ripe for plunder.

The young marquis was delighted with the soundness of the plan, "And at the end of the six months we can, perhaps, renegotiate a new contract."

Although we both smiled and nodded, we knew that such a contract would depend upon any other offers of work. We were now in Italy where there were many city-states that would happily pay for our services. So long as gold continued to roll in, we would serve Montferrat.

Chapter 20

Italy 1361

I summoned my archer captains. We had been given a large house whose owner had defected to Milan. The marquis suffered no dissension in his lands. The land was extensive but unsuitable for farming and was largely run down. That did not bother us. Once my men had joined me and with Michael and Dai in attendance, I outlined my plan. "We need Chieri and Torino to be thoroughly scouted out. I need to know where all the roads are and where are the places we can both block and ambush. I want somewhere we can fight the Savoyards. Robin, I need you to use all your expertise to enable us to find out where they will come when they do try to rid the land of us." He nodded and I knew it would be done. "The rest of us will repair the house and prepare for a war." Albert just stood and allowed me to give orders.

The scouts took just three days to find all that we needed to know. "When they come it will be from the north-west. It is the shortest route, but they have to pass over a small range of mountains and through woods. There is a place which would block them, Reaglie, and we would be able to fill the forests with archers and you and the men at arms could hold them. The Savoyards would only have a one hundred and fifty pace frontage. It is also close to Torino and means we would be fighting in Savoy."

"And if they chose not to come that way and picked a route which would allow them to bring superior numbers to bear?"

"Then it would be from the west. It would be a longer way for them to come and there would still be places to ambush them for the roads around here twist and turn through rocky passes. It is just that the second route has fewer trees." He smiled, "Either way we would hold the advantage."

"Good, then tomorrow we twist the nose of the Count of Savoy and see how long he endures it before he tries to swat us away."

We used the five-column strategy we had employed in France. It had seemed to work there. I led one, Albert a second, Michael a third, Robin the fourth and Karl the fifth. The choice of Karl was mine and it was to try to win over his vote and that of the Germans he led. Each column had archers for we had almost four hundred of them. The pages went as horse holders and the men at arms were distributed evenly too. The raids in Champagne and Burgundy had honed my men's skills so that we were able to cover large areas, taking all that there was to take and without losing a man. On the first day, I rode with my column to Pino Torinese. It was the closest town of any size to Torino and as such had the greatest risk. Once more I was trying to win votes. Albert chose an easy target not far from Casale Monferrato; men liked to follow strong leaders.

The settlement I raided was a cross between a large village and a small town. It was on a high piece of ground and the town wall was an illusion. A horseman could leap it. Ned led my archers to cut off the town from Torino and then we swept in. We would collect the animals in the fields later. Our first task was to take armed men and find treasure. The more men we could eliminate the fewer we would have to face when the Count of Savoy came to do battle. Saviliagno had been a shock to him and he would, I knew, want to bring enough men to rid his land of us. The Savoyards defended their walls, gates and fields but when horsemen leap over your walls there is little that you can do. Once we had opened the gates then we disarmed those who still remained armed and began to take all that we could. There was new season wine as well as wheat and rye flour. We dug in their kitchens to find the treasure. The rich men of the town had their homes almost emptied. By the time Ned and the archers joined us we had finished, and we started to collect the animals and drive them back to our camp. We had lost none, and the Savoyards had suffered fewer than twenty casualties. However, they were now weaponless and had seen how futile their small walls were.

That evening I met with the other captains and Albert to share what we had learned. As we had expected, the first day would be our easiest for they were not expecting us. From now on it would become harder. My second raid was on Pecetto Torinese and although it was just a few miles from our first raid as well as being close to Torino it was not particularly well guarded. However, it brought us our first serious confrontation with the count's horsemen. Ned had ensured that we were not disturbed as we raided but he had, when he brought his men back, left four men on watch. It was they who reported the arrival of a column of light horsemen made up of feditore and men at arms. Later we deduced that they were just a patrol looking for us. That they discovered us proved a mistake… for them.

The archers hurried back and shouted a warning. We had the walls and the gates. Leaving the gates open I joined my archers on the walls. Dai and Giovanni waited with a dozen men at arms just inside the gates. The twenty men galloped down the road and I could see that they were prepared for war. The eight men at arms had helmets with visors and all twenty of them carried lances or spears. Ned commanded the archers and I stayed on the walls so that I could see the mettle of the opposition. The villagers and armed men we had seen were hardly representative of the armies we might face. The spurs on the leading horseman told me that he was a knight. He carried no banner, but his orange and white diagonal stripes were distinctive. I wore no helmet. I saved that for battles, and I preferred to have an open view. They did not slow as they neared us, they rode towards the gates. Ned's command and the sound of the forty arrows were almost simultaneous. Half of the saddles were emptied. The knight either bore a charmed life or he had very good plate for he survived the first shower. Three of the feditore towards the rear were quick-thinking enough to wheel their horses and flee. The horse of one of them was rewarded with an arrow to the rump from the next flight. The knight was the only other to survive. He, too, wheeled his horse. One arrow struck his cantle and a second penetrated his back plate, but the man showed courage and skill as he retained his seat. His lance and shield lay with the dead men he had led. The arrow would be clear evidence for the Count of Savoy. Only English archers had such skill and that meant the company he faced was The White Company.

We had horses, weapons, and plate as well as food, animals and coins. I made the decision not to raid the next day. This was for a number of reasons. I did not want to overtire the horses nor the men but more importantly, I wanted the Savoyards to be uncertain about our next move. The marquis was delighted with our success. The animals and the food went to his people and he saw our pay as money well spent. His citizens were not being raided and prevented from working. If we had not been there, then in a few weeks' time they would be. We had raided earlier than was usual and we had caught the enemy unawares.

The next few days we raided but the Savoyards refused to react. We had increased our raids so that we had twenty-five miles of Savoyard land under our control and we had raided beyond that. Pino Torinese was still the furthest we had raided, and I had the germ of an idea fermenting in my mind as I rode back to Casale Monferrato. I gathered my men and put it to them. "I would threaten Torino itself."

As I had expected I had opposition from the cautious Albert. He still called himself the Captain of the White Company, but all knew that it was I who made the military decisions.

"Why? We are doing what the Marquis wishes and keeping the Savoyards under pressure."

"And what of Milan? You have seen the army of Montferrat. They are popinjays, finely dressed but not an army for war. While we are in the west what is to stop the Visconti from attacking in the east? Casale Monferrato is as close to Milan as Torino is to us. The count is proving to be too cautious. Robin identified the place we ought to fight them. The difference is that this will not be an ambush. Other than that it is perfect. What have we to lose?"

It was Albert I was convincing. My English captains, not to mention Karl and Giovanni all trusted and believed in me. They had been with me in Champagne and Burgundy and knew that I could win.

"Let us raid some more, John, eh?"

I shook my head, "No, Albert, the day after tomorrow we ride to Torino and attack the bridge. We will use men on rafts which we shall build tomorrow at the river side. Our company will be arrayed close to the bridge and use the trees and slopes for cover. If the Savoyards let us alone then I will ride and demand tribute from them. At the very least we will have a profit."

Giovanni smiled, "But you think that they will give battle."

"The Count is young and there will be Savoyard soldiers who think they can deal with a mercenary who has no honour and merely robs churches and steals coins from ordinary citizens." I was quoting what I knew others had said of me. It did not bother me. "Come, Albert, if I fail then you can make all the military decisions from now on."

That was the argument which convinced him for he thought I would lose face and no longer be a threat to him.

I chose my men for the rafts carefully. I used the best men from Peter's company of archers. They were all young and quick thinking. The day before I rode with them myself and ten men at arms and we hewed trees upstream from the bridge. I wanted just two rafts. The men who would go with Peter were all good swimmers, but I planned on being close myself with their mounts. It was late afternoon when we had finished the rafts. We had brought dry kindling and oil with us. The oil had been taken on the raids. After hiding the rafts my men at arms led the archers' horses back with us. They would camp close by the river. We had chosen the most deserted stretch of water we could find.

As we rode back Dai asked me about his promotion, "Sir John, am I ready to lead a lance?"

I smiled, "I suppose that the fact you ask would mean that you do not think so, but I do not believe that you are as confident as I was at your age. I would have demanded to be promoted. When the next archer joins us and a spearman who wishes to be a squire then you shall be a lance and serve in Captain Michael's company."

He nodded, "Then I am content, Sir John."

It was dark by the time we reached our temporary home. I had ridden Mary to the river, but it would be Roman I would take to what I hoped would be a battle. I slept barely three hours for we had an early start planned. We left Casale Monferrato in the middle of the night as the first prayers were being said in the church there. The Marquis asked to come with us. He was our paymaster and I saw no reason why he should not but, as we passed through his gates, I said, "Marquis, I know that you pay us, but you are paying us to be soldiers who fight for you. You must trust our judgement. Our men will not obey your command!"

"I know." He looked over his shoulder. Albert rode with his Germans, "The same might be said for Captain Albert. This is your plan is it not?" I nodded. "Yet you do not lead The White Company."

"Albert is older, and we joined him. I am content and there are no arguments between us." It was a neutral answer which belied my plans. We passed through Pino Torinese and I said, "You will wait with the main army, my lord, hidden by the trees when I ride down to my archers."

"Of course."

We had, of course, scouted out where we would face the Savoyards. The trees were less than two miles from the bridge. The army would wait there until the bridge was fired. It did not matter if the fire failed to destroy the bridge. I did not expect that as an outcome. I wanted them to fear that we could destroy it. I had with me a trumpeter and he would give the signal to Albert and the army. When they heard it, they would move to within half a mile of the bridge. We would have plenty of time for if the Savoyards chose to give battle it would take some time to prepare their army and cross the bridge. I did not expect a battle any time soon.

Dawn was breaking when we neared the bridge. Like all such important crossings, it was guarded. The twenty men I led had the archers' horses and they tied them to the lower branches of trees just four hundred paces from the bridge. Then, still mounted, we edged our way not down the road but through the trees. The light of the new sun would be in the eyes of the sentries, but I counted on the fact that a fire would grab their attention quicker! We waited in the eaves of the wood and behind a dwelling of some type. I could hear movements in the house and then I smelled smoke. It was not coming from the house but the river. When I heard shouts then I knew that the archers had been seen.

"Now, Hawkwood!" I spurred Roman who leapt towards the road. His hooves found purchase and I galloped towards the surprised sentries. They were torn between looking down at the river and the rafts and the horses and mailed men who rode at

them. I saw one begin to load a crossbow and I rode at him.
Roman was a warhorse and, snapping and snorting, he went for
the man. As the crossbow came up my sword slashed down and
split his skull. My men at arms were amongst the sentries and it
was like a pack of wolves in a sheepfold. Those that could, fled,
and my archers scrambled up the bank.

"Keep moving! Your horses are tied to the trees!"

We chased the men across the bridge and then, hearing the
horns from inside, I ordered my men to fall back. It was not a
moment too soon and I felt a bolt strike my backplate. Once
across the bridge, I reined in. Although the bridge had stone
anchoring it to the riverbed, there was wood in the supports for
the road. The Savoyards were not going to allow us to destroy
their bridge and horsemen raced from the gate in the city wall. If
they expected us to flee then they were in for a shock and we met
them where the bridge met the road. I unhorsed one rider who
tumbled backwards into the river. I saw John of Stroud speared
in the side and I shouted, "Fall back! Ned!"

As we headed down the road the arrows from Ned's men fell
amongst those pursuing us and they halted. I heard an order
shouted. I guessed it was for crossbows. We waited until Ned
and his men had mounted and then headed up the road. I heard
hastily sent bolts striking the foliage, trees and even one back
plate but there were no shouts.

"Sound the horn three times."

The signal having been given, my men would be forming
their battle lines. William of Ely was at the rear and it was he
kept glancing under his arm to see the pursuit. He called out his
observations. "They are two hundred paces back, my lord."

That was too close, and I spurred Roman so that we would
extend our lead. The road rose from the river and it would sap
energy from our horses' legs. In our case that would not be a
problem as we would be standing to await the Savoyard attack if
it materialised. The Company was still forming its lines when we
drew near. The men at arms sat on their horses and they filled the
road and open ground on either side. I saw archers hurrying into
the woods. Ned took his archers off the road and headed to his
appointed place on the left flank. I led my men to fill the gap left
by Albert in the centre. I saw the marquis and his bodyguard

with the horses. He was mounted and plated but there was no helmet. It was as though he was watching a tourney held on his behalf. He waved at me as I stopped. Waving back I reined in and patted Roman, "Well done!"

Albert asked, "And?"

I pointed down the road. The smoke spiralled up, "The bridge has been set afire. They will douse it, but they pursued us."

The two hundred or so men who had ridden after us, had come into view and they had stopped. Albert nodded, "Now we see if they do that which you intend."

"Joseph and ten archers are at the other bridge that they can use to cross the river. If they do not come here to attack us and try to outflank us, we will have a warning."

"And if they do not attack at all?" The half-smile on his face told me that he hoped that would be the case and then there would be no challenge to his authority.

"Then, in two days' time, I will ride to the city and demand tribute."

He laughed, "The Count of Savoy may be young, but he is not a fool. He will not agree."

"He may be young but if you look down the road at the men who observe us you will see spurs and greybeards. They are not young, and they will be looking up the road. All that you can see, from their position, is our front ranks. They may think we have a vast army. Remember, Albert, when we raided, they only saw a fifth of our forces at each place. They will have exaggerated the numbers when they sent to the count. He will want true numbers. They may not attack today, in fact, I will be surprised if they do but tonight he will send scouts to count our campfires and tomorrow will be a truer test."

The horsemen stayed for an hour while they tried to count us and then turned and headed back down the road. I dismounted and shouted, "Make camp! Captains to me!"

Albert dismounted and said, "I should be the one to give the commands!"

Without looking at him I said, "Then command! I do not wait." I waved over one of the pages who eagerly took Roman. Taking a coin from my purse I said, "Walk him to water, slowly, let him drink and then, when you have taken his saddle, groom him and give him a blanket. Then you can let him graze. He is my horse and deserves the best grazing. Alright, Jean?"

I think the boy was shocked that I knew his name. He nodded and said, "I will take good care of him, Sir John, and you need not pay me."

I nodded, "I know but I do so because I want to! Now go and I will not need him until tomorrow. Sleep close by him this night and watch him for me."

The marquis and his bodyguard had come to join us. He looked disappointed, "Has your plan failed, Sir John?"

His doubt was more understandable than Albert's. "Not yet, my lord, but, in any case, the plan is flexible enough to deal with anything Count Amadeus comes up with. I am just sorry that you will have a night sleeping rough."

It was as though he suddenly realised there was neither a tent nor a building for his bed. "Oh!" His bodyguards also looked as though they had no idea what to do.

"Peter of Poole!"

My man at arms and his son, now almost ready to be a man at arms, hurried over, "Would you and your pages show the marquis how to improvise a hovel?"

Peter grinned, "Aye, my lord!"

We had brought no tents and the men had made hovels. The advantage of having just a handful of noble-born men at arms was that they all knew how to rough it. The marquis was the exception, and he did not look happy. He was already regretting his decision to accompany us. War was not all about victory and triumph! The archers scoured the woods to hunt game and birds of any type and soon the air was filled with the smell of pots simmering with all manner of beasts and birds.

Albert did not let me out of his sight and when the captains arrived, he stood at my shoulder as I gave them instructions. It was disconcerting but I allowed it. "Have one in twenty of your men sleep today for tonight I want them in the woods lower down the slope. Choose the best killers you have for I want the Savoyard scouts dead. The more uncertainty in their minds then the more certain am I of victory." Even Albert's German captains were happy with my reasoning and they nodded and returned to their camps. I turned to look at Albert.

He shook his head, "You are too confident, John, and one day you will overreach yourself."

"Perhaps but it will not be this day!"

I slept in the late afternoon and that night, to the great surprise of some of the other sentries, I headed down to the woods. I wore no spurs and my coif hung around my shoulders. I had my cloak, and its cowl hid my face. I descended to within four hundred paces from the bridge which was now guarded. The Savoyards had doused the fire and there were forty or more men camped there with a pair of braziers ruining their night vision. I looked to my left and right and saw, on one side, a man at arms, a shadow forty paces from my right and, on the other side of the road an almost invisible archer. I nodded at both. I leaned with my back to a tree and the river. I slid down so that I was seated on the ground and I listened. This would need patience and listening skills. I had both. The men at the bridge were speaking to each other but at that distance, it was a murmur. Time passed and the murmur died. It was then I heard the footsteps on the bridge. Men were marching along it. That told me the Savoyards were not using those who knew the woods to do their scouting but warriors. I slowly rose and looked to my right. The man at arms was sitting with his back to a tree. He had heard nothing, and I picked up a pinecone and threw it at him. It struck his cheek and he turned, angrily. He saw me and I pointed to the bridge. He nodded and stood. The archer nodded when I turned to look at him.

I drew, not my sword but my long-bladed dagger. Ensuring that the cowl was over my face I peered around the tree. I saw shadows moving from the bridge. The shadows were silhouetted by the light from the braziers and could be seen as men. The warriors who were heading into the woods would take some moments to accustom their eyes to the darkness. My men and I had been in the woods for hours. I estimated that there were twenty men. Whoever sent them would assume that we had sentries and expect some men to fail to return. Whatever numbers they managed to count would be a very rough estimate. They would assume ten men to a campfire. We had lit more fires to confuse them. I heard the man who was heading along the edge of the wood. As I had discovered when we had taken up our position, there was a great deal of debris on the ground. They were wisely ignoring the open ground and the road. I guessed they assumed we would be watching there. I was able to gauge his progress from the sounds he made but when he was forty paces from me, I saw his shadow moving. I did not move and knew that I would look like part of the tree.

I knew how to kill and kill quietly but I could not count on all my men having the same level of skill. As the shadow approached, I saw that it was a feditore. They were the warriors who aspired to be knights and men at arms. They wore a mail hauberk and normally had a kettle helm. This one had no helmet and I saw that he had his coif around his shoulders. He was listening. I also saw that he was looking where he placed his feet. All the Savoyard scouts would be working on the assumption that our sentries were much higher up the slope. The wind was coming from the river and I could smell the wine on his breath. He had fortified himself for the task. It would take my smell up the slope. Putting my back to the tree and facing up the slope I let the man pass me. I had been an archer and my left arm was as powerful as most men's right. I stepped forward, grabbed his head, and pulled back, exposing the man's throat. I dragged the razor-sharp blade across it and gave him a quick and merciful death. I was glad I was not wearing my white jupon for there was a great deal of blood. I lowered his body to the ground.

I heard a scuffle from my right and then silence. I saw the man at arms lower the body of another scout to the ground. Had there been a greater noise then he would have had to endure my wrath. I glanced down the slope and saw no more shadows moving up to our camp. That meant all the Savoyard scouts were committed and were in the woods somewhere. I had chosen my position with care for I would stay watching until dawn. Any scouts who evaded observation and attempted to return to the city would have to cross the bridge and I wanted Count Amadeus blind!

The cry, when it came, was from my left and appeared to be at the edge of my line of watchers. That brought a reaction. I looked down the road and saw that the men at the bridge had heard it and they had armed themselves. The sound of steel on steel could be heard and then I heard the sound of feet running back to the river. I counted just three scouts who made it. The men at the bridge stood to. I whistled and the archer turned. I mimed for him to check on our sentries. He disappeared. The man at arms was looking at me and I mimed for him to do the same.

It was the man at arms who returned first. He came close to me, "All of those who tried to pass are dead, Sir John."

"Take my place here while I speak with the ones on the other side of the road." I slipped across the road. The bridge sentries would see a moving shadow, but it mattered not, they now knew where we were.

I reached the archer as he was returning. "Johann is dead, but the rest of the Savoyard scouts were slain."

"Take his body back to the camp. Have the rest of the sentries move up the slope. I want them on the edge of our camp."

I returned to the man at arms and gave him the same instructions. I waited until I was alone and then I moved back up the slope. We had hurt them and when dawn broke no more scouts had come. They did not know our numbers.

Chapter 21

Dawn came and we saw no further scouts. I went directly to bed having left Dai with orders to wake me at the first sign of movement. Our mounted scouts half a mile from our camp would deter any enemy. I was woken at noon although, to be honest, the noise of movement had begun to stir me before then.

"Sir John, the Savoyards are coming. They sent some scouts about an hour since."

"Why did you not wake me then?"

"Albert said that you needed your sleep and besides, they did not progress beyond the line of mounted scouts."

"Next time obey my orders and not Albert's. And their army follows?"

He grinned, "Aye, Albert had the men stand to and we watched their ponderous approach. The men at arms are all mounted."

Michael approached. His armour was burnished so that it glinted in the bright sun. It was not just our jupons and surcoats that marked us as The White Company, our plate looked white too! "They will not be able to form their battle lines for an hour, Sir John."

"Good, then I have time to bathe, eat, drink and dress. Come Dai, today you shall be my squire."

The marquis, looking more dishevelled than I had seen him came over with his bodyguards. "I see, Sir John, why your men see you as their leader. You fought in the woods last night?" I nodded. "Why? Surely you can command."

I said, "Firstly, my lord, I trust my own eyes better than any and a leader who is not willing to do as his men do is no leader. My men know that I do not ask them to do anything that I would not do!"

"I can see that!"

"And now, my lord, I must prepare for battle. Count Amadeus and his men will be given a taste of English bowmen this day!"

It proved to be more than an hour before the Savoyard army was ready. By that time I was totally refreshed and wearing a new surcoat, for we would be fighting afoot, I rode Roman to join the others who were also mounted. I waved a vague greeting and then peered at the Savoyards who were more than three quarters of a mile from us and moving closer albeit slowly. It was far enough so that they could resist a charge by our horsemen and wide enough for them to array their men. On their flanks, they had spearmen, archers and crossbows. They had few archers. I estimated that there were almost four thousand of them, two thousand on each flank. In the centre, they had their knights, men at arms and feditore. There were two thousand of them and they were all mounted with lances. The pits that had been dug in the night and in the morning by my men were disguised by sods of earth placed on piles of twigs. To a less than vigilant eye, the ground would appear flat, but a horse would break the twigs and make its rider tumble. We had no intention of risking our horses in a cavalry battle.

I turned to Joaquim who had the horn. "Sound it twice!"

The signal would confuse the Savoyards. They thought we intended to attack, and their own horns were sounded. Shields were pulled up and some of their crossbowmen and archers wasted missiles. The signal was for the pages to take our horses. Jean ran to me carrying my favourite poleaxe. I nodded to him, "Roman was well-groomed, Jean, I have high hopes that one day, you will make a horseman." He grew a foot at the praise and proudly led away my warhorse.

We stood in three lines with the third one made up of archers. It was thinner than I would have liked, and I hoped that the slope would aid us. The Savoyards would be looking for my archers. More than two-thirds were hidden in the woods on the flanks and it was they who would do the serious damage. Knowing we had archers in front of them, the Savoyard horsemen would use their shields as well as good plate and mailed horses to minimize casualties. The ones on the flanks would have softer targets. The archers behind our two lines of men at arms would use their arrows on the flanks which were less well protected. The sudden dismounting manoeuvre appeared to throw the Savoyard plans into disarray and instead of attacking while we were forming lines they debated what to do. Their horses were becoming restless and even just standing there they were tiring. They had walked up a steep hill and had not been watered. They had been ridden and not led. We waited patiently. Our front two ranks all held pole weapons. One in two of the men in the second rank held a long fourteen-foot spear so that there was almost a double line of blades facing the enemy. I doubted that the Savoyards had fought in many such battles and there was an assumption that heavily armoured men on mailed horses would simply sweep over a dismounted enemy. The reality was that horses would try to avoid running into an obstacle and they were too heavy to be able to jump.

The order was finally given and the two wings advanced. The Savoyard commander, whoever he was, wanted his missile men to be able to weaken us. Having been there for two days my archers knew the range well and as the crossbowmen knelt and archers who were inferior to English longbowmen drew their bows, my archers sent their arrows first. The flank archers commanded by Robin and Martin did not loose and the relatively few arrows sent to decimate their crossbows and bows must have encouraged the Savoyards. They came on. The bolts and missiles they sent were blocked by the shields of those of us in the front rank. Soon there were no missiles coming our way and the horns sounded to initiate the Savoyard attack. The horsemen had four hundred paces to travel and their commander tried to keep a straight line. He had planned on timing all three elements to strike at the same time and it was a good plan. I swung my shield around my back and held my poleaxe with its butt in the soft earth.

The pits were in the centre, about two hundred paces from our front line. The archers in the flanks were three hundred paces from the horsemen which meant that we would have to fight hard in the centre where our arrows would have less effect. Our job was to hold. I knew it was one reason Albert was unhappy. He did not like being in the front rank and preferred to direct the battle from the rear. My presence meant he had no choice in the matter. The horses hit the pits just as the flank archers struck and the ones behind us switched their aim to the mounted men. Some of the men on the flanks fell into the pits and that caused confusion. When horses hit the pits then legs were broken, or horses tumbled, and a mailed horse is both heavy and a substantial obstacle. A rider flying from its back is lucky to avoid injury. Along with the arrows it was as though we had pulled up a tripwire. Horses and men screamed. Our archers could loose five arrows in an incredibly short time and we had plenty of arrows. Here we had no problem sourcing bodkin arrows and even when they did not kill they caused injuries and loosing from the flanks meant horses were wounded for it was their heads and necks which had the most protection. A thick caparison was useful, but a bodkin would slice right into it. The pits stopped just forty paces from us, but they had done their job and broken up the line.

"Brace!"

I jammed my foot against the haft of the poleaxe. On one side of me was a fourteen-foot spear and on the other a pike. Had there been more than one horse coming at me then I might have been injured but the knight with the green and white stripes was alone; his companions had fallen. I saw two arrows in his shield and one in his cantle. He had been lucky, but that luck was about to end. He pulled back his arm to spear me with his lance. I was gambling on my quick reactions rather than a shield to prevent injury. I had both hands on my poleaxe and the axe head could easily deflect a lance that wavered up and down as well as side to side. In the end, it did not come to that. The spear made the warhorse jink to the side and the lance went between Giovanni and me. I saw the side of the head of the horse and I swung the hammer head into its skull. Even the mail shaffron it wore could not save it and I think the animal died instantly. As it was already turning away from the spear it fell, not into us, which would have been disastrous but across the path of a second knight. The rider of the first horse fell backwards and his horse landed on him.

The two flank attacks had now struck and both front lines were engaged. The Savoyards outnumbered us, but it was then that Robin and Martin launched their own attacks. They left the forest to send arrows at close range to drive through even good plate. I picked up my poleaxe and stepping forward shouted, "Charge!" It sounded like madness for we were outnumbered but the Savoyard horses had all stopped. That was partly a lack of water and tiredness, but it was also the fact that there was a wall of dead, dying and badly injured horses before them. They could not move. A lance is of most use when a man at arms is charging. When their knights and men at arms tried to stab us with them there was no power while our pole weapons were deadly. I hacked through the leg of one knight. It was as though the plate was not even there. As a second man at arms struck my chest with his lance, I swung the head of the hammer to smash his kneecap to a pulp. It was the same all the way along the line and when I heard the Savoyard horn sound I was not surprised. They were falling back! The horsemen tried to disengage first, but my archers had almost closed the gap and they would have to fight their way through archers whose bodkin arrows could not fail to kill at such short range. I saw some knights surrender rather than risk certain death. The men on the flanks tried to take to the woods and on the two sides, it became a confused mêlée. In such a fight it was my men, the professionals, who would emerge victorious.

"Joaquim, sound 'Horses'!"

As the strident notes echoed, I knew that the pages would be rushing to see who could fetch their horses the quickest. Jean was fast and I was almost the first to be on the back of my horse. Many have questioned why we all wore white and seemed to ignore the fact that it was my livery but now there was an even more important reason. I discarded my poleaxe, swung my shield around and drew my sword. Like the rest of my horsemen, we all wore white. My archers knew that any man they saw not in white was an enemy. We would suffer no accidental casualties.

"Charge!"

It was not really a charge for we were not together, but my men all followed me down the road to pursue those who had escaped my archers. Our horses were fresh and had been watered and fed. The Savoyards were tired and thirsty. We began to catch them. I killed few but preferred to smack them on the side of the head with the flat of my sword. Knocked to the ground many were injured but all would be taken by Robin and our archers who were following behind. It did not matter that they did not surrender to Sir John Hawkwood. We were The White Company, and we shared our profits! There were a hundred knights ahead of me when we reached the bridge and I had with me, Michael, Sir Eoin, Giovanni, Harry, and Karl. A better set of knights I had yet to meet and as the Savoyards galloped through the gates of Torino, we simply followed before they could be closed.

"Secure the gates!" I did not mind if they made their castle and defended it against us. If we held their town then we had won! It was a short and bloody encounter at the gates. The Savoyards there knew what it meant if we held them, but it was boys against men. Had they had plate or even mail it might have been a more even contest but bravely though they fought we killed them, and it was our archers who reached them before their men on foot. They surrendered and we disarmed them. By the time darkness fell we had the city, and I did not mind that many had fled into the imposing fortress. We ate well and we all had beds for the night.

The Marquis beamed when he joined us, "You were right Sir John and this is a great victory!"

"When the Count surrenders on the morrow then it will be a great victory, my lord!"

Albert was good at this sort of organisation and he assigned men to watch our camp and to guard the walls. A third group guarded the disconsolate prisoners. I smiled at the discomfort of the knights and nobles who had to endure the same conditions as the ordinary soldiery. Even our pages had to stand a watch.

The next morning I rode with Albert and the marquis to speak to the count. The streets through which we passed were deserted. Any of the citizens who had not fled into the fortress hid in their houses. It did not bother us.

Albert spoke for us but the presence of the marquis was important, "Count Amadeus, we have your town, and we have many prisoners. We have no wish to cause you further harm. For ten thousand florins we will return your men and leave your land."

"That is all?"

I spoke, "Not quite, all. You will also swear that you will not attack Montferrat." I gestured towards the marquis. "The consequence of that would be a return of The White Company."

He was a young man. I guessed it was only a year or so since he had begun shaving and if the truth were told a cat could lick his whiskers off, but he was a leader. I saw him speak to a churchman and what looked like the mayor then he spoke. "And if I agree to your terms?"

Albert smiled his silky smile, "Then we shall leave, Count Amadeus."

"It will take time to gather the money."

I said, "If you will have your Bishop fetch a Bible then a simple oath will suffice for now. I know you do not wish us to return."

A Bible was fetched, and he swore the oath. We headed back to Montferrat.

Albert preened as he rode on his white charger riding behind a triumphant marquis and his bodyguards at the head of our column of men. Although they had done nothing to achieve the victory, I was happy to let them ride as though they had. I had different aims!

The Marquis threw a huge banquet for my captains and Albert and I flanked him. He was effusive in his praise. He said, "I would not have believed you could have so complete a victory and lose so few men."

"And," I added, "you have his sworn word that he will not attack you again. Unless, of course, you attack him!"

He shook his head, "We are not warlike and that is why we hire men such as yourselves."

The tribute arrived a week later. We had taken arms, armour and horses and I knew that if we stayed in Italy then we would need to buy somewhere which we could use as a base. When the marquis heard what we needed he immediately offered us a large manor close to the Milanese border. It was far better than the run down one we had lived in before and could be made into a stronghold. He gave it to us for he asked us to extend our contract to a year. I was happy although Albert was suspicious. I took it for what it was, a way of protecting his land for longer and encouraging us to stay after the contract was over. It was not as close to a large town as we had enjoyed at Bordeaux, but we had plenty of space and my captains all had the kind of accommodation they deserved.

We were halfway through the contract when we were visited by Luchino Novello, Visconti of Genoa, the son of Galeazzo

Visconti. Our victory over Savoy had made the Milanese think twice about attacking the relatively weak Montferrat. We had made no secret of our presence and our home was just a couple of hours from the Milanese border, another reason why the Marquis had been so generous.

Luchino was an arrogant young man. He arrived with all the trappings of a rich young noble and was escorted by nine men who were dressed equally finely. The tenth looked like a real soldier. Albert was impressed and fawned all over him. The hall in the house we had been given was not huge and there would not be enough room for all of us. I took the decision to make it a small meeting. "My lord, our hall is small. If your men would go with ours, they will be given wine and food."

I nodded to Robin who took my meaning immediately, "Aye, lord! My good fellows, come with us. We have some fine Savoyard wine you might enjoy!"

I could see that neither the Genoese lord nor his men were happy about going with Robin whose Italian was as rough and ready as the clothes he wore but he nodded and his men obeyed. The Milanese lord followed a frowning Albert along with the single older warrior from his entourage. We did not employ servants, we used our pages. We had found more orphaned boys in Casale Monferrato and four of them had come with us. They fetched wine and food.

Albert continued to simper before the Milanese lord, "My lord, how may we be of service to you?"

Before Luchino could answer I stated the obvious, "For we are contracted to the Marquis of Montferrat and we have taken his gold."

Both Luchino and Albert frowned at my words. The young Visconti turned his attention from me back to Albert, "Lord Sterz, we would employ you and your company to help us to take Pavia. The matter is urgent, and we cannot wait for your contract to finish. You will be paid well."

I saw from Albert's face that he had decided to accept. I knew that he admired the Visconti family and saw them as the most powerful clan in the land. He had often said that if we were to work for them, we would be guaranteed a richer life. It was one reason we had not acted aggressively towards the Visconti. I allowed him to dig his own grave.

"My lord, I am sure that we can come to some agreement with the Marquis of Montferrat. What is the price you are willing to pay to hire the finest company in the land?"

The Visconti lord smiled, "The figure may seem paltry, just five thousand florins but that would be for a month-long contract and Pavia has many rich men who would pay a healthy ransom. At the end of the month, we would renegotiate the contract with more favourable terms."

I smiled and the two men thought that the smile emanated from my tacit agreement. They were wrong. I now saw this plan for what it was. The Visconti were offering us a tiny sum to draw us from Montferrat so that they could then swoop in while it was undefended and take it all almost bloodlessly. Once they knew that we were coming to the aid of Montferrat they had sent a member of their family who was from Genoa to throw us off the scent. We had heard that the Visconti wished to take the city-state of Pavia, which was one of the smaller, although richer, city-states in northern Italy.

"So we are agreed?"

"No, my lord, we are not!" I turned to Albert, "Come, Albert, we must speak alone." I stood, "My lord, enjoy the wine we will not be long."

Albert was not happy but as I swept from the room, he had little option but to follow me. I carried on out of the house and into the open. I waved away the men who were practising there and turned to face an angry Albert.

"What do you mean by this? I am the leader, and we can take the money we were given by the Marquis and make ten times the amount from Pavia!"

I kept my voice calm, "Albert, we are successful because of a number of things. One of them is that we keep our word. When we were in Champagne, we kept the land safe and we were trusted. If we begin to break contracts, then we will not be trusted. Can you not see that this is a ploy so that Bernabò Visconti can take Montferrat?"

He shrugged, "He is a bigger fish and Montferrat will fall sooner or later or do you envisage staying here forever?"

"No, and at the end of the contract I would suggest we head deeper into Italy and find another paymaster, but the Visconti are cheap. Five thousand florins is an insult."

"Nonetheless I am the leader of The White Company and we will fight for the Visconti."

That was the moment I decided to take over. I had bided my time and left it too long, but things had come to a head. I meant what I had said, we could not break contracts! Albert turned on his heel and went back into the hall.

I closed the door behind us.

Albert said, "I am sorry about that, my lord. We are agreed and The White Company will accept the contract."

"Good I…"

I had not sat down nor moved from the door. I said, "No, Lord Luchino, we will not. Albert here will no longer be leading all of the company." The three of them stared at me although the older warrior just looked curious rather than angry. "Lord Luchino, the success and reputation of the company are based on a number of things. We keep to contracts, we have discipline, but the most important reason is that we have mounted archers and they are all English. And, my lord, they are all loyal to me. You may employ The White Company, but it will not have its most potent part. The archers and the English elements will be here and we will fulfil the contract we signed."

I strode from the room and went to the yard. Dai and Michael were practising. Robin was entertaining the Italians. I waved over Michael and Dai. "Gather every man. Robin is entertaining the Italians and I need him too."

Michael looked worried, "What is amiss, Sir John?"

"We need a vote. Albert intends to break our contract here and I would extend it." They nodded and hurried off.

One of the reasons we liked the gifted lands given to us by the Marquis was the fact that there was a huge paddock. The owner had enjoyed hosting tourneys. It was a place where we could practise our manoeuvres. It was also a place I could address a large number of men. I waved over Henry and Stephen, they were drilling some of the pages who were progressing to the next level, spearmen. Martin was already training the ones who might become archers.

"Have a wagon brought into the practice ring. I need to speak with the men!"

I strode alone to the centre of the ring. William must have been told by Michael what I intended for he came running from his office. "What is going on, Sir John? It is as though an ant's nest has been disturbed."

"Walk with me and I will tell you." By the time the wagon was fetched and the men began to assemble, I had given him all the facts. "So, William, you are the bookkeeper, what do you say?"

He smiled, "That is easy, my lord, we do not need Albert and I can tell you that the vote will support you. The men speak to me," he shrugged, "I pay them, on your behalf, and I am the one they see when they get their pay. They know who the true leader is, and you are right, we cannot break contracts. That is a path which can lead to disaster."

I climbed up on the wagon and held my hand out for William, "Come and join me." I believed him but it would do no harm to have the man who paid them standing next to the man who would lead them.

The men were assembling and there was a buzz of conversation for we had not done this before. Robin and my captains had spread themselves out to encourage all to vote for me. I saw Albert hurrying over. He must have heard the noise. The Italians had also emerged and were mounting their horses. I smiled for it meant they feared me and were looking for an escape if things turned ugly.

"What in God's name do you think you are doing, John?"

I held my arm out, "Come and join me, Albert. It is time we decided who really runs this company."

His face fell but he took my arm and I hauled him up. I made certain that William was on my right and Albert on my left. I held my hands up and silence fell. I could hear the horses of the Italians as they stamped and snorted. "Men of the White Company I have called you here not to hear speeches but to give you a simple choice. Lord Albert and I have a disagreement. He wishes to break this contract and go to serve Luchino Novello, Visconti of Genoa." I pointed to the Italians. "I believe we should honour the contract. I wish to challenge Albert Sterz for the leadership of the company." I turned to Albert, "Do you wish to say anything?"

He was white with anger, but he had been outmanoeuvred and he knew it. "All that I will say is that I will be going with Lord Luchino Novello, Visconti of Genoa and taking with me all the men who vote for me." He turned to me, "You can stay here with the handful of dogs who will vote for you."

It was a huge mistake. I knew from William's words that even some Germans preferred me, and this would tip the number who would support me. He had insulted more than half of the company.

I nodded. "All those who wish to support me, stand on this side." I pointed to my right. I saw men looking at William. It was soon clear that the vast majority all supported me. The pages were all there for they had a vote and to a boy, they all joined my side. Every English warrior, Italian and Spaniard also followed. When some Germans, led by Karl, walked to my side I saw Albert's head droop. He had eight hundred men who had remained loyal but fifteen hundred had voted for me.

Ignoring Albert I said, "I accept your decision. I will be the new Captain of The White Company and we will fulfil the contract!"

I saw the Italians mount up and ride away. They had seen what happened and heard the cheer. They had failed to open the door to Montferrat. I did not doubt that they rode directly to Bernabò and Galeazzo to tell them of their failure.

Chapter 22

1361 Montferrat

It took three weeks for everything to be sorted. William proved his worth as he blinded Albert with figures. As Albert was walking out on the contract, he and the men who followed him lost some of the money which we had been paid by the marquis. The corollary of that was that the rest of us would have more money. There were joint funds from the company and William just divided that sum by the members of the company. That caused disagreement with those leaving as the pages were each entitled to some of it, but Albert knew he had to capitulate. The last thing he needed, with so few men, was the bloodbath that would ensue if he tried to take the money by force. The animals, armour and weapons were a problem more easily solved.

The day before he left, I had a meeting with him alone. I wanted neither misunderstanding nor animosity between us. I had never liked Albert, but I recognised his qualities. "Albert, I have always got on with you and we have worked well together. Despite our differences, we have always managed to succeed."

"And yet you ousted me!"

"You were deviating from our rules, the rules which we devised, and which have seen us grow and go from strength to strength. If ever you choose to rejoin us, then the door will ever be open. You may even challenge me for the leadership if you wish."

He gave me a rueful smile, "And if I won then you and your English archers would simply walk away." I shrugged. "I thank you for the offer but at the moment there is a bitter taste in my mouth, and I cannot see that day dawning."

"And I can understand that. There is something else, however. Do not take a contract to fight against us. If you do then you will, in all likelihood, die. This contract with the Visconti is one thing but when you have Pavia, do not think to join a fight to take Montferrat. At least not until we have taken another contract elsewhere."

"I cannot promise that."

"Then let us hope we never have to face each other for I know the outcome and, deep inside you, so do you."

There was sadness when the largely German contingent left. Men had made friends. There were shield brothers who had stood together and shared common hardship but left they did. I wasted no time in reorganising the company. I promoted others to become captains. Karl led the German contingent, Giovanni the Italian and so on. I found a Hungarian to lead the Hungarian contingent. The other companies were dwarfed by the English Company which contributed two-thirds of our men. I also initiated patrols along the border with Milan. When I was sure that all was quiet, for Albert and the Visconti family were besieging Pavia, I left with William and ten handpicked men at arms, including a newly promoted Dai and we headed for Bordeaux. I had decided to gather all my personal treasure. Half would be sent to my father-in-law in England. I knew that I could trust him and the rest I would take with me. I intended to buy somewhere in Northern Italy. I now saw the possibilities which were there. The armies were so small that my company could fight and defeat almost any of them. I left Michael and Robin in charge.

We did not ride wearing our white jupons; we had made too many enemies. Instead, we had red and blue ones made and travelled anonymously as Sir Walter of Greenham returning to England after fighting for the Emperor. We avoided any place we had raided and that added four days to the journey. I would have gone by sea, but Genoa ruled that and I had made an enemy of its ruler!

It was well over a year since we had left France and I wondered at the changes in my children not to mention Elizabeth and the farm. We had received neither news nor men for the last eight months but as we had been so far away that did not surprise me. Gascony seemed almost alien to me as we rode towards my farm. War had ended with the treaty of Bretigny and many of the men alongside whom I had fought were now in Spain where there was another war being fought by King Edward.

The sentries on the gate were new but the peaceful nature of the land meant that the gates were open, and no weapons were pointed at us. "Yes, my lord?"

"I am Sir John Hawkwood."

I had intended to say more but the man paled and stammered, "Ye, yes Sir John, pray enter."

I rode into the once familiar cobbled yard and dismounted. A much older Roger of Norham, with a baby in his arms and what I took to be Thomas and John behind him stepped into the light. He beamed, "Sir John, we were not expecting you!"

I smiled. I had come to terms with what I had deemed to be disloyalty and now remembered all the times I had fought alongside Roger. "Good to see you, Roger, and I wanted no fuss as I just came when we had no war to fight. I take it the babe is Roger?"

"Aye, lord and a fine warrior he will make. He has an arm that can hurl his food clear across the room! John, Thomas, say hello to your father."

They both appeared dumbstruck and just nodded.

I understood their shyness, but it still hurt, "We will get to know each other over the days I am here."

"You are staying long, Sir John?"

"I have business to conduct. It may be a week, it may be a month. It all depends upon Captain Jack." Dai and my men had returned from stabling the horses and I noticed that Elizabeth had not put in an appearance. "Where is your wife?"

"Come inside and see her yourself. She is with child again but this one is not going as well as the other three. She feels unwell and is lying down but your arrival and that of her brother will be the best medicine she can receive."

I entered the house which felt both familiar and strange. I saw the touches made by Roger and Elizabeth. This was their home and they had made it theirs. It was mine no longer. The distance between my sons and me was also disconcerting. They did not know me and there was no reason why they should. John had been little older than young Roger when I had last seen him.

Considering that Elizabeth was supposed to be having a difficult pregnancy she looked remarkably hale to me. She beamed when she saw me and tried to rise. I held up my hand,

"Hold, Elizabeth, you have no reason to be on your feet." I stood to the side so that she could see her brother. "And see, I have brought William to visit with you."

He knelt and embraced her. Roger handed his son to a nurse and said, "Come, Sir John, while they have a reunion, I will take you to meet the new men."

I nodded, "And they will be needed." As we headed to the warrior halls, I told him all that had happened.

He stroked his chin, "I never met this Albert, Sir John, but from what the others said of him I did not like him, and I believe you are well rid of him."

"Perhaps but he knows how we fight, and I would hate to face him across a battlefield." The men had seen us approach and they all stood as though at attention. The sentry on the gate must have warned them who I was. "And these are the men?"

"Aye, Sir John, and they are good ones. They are champing at the bit, too. Four have been here a year and were considering making their own way to Italy."

"That speaks well of them."

"There are twenty-one archers and ten men at arms. We also have ten of the Bordeaux boys."

"And mounts for them all?"

He shook his head, "I did not want to go to the expense if we did not need them, but they are in plentiful supply and I can have them for you in three days."

"Good, and William will settle our accounts." I addressed the men, "Speak with the men I brought, and they will give you a flavour of our life in Italy." They all gave a little self-conscious bow. I smiled and shook my head, "You will not need to bow and scrape to me. We are one company, and we share all the dangers and rewards. You just need to learn to obey me instantly!"

As we headed back Roger said, "All of them came from England. It is peaceful there and there is no profit."

"And you should know, Roger, that my visits may well be even more infrequent. I plan on sending most of my treasure to England. I hope to buy more land there so that, one day, I might retire there. I have a house already and another would earn me a good income. I will empty my treasure here. From now on send any men to me directly. They can travel by ship for Genoa is handy and whilst I cannot use it, they can."

"Of course, my lord." He paused, "All is well now between us?"

"All is well, Roger, and I am sorry that I behaved the way I did. Pride!" I shook my head, "I have many sins on my conscience but that one sits heavily."

Over the next two days, I went everywhere with my sons. Dai either carried Thomas or held his hand. We mainly rode as I went into Bordeaux to discover when Captain Jack was arriving and to buy both cloth and supplies that we needed. Montferrat had most of the things we needed but Bordeaux had treasures and treats which would make our lives better. And I indulged my sons. I confess I tried to buy their love and bought them whatever took their fancy. I could have saved myself the coins I spent for Dai's innate sense of humour and fun allied to the joy of being off the farm meant that the two of them giggled and laughed the whole time we were together. I realised then how much I owed to Dai. When I found it hard to talk to the boys, for they were not adults, Dai would show me the way. He could make silly noises and pull faces which had the boys in fits of giggles and because I was close by they saw me as fun, by association. I was under no illusion, by the time my men and I left for home the boys would miss Dai more than they would miss me. I was a practical man and at the end of our time together they were looking forward to the time they could be with The White Company, but that was because they would be close to Dai. I would have to ensure that Dai stayed alive until they did so.

We stayed an extra week as Captain Jack was not in port. It gave me the chance to write a letter to John and give him my requests. I wrote the letter twice for when I showed the first version to William he commented, "Sir John, you have not asked about your daughter. I would begin with that."

He was right but then once I left the world of war I was out of my depth. We gave Captain Jack the letter and the chests of gold I wanted to be delivered. I paid him five florins to deliver it. He was not going to take it at first and I had to persuade him. It was not as if the coins were hard to come by.

My business concluded I should have hurried back to Italy, but I did not. That was partly because I did not wish to be parted from my sons but also because there was news that was of great importance to me. Prince Edward had married the year after the Treaty of Bretigny and he had just been made ruler of Aquitaine with Sir John Chandos as his lieutenant. Roger pointed out that it could have been me, but I had burned that bridge many years earlier. The prince had been charged by his father with ridding Aquitaine and Gascony of the Free Companies who plagued the region. I did not agree with the use of the word plagued for I was one of them but it was how the merchants in Bordeaux saw them. I was glad that I stayed for I now knew that I could never return to this part of France. My future and that of the company I led was now in Italy or further east at the very least. We also benefitted from the dissolution of one such Free Company. It was one that had been led by Sir Robert Knolles, but he had moved on to bigger and better things. Taken over by Jacques de la Rochelle, a man who had served with Arnaud, they had been the scourge of the Dordogne. Their leader was executed, and the rest ordered to quit Gascony. Sir John Chandos was a ruthless man. We benefitted to the tune of fifty-two English archers and fifty men at arms: half of them Hungarians. They were all mounted and were happy to sign William's papers. My reputation along with that of my company was reaping the reward. Albert would have loved to have the men who joined me, but the men told me on the journey east that it was my name that convinced them to join. They saw me as a just and fair captain. I was not so sure of that!

The extra men were the reason we had to leave for the farm could not accommodate them and Elizabeth arranged a hurried farewell meal for us. It was a feast, but it was tinged with sadness as well as great joy. We all knew that such events would happen less often in the future. I planned on leaving John and Thomas with Roger until Thomas was seven. At best I would have five such visits and after that, none. When we left the next day Elizabeth was tearful for her brother was leaving and Thomas and John were inconsolable. The tears were mainly for Dai but when the two of them each grabbed my leg I felt my throat tighten. I did not look back for I did not wish to unman myself.

The journey back was slower for we had a wagon and more men. Although we were not a free company in the true sense of the word, there were less than one hundred and forty of us, we were treated well in Gascony for we were seen to be leaving their land. Provence was a different matter and we had to pay for everything. I used William to ride ahead with a few guards to negotiate our passage. Savoy was now an easier country to cross. We had defeated them and, when I rode through their land this time, I had my men wear their new white jupons. The effect was to make every village and town through which we passed, bar its doors. We stopped in Casale Monferrato to speak with the marquis and it proved to be a judicious visit.

My men were accommodated and Dai, William, and I dined with the marquis. "Giovanni Acuto."

John the Sharp was how the Italians addressed me. It meant I was cunning and I took it for a compliment.

"Yes Marquis?"

"I have heard disquieting rumours about the Visconti."

"Luchino Novello?"

He shook his head, "No, he and the ingrate, Albert Sterz, are still awaiting their ransoms in Pavia. It is his cousin Marco, the son of Bernabò. He tried to hire von Landau and the Great Company to attack my lands."

They were the largest company in Italy and were largely German. Albert hated von Landau and that alone would prevent him from joining up with his countryman. "You say tried. I take it he failed?"

"He either could not afford him and his men or they disagreed. I have heard that he is hiring bandits to augment the Milanese army he leads. His uncle, Galeazzo, controls the large part of the army and his father, Bernabò, is so tight-fisted that he does not have a large army."

I nodded, "Then they will have to pass our base to do any damage. Have I your permission to ride Milanese land to gather intelligence?"

"Of course, and I also want to bring my army to fight them should they be foolish enough to attack us."

I did not like that. They were not professionals. "You need not do that, Don Giovanni."

He smiled, "I am not a fool, my friend. I have no intention of trying to usurp your authority nor of getting in the way, but it is my land and I would like my men to see how you fight. One day you will leave me. Florence and Venice can pay far more than I can When that day comes, I would have a better-prepared army."

I smiled, "Then if you agree to place your army under my command, we have an agreement."

"Good. I will send two of my nobles to return with you. They will bring me the news and you can use them to send for me when we are needed."

"Of course." I was not entirely happy but having an extra couple of thousand men might be useful.

Chapter 23

We had so much to do when I reached my home that there were not enough hours in the day. The first thing I did, after we had assigned the new men, was to hold a council of war with my captains. It was much easier now that Albert and his dissenting elements were gone. The atmosphere was more conducive to a positive outcome. I told them of the news from both Gascony and Casale Monferrato. William had made lists of the new men and assigned them to lances. We had travelled in lances on the way east and now William allocated the new men to captains.

"We will now patrol aggressively. Marco Visconti has tried to hire warriors. I do not want him to hire Albert for he knows how we fight. As he and Luchino Novello are still raiding around Pavia I would rather Marco makes the attempt sooner, rather than later. Cross into Milanese land, take military prisoners and animals but do not risk losing any men. I wish to provoke the bear and not hunt it."

I left Robin and Michael to organise the new patrols and I began to practise with the new men. It helped me hone my skills and told me much about their quality. In the main, I was pleased with them and I told their captains the ones who needed work. We had a system and only a fool would ignore it.

The first reports came more than a month after we had returned. They came, ironically, from one of Albert's men. He sent a messenger to speak to us. I think it was to gloat about the one hundred and eighty thousand florins they had extracted from the Pavian citizens, but I did not mind. In the first place, I knew that he would have to share that with the Visconti and secondly because the information he gave me, ostensibly the main reason for his visit, was valuable.

"Captain Sterz says to warn you that an army of four thousand Milanese is heading towards Casale Monferrato along the Po valley."

That told me much. The Milanese would have to pass through Pavia which they now controlled and I now saw the tentacles of the Visconti octopus. They would have to ford the river and the best ford was just fourteen miles from our home.

"Tell Lord Sterz that I thank him and hope that one day we will fight alongside one another again. We will be ready for him when he nears our home!" I had no intention of giving more information to someone who was working for the Visconti. I trusted his information for he knew that my vengeance would be swift if he betrayed me but, equally, he might well pass on to his new masters my plans. This way they would not expect me fifteen miles from where they thought I would wait.

My council of war was a short one. I left fifty of my men at arms and the boys who were not needed as pages to guard our home. William would command. We sent word of our intentions to the marquis. The rest of us, all mounted, headed down the mighty Po to the tiny hamlet of Bassiargno. I knew the ford having explored the land the previous year and, in truth, it was not really a ford for the river was almost one hundred paces wide and so deep that it had to be swum. It could be swum by horses and the enemy army could build a pontoon or raft bridge very quickly. The alternative and the safer crossing was so far away that it did not even bear consideration.

We did not have far to go, and I had time to assess the potential battlefield. While my men made camp and planted stakes to prevent us from being surprised, I rode with Michael and Robin to the bluffs above the river. There were trees and shrubs both on the slopes and the crest. That this was used as a crossing was clear for there was a path that twisted and turned up the slope. The lack of wagon ruts told me all I needed to know, it was used by horses only.

Robin rubbed his chin and pointed to the crossing, "Put my archers here and there will be no need for battle, Sir John. Even horsemen swimming their horses would be moving so slowly that we could empty every saddle. If they build rafts, then the same would be true."

I nodded but my mind was a couple of moves ahead, "If we were raiding the Po valley what would we do?"

Michael said, "Scout out every crossing of the river."

"Make sure that we held them when we found them." Added Robin.

"Exactly, and if we intended to cross an army at one then we would have scouts there guarding it. Can you see a sign of a single scout?"

Robin chuckled, "You are an old fox, my lord. It is no wonder that the Italians all call you sharp." His smile turned to a frown. "Did Albert deceive us? Is this a trap? I will gut the bastard the next time I see him."

I shook my head, "Had he wished to deceive us he would have said nothing at all, and the Milanese would have been at Casale Monferrato before we even knew it. No, Robin, Albert sent his message in good faith. A part of the Milanese army might have been at Pavia, but the rest were elsewhere." I looked behind me.

Michael asked, "You think they have crossed already?"

"Perhaps, but we saw no sign of them on our way south." I pointed down the twisting river. "If they do not intend to ford here then they crossed further east and will be on this side of the river already."

We headed to the small river which fed into the Po, the Tanaro. There was a small stone bridge that crossed the river. It was not wide and looked to be for local traffic. I could see another hamlet not far from the bridge. I turned and estimated that the bridge was just under a mile from Bassiargno. I whipped Roman's head around and rode towards the hamlet. The road which passed through it was a relatively good one and passed a wood which tumbled down to the Po. The Roman Empire had built well. I regretted then that we did not have maps. It was an oversight and one I would remedy if we emerged successfully from this dilemma. The bridge over the Tanaro meant that the road headed north and west to the hamlet.

"We use this as our bulwark. Michael, have the men move the camp to here. We can use the buildings, small though they are as our bastions. We will place our men at arms in a line to the bluff. Robin, your archers will need to be flexible. It goes without saying that they will be in line behind us and in the village, but I want some to cover the crossing in case I am making up problems which do not exist. I saw a large animal pen on the other side of the village. We will put the horses there and just use a dozen of the young boys to watch them. The rest can use their slings."

They both nodded and we turned our horses around to head back to the village. Robin said, "If you are right then Albert was deceived too."

"And that means that he may well have been deceived about their intentions. You two carry on with your tasks and I will speak with the headman."

I dismounted. The hamlet had no more than half a dozen houses with tended fields all around and I guessed that the river's proximity made this a good and relatively safe place to farm. All that was going to end. A man who looked to be about fifty with a grey-flecked beard emerged from a house as I approached; my jingling mail had alerted him. The rest of the doors remained closed.

He saw my spurs and bowed, "My lord. I am Luigi Bassiargno, and I am the headman of the village. Is there a problem?"

"There may be a battle, my friend. I serve the Marquis of Montferrat and I have heard that a Milanese army is heading along the Po."

"They will cross down there," he pointed along the valley, "at Tornello. It is twenty-five miles away. Then they will cross the bridge over the Tanaro."

"You seem knowledgeable about such matters."

He smiled, "I was not always a farmer and I have served the lords of this land. They will come that way."

I believed him, "What about the fords?"

He laughed, "In high summer when the river levels are down, perhaps, but not at this time of the year."

"I intend to defend your village, but I do not want you harmed."

He nodded, "We will stay here until we see their flags. Then we will have time to leave."

I admired his stoical nature, "You are calm about this."

He shrugged, "Your presence means that the Milanese, even if they win, will have a bloody nose. If you were not here, then all would be taken, and our women violated. You will be the ones fighting and not us."

"We will share our food with you. It is the least that we can do."

"Thank you, my lord."

We had barely begun to embed stakes and the cooking food had just begun to boil when we saw their scouts. They crossed the bridge over the Tanaro. It was exactly as Luigi had said and we saw the Milanese army as they started to erect their own camp. We had barely arrived in time. Had we delayed our departure by even a few hours then Bassiargno would now be in Milanese hands and the choice of the battlefield would have been the decision of Marco Visconti.

"Robin, mount fifty archers and ride towards the camp they are building. Discourage their scouts from coming any closer. I do not wish them to know our numbers although Albert may well have given them a good idea."

"Aye, Sir John."

He also mounted ten pages who would act as horse holders and they accompanied him. I looked at the sky. It would be dark in an hour or so. I doubted that they would make a night attack but as we had yet to finish our defences, I doubted that my men would get much sleep. I mounted Roman and with Dai accompanying me I rode closer to the Milanese to assess their numbers. I now had a clearer view of the bridge and I saw that their feditore, about three hundred of them, were standing in a line behind the hundred or so light horsemen who were their scouts. Horsemen, knights and men at arms I guessed, were now crossing the bridge. They could not begin to build their camp until their baggage arrived. I was fifty paces behind Robin and his dismounted archers. The Milanese scouts were well within range and had Robin ridden just a little closer to the river then so would be the bridge. Neither Robin nor I wished the battle to begin just yet. We needed defences in place for it was already clear that we would be, once again, outnumbered. More men at arms had already crossed the bridge and the main body of soldiers were still coming. Two knights detached themselves and rode to the mounted scouts. After a brief conference, the knights led the light horsemen at Robin and his archers. It was a mistake. The shower of arrows unhorsed riders and one of the knights fell from his horse. Robin had decided to discourage them forcefully.

The light horsemen wheeled around and leaving fifteen of their number on the ground they and the knight headed back to the safety of the bridge. The feditore, protected by shields, advanced to the dead horsemen. Robin wasted no more arrows but waited for night to fall.

"We have seen enough, Dai, and we have much work ahead of us."

This would be the first battle in which I led The White Company. True, all of the other battles had been directed by me but I had been aware that I had first, Arnaud and Albert looking over my shoulder and then just Albert. More than that all the men I had not trusted had gone with Albert and now I felt confident about all of them. My tactics and my strategies had all evolved from the men I had followed in battle, the Duke of Lancaster, the Captal de Buch and Prince Edward. I would evolve my own style, but I felt comfortable fighting defensive battles. Accordingly, we planted stakes behind which we could defend. The battle would be fought the way we had fought most battles: we would let my men at arms, me included, bear the brunt of the enemy attack while our archers whittled them down to size. The ground suited us. The woods filled the land on our left flank all the way from the Po to the Tanaro. We had five hundred paces between the hamlet and the trees. I knew that the Milanese did not have troops who liked fighting in the woods and I placed my pages and a company of archers there. Our right flank had the village as an anchor and there I placed another company of archers and men at arms. They were placed obliquely to the enemy line of attack and would prevent us from being outflanked. All night my men toiled to bury sharpened stakes before us so that we had, as we had enjoyed at Torino, a wooden wall behind which we could fight. The five hundred pace frontage would be defended by a thousand men at arms and that meant our line would be just two deep. I hoped it would be enough. I had sent a rider to the marquis as soon as we had seen the enemy at the bridge but I knew that they could not get here until the late afternoon. The marquis would be keen to fight a battle and if he had mobilised his men when my first messenger reached him then he should be on his way. However, none moved as quickly as The White Company. If the Milanese tarried, then they might arrive in time to swing a losing battle, but I was not confident that we would have any assistance.

Luigi and the villagers left their homes in the early hours. They had dug up their treasure and pulled handcarts with all that was valuable to them. Pellizzari was just two and a half miles away and they would be there as their neighbours awoke. Most of my men managed an hour or two of sleep but my captains and I did not. We all knew the importance of this day, our first real battle without Albert and his men. It was clear to me now that Albert had been offered his contract to weaken Montferrat and that Marco Visconti was a wily and cunning leader. The men were roused and fed before dawn. At that time we had no priest with us and so the men just prayed alone. No man goes to battle without some attempt to confess to sins. We knew that we were all sinful men. Our trade broke one of the commandments each time we went into action!

This was the first time I had fought the Visconti and I learned much that day. That they would give battle was obvious as they formed themselves into battle lines. They did not make the mistake of the Savoyards and their men were dismounted. Perhaps Albert had advised them how we would fight. It mattered not. An advance on foot would allow my archers a longer time to thin their ranks. Marco Visconti had divided his dismounted men into six blocks. Each one looked to be about six hundred men strong. I calculated that by looking at the frontage of each one, a hundred men, and multiplying by the ranks deep, six. There was another block of mounted men, but they were at the rear, close to the bridge. The front ranks of the six blocks were all filled with men at arms and the feditore supplied the next two ranks. The last two ranks were arrow fodder: men without armour and a wider range of weapons. Before them was a screen of two hundred light horsemen, armed with javelins and two hundred crossbowmen. It became clear that there would be no negotiation and a horn signalled the light horsemen and crossbowmen to move forward. I saw then that Marco intended to send his blocks of men two at a time for while four remained. If the first two blocks failed then, I deduced, another two blocks would be sent in. The horsemen were a threat should the enemy break our spirit.

We all had pole weapons, but the javelins and crossbows meant we needed our shields. I was never one for rhetoric before battle, but I was aware of the moment. I stepped between the stakes and stood with my back to the enemy. The horsemen were trying to keep the pace of the crossbows and it was not bravado. I calculated that I had enough time.

"Men of The White Company, today, for the first time, you fight under my sole captaincy! Let us show these Milanese that despite their numbers, they are no match for us." I heard the hooves behind me, and I saw my archers with drawn bows. Raising my sword I shouted, "Hawkwood!"

Every man shouted it out too and then I saw the arrows fly over my head. As I walked between the stakes, I felt something strike my back. It could have been a bolt or a javelin but as I felt no pain, I did not turn but I kept walking to my allotted place. I heard cries as men and horses were hit by plunging arrows. When I did turn, I saw a field littered with bodies and horses meandering around, riderless. Some of my men had bolts in their shields and I saw embedded javelins. Just five feet from me lay a javelin and Michael said, "That was the javelin which hit your backplate."

"Was it?" I sheathed my sword and walked back to pick it up.

The Milanese screen had done its job, but no more javelins and bolts would be sent in our direction for the survivors were fleeing. The advancing men at arms were now within three hundred paces of us. They were aiming to hit the right side of our line, close to the hamlet and I had been right to place men there. The Milanese would have a shock if they thought they could sweep around us. Our archers had now switched targets and changed arrows. They waited until the plated men at arms were close enough for their bodkins to do damage. The fact that no arrows were sent in their direction seemed to encourage the Milanese. Robin and my longbowmen were merely biding their time. The arrows began to fall when the men at arms were just one hundred and twenty paces from our stakes. Not every arrow was a mortal strike. Many of them hit arms or helmets but enough struck men in the front four ranks so that gaps appeared and when more arrows fell within two or three steps then the gaps became bigger. The pages with slings then found the range and the sound of their stones on metal sounded like hailstones. I heard a Milanese horn and saw the next two blocks advancing. They were using the blocks like punches and the last one would be the horsemen. They wanted successive fresh men to hit the same place and to weaken it. As the survivors in the front ranks reached the stakes they began to pull them out. I still had the javelin and as a Milanese man at arms tried to wrest a stake out, just fifteen feet from me I hurled the javelin which struck him in the face. He had raised his visor, the better to see the stake. It cost him his life. I slipped my shield over my left arm to hang there protectively and held the pole axe ready for when the first men made it through the stakes.

We had the advantage that we were a solid line of men, but the Milanese would be forced to break up their line and there would be no cohesion. Robin and our archers had done a good job and most of those who were plated, mailed and had survived, had arrows sticking from them. The plate, mail and gambesons stopped them from incapacitating them, but they would impair their ability to fight well. The first man at arms to make it through the stakes had a shield and a mace. He was a knight. His shield had so many arrows in it that it was a danger to me! If he could close with me then his mace could deal a deadly blow. Luckily, he had his visor down and failed to see the poleaxe as I swung the hammer at his helmet. The helmet was well made but I dented it and while it did not kill him immediately it not only stunned him but also jammed the visor shut and, I think, prevented him from seeing as well as he might have wished. As he blindly stepped forward and raised his mace, I rammed the spike under his arm and blood spurted. Pulling it out I swung my poleaxe head at the bottom of the helmet. It was a powerful blow, and the sharp blade tore through the mail coif and into his neck. He subsided to the ground and lay there as an obstacle to those behind.

The next men who came were not men at arms and had mail covered by padded jackets. They were feditore and held long spears in two hands. I slipped my shield from my arm as it was not helping me and there were no more bolts or javelins coming in my direction. More of the stakes had been pulled out but the men who had done so now lay dead, pierced by arrows. I saw the next two blocks as they marched across from the river towards us. There were still two blocks that remained to be committed but they were the weaker ones. As I readied my poleaxe, I saw that our right flank was holding, and our archers were able to thin the ranks of the feditore as well as those who were at the rear of each block. I glanced down our line and saw that we had lost few men. We had the advantage, still, of cohesion.

The men with the spears obviously thought that they held the advantage but beneath my jupon, I wore Balin's very expensive and well-made breastplate. I did not intend that it should be tested but I was confident that if it was it would pass the test. I waited until the first spear was thrust at me before I swung. I smacked the shaft with the head of the hammer and then, as I stepped forward, I swung the axe head at the feditore's skull. He wore a kettle helmet and a coif. The poleaxe hacked deep into his skull and the spear fell from his lifeless hands. A Milanese horn sounded as the first two blocks began to fall back. At least I assume that was the plan but as most of the men at arms and knights lay dead or wounded and the ones who turned were not well protected and so they ran. When arrows hit them in the back they panicked and ran towards the two advancing blocks. They were trying to get to their bridge. Many were impaled on the weapons of their comrades and they also broke the solid ranks. It allowed my archers to send bodkins at stationary men.

Marco Visconti then sent in his last two blocks of infantry. It was a desperate gamble. I picked up the long spear which lay before me and I rammed it at an angle into the ground. It was an avoidable obstacle, but it might distract an enemy long enough for me to kill him. Seeing what I did others copied me. Archers raced out to fetch undamaged arrows and pages picked up stones. The next two blocks were less than one hundred and fifty paces from us when our lines reformed. This time they had fewer stakes to negotiate and were slightly closer together. I noticed that not as many of the front ranks were as well armoured as the first had been. All my men had plate armour and good helmets. It made a difference.

This time some of those who advanced had similar weapons to us. In such a duel it was the one with the most skill who would win. We had fought regularly and practised every day against men of similar skill to us. They had not and that became apparent when a knight with a poleaxe advanced to fight me. While we both held them at an angle, he had his hammer as the weapon he would use to strike at me. I had an axe for I saw that only the head was protected by metal. I could also tell that he was aiming at my head. I was aiming at his shaft. The shaft was closer to me than my head was to him. The axe head sliced through the wood and the now useless piece of metal fell to the ground. As he dropped the shaft, his hand went to grab his sword and that allowed me the time to lift the poleaxe and turn it so that the head of the hammer could be used. His sword was halfway from its scabbard as the head smashed into his helmet. He began to fall, and I hit him a second time. The first blow had weakened the metal and the second smashed into his skull.

Our archers and the pages on the left had now moved close to the right flank of the two blocks and with a barrier of dead and dying men they had protection and their missiles hit the right side of the men at arms, feditore, and the ones at the rear. As many were engaged with my men at arms on our left they were being cut down in huge numbers and this time they did not wait for a horn to sound the retreat. The block on the far right was down to a quarter of the number who had begun the attack and they broke and fled. The ones fighting in the centre and on our right had lost fewer men but the ones who were not men at arms saw their comrades flee and joined them. That exposed the men at arms fighting us to arrows and stones as well as our deadly pole weapons. I rammed my spike into the face of a feditore with such force that it emerged from the back of his skull and I had to twist it free. As I did so the next man was sprayed with blood, bone, and brains. It takes a strong man to ignore such a shower and as he turned the axe-head drove into his face. The block broke.

Lifting my visor I saw then that the last two blocks which had begun the march across the open ground to us had halted. They were of equal number to us, but they had seen their fellows perish. A knight on a white charger rode forward to speak to them but he must have been unsuccessful for they began to withdraw. Had I had the men of Montferrat with me then I might have considered a charge with mounted men but, as it was, we would stand and take the final attack.

I looked at the sky and saw that it had passed its zenith. I picked up the waterskin from where it lay and drank deeply. The knight who had tried in vain to make the last two blocks of men advance shouted something and I saw his mounted men at arms and knights form a line. At first, I thought they might charge. Across a battlefield littered with the dead and dying that was a mistake. Then I saw that they were shepherding the broken groups of men into two new blocks.

I turned and shouted, "They are going to attempt a larger attack. How are we for arrows?"

Robin's voice came from my right. He had begun the battle on the left, but he must have decided that he was needed on our right flank, "We have enough to end this battle, Sir John!" His confidence was inspiring.

It was clear that there would be no attack for a short time and so men took the opportunity to empty their bladders. Others did as I had done and drank. I saw two archers run from the woods, lower their breeks and empty their bowels. Fighting a battle was hard enough without being uncomfortable.

"It seems, Michael as though the Visconti are desperate to rid their land of us."

"I will take that as a compliment, Sir John." There was a slight pause. Michael had come a long way since we had found him, but he still needed to be more confident. "Can we hold them?"

"I think so, but it will not be as easy as they are attacking with more men this time but at least one of the blocks is made up of men who have fled once, and it may not take much to break them again! We just keep doing what we have been doing."

It took some time for the Milanese to bring some sort of order to their men. This time they did not echelon them as they had in their first attacks but placed them in one long line, three blocks long with their horsemen in a double line behind. I heard the sound of the men being exhorted by their leader but the wind from behind us took his words away from me. He occasionally turned to wave at us and, I dare say, to insult us. Finally, when they gave him what sounded to me like a weak cheer, they began to advance and he rejoined his horsemen.

"Ready!"

Our cheer seemed much louder to me. I knew that we were resolute and had more skill but now we were facing at least one thousand men who were fresher than we were. The wind which had taken away the Visconti voice now took our arrows further and Robin ordered the archers to loose at a longer range. Men were hit, although this time the front ranks held shields above their heads, they had learned to fear the longbow. They were not attacking with pole weapons but swords, spears, and hand weapons. Fewer men were hit although on our left flank the archers were able to use a flatter trajectory and the pages' stones smacked into unprotected sides and the right-hand block was thinned more than the others. The last attack had taken more of the stakes so that it was almost a solid line of men who came at us. We trusted our archers and they had great skill. They kept the arrows falling even when the Milanese were just ten feet from us. In truth, the front rank might have been safe but when arrows fell and hit those in the third rank then the others kept their shields high. I swung my poleaxe in a wide arc. I connected with one helmet and then an arm holding a shield. Another walked into the spear I had embedded but there were so many of them that the dead men were propelled forward by the sheer weight of numbers behind.

Then I heard a horn, and it did not come from the Milanese. It came from our right. I also heard hooves thundering on the ground and I wondered, for I could not see if the Milanese had been clever and used a flanking charge of horsemen. It was when I saw the Milanese horsemen begin to move from left to right to face a new threat that I deduced that it was Marquis Giovanni and the men of Montferrat. I hoped the young noble knew what he was doing. Whilst the attack would relieve us, if he was swept from the field by the Milanese then all would have been in vain.

Robin's voice rose above the sound of battle, "Switch targets to the Milanese horsemen!"

I shouted, "Push back their men at arms!"

Holding the poleaxe in two hands I rammed it at the middle of the feditore before me as I stepped on the dead men at arms. I twisted the spike as it entered his middle, bursting his mail links when I did so. I kept pushing and the dying man was shifted backwards as my men pushed my back. I heard the clash as the two sets of horsemen crashed into each other. This was maddening. I could see nothing, and I realised that the front rank was no longer the place for me! I needed to be able to see the whole battle and direct action. I could do nothing about that, and I swung my axe head diagonally to rip into the neck of the warrior before me. He wore only a padded jacket and the axe tore open his chest. My other men at arms were enjoying the same success and as we were now fighting their secondary troops, we were hurting them more than they hurt us. They broke. This time it was truly a rout, and they fled the field. My men at arms were too weary to pursue and so we just took prisoners or put the badly wounded out of their misery.

It was our archers, loosing at the mounted Milanese men at arms who enabled the marquis to drive them from the field. Our archers also raced after the fleeing men on foot and we took many prisoners. By the time darkness fell the field was ours and we had enjoyed an unlikely victory. I had hoped to merely hold them, but Marco Visconti had been defeated and I had made another enemy!

Epilogue

We took many prisoners, and the ransoms were high. Thanks to the Visconti victory at Pavia we knew they had a great deal of money. When the marquis met with Marco Visconti he did so from a position of power and, for one so young, he negotiated well. Many nobles had been slain but it also created a problem for us. The Milanese now knew that they had to fight fire with fire. When next they came, and come they would, it would be with mercenaries of their own. They had lost too many rich nobles and impoverished others for them to do anything else. We had lost men and they were good ones too. I was a practical man and as the ones we had lost were men at arms then they could be replaced far more easily than the invaluable archers.

It confirmed with Marquis Giovanni that we were needed, and he increased our pay. We had made enemies but that, at the time, did not worry me. We had won another battle and the reputation of The White Company was intact. More men would flock to fill our ranks and with the treasure we had taken and the pay from the marquis we could continue to recruit. This had been the first time I had truly led The White Company and I had learned from it. I would no longer fight in the front ranks. As I had been hewing heads, I had realised that I did not need to prove myself in battle. I had done so many times. Robin had shown me the way. He had changed position because he saw a new danger. From now on I would use my captains. They had all been trained by me and I had to trust them. They were the men of The White Company and they were the best warriors to be found anywhere. I was content but I still had a personal matter to settle. Count Konrad Wirtinger von Landau led a company in Italy and that meant he was within my grasp. The death of my banker and the theft of my fortune would be remedied. I just did not know how yet.

The End

Glossary

Battle- a military formation rather than an event
Bastard Sword-One requiring two hands to use. The shield hung from the left arm
Bevor- metal chin and mouth protector attached to a helmet
Brase- a strap on a shield for an arm to go through
Brigandine- a leather or padded tunic worn by soldiers; often studded with metal
Centenar- the commander of a hundred
Chepe- Market (as in Cheapside)
Chevauchée – a raid on an enemy, usually by horsemen
Cordwainer- Shoemaker
Feditore-an Italian warrior
Gardyvyan- Archer's haversack containing all his war-gear
Glaive- a long pole weapon with a concave blade
Guige strap– a long leather strap that allowed a shield to hang from a knight's shoulder
Harbingers- the men who found accommodation and campsites for archers
Hotel de Ville- Town Hall
Jupon – a shorter version of the surcoat
Mainward-the main body of an army
Mêlée - confused fight
Oriflamme – The French standard which was normally kept in Saint-Denis
Pavesiers - men who carried man-sized shields to protect crossbowmen
Rearward- the rearguard and baggage of an army
Rooking - overcharging
Shaffron – metal headpiece for a horse
Spanning hook- the hook a crossbowman had on his belt to help draw his weapon
Vanward- the leading element of an army, the scouts
Vintenar- commander of twenty

Historical note

John Hawkwood was a real person but much of his life is still a mystery. At the end of his career, he was one of the most powerful men in Northern Italy where he commanded the White or English Company. He famously won the battle of Castagnaro in 1387. However, his early life is less well documented, and I have used artistic licence to add details. He was born in Essex and his father was called Gilbert. I have made up the reason for his leaving his home but leave he did, and he became an apprentice tailor. It is rumoured that he fought at Crécy as a longbowman and I have used that to weave a tale. It is also alleged that he was knighted by Prince Edward at Poitiers. The Duke of Clarence was almost 7 feet tall and Prince Edward was also a tall man. I am unsure when he began to wear his black armour but I chose Christmas 1357 as the date.

Let me get the hasty wedding out of the way. Sir John Hawkwood had two wives and one was English. As there is little evidence of him in England after 1357 he had to marry before then. That he was married, although I could not discover to whom, is attested by the fact that he had a daughter and she married into the prominent Essex family the Coggeshales. His granddaughter was Alice Coggeshale and she married well. I used Antiochia as the name of his wife.

For those readers who do not like John Hawkwood then all I can say is that all the bad things he did were not made up by me. He did run a medieval protection racket for a while but that just helped him to gather a company that, eventually, became the greatest force in Italy. If you find him flawed then I have done my job and painted a portrait of a real and complex man.

Most of the incidents I used really happened. The battles of Beaune and Torino are fictional, but the Duke of Burgundy was forced to pay a huge sum of money to Prince Edward to rid his land of the companies. The hailstorm happened as I described and ended Prince Edward's hopes of continuing his raids. The tiny county of Montferrat was hemmed in by both Milan and Savoy. It was The White Company who saved it from extinction.

Griff Hosker
April 2021

The books I used for reference were:

- French Armies of the Hundred Years War- David Nicholle
- Castagnaro 1387- Devries and Capponi
- Italian Medieval Armies 1300-1500- Gabriele Esposito
- Armies of the Medieval Italian Wars-1125-1325
- Condottiere 1300-1500 Infamous Medieval Mercenaries – David Murphy
- The Armies of Crécy and Poitiers- Rothero
- The Scottish and Welsh Wars 1250-1400- Rothero
- English Longbowman 1330-1515- Bartlett and Embleton
- The Longbow- Mike Loades
- The Battle of Poitiers 1356- Nicholle and Turner
- The Tower of London-Lapper and Parnell
- The Tower of London- A L Rowse

Other books by Griff Hosker

If you enjoyed reading this book, then why not read another one by the author?

Ancient History

The Sword of Cartimandua Series
(Germania and Britannia 50 A.D. – 128 A.D.)
Ulpius Felix- Roman Warrior (prequel)
The Sword of Cartimandua
The Horse Warriors
Invasion Caledonia
Roman Retreat
Revolt of the Red Witch
Druid's Gold
Trajan's Hunters
The Last Frontier
Hero of Rome
Roman Hawk
Roman Treachery
Roman Wall
Roman Courage

The Wolf Warrior series
(Britain in the late 6th Century)
Saxon Dawn
Saxon Revenge
Saxon England
Saxon Blood
Saxon Slayer
Saxon Slaughter
Saxon Bane
Saxon Fall: Rise of the Warlord
Saxon Throne
Saxon Sword

Medieval History

The Dragon Heart Series
Viking Slave
Viking Warrior
Viking Jarl
Viking Kingdom
Viking Wolf
Viking War
Viking Sword
Viking Wrath
Viking Raid
Viking Legend
Viking Vengeance
Viking Dragon
Viking Treasure
Viking Enemy
Viking Witch
Viking Blood
Viking Weregeld
Viking Storm
Viking Warband
Viking Shadow
Viking Legacy
Viking Clan
Viking Bravery

The Norman Genesis Series
Hrolf the Viking
Horseman
The Battle for a Home
Revenge of the Franks
The Land of the Northmen
Ragnvald Hrolfsson
Brothers in Blood
Lord of Rouen
Drekar in the Seine
Duke of Normandy
The Duke and the King

The White Company

New World Series
Blood on the Blade
Across the Seas
The Savage Wilderness
The Bear and the Wolf
Erik the Navigator

The Vengeance Trail

The Danelaw Saga

The Dragon Sword
Oathsword (due out in October)

The Reconquista Chronicles
Castilian Knight
El Campeador
The Lord of Valencia

The Aelfraed Series
(Britain and Byzantium 1050 A.D. - 1085 A.D.)
Housecarl
Outlaw
Varangian

The Anarchy Series England
1120-1180
English Knight
Knight of the Empress
Northern Knight
Baron of the North
Earl
King Henry's Champion
The King is Dead
Warlord of the North
Enemy at the Gate
The Fallen Crown
Warlord's War

273

Kingmaker
Henry II
Crusader
The Welsh Marches
Irish War
Poisonous Plots
The Princes' Revolt
Earl Marshal

Border Knight
1182-1300
Sword for Hire
Return of the Knight
Baron's War
Magna Carta
Welsh Wars
Henry III
The Bloody Border
Baron's Crusade
Sentinel of the North
War in the West
Debt of Honour

Sir John Hawkwood Series
France and Italy 1339- 1387
Crécy: The Age of the Archer
Man at Arms
The White Company

Lord Edward's Archer
Lord Edward's Archer
King in Waiting
An Archer's Crusade
Targets of Treachery (Due out August 2021)

Struggle for a Crown
1360- 1485
Blood on the Crown
To Murder A King

The White Company

The Throne
King Henry IV
The Road to Agincourt
St Crispin's Day
The Battle for France
The Last Knight (September 2021)

Tales from the Sword I

Conquistador
England and America in the 16th Century
Conquistador (Coming in 2021)

Modern History

The Napoleonic Horseman Series
Chasseur à Cheval
Napoleon's Guard
British Light Dragoon
Soldier Spy
1808: The Road to Coruña
Talavera
The Lines of Torres Vedras
Bloody Badajoz
The Road to France
Waterloo

The Lucky Jack American Civil War series
Rebel Raiders
Confederate Rangers
The Road to Gettysburg

The British Ace Series
1914
1915 Fokker Scourge
1916 Angels over the Somme
1917 Eagles Fall
1918 We will remember them

From Arctic Snow to Desert Sand
Wings over Persia

Combined Operations series
1940-1945
Commando
Raider
Behind Enemy Lines
Dieppe
Toehold in Europe
Sword Beach
Breakout
The Battle for Antwerp
King Tiger
Beyond the Rhine
Korea
Korean Winter

Tales from the Sword Book 2

Other Books
Great Granny's Ghost (Aimed at 9-14-year-old young people)

For more information on all of the books then please visit the
author's website at where there is a link to contact him or visit
his Facebook page: GriffHosker at Sword Books